GRUMBLER'S RIDE

Satan's Devils MC - San Diego Chapter #2

COPYRIGHT

PRODUCTION ACKNOWLEDGMENTS

Cover Design by Wicked Smart Designs

Edited and formatted by Maggie Kern @ Ms.K Edits

Proof reading by Melanie Darrow

Photographer: Golden Czermak of Furious Fotog

Model: Fred Dibella

CAST OF CHARACTERS

Officers

Lost – President

Dart – Vice President

Grumbler – Sergeant at Arms

Salem – Enforcer

Scribe – Secretary

Bones – Treasurer

Blaze – Road Captain

Hard Token – Computer Expert

Patched Members

Brakes

Deuce

Dusty

Keeper

Kink

Niran

Pennywise

Reboot

Snips

Prospects
Connor
Curtis
Wrangler

Old Lady's and Children
Alex (Dart's): Tyler, Isla
Patty (Lost's): Beth, Connor

Club Girls
Cindy
Eva
Pearl
Tits

Members Out Bad
Bastard
Crow
DJ
Rattler
Tinder

Deceased Members
Bird (ex-Prez)
Gator
Poke (ex-SAA) Dispatched to Satan
Shark
Smoker
Snake (ex-Prez) Dispatched to Satan

SATAN'S DEVILS MC

CHAPTER ONE

Grumbler

The whirr of the tattoo gun ceases as Blaze switches it off. "Gotta say that looks good, Brother, even if I do say so myself. Here, what do you think?"

Covered with tats as I am, the only spot I had free was under my left shoulder blade. As I can't see it myself, Blaze takes a pic then passes me his phone. I eye the image he shows me and give a satisfied nod. It turned out better than I'd hoped, though I should never have doubted Blaze's skills. In addition to my other tattoos, I now sport a skull smoking a cigarette, a tribute to the much-loved brother we'd lost a few weeks back.

Jeez, how I miss Smoker. He'd been my club brother for nearly thirty years. After the business with Snake and losing nine members three years back, he and I had been all that remained of the old guard. It was easy to figure out how Smoker got his handle. I can't remember seeing him without a pack of cigarettes close at hand. Unsurprisingly, it had resulted in him receiving a terminal cancer diagnosis shortly before his death, but that hadn't been what killed him. He hadn't faded away, which had been the eventual outcome as he'd refused treatment. It had been his time, he'd accepted that. But instead of having those last few months with him, time I needed to prepare myself for his loss, he'd been shot. I'm still smarting from being robbed of those last weeks with him, a few more rides together, and evenings spent just shooting the shit.

Truth be told, I'm not sure if a couple more months watching him go downhill would have helped either me or him, seeing him suffering and being unable to do anything to help. Smoker would probably have preferred the end that he had. He'd died sacrificing himself for the club. Doesn't mean I don't still miss him like fuck though, which led me here today, honouring him in the only way I can.

"You know the drill. Want me to go through it again?" Blaze asks while cleaning his workstation.

Barking a laugh, I shake my head. With more tattoos than I can count, I don't need him to go through the aftercare routine. I could probably teach him a thing or two about looking after newly inked skin.

"You heading straight back to the clubhouse?" He squirts more disinfectant onto a rag.

"Fuckin' right. There's a beer with my name on it. You ready to come, Blaze?"

"What d'you think I am, a part-timer like you?" Blaze chuckles at the expression on my face. "I've got another client coming in soon."

Blaze does good work, with the result that the tattoo parlour brings in good money for the club. Seeing him preparing for said new customer to arrive, I wave my hand in a mock salute and leave. Bypassing the reception desk with just a nod at the pretty young thing sitting there—Blaze does the brothers tats for free—I emerge into the brilliance of a late summer's day in San Diego.

Taking my shades out of my cut, I slide them on, then go to

my Harley that's parked patiently waiting for me outside. For a moment I stand, admiring it from a distance.

I've no woman or family, never wanted one if truth be told. The only thing I need in my life is my bike. All my spare money goes to maintaining it. A few months back, I'd had a spill and ended up dirty side down, hurting my baby as well as nastily breaking my leg. I don't know which wound was worse. As usual, I inspect the Harley with a critical eye, seeing if I can spot a remaining scratch which hadn't been fixed, or a dent that's managed to hide up until now.

My brothers joke with me for having every Harley accessory known to man and then some. Each chrome addition I polish until it gleams. My normally dour expression lifts at times such as now, when I spot the sun glinting off the 'Live to Ride' plate covering the air filter.

It's a beautiful machine, my sole mode of transport, and the love of my life. Without my cherished motorcycle or my club, what would I be? A grumpy old man growing sourer by the day.

I saunter over to it, swing my leg over the saddle, grimacing at aches which weren't there before the surgeons had to pin my leg back together, and lean forward to put my key in the ignition.

"Hey! Hold up."

At the man's shout I raise my head, looking around to see whose attention the voice is trying to attract. There's no one around but me and the hippy type, one of the many we get in Southern California, running down the road heading straight toward me, a card of some sort held in his hands.

I frown, wondering what he could want. I could ignore him, press start, then kick down into gear and leave him in my dust but admit I'm curious as to why he's yelling at me. I'm blocking no one in, and am, for once, legally parked.

When he gets close enough to speak, I say nothing, just lean my arms over the tank and raise an eyebrow.

He's out of breath as he pants out, "This your bike, man?"

I admit to feeling a sense of pride as he's all but drooling. "She's mine."

"She's a real beaut." His eyes take in everything from the eagle on the front fender, to the ornate license plate holder on the rear. "Must take you ages to keep the chrome gleaming like that."

I admit I prefer to keep her neat myself, but if I don't have the time, one of the prospects will do it. They know if there's as much as a smear of polish left when they've finished, they'll be in for a world of hurt. I tell him none of that. He can look and admire, but he's not going to get anything else.

By now he's realised I'm not the talkative type and stops waiting for me to answer. "The name's Devon Starr." He puts the card he was holding in his other hand and stretches out his right. I stare at it, but I don't take it.

The man doesn't look like a fed or a cop, but you can never be too careful. I haven't lived the biker life for thirty years without becoming ultra-cautious.

For a moment, he looks dumbfounded, but he recovers fast, now shoving his card toward me. Idle curiosity makes me take it.

Devon Starr. Photographer.

Hmm. Perhaps he wants to take pictures of my bike? In my head, I have an image of my beloved machine on the cover of a magazine, or perhaps a centrefold spread. My heart starts beating faster—now, that, I could go for.

I raise my eyebrow again.

"My photos are used on the covers of novels." He preens a little. "Many authors come to me for the right picture."

"Novels?" I frown, my dream of seeing my Harley in a

magazine for bikers disappearing. "What kind of fuckin' novels?"

The photographer shrugs. "Anything they want. Some action and adventure, but mainly they're romance." He must notice my perplexed expression. Why the fuck would he be interested in my bike? I can't see how that can sell love stories to women until he adds, "MC, motorcycle club romance is all the rage at the moment. People are crying out for pictures of hot bikers and hot bikes. And your bike is hot, man."

My lips curve slightly. "You want to take my picture? You think it will sell books?" Jeez, I haven't had a compliment like that in years, if ever.

"Er…" Devon looks a bit taken aback and shifts from one foot to the other. "Ah, no. C'mon, man, you're not exactly the ideal of what young girls go for. Your bike, yes. Fuck, hell yeah, but you? Nah. The age bracket isn't right."

Raising only my eyes, I look up at him through my hooded lids. "So, let me get this right. You want to use my bike. Presumably with another model."

His head bobs up and down. "Yeah. That's right. That's what I want to do. I've thought of the perfect place to do it, the beach. We can roll it onto the sand and…" his voice trails off, probably at my expression of what blown sand could do to my tank, and as for rolling darn near seven hundred pounds of bike over soft ground, there's no telling what damage it would do.

Devon hastily backtracks. "On the sidewalk, with the sea in the background. I'm sure we can find somewhere to show it off."

"And this other model? What would he do?"

"Sit on your bike—"

Seeing red, my tone reflects it. "Ain't no one going to be touching my bike except me. Big fuckin' disrespect right there. No man ever touches another man's ride."

The photographer seems unfazed. "Well, perhaps he can

just stand beside it. That would do. We could make it work. What do you say, man? This motorcycle is wonderful. I really must get it in a shot."

I haven't survived being sergeant-at-arms for the Satan's Devils MC without having a few wits in my head. Even if my body's a bit slower nowadays, my brain still works fine. Pulling a pack of cigarettes out of my cut, I tap one out. Nowadays, I rarely smoke, but it helps me think when I do.

Cupping my hand around my lighter, I put the flame to the tip and breathe in deeply. As I'm putting my Zippo back in my pocket, I ask lazily, "These models of yours, they get paid?"

"They wouldn't do it for anything else," Devon scoffs. "They don't get a modelling fee per se, but when a photo is sold, we share a fifty-fifty cut."

"Yeah?" I take another drag, then blow smoke out. "Okay, I'm interested. What do the photos sell for?" My new smartphone takes some darn good shots. I'm half considering if that's something I could do myself. Our computer guy Token would help me set up a website, I'm sure.

The photographer goes quiet.

I nod and tap the pocket where I'd placed his card. "Presumably your rates are on your website."

He sighs. "Six hundred dollars for a single model. Eight hundred for two. I take fifty percent, the model or models get the rest."

That sounds quite lucrative for not doing much. "Uh-huh." I push up to a seated position, folding my arms over my chest. "Let's say I'm interested. But if I let you use my bike, she gets an equal modelling fee."

"What?" His eyes go wide. "Your bike's not a fucking model. It's a prop." I lean forward and my fingers hover over the push button start. When he's quiet, I push it hard. "No, wait a minute," he yells over the sound of the engine.

I turn it back off as he eyes my bike once again. If he wants an example of a tricked-out Harley, he'll have a long way to go to find one better than mine. *And* find some asshole who's prepared to have him take photographs of it for nothing.

I wait, my face turned toward him with one eyebrow raised.

He pinches the brow of his nose and then walks around the bike. "Look, how about I give you a hundred dollars for each picture sold?"

"How many will you sell?"

"Maybe none," he replies, honestly. "Your bike on its own won't help sales. It depends on the appeal of the models. If they prove popular, then we're looking at single or double digits."

So, I may get nothing, or I may get a hundred dollars if I'm lucky—maybe even get up to four figures for doing nothing at all.

"Let me get this right. I bring my bike to a photoshoot, you take pictures, then I sit back and wait for the money to roll in, or not, as the case may be."

"That's right, man." He looks overeager, as if he's got me on the hook now, and to be honest, he probably has. I'm proud of my baby and enjoy showing her off.

I'm assessing the situation and really can't see any harm in it. My brothers are unlikely to find out. The types of books the picture of my bike would appear on aren't ones that would interest them at all. Why read about the life when you're actually living it? We'd watched *Sons of Anarchy*, sure, but only for a laugh. All that violence and death was unrealistic.

Hmm. That was before the business with Snake, our ex-president who betrayed the club. Living through that had shown perhaps our life is just as treacherous and brutal. Things have settled down now, of course. Though I suppose recently stopping a trafficking pipeline across the border isn't exactly quiet, but we don't often do shit like that, thank fuck.

That last escapade had my current prez, Lost, finding his old lady as a result. The only downside was that Smoker had been a casualty.

A cough brings me back to the present. As I come back to myself, I realise, like the old man I am, I've gone down the rabbit hole of mental reminiscence.

I turn to the photographer and give him my terms. "Two-fifty per sale."

His mouth opens wide. "Man, that's going to break me. I've got to pay the models as well."

"How long does the photoshoot last?" I query. "An hour, two?" When he nods, I say, "And for two hours work you just sit back and let the money roll in?"

"There's the editing, the loading of photographs onto my website, promotion, running ads. There's a lot more to it than just taking shots with my camera." Twin spots of red appear on his cheeks as though I've insulted his manhood.

Once again, I reach for the start button. I'm not bothered one way or another, he's the one with the most to lose.

"Two hundred, and that's my last offer."

There it is. I turn and grin at him, giving him a chin lift. "Two hundred." I spit on my palm, then hold out my hand for him to shake.

He stares at it as though it's a poisonous snake, then tentatively reaches out to take it. His grip isn't firm, allowing me to take the opportunity to show him I might be old, but my strength hasn't gone.

"Give me your cell, and I'll call you when I've got the models lined up."

Rattling off the number I know by heart, I wait until I'm sure that he's got it. Then I don't dally, starting the engine, kicking down into first, and pulling away with a loud roar of my exhaust.

On the way back to the clubhouse, I'm grinning. If this

comes off, there might be some easy money for me in it. I take my hand off the clutch and stroke the tank of my baby. After all, she'll be doing all the work if you can call it that. All she'll need to do is sit there and look pretty. And boy, she can certainly do that.

CHAPTER TWO

Grumbler

"Moving to the next point for discussion. Alder." Lost, our prez, looks around at all the members gathered in church. "Those loose ends we thought might be hanging? Well, Utah assures me there's nothing more to worry about. I'm tempted to now remove this item from the agenda."

"While we might not want to discuss it weekly at church, we should still keep our ears and eyes open." Wearing my sergeant-at-arms hat, I look out for all the members of the club, and that includes old ladies. "I'm not sure I trust our Mormon brothers."

Dart, the VP, barks a laugh. "They're based in Utah, that doesn't mean they're Mormon."

I shrug, reserving judgement about anything to do with that club. Whatever that chapter is, they aren't normal, or not like us anyway. We'd always thought they weren't any different, but as it turned out, what we'd assumed had been wrong.

That all came to light a few weeks back when Prez and the VP had flown to an emergency meeting in Utah called by

Drummer, the mother chapter prez. When they'd returned, what they had to say had blown our minds.

Our Utah brothers, who to my mind are lucky to be able to still call themselves that, have been pulling the wool over all the other Satan's Devils' chapters' eyes. Having led us to believe they had no computer expert, or certainly not one the calibre of our guy, Token, the opposite was in fact true. More than that, technical expertise was the main focus of the chapter. Oh, and that comes along with a sideline of rescuing people who'd been kidnapped, together with putting an end to human trafficking wherever they found out about it.

Topping that, their president was a double amputee and couldn't ride a bike, not to mention, to hide that indigestible fact, his VP had swapped out his rag to make everyone else believe he was the prez when meeting other clubs.

It hadn't been a short-term deception. Instead, they'd been fooling all the other chapters for ten years.

Once things had come to light, as deceit and lies so often will, Drummer had called a meeting of all the chapter prezes and VPs, and together they'd sorted the whole mess out, to theirs, if not my, satisfaction.

Emotions had run high after Lost and Dart had returned and informed us of what had been discussed and what was agreed. Pip, the man who couldn't ride, was relegated to being the club advisor, and Snatcher, who'd we thought was the prez all along, became that for real. Oh, and this one really sits in my craw—what I can't understand is that they'd allowed a woman member, and she had become the fucking enforcer no less.

I don't care what her fucking capabilities are, no way are we allowing females into the San Diego club. Though apparently, Satan's Devils regulations don't prohibit it, just lead to the assumption we are a males-only MC. Women members? *Over my dead fucking body* comes to mind.

Once we'd absorbed all that, there was more. The fucking icing on the cake was that the sniper who took Alder out, the man our prez had a very personal reason for wanting to question and had been robbed of the chance by the bullet to his head, was none other than Stormy, a member of the aforesaid Utah club.

Alder had been after Patsy, Lost's old lady now, but we didn't know for what reason. In case there was anything that hadn't died with the man, Lost had needed to learn what he could before he dispatched him to meet Satan. Was anyone else coming for Patsy?

Stormy's admittedly impressive head shot from a distance had stopped us getting answers that would give Prez and Patsy peace of mind.

"What's the news about Stormy?" Salem, our own enforcer, asks, as though he's plucked the thought out of my head. Yeah, he too was robbed of a chance to put his skills to use. He also has no love for the man he'd never met.

"Still in the wind," Prez answers, his face grim.

It had transpired that it wasn't only us who had issues with Stormy, even his own chapter hadn't been impressed with his behaviour. He'd gone rogue, had acted without his prez's agreement, not once, but twice, causing a rift with the other chapters. He had to be punished.

If left to me, he'd have been sent out in bad standing, but the assembled presidents and VPs at that meeting in Utah agreed that he was to indeed lose his patch, but would have a chance to regain it if he went back to being a prospect for six months and proved himself all over again. Oh, and a beatdown had been ordered as well, but before the sentence could be carried out, leaving behind his precious cut, Stormy had taken off on his bike and disappeared. No one has seen or heard from him since.

"It's been what, four weeks now?" Salem's frowning. "What's Snatcher doing about it?"

Lost grimaces. "You'd think with all the tracking skills Utah has, they'd have been able to find him, but they can't find a trace of the man. Snatcher's losing his patience, but he's giving him three months to get his head straight and still hopes he'll come back. If he doesn't put in an appearance and take his punishment like a man, he's out bad."

Dart growls. "He'll deserve it."

"Getting back to Alder." Token raises his hand. "I got Utah's man Duty to send me all the information they had. I've been through it a few times, and I think they're right. Alder's organisation died with him, and I concur Patsy is safe now."

This is good news. I like Lost's old lady. She's a good influence on the prez. He seems to have grown in self-confidence since she's had his back. When I'd first met her, I had my doubts as to how she would settle into MC life, but she's surprised me. She's only a few years younger than me, will become a grandmother in a few months, but her outlook on life is youthful, if not downright surprising at times. She doesn't blink an eye when Kink brings one of his 'pets' naked into the clubroom, she just laughs.

"I'll cross the item off the agenda." Lost circles back to the suggestion he'd made a few minutes before, while breathing out a sigh of satisfaction. There can be no doubt about how much he feels for Patsy and wouldn't want to lose her. "Any other business?"

I glance around, hoping there's not. It's been a standard meeting. Updates from businesses have been given and discussed, Salem's new premises for customising bikes is up, running and doing well now, the tattoo parlour's gaining in reputation, the shop selling bike apparel has increased its profits and our bar is proving popular with weekend warriors and non-bikers alike. All good stuff. But if anyone raises their hand in this part of the meeting, it's usually because something is off. Me? I'm all for a quiet life. Long may it continue.

I glance across at Niran when no one speaks, I raise my chin to him. When I was injured and recovering, Niran had become my right hand, taking on my duties as sergeant-at-arms. We'd developed a good working relationship, and I rely on him a lot now. We've become good friends, though subject to jokes about only having two good legs between us. One of mine is fractionally shorter than it was before—the leg still aches and I need to favour it which give me at times a pronounced limp. But at least it's flesh and blood. One of Niran's is prosthetic. Saying that, though, even given his disability, Niran's nimbler now than I ever was.

Lost bangs the gavel. "Church is over," he declares.

En masse, everyone stands and starts walking out of the meeting room, as normal with the predictable thing on their minds, getting a drink in their hands. I push myself up from the table, not surprised to see Niran waiting for me to stand.

"I went through the inventory earlier. We're looking good, Brother," Niran enlightens me, and I'm glad he's taken the stock check off my hands. Seems like we don't need to order more ammunition right now. It's worth keeping an eye on. Brothers use it for target practice most of the time and it's not unusual to find more than a few rounds missing. The last time we used it in earnest was when we were shutting Alder's operation down.

"Thanks for doing that." I give him a chin lift.

"I'm trying to get the brothers to note what they take out, but I think herding cats would be easier."

I grumble at the laziness of my brothers as I follow the big Black guy out.

Niran's attention is soon caught by Pennywise, and as he wanders off in that direction. I make my way to the bar, having to wait while Connor, Patsy's son and our new prospect, is run ragged trying to make sure drinks land in the right hands.

"Whisky," I tell him when I reach the front.

He puts the bottle of beer he was going to hand me back down. Fuck knows why, but I feel like downing a Jack Daniels tonight. Raising my shot glass, I turn, sipping it gently, and take in the sights. Pearl, one of the sweet butts, is swinging around the stripper pole, and I take a few seconds to admire how her lessons with Alex, Dart's old lady, have paid off. She's elegant and so damn fucking sexy. Even an old man like me has to admire her skills as she continues to dance while gracefully stripping her skimpy clothes off. That part of the lesson I suspect, Alex hadn't demonstrated.

"Enjoying the sights, old man?"

"Less of the old," I snap at Eva. Eva's an interesting girl, being a full-time nurse at the local hospital, and part-time club whore. She works both of her jobs enthusiastically. She's got a son the same age as the VP's, and somehow, while living apart, shares parenting amicably with her ex. I sometimes wonder how much he knows of her extra-curricular duties.

"You want to go upstairs?" she asks in a sultry voice.

She also knows my preference. I'm too ancient to show my skinny and less-than-perfect ass in public now. Although in days gone by, I was certainly not averse to giving a demonstration to my brothers, showing how satisfying a woman should be done. Nowadays though, I don't have as much interest in getting off as I used to. Who am I kidding? Sometimes I can't finish is the polite way of putting it, and the whores here don't get me so hard anymore.

During my many years at the club, I've seen club girls come and club girls go. For a while they join us, sharing their bodies, getting a bed and food for free, and seem to enjoy the loving they get from us bikers. But in the end, they all move on, their dreams of snagging their own old man always failing, as brothers don't want anything permanent with someone who's been biblically known by every male in sight. The result is that the club girls seem to be getting younger in direct correlation with how I'm growing old. Eva, who knows the score, who has more respect due to her profession, has stayed longer than most. She's mid-thirties now, so when I want to shove my dick into a hole, it's usually hers I go for without having to think I'm baby snatching, though, I can't even remember the last time I'd been there. Cindy, Pearl and Tits are in their early twenties. I avoid them like the plague, as all they do is make me feel like a dirty old man.

"Nah, not tonight, Eva." I turn her down, but she isn't surprised. Eva knows me well and takes no offence at my refusal.

When I was younger, I used sex as a release on almost a daily basis. Now I don't have the same need or urges anymore. A drink, a good conversation, maybe a game of pool or cards I find just as, if not more, satisfying. Of course, until recently, I spent most of my evenings whiling away the time with Smoker.

Maybe I've just become bored with the easy pussy here.

Prez, I notice, is deep in conversation with his old lady, his arm around her, holding her tight to him. As I take another sip of my whisky, I ponder how I never expected him to find his one.

I'd already been in the club as a member for fifteen years or more when Snake had brought him back to the clubhouse. I'm not sure of the whole story there, or how the then VP had come across him, but the handle he'd already picked up had suited him. I'd never seen a man so lost. When I'd gotten to know him, I'd collected bits and pieces and put them together. That his business had failed was common knowledge, but that he'd been burned by a woman was not. Still, he proved himself as a prospect, and when Bird had died and Snake took the role of prez, no one was surprised to see Lost in the VP seat.

Lost, I know, thinks Snake put him there so he could run the club while Snake carried out his more nefarious business. Maybe he did, maybe it just worked out that way. Snake had fooled us all, and so had a number of the other brothers. It's down to Lost and Dart that we managed to pull ourselves back from the brink and keep going.

It had been bad, the betrayal devastating, making more than one of us reconsider our future. For a time I'd thought I was going to have to start all over, even going so far as to revisit my old roots and see if there was anything there for me. I had reconnected with old friends, but that's as far as it went. My problem was clear. I didn't know how to exist outside of the MC world, so I'd been hoping there was another club or chapter of the Satan's Devils who'd have me. In the end, thank fuck, that hadn't been necessary. Somehow, we'd managed to put distrust behind us and move on. In my view, we're a better club for it.

The final piece of the puzzle for the prez was finding Patsy. If having an old lady is what you want, and in Lost's case it seems to be, then he certainly got his reward. As an old lady for a prez, he couldn't do better than her. And with her beside him, he's put his self-doubts in his rearview.

My chance of finding an old lady has long gone. When I was younger, I was all for the variety of pussy, never wanting to be tied down or having any desire to come home to that one special lady. If there was someone out there for me, well, I never found her, though I have to say I hadn't gone looking. I'm staring at the big six zero coming up in three more birthday's time and have long accepted I've been single this far, I'll stay that way until I die. Not that I regret it, I've never pictured myself with a lady in my life and don't expect I'll change my mind now.

Sex? Eva would provide that if I had a need for it. Food, I cook for myself, eat out, or see who's cooking in the clubhouse that night. I'm not a cuddler, and even if I were, I've a pillow I can hold in my arms. Nah, I do alright. Still, it can't be denied, Patsy's put a smile on Lost's face, much like the expression I wear when I set eyes on my bike.

Knowing I need to get myself out of my head for a while, I leave the clubhouse, noting it's a nice evening for a ride. I get on my bike and ease out of its parking spot, then head out of the compound and make my way down into the city.

CHAPTER THREE

Grumbler

It's another glorious morning in San Diego, the sun shining out of a cloudless blue sky. Sometimes I wonder what it would be like to live somewhere where you couldn't ride all year around, Utah perhaps. I shudder, knowing I would hate it. The only bad thing about our climate is that it appeals to everyone, which is why Southern California is getting so fucking busy now. Traffic flowing freely on the freeways is a distant memory. Thank fuck I ride a bike and lane splitting is allowed, else I often think I'd never get anywhere.

"What's up with you, Brother?" Salem kicks out a chair and sits down opposite me, placing his coffee on the table.

"Not a lot," I answer honestly. I'm just letting a very edible breakfast of bacon and eggs digest, the cooking of which Patsy supervised. Under her tuition, the food in the clubhouse has taken a huge step forward. Eva's cookery skills are okay, but she's not always around. As for the rest of the sweet butts, their food is only just edible. Dart's woman isn't around much, not since she's had the baby, and tends to focus on her kids.

"Where did you disappear to last night?"

"Same as always, Brother. Out for a ride." The truth, but maybe not all of it. It seems to suffice as he changes the subject.

"Lost and Patsy are going out looking at houses."

At Salem's announcement, I narrow my eyes. "Kind of got used to her living in the clubhouse."

"Chow's improved, that's for sure." Salem grins. "Still, it shows he's starting to believe no one's after her anymore. Must be a relief for them both."

I can't see what's wrong with living at the clubhouse. Sure, I've got my own house, but I rarely visit it. It had seemed the right thing to do years back, but I admit, I feel lonely staying there. Fuck knows why I keep it, but the mortgage is paid off, so may as well hang onto it. Perhaps ready it for a time when I can no longer ride and need to leave the club, but hell, I'd prefer to go out with my boots on, and riding on my baby. Thinking of which I pose a question, "I'll be heading down to the Harley store later, you want to come for a ride?"

"Nah, I've got to finish up that custom build. The owner wants to pick it up this afternoon. And I don't know why you're bothering, you can't fit anything else on that bike."

"Could still change something," I tell him, while seriously thinking about it.

"What are you two planning, world domination?" Pennywise comes over, puts his hand on my shoulder for a second, then moves over to Salem and slaps him none too gently on his back. It makes Salem's coffee spill over the table.

"Prospect!" Pennywise yells. "Clean this fuckin' place up." He points to the puddle of spilled beverage, and Connor comes over at a run. As any good prospect should, he cleans up the coffee carefully and with a smile.

"Grumbler's off to the store again." Salem nods at me.

Pennywise rolls his eyes. "What are you looking at now?"

"Fishtail exhausts," I tell him, having decided.

"You added new pipes when your bike was rebuilt." I just shrug. It's my bike and my money, I can do what I want. I don't need to explain myself to anyone.

"Leave him alone, Pennywise," Salem admonishes him, which is alright for him to say, he was just criticising me himself. Brothers. Got to love 'em.

My phone pings. As I take it out of my pocket, my eyes crease as I see a number I don't recognise. Pennywise and Salem start discussing the paint job the enforcer is working on. I open the text. A light bulb goes off in my head as I realise who it's from. It's the photographer I met a week or so back. As he hadn't contacted me, I'd forgotten he'd wanted to take pictures of my bike, and, as time had passed, thought he was no longer interested. It seems I was wrong.

The message asks if I can meet him this afternoon at three. He names a scenic spot coincidentally up the road from the old airfield where our compound is situated. It's a good place, views out over the Pacific will make a good background, and, unlike the beach idea, a bit of gravel, but no fucking sand.

I purse my lips, considering it. I can still stop off at the store and have plenty of time to make the meet. What have I got to lose? Can't see a downside to this, and the upside is, that for a nice ride out and an hour or so standing around, I might end up with some dollars in my wallet. I stab at the keyboard and laboriously tap out my reply.

Grumbler: I'll be there

"I hear that you're heading out to the store?" Niran's deep voice barks from behind me.

"Yeah. I'm heading there now. You wanna come with?"

"Not that I can afford anything," Niran laughs, "but I'm up for a bit of window shopping."

Standing, I slap his back. "You'll end up buying something."

He gives that throaty chuckle of his. "You're a bad influence, old man."

I show him my middle finger at the reminder.

It's a pleasant way of wasting a couple of hours on a Saturday morning, though the outcome is surprising. I can't find the exact exhaust, which I think would enhance my bike. Niran though, he ends up with a black cam cover for his hog. I yank his chain that my love of customising my bike has rubbed off on him.

We drink the free coffee and have a chat with a couple of bikers who've stopped in, taking the opportunity to slip them one of the club's auto-shop cards while singing Salem's praises and showing them some pictures of jobs that he's completed. Niran also plugged the store we own next to our auto-shop for non-branded apparel and parts which work out cheaper. Then we finish up by discussing some of our favourite rides in the vicinity. We've had a nice chat with like-minded folks and maybe have drummed up some business for the club. Niran and I exchange satisfied grins as we go out to our rides.

"What are you doing now, Brother?"

"Going back to the club. You?"

Niran looks down at his tank for a moment. "I think I might take a ride. It's a nice day to get the breeze on your knees. Sure you don't want to come?"

I would, if I hadn't got that darn photoshoot this afternoon. I consider blowing it off, but if I give my word, I normally keep it. But I won't be sharing what I'm doing with Niran or any of the other nosy assholes. Brothers will be brothers and I can just imagine what they'll say if I let them know pictures of my bike might end up on covers for romance novels of all things. So I content myself with a non-explanation.

"Nah, I'm good, Brother."

Amicably, we part ways. Niran zooming off, with me looking longingly after him, thinking for a moment perhaps a good ride out with my brother might be preferable to the unknown, or what I suspect will be standing around, watching a photographer take pics.

Still having time to spare, I return to the clubhouse. Heading to the kitchen, I make myself a sandwich, then return to the bar area to eat it. Scribe, Brakes and Reboot are there, playing cards. They offer to deal me in, but on checking my phone, I see I haven't got time to get involved in a game, so I settle myself by just watching on, keeping an eye on the time to ensure I'm not going to be late.

When the digits show me it's time to leave, I stand and stretch, bouncing my bike key in my hand.

"Where you off to?" Pennywise, entering the room calls out.

I pause, when directly challenged, I don't want to be evasive or lie. So I tell him the truth, yelling back my answer while grinning widely. "I'm going to pimp my ride."

Pimp my ride. I'm still chuckling to myself as I go out of the clubhouse and swing my leg over the saddle.

Pointing my bike up away from the city, I settle back to enjoy the short journey, the feeling of the wind and sun on my face, and the pavement rushing past beneath my wheels spells freedom to me. When I arrive at the scenic overview, it's with time to spare. Pulling a rag out of my pocket, I go around my baby, making sure there's not a speck of dust or a smear of grease on it. Stepping back, I view it with critical eyes. It's gleaming and perfect, even if I say so myself.

A car pulls up. I half turn my head that way, seeing a girl who looks very damn young getting out of the passenger side. She slams the door, making me wince. My attention caught, I watch her stomp stubbornly away with folded arms making me wonder what's got her goat. Intrigued, I focus now on the driver's side. A moment passes, then another, then that door opens, and an older woman steps out. I notice her face is flushed and red. When she catches my eye, she looks away fast, but makes no move to follow the girl.

Not my business.

Spying a bit of dust that's dared to land on my bike, I take out my rag once again.

Another rumble of tyres on gravel makes me look up. As I do, I see that it's Devon Starr. His car is newer, posher and what somehow doesn't surprise me, flashy. When he gets out, he's wearing khaki shorts and an open-necked shirt. He walks over to me, eyeing my bike, then the location he's chosen.

Without a 'thanks for coming' he's all business from the get-go. "Can you park your bike over there?"

I glance at the ground, then at the space he's pointing out. "Sure." It's only a few feet away, so I paddle walk my bike over, kick down the stand, and dismount it again.

As I do, I notice the young girl watching me with something now akin to horror on her face. She takes a step toward Devon, her eyes wide. "Is this him?"

"What?" Devon follows the direction of his eyes, then barks a laugh. "No, pet. This isn't who you're posing with. This is just the bike's owner."

The look of relief on her face is almost comical, making me chuckle as I realise, she mistook me for a male model. Well, I suppose that I could be, were it a May/September romance. Fuck it, I could be this little thing's grandfather, maybe even able to add a great before that.

Devon glances at the expensive watch on his wrist, and frowns. "Where the fuck is he?" he mumbles. He taps the device as if it could be showing the wrong time.

I take out my pack of cigarettes, tap one out, then spying

the older woman glaring at me, walk over to the guardrail to light it up. The smell from the cloud of smoke surrounding me reminds me of Smoker. Days like this, we'd often take off and ride to nowhere in particular. Of course, he'd have probably been on his third or fourth cigarette by now—one at least smoked while he was riding, the wind taking more of the nicotine than he drew into his lungs. For a moment, I stare out at the view, lost in my memories. I miss the old bugger. Tapping my fist against the railing, I mentally ask, *why, Smoker, why? Our time was cut short too soon.*

Spitting gravel pulls me out of my head. Turning, I examine the new arrival who's just getting out of a Honda Civic. It's a young guy, not much older than the girl. He's wearing jeans and a shirt that's flapping open, allowing a sculptured chest to show, suggesting he works out but has only managed baby muscles so far. My expert eyes tell me he'll need a few more years under his belt before his body matures. Still, perhaps it's the look the women go for.

Devon walks over to meet him, his gesticulations suggest he's berating him for being late, then he turns and waves toward the girl. "Come on, let's get started."

Thank fuck.

Devon sets a camera up on a tripod, then positions the girl and the kid to stand next to my bike. Instantly they do. I see the kid's hand reach out toward the handlebars.

"Don't touch the fuckin' bike," I growl, in my best sergeant-at-arms voice. I swear the kid jumps back at least a foot.

The photographer turns to me and glares. When I raise my eyebrow, he turns back. I place myself with my back up against the trunk of a tree, one leg bent with my instep against the bark. I'm near enough to see if anyone so much as breathes in my bike's direction. It's then I notice the older woman again. She's staring as avidly as me, but not on the same bearing. No, her eyes are fixed on the girl, and specifically the arm the young guy has just placed around her.

Her reaction is as fast, and much the same as mine, when the boy's hand strays too close to the girl's tit.

"Mom!" the girl admonishes. "You're embarrassing me."

Devon raises his eyes to the sky as if asking for divine intervention. He turns, spares a disdainful look at both me and the woman, then brings his attention back to the models. "Turn to face each other, lean in as though you're going to kiss." He casts another glance in who I know now is the girl's mother's direction. "But don't let your lips touch. Close your eyes, Alicia, lift your face, that's right, give a little smile, purse your lips as though you're really anticipating this. No, Owen, don't close your eyes. Put a little heat in them."

While keeping a close eye on what they're doing, I move until I'm standing next to the girl's mother.

"Name's Grumbler." I tip an imaginary hat as she glances toward me.

Just as quickly, she looks back to the scene playing out in front of us. "Mary," she offers. Then confides, "I hate this."

I kind of got that impression. "Your girl do this often?" She frowns. I nod to the pair. "Model."

"First time," she admits. "I tried to dissuade her, but Devon Starr there was most persuasive. Apparently, she was just the type he was looking for. He turned her head. Wasn't much I could do about it, except come along to make sure it was all above board and that she was safe."

The actions of a good mother in my eyes. But I frown a little. "Starr approached me much the same way. Well, not that he wanted me, but my bike."

"Hey, Grumbler." Devon's walking across the gravel, making a beckoning gesture with his hand. "Lend Owen your vest thing for a moment, will you?"

What. The. Fuck? I go completely still. "My vest thing?"

"Yeah, this." His finger reaches out to touch my cut. He screams like a bitch when I grab his offending digit and my hand pushes back hard.

"No fuckin' way. No one touches my cut," I spit out, and certainly not a pimply faced kid.

CHAPTER FOUR

Mary

"**M**om."

Just one word and I know exactly what mood my seventeen-year-old daughter is in. She's at that age when she knows everything and can do anything she wants—in her own head, anyway.

Trying to stay calm, clenching my hands to keep myself from screaming, then, as patiently as I can, I explain, "A photographer approached you on the street, Alicia. He told you, you're an attractive girl. He said very flattering things about you..." I hold up my hand, "and I agree with every word. You are photogenic, and I'm sure would make a good model. But you have no idea who this man is."

"He gave me his business card."

I refrain from rolling my eyes. My know-it-all daughter can be very naïve, especially when she wants something. "Anyone can have cards printed, darling. Doesn't mean they are who it says they are."

Her face is set and sullen. Lips forming a pout, she tosses back her hair. "I trust him, Mom."

There we have it. My daughter can't possibly know enough about the man to know whether to trust him or not. I was incensed that a stranger had even talked to her, let alone her giving him her cell. A number that was called a couple of days ago, and it seems we've been arguing ever since. Well, not that it's particularly unusual, I suppose if it wasn't about that, it would be something different. My sole purpose in life is to ruin hers it would seem.

It had been Devon Starr who'd called her. I wish I knew someone who could investigate his background for me, but I do not. Limited as to what I can do, I've googled his name, and sure, there is a photographer with that handle. He's got a legit looking website, an Instagram account, and a Facebook profile. His pictures range from fairly innocent to suggestive poses which I wouldn't countenance Alicia modelling for. There's no full nudity that I could see, but certainly models in their underwear. He doesn't seem to have any physical premises, so I presume he hires a studio when he needs to.

This is the man who's set up a meet with my daughter. Unlike her, I'm unfortunately well-versed in the ways of the world. You tend to be savvy when you've got sole responsibility for bringing up a child. There are bad people to be found anywhere, and it's my job as a parent to keep her safe from them.

My daughter is pretty, her face expressive, her eyes large, and her lips full. While I agree she's the perfect candidate for being photographed, she could also easily be a target for being abducted and stolen away.

All this I've tried to explain to her, but, to her mind, I'm being overly cautious.

"I can't see the problem. I haven't said you can't do this, Alicia. All I've said is that I'll drive you there."

"Mom. I'm seventeen. I can drive myself." She gives another toss of her blond hair. "What's it going to look like when I turn up with you in tow?"

Some days I regret her learning to drive, but I've still got control when it's my car she's driving. "You're going nowhere without me to chaperone you." My voice is now firm. *Don't lose your temper,* I remind myself. "I either come with you, or you don't go at all."

"You can't stop me." Again, I'm afforded a head toss. "I'll get an Uber."

Oh no, she won't. I breathe deeply and keep my voice even. "You'll need a parent or guardian to sign any modelling contract on your behalf."

Her eyes go wide. "You wouldn't say no."

"Try me." I can't stop the challenge coming out of my mouth. *Damn.* I didn't mean to come over as forcibly as that, but reasoning isn't working.

She stomps her foot. "I hate you."

"Seriously? Alicia, I know you hate me right now, but I'm only doing this because I worry about your safety." Again I make an effort to swallow my annoyance down. "What's the problem? I'm coming with you. I'm not going to interfere," *unless someone puts their hands where they shouldn't be.* "I'll keep in the background, and you won't know I'm there."

"You'll embarrass me."

"What? By just standing watching?" I really can't see why she's so upset.

"This is my chance, and you're going to blow it for me."

Her chance? I could explain her modelling for a romance novel cover is not her ticket to Hollywood, but I'm sensible enough to keep my mouth shut.

If Devon Starr is legit, if he doesn't pressure her into poses which are too suggestive, or wants her to take off her clothes, then honestly, I don't see there's too much of a problem. If her photos sell, then she could end up with some pocket money. I'm realistic to know that there are a lot of ifs, and that this isn't the start of a career.

I've done my best raising Alicia, trying not to impose my dreams over hers, and instead encouraging her to be her own person. It's been hard raising her for the last seven years on my own, but I've tried my best to raise an independent thinking girl. Sometimes I think I've been almost too successful. It would have been nice to share the burden at times instead of always having to be the disciplinarian, but in that, I'm on my own.

I love her so freaking much, but that doesn't mean we don't clash at times—times, like now.

"Oh have it your own damn way. Come with me then." Alicia stomps her way down the hall leading to her room, mumbling something I expect I'm glad not to be able to hear.

Half an hour later, I blink, half-close my eyes, then open them fully. She's standing, one hip jutted out, her mouth set, her eyes sparking a challenge. She's wearing a sports bra, her midriff is bare, and she's got on shorts which can only have been made by cutting off too much leg from a pair of old jeans. It's not the damage to the pants that worries me, I know they're an old pair that got ripped, it's the fact you can see her ass cheeks.

She could end up on a book cover just like that.

Why should I care? Clothes shouldn't define you. During my younger days, my parents would tell me of all the dire things that could happen to me based on the clothes that I wore. Unfortunately, that seems to have become fixed in my head, warring with the eternal question of why young females should be responsible for the apparent uncontrollable urges of men.

What Alicia is wearing makes her look sexy, something to be objectified. But isn't that exactly what the photographer wants? For women not so blessed, or perhaps wizened with age, to see her and dream of themselves in her image? To be someone attractive to men?

I can't think of my daughter in that way. Underneath the makeup and the clothes she's chosen for today, she's still my little girl, the baby I once held in my arms. Often I wish, I could have kept her that age. It was far easier.

She raises an eyebrow, making me realise I haven't said a word, but I find it impossible to tell her *you look nice.* Contenting myself that I'll be there with her, I pick up my keys. "Come on, we better leave now if you don't want to be late."

"This is so freaking embarrassing," she says, storming past me, then opening the front door and exiting the house. "Stupid. I'm not a child."

Oh but you are, I reply in my head.

It's a fine balance not wanting to scare your child but wanting them to be aware of the many evils in the world. Perhaps I haven't adequately set the right balance. Am I a failure or just the typical parent of a wilful teenager?

Backing the car off the driveway, I make my way through the city then up and out into the countryside that surrounds it. The temperature starts to rise as we begin to climb, as shown by the digits flicking up on the console, and the air conditioning starts to work harder. In direct correlation, Alicia's mood, which had commenced poor, sours the more miles I drive. After I'd made one comment about how it was nice to get out of the city for a while, and she'd refrained from answering, I stay quiet.

Eventually, my GPS tells me I've arrived, and I pull off into a paved parking area, immediately spying I'm not the first to have arrived. There's an impressive gleaming Harley parked up, and an older, weatherworn and heavily tattooed biker standing beside it. At first glance, he seems quite harmless. As he turns, presumably to check out who's in the car, then when he swings back around to look out over the scenery, I see his leather vest has patches on the back of it. Satan's Devils MC, says the top one, the bottom, San Diego, and the middle patch is an emblem of some sort, the grim reaper with a scythe looming over what looks like three demons.

It's scary as hell. I swallow, wondering whether it's best to turn around and make a run for it.

But any chance of escape is soon lost. Alicia, completely oblivious to any danger, gets out of the car and storms off as though wanting to put distance between us. Telling myself I'm overreacting, I decide the best thing to do about the biker, who's clearly in some sort of club, is to ignore him. Maybe he's just stopped off to look at the scenery and will soon move on.

I start hoping Devon Starr arrives quickly, and then the biker will be gone. I find his presence unnerving. I know nothing about motorcycles or the people who ride them. Alicia's father was into muscle cars.

Ah, another car is pulling in. Alicia's face brightens when she sees the man driving, and I recognise him from his Facebook profile. It's Devon, the photographer. He greets Alicia with a nod of acknowledgement, then goes over to talk to the biker, who's soon moving his motorcycle to a spot that's just been pointed out. It dawns on me it must be a prop for the photo shoot. My mind's eased that the biker has a good reason to be here.

Then we seem to be waiting again. Devon's getting impatient, tapping his watch, while the biker smokes a cigarette, politely moving downwind of me when he reads my disgust.

At last it becomes clear who the delay is for.

My eyes fall on the newcomer and I can't stop the roll of my eyes. Jeez, does this kid think the sun shines out of his rear or what? Every movement seems practised, starting with the way he exits the car. His walk is fluid, the way his hips flex looks like he's been coached on how to move sexily as he saunters across to Devon and my daughter. Warily I watch Alicia's face, seeing her eyes are wide, her mouth open, and her cheeks flush. The kid's demeanour might be wasted on me, but not on her.

Devon exchanges a few words, presumably about the newcomer's tardiness, though the kid doesn't look very contrite. Then he kicks into professional mode, posing his models as he wants them. My eyes are sharp, watching for any impropriety. It's undeniable there's chemistry between the pair, or on Alicia's part, definitely. The photographer seems to know what he's doing, and positions them just right, telling them what expressions to wear, making heat beam out of them.

I suppress a smile as it becomes clear the biker is very protective over his motorcycle. I do grin at the way he snaps when the kid tries to touch it, but soon I'm frowning, feeling a similar emotion.

"Hey, watch where you're putting your hands."

"Mom, you're so embarrassing." Alicia's not impressed at my interruption, but that kid, who appears to go by the moniker, Owen, had been about to caress her breast—not on my watch.

So intent on viewing her, I don't notice the biker's moved closer, until he announces himself. "Name's Grumbler."

I glance at him quickly, then put my eyes back on my daughter again, but I do respond politely. "Mary," I tell him. Then to explain my rudeness in not paying attention to him, I confide, "I hate this."

"Your girl do this often?" When I frown, confused, he points toward his bike. "Model."

"First time." Then it all comes rushing out. "I tried to dissuade her, but Devon Starr there was most persuasive. Apparently, she was just the type he was looking for. He turned her head. Wasn't much I could do about it, except come along to make sure it was all above board and that she was safe."

His eyebrows draw down. "Starr approached me much the same way. Well, not that he wanted me, but my bike."

"Hey, Grumbler." Devon's walking across to us. He's making a beckoning gesture with his hand. "Lend Owen your vest thing for a moment, will you?"

The biker beside me freezes and repeats in a voice dripping with disdain, "My vest thing?"

"Yeah, this." The photographer's finger reaches out to touch the vest of the man standing beside me, then screams when Grumbler grabs hold of it and twists it away.

"No fuckin' way. No one touches my cut," Grumbler spits out.

Devon raises his hands in defeat. "Fuck, man. What is your problem? I only asked."

"Well keep your fuckin' questions to yourself, or I take my bike out of here and ride."

My mouth quirks as I watch the scene play out, wondering if the biker will make good on his threat. It's obvious that Devon doesn't like not being in the driving seat. It's also blatantly apparent that he wants the motorcycle as part of this shoot, as with a shake of his head, he walks back to what he can control, the human models if not the mechanical ones.

"Why didn't you let him borrow your vest?" I ask after a moment for conversation as much as anything else. I'm starting to get bored as shot after shot is taken.

"It's called a cut." His voice is deep, gravelly, as he speaks from my side. Like me, he's staring avidly ahead, keeping as careful an eye on his bike as I am on my daughter. "I earned the right to wear it, it's mine. Big disrespect to even touch it."

"Like your bike?"

"Yeah, babe. Never lay your hand on a man's ride." He spares a glance for me, waiting for some reason for that statement to sink in. Eventually I nod, duly noting that if I ever come across another biker, I'll make sure to keep my hands away from his motorcycle.

"It's something else, isn't it? Your bike?" Even I, a non-rider, can appreciate it for what it is.

"You like motorcycles, darlin'?"

Risking a quick glance to the man at my side, I notice he's also turned assessing eyes in my direction. "No," I reply honestly. "I've never had anything to do with them. But the way the sunlight's gleaming off yours, it looks special."

"Why, thank you, ma'am."

I've pleased him by saying the right thing. After that, a few minutes pass in silence. Surprisingly, they're not uncomfortable.

It's finally him who speaks first. "So this was your daughter's idea? To get into modelling?"

My eyes narrow as Owen pulls Alicia into him, but this time my nonverbal warning is sufficient, as the pair are posed decently enough, even for a mother's critical viewing. "Hopefully this is just a one-off."

"I like that you're chaperoning her," he tells me, seriously. "Girl her age could get into trouble without someone watching out for her. Her dad have anything to say about this?"

"My husband died a few years back."

"I'm sorry," he commiserates automatically.

I shrug. So am I, but I've had to learn to deal with it. "Maybe it makes me overprotective, knowing I'm all that she has."

"That you're here with her shows you're a good mother. How old is she?"

"Seventeen."

I hear him chuckle. "I don't envy you that. She's strong-willed, isn't she? Got attitude. Saw that as soon as you arrived."

He's got that right. "She's pushing boundaries, thinks she can run before she can walk." He seems to understand kids. "You got any children?"

"No, thank fuck." Those three words are filled with heart-felt relief.

"Okay, that's a wrap," Devon calls out. "Got everything I need for today." He turns and stares straight at the biker. "Fucking shame I couldn't get any shots on the bike, you sure you won't reconsider?"

Grumbler's expression is all the answer he gets and needs. Devon sighs and shakes his head.

"What happens now?" I ask, looking out for my daughter's interests.

"The photos will go on my website. If one is purchased, I'll be in touch."

Alicia comes bounding over, her eyes sparkling. "Will it be soon?"

Devon's shoulders rise and fall. "Could be, I took some nice shots. But I have to prepare you, it may be never. It depends if someone's writing a book that's got the likes of the two of you as characters. Authors like to match the models to the people in their books."

Owen taps my daughter on the shoulder. She moves around me to our car, reaches in and takes her phone out of the glove compartment where she'd left it. She hands it over to Owen, who taps something into it.

He's giving her his number.

As I'm trying to process what I think of them exchanging contact details, Grumbler nods toward Devon. "You've got my cell. I'll wait for your call."

"Might not sell any at all," Devon warns again.

Ignoring him, Grumbler's eyes narrow as they settle on the two youngsters, then he turns to me. "Nice to meet you, Mary."

He glances back at Alicia once more, then leans in, saying with a chuckle, "Good luck."

He strides away, and it's then I notice he's got a slightly uneven gait, but it doesn't seem to hold him back as he goes to his bike and swings his leg over it. Then an ear-shattering roar pierces the air as he starts the engine. With a salute, he turns the bike, eases out onto the road, then accelerates and disappears.

CHAPTER FIVE

Grumbler

Club life continues as normal. My phone has remained quiet with no texts or calls from the photographer, so I guess that means I won't be making a fortune from pimping out my bike. I often smirk as I remember how he'd assumed I'd let a pimply faced kid borrow my cut and sit on my ride. Hopefully he learned his lesson.

The shoot itself hadn't been much bother, just meant I'd been hanging around for an hour or so, and it had been an experience seeing how photographers worked. I had checked out his website and had been impressed by some of the pictures he's taken. My bike had looked damn hot. If I hadn't kept the whole affair secret, I'd be tempted to ask Token if he could download one and take off the watermark so I could keep it and frame it. Surely I was entitled to something? But it would open a huge can of worms were I to ask him.

So I keep quiet. Now, once again, Friday's come around, and we're seated in church.

"What's the latest from Utah?" Salem asks once the formal business items have been discussed. "Any sightings of Stormy?"

Lost wipes a hand over his face. "Spoke to Drummer a couple of days back. There's still been no sightings of Stormy. He hasn't gone back to the club."

"They gave him three months, didn't they?"

I seem to remember discussing that a few weeks back. Three months was too long in my view. As soon as Stormy had dropped out of sight they should have declared him out bad. Last time this topic had come up must have been about the time I pimped out my bike, and that was what, six weeks or so back?

"So he's got, what? A couple more weeks?"

As Salem's voice booms again, I realise I've been lost in my head, and completely zoned out of the meeting. I try to look as though I was paying attention the whole time, and prompt, "So, then…?"

"He's out bad, and everyone will be on the lookout for him." Lost nods my way.

I might have felt sympathy for the man who'd been bounced back to prospect if it wasn't for the fact he'd taken a kill which should have been ours. Also, who could have respect for someone who'd run rather than stay and face a beatdown? Not me, that's for certain.

"Snatcher hasn't got a choice," Lost continues. "Drummer's still keeping a close eye on Utah. If Stormy's not kicked out, then Snatcher will be going against the Satan's Devils' conditions for them continuing their charter. He won't sacrifice his club for the benefit of one rogue member."

"They keeping their noses clean in everything else?" Pennywise asks, tucking his shoulder-length dark hair over his shoulder.

"Seem to be," Lost confirms.

Bones sniffs and rubs at his nose. "How's their new enforcer doing?"

His query makes us all grin.

Lost smirks. "Apparently scaring the shit out of everyone."

Now there's outright laughter. I sit shaking my head. If nothing else, that alone proved that the Utah club were out of their fucking heads. Not only did they patch a woman member, they made her their fucking enforcer. Bunch of fucking pussies if you ask me.

Dart raises his hand. "Alex was asking—"

"She's not joining," Salem says fast, his eyes widening in horror.

Dart rolls his eyes. "Alex was asking about that beach run that was suggested the other week. That still in our plans."

"Fuck yeah," Reboot says, thumping his hands on the table.

"Could do with a club ride," Niran agrees.

"I'm down for that." Brakes gives a thumbs up.

"Okay," Lost looks around, "Patsy and Alex will take the lead on getting the food sorted, and we'll set a date now. Weekend after next work?"

From the nods of agreement, it does. Sounds good to me. A club ride topped off with a beach barbeque. Exactly the kind of shit that a man joins the club for. I'm looking forward to this—me, my bike, my brothers. Good food, good company and if we go to the beach that we normally do, a good fucking location with a paved parking lot.

Another church meeting done and dusted. The weekend proceeds like others before it. This time I do ride out with Niran when he suggests, which puts me in a good mood for the work week. Monday to Friday I'm a mechanic working at our shop. I get my head down like any other employee, but truth be told, I love my job. It's not work when, as a member of the Satan's Devils, I'm also my own employer and invested in making this business a success.

When Salem opened this workshop in the second hangar, it was so he could work on the customisation jobs, but truth be told, our auto-shop in town has proved so popular, having the space here, we also use it for overflow work. I prefer working at this location. It's only a short walk from the clubhouse, preferable to riding through traffic.

In the seven weeks since my bike's been photographed, not a lot has changed. I'm still toying with the idea of replacing the exhausts, but the ones I've got now do the job fine. Still, I do love tinkering with my ride. If I'm not working on it, I'm reading about parts and what difference they'd make to the look or the performance.

Though each day in the club is much like another, Friday comes around once more. Like anyone else, I'm already starting to wind down, which is why I'm sitting, flicking through a magazine, drinking a cup of coffee having just completed replacing a burned-out clutch on a car. It was a bit of a pig of a job, and so I had given myself a few minutes off. A scuff of a boot on the floor gets my attention.

Looking up, I roll my eyes. "I take a breather and get caught by the boss."

Prez barks out a laugh. "So this is how you spend your days. Always suspected you slacked off on the job."

I raise my middle finger toward the prez. He knows I put in my hours. "You need anything, Prez?"

"Nah, just dropped off Patsy's car. Needs an oil change and one of her tyres is wearing a bit low."

He'd be worried about that. Lost would do anything to keep his old lady safe.

"Hi, Grumbler." Patsy puts her head around the door, doing that little finger wave women are apt to offer.

Lost turns and directs himself to her. "Wait here for me, babe. Just need a word with Scribe about your car."

When she nods, Lost disappears. Then Patsy's eyes sharpen as they turn toward me. "I thought Salem did a custom job on your tank."

Tilting my head sideways, I put aside the parts manual and look up, surprised by her statement. "He did. Why?" I get to my feet, grimacing as my leg's stiffened in just the minute or so I've been sitting down. I place my hand on my desk, thinking about the work that had been done on my bike. The enforcer had done a fucking good job.

"Does he do the same for other people? Or is someone copying his style?"

I bristle. My bike's a one-off, and if Salem has done the same paint job on someone else's bike, I'll want to know why before his teeth meet my fist.

Instead of elaborating, she fumbles in her purse, digging down deep like women seem to do, then with an exclamation of triumph, pulls a small tablet out. She taps the screen and slides her finger across it, then passes it over to me.

In big letters there's a title, *Death Ride,* and the author's name, Fara Weir, is underneath. And there, in pride of place, is my fucking bike—one of the pictures that had been taken weeks back. I slide the screen and quickly find the details I need.

Photographer: Devon Starr
Models: Alicia Styles and Owen Leesom

There's no fuckin' mention of my bike, not a tribute or thanks for me allowing it to be used. Should there be? Fuck if I know. Maybe there should and perhaps Starr is as fucking dirty as I originally suspected he might be. One thing is blatantly obvious, he's shafted me. I'd had no contact from the day he assured me he'd be in touch if a picture using my bike was sold, but no such contact had been made, which meant I was out of pocket two hundred bucks.

Taking my phone out of my cut, I snap a picture of the cover that Patsy's shown me. As I do, I notice she's standing with her chin raised, her head leaning more toward her left shoulder than the right, and her expression is pensive. Slowly a grin spreads over her face.

"I take it from your reaction that this," she taps the screen of her e-reader I've just handed back, "is *your* bike."

I might be a biker, but I live by a code. Unless it's to protect my brothers, I don't like to lie, especially not to my president's old lady, so I keep my mouth firmly shut.

Her grin widens, and she reaches forward and touches my arm. "Your secret's safe with me." She starts to turn, presumably to go off and find her man. "It's a good picture, Grumbler. Really shows off your bike." Then she disappears out back, ignoring the fact Lost had told her to wait—just like a woman.

Gazing after her, I narrow my eyes. Sure, she'll keep a secret from her man. Of course she won't. But Lost's a good man. He'll guess if I haven't said anything that I won't want it common knowledge that I literally pimped out my ride.

Still, I've got heavier shit to deal with than being the butt of a fuckload of jokes if were the truth to come out, like this asshole of a photographer taking me for a ride. You do not cross a Satan's Devil and he's going to learn that. I think it's time I go and pay him a visit. First of all, though, I'll have to find out where he resides.

Following the path Patsy took earlier, I call out to Scribes that I'm calling it a day, hang up my overalls, then walk back to the converted hangar which is our clubhouse, and take the stairs up to the place that I call home. To some it wouldn't be much, a room containing little more than a closet, a desk and chair, and of course, a large king-sized bed. Off to one side is a door leading to a private bathroom. On the desk is an ever-growing pile of bike magazines and parts manuals. Taking out my wallet, I look inside. No card.

I go to the desk and then rummage through the drawer. Coming up blank in both places, I rack my brains. *What did I do with it? Damn it.* Suspecting I tossed it, I look into the garbage can. *Empty.* Well, if it wasn't Wrangler, Curtis and Connor wouldn't have a chance at getting patched in.

Moving the pile of periodicals aside, I open my laptop. It takes a few moments to come to life and I tap my fingers impatiently. As soon as I reach the search engine, I enter Devon Starr's name. I find a load of social information about him, but there's no physical address anywhere that I can find. Fuck. My immediate idea of riding to find him and literally shaking my money out of him goes straight out the window. He has an email address on his website though, and Facebook invites me to send him messages through the app. I pause, wondering what to do next. If I try to contact him, he'll know I've found him out. I might put him on his guard. Even if I don't, I'm far from being a patient man. Instant gratification is more my style, and I don't want to be reliant on waiting on an answer.

I need help.

Christ. If I ask my brothers for assistance, I'll have to wait until they pick themselves up from the floor where they'd fallen laughing after seeing my bike on a romance novel. Then they'd crack up again at how I'd been taken for a fool. Not that I'd blame them, I'd do the same if the boot was on the other foot. So what do I do? Put it down to experience? That is not my style. It strikes me that if Lost's old lady hadn't a penchant for devouring any novel that mentions an MC, I'd never have known my photo had been used and had proof that I'd not been paid.

Trust Patsy to like reading that rubbish, it had gone out of my head that she did. But I had known, I'd even once asked Lost if he minded her filling her head with rubbish about fictional clubs, and people writing about shit they knew nothing about. For some reason, a broad grin had spread over his face, then he'd given me a knowing wink and had changed the subject.

Glancing down at my phone and the pictures I'd taken of

the book on Patsy's e-reader, I wonder if there's something else I could do to locate the photographer without emailing him direct. Then I see something else I could try. Fara Weir, the author, has a website, perhaps she might know more.

Not holding out much hope, painfully slowly, hunting and pecking out each letter, I compose an email.

Dear Ms Weir (well I suppose I should be polite)

I'm looking for some fucking help. My motorcycle is featured on the cover of your book 'Death Ride'. I am trying to locate the photographer, Devon Starr.

Do you know where I could reach him?

The bastard hasn't paid me what we fuckin agreed. Any help to locate him would be appreciated.

Fucking Warmest regards

Grumbler Bart Winslow

After removing some of the words that I'd typed, I take a breath and press send.

Having no expectation of a speedy response, I stand, stretch, and move to the window. I'm so wound up, if I were to go downstairs, anyone would be able to see that I'm grumpier than normal and all the nosy fuckers would want to know why. Right now, I don't want to tell them.

A ping from my laptop gets my attention. *The author couldn't have replied so fast, could she?* Nah, it's probably a spam email of some fucking sort, the kind Token sometimes warns us about. No one's going to make me rich quick, and I'm not related to a long-lost Nigerian prince.

Not feeling particularly hopeful, I sit and look down at my emails again. Top of the list is one from Fara Weir.

Hi Bart

Your motorcycle is stunning, and with the models was so right for my book. As for Devon Starr, I'm sorry, I know little more than you. All my dealings have been via email. Being his friend on Facebook, I think he's based in California, but that's all I know. I bought the photo a few weeks ago now and have heard nothing further from him. As I paid in full, I don't expect to. Sorry.

All the best

Fara xoxo

What the fuck does *xoxo* mean? Is it some secret code? Shrugging it off, I sit back, linking my hands behind my head. My gut tightens telling me I won't be able to let this drop. No one takes the sergeant-at-arms of an outlaw MC for a fool, especially not some skank of a photographer.

But without more detail, my hands are tied.

So, I muse, closing my eyes. I've got three choices. Contact him directly by email, which I'm sure wouldn't work, but maybe it would be amusing to show him I'm onto his game and that he's been caught out. So, he might come up with the money he owes, but what's stopping him doing it again? How many other pictures will he sell? I'll never find out, unless Patsy reads all of them.

Or I could let it go, learn a lesson not to pimp my bike out again, and let Starr get one over on an ignorant biker. It's not my favourite choice.

My final option is to involve Token, a man who keeps our data secure but when it comes to verbal information about any of us, cannot keep his fucking mouth shut. If I come clean and let him know why I'm tracking the photographer, it will be all over the club before I've finished my explanation.

I view the screenshots of the book's information once more. *Alicia Styles and Owen Leesom.* Maybe I could find them instead? Maybe they got their payment from Starr, and maybe there is some way to track him down that way. At the very least, they might provide me with more information.

I don't feel particularly comfortable chasing down kids, but there is an adult I can try to find. But what was the mother's name? My eyes narrow as I think back to the brief conversation we had. *Marie? Martha?* Mary, that was it. Mary Styles, if she still has the same name as her daughter. I recall she'd mentioned an ex. If it had been an acrimonious parting, she might have returned to her maiden name, but for now, I could work on the principle that she'd hadn't. Hold on, hadn't she said he was dead? She had, and in that case, it's probable she kept his name.

My hands still linked behind my head, I tap my fingers together. Now surely, I can come up with something plausible to get Token to track her down. I've just got to come up with an excuse of why I, a confirmed bachelor, want to find a woman who I've only met once. If I can't think of a good one, he'll tease the shit out of me.

I glance down at my phone. I've still got an hour before church. Time to go see what food's on offer and consider how best to approach Token. Maybe I'll talk to him after the meeting if I've come up with an explanation by then.

I close my laptop and stretch as I stand, wincing as my bones creak. *Fuck, I'm getting old.* Rolling my shoulders to loosen them, I grab my phone, slip it into my pocket, then go out the door.

Hearing voices coming up from the clubroom, I descend the stairs, my nostrils twitching as an aroma hits me, and I identify it at once. I'm not disappointed when I see my brothers opening boxes of pizzas.

"Hey, Grumbler. Got your favourite here."

Making a beeline toward Salem, I give my brother a grateful chin lift as he opens a box revealing a meat lover's delight or some fancy title or other. I don't care, not as long as it's fit for a carnivore. I take a large slice, then reach for another, piling one on top of the other. Salem grins and shakes his head, pushing the rest toward me.

"Take it all, there's plenty more."

There probably is. We usually over order so no one goes hungry around here.

"Hey, asshole." I swing around as, before I can claim the box, a hand reaches past me. "Get your fuckin' own."

Pennywise pretends to rub the hand I just slapped. "But man, I want this one." He pouts.

He's just fucking with me. It's par for the course. The MC is one big family, and like any siblings, we squabble, tease and plague the fuck out of each other at times. At the end of the day though, we have each other's backs. I can't imagine any other life. My blood family were good for nothings, dad was a drunk and my mom not much better. Dad had died early on—a burning cigarette had led to a house fire which my mom, my brother and I luckily escaped. Mom used her new freedom to find a replacement. The first one wasn't too bad, the one after, well, we never saw eye to eye. A decade or so back she'd succumbed to a heart attack. If I were a crier, I'd shed more tears about Smoker who'd recently passed rather than the loss of my blood family.

My brother? Well, we'd never seen eye to eye, different in almost everything. There was no animosity between us, but no love either, and we'd followed different paths in life. Growing up, he'd escaped into books whereas I'd been dyslexic—not that I'd had that diagnosis at the time. Consequently, despite our neglect in childhood, he'd gotten good grades and went on to live a corporate life. I, I'd found, had been better using my hands and was hired as a mechanic. I worked from when I was sixteen, bought my first motorcycle just two years later, and then my world fell apart.

I ended up serving my country. Not that it was bad, per se, but it wouldn't have been my choice and fucked up my other life's ambitions. But when life serves you lemons, you make lemonade or else you might as well roll over and die. I'd done my time, but when I got out, things weren't the same. I had pulled my bike out of storage and tried to make the best of having nothing else—no dreams, no aspirations, no job.

One day I'd stopped off at a biker bar which members of the Satan's Devils MC were using as a watering hole on one of their rides. They'd been looking to take on another employee in their auto-shop and my knowledge of anything mechanical matched what they were looking for.

I'd jumped at the chance, my original skills honed by my time spent in the Army. Then I'd listened, learned, and after hanging around, became a prospect. The rest, as they say, is history.

Suddenly I lurch forward. "You eating that pizza or just staring at it?"

"Mind your fuckin' business," I growl, rounding on Snips. "At least I *can* fuckin' eat it."

"Not fair, Brother, not fair." Snips face falls, but I've got no sympathy for the man.

"Just go to the dentist and get that fuckin' tooth taken out." He's been in pain for weeks. I sigh. Seems like we'll have to drag him there ourselves. It won't be the first time.

"You know how I feel about dentists," Snips complains.

We all do, he's told us enough. But hell, last time he'd suffered with an abscess for weeks and his face had puffed up like a hamster. Still, he had rather put up with that pain than get the root canal work done. Then we'd sneaked some sedatives into him and managed to get him there. Did we get a thank you? Like fuck.

With a wary eye in my direction as if I'm going to drag him there now, Snips sidles away, and now, at last emerged from my reverie, I down the two pieces of pizza in my hand. Then, I go back for more.

I'm licking tomato sauce off my fingers when I hear the summons to church and follow my brothers there. Passing

Token before going to my seat at the right hand of my prez, I lean and speak into his ear.

"Need some help, Brother. Speak after?"

"Sure, Grumbler."

"Online ordering still beyond you, old man?" Scribe, over-hearing, calls out.

I show him my finger. Nah, I've got that shit sorted now, but it had taken me longer to get used to it, letters and numbers get jumbled sometimes and I have to concentrate to get them straight. But I don't mind them pulling my leg about it, isn't that what brothers are for?

CHAPTER SIX

Mary

"You coming with us for a drink after work?" Kristen calls out as I walk past her cubicle.

On a Friday evening that sounds great, and I normally would but not tonight. "I can't." My eyebrows draw down.

"Alicia?" Terra, coming up alongside me asks, her voice sympathetic.

"She's grounded again," I confirm, my expression showing I've once more failed at being a mom.

"One day that kid of yours is going to appreciate everything you do for her."

I sigh and give a weak grin toward Kris, thinking that day will probably never come, or that it's so far off, I can't see it.

"Come talk to Momma Terra. What's she done this time?"

It's Friday afternoon, and my work is about done. I've finished preparing a disposition that will get to where it's supposed to be on time. I'd translated the residents' objection to the heavy-handed approach by a land developer into legal speak that will hopefully sufficiently impress a judge. I can spare a few moments to speak to my friend.

Terra is in her fifties and never had children of her own. Whether she wanted to and couldn't, or whether she'd made the wise decision not to burden herself like it seems I have done, I've never enquired. But she does like hearing about my daughter, maybe to confirm she'd made the right choice in her life. Kristen, in her early twenties, is still looking for Mr Right, for now settling on Mr Right Nows, which none of us mind, as she usually spills all the salacious details as she continues her search.

I'm not surprised when I pull up a seat next to Terra, Kristen leans over the partition to listen as well.

"Remember those photographs she had taken a month or so back?"

"Seven weeks," Kristen corrects. She's a bit anal retentive and remembers details like that.

Nodding, I continue, "That's when it started, the photo-shoot with the motorcycle." My voice trails off as I remember that was the day I'd met a real-life biker. He'd scared me at first, but when I'd spoken to him, I'd found him not what I expected. Polite, if a bit gruff, and overprotective about his bike and his cut. But then I'd been the same way about my daughter. Still, it turned out, being close to someone wearing a one-percenter patch hadn't made me feel in danger of my life. I'd been more suspicious about the photographer… there was a word for someone like him. Sleazy, that's it. I hadn't trusted him. It wasn't his profession, but the man himself.

Kristen waves her hand, obviously trying to hurry me up.

"Well, a couple of weeks back she was offered another photoshoot, studio work this time. I again went with her. There was another man in his late twenties, early thirties, perhaps." My eyes glaze as I remember thinking the pairing of the two models was only this side of tasteful. The age difference too apparent. "Once again, Alicia kicked off, said that she didn't need me there."

"Why are you only telling us now?" Terra hits my shoulder lightly.

I grimace. "I don't want her modelling for him anymore. Didn't want you two to say I was being too cautious."

"We'd never say that." Terra looks at me, while Kristen shrugs, letting me think she might be in camp Alicia. "Did anything happen?"

I huff a little. "Let's just say I'm glad I went. If I hadn't, well, I can't say for certain, but the looks Devon kept giving her made me think he was visualising her with her top off." I look at Terra, then at Kirstin. "She's only seventeen for goodness' sake."

"Far too young for her to be showing her body off." Kristen's head is now bobbing up and down in support.

"But he didn't actually come out and ask?"

I direct my reply to Terra, "No, but that could have been because I was present. Nothing gave me any confidence or let me want to loosen the strings. It wasn't even his studio, just somewhere he rented by the hour."

"Did she ever receive payment?"

I shake my head. "Presumably, none of the pictures have been sold. It has been a lesson that perhaps modelling isn't as lucrative as she first thought." I may have pointed out to her getting a part-time job in a local store might bring her in more money than standing looking pretty for a couple of hours. Lead and balloon come to mind when I think of how that went down.

"I was a pain in the ass as a teenager," Kristen informs us with a grin. "I objected to anything just because. Teenage hormones are the pits. You feel off balance and hit out at the closest thing, which normally happens to be mom or dad."

"I remember being a perfect angel," Terra disagrees.

She gets two pairs of rolling eyes directed toward her.

"I know it's a teenage thing, that her body's telling her she's an adult, yet in her head she's still not. I keep making allowances for her, but my patience is running thin." Thank goodness I'm a working mother and I can get out of the house and think about something different for a while. I'd go mad if I was stuck at home dealing with her moods all the time. The weekend ahead is going to be hard if I'm going to stick to my guns. Me and Alicia having one-on-one time for forty-eight plus hours is not my idea of fun. "I'm not letting her out of my sight this weekend."

Terra translates accurately. "So, what's she done to get grounded this time?" She's right. It's far from the first.

My lips purse, I breathe air in, half of me wanting to keep quiet. "I didn't know, Owen, the first model she was photographed with, the day they posed with the motorcycle? Well, he's been texting her. They've gotten quite friendly." Too friendly in my opinion,

"Go on." Terra reaches for a bottle of flavoured water, opens it and takes a sip. "What does friendly mean?"

"Friendly enough that I caught her texting him a topless photo of herself." The words leave my mouth in a rush, and I blush as I look first at Terra, then Kristen, wondering how they're going to take that bit of information.

After a moment's silence, Terra goes first. "Uh-uh. I'm so freaking glad smart phones weren't around when I was a kid."

Kristen's gone redder than me. "Um… Sounds like something I might have done."

"Might have? Or did?" Terra questions her.

The tone of her face goes darker, giving me the answer without words.

"Were there any repercussions?" I ask, wanting to be reassured.

"Not in my case, but seeing the dangers of sexting nowadays, I got lucky. It was only the once, and I trusted him when he said he deleted it."

Terra pats my hand reassuringly. "I'm sure you've got nothing to worry about. Owen's just a kid—"

"He's twenty-one." My brow creases. "That four-year age difference is immense when you're talking about a high school girl."

Again Kristen refuses to meet my eyes. Thinking she might have some tips on how to handle a teenager who thinks she's older than she is, I ask her directly, "How did you get on with your mom?"

"Honestly? My mom didn't care what I did. I made a few mistakes, learned from them the way you do."

I'm not sure what she's saying. I tilt my head. "So, are you suggesting I back off and let Alicia find her own way?" I'm not sure I could even do that. Isn't it a mom's job to guide their children right?

"Hell, no." Kristen looks aghast. "I said I made mistakes, and I don't want to go into them. Learning from them was hard. It would have saved me a whole lot of heartache if I'd not gone down the road that I had. I'm lucky that I pulled myself out. I wouldn't wish what I'd gone through on any kid."

Kristen has, as she puts it, turned out fine. In fact, if we hadn't had this conversation, I'd never have thought she'd had anything but a perfect past. Quickly, I think back over my inter-actions with her when she started at the firm a year or so back, and then remember there were times when a bleak look would come over her face, and she seemed closed off. That appears less often now, so rarely that I hadn't thought about it in ages.

"Maybe you should get Kristen and Alicia together." Terra looks shrewdly at the younger woman. "Get her to explain some of the seedier sides of life to Alicia."

It's an idea, but… "I don't think Alicia's in a space right now where she'd listen to anyone."

"No one could have told me," Kristen puts in. "I'd have known better, I always did. I was cleverer and knew more than anyone. In fact, I lost my best friend as I wouldn't listen to her warnings. But getting back to Alicia, you said you caught her sending a picture. Did she actually send it, or did you stop her in time?"

On that occasion I had. I'd walked into her bedroom to drop off some clothes that I'd just taken out of the dryer and folded, and got the shock of my life when I found her half naked in front of the mirror. "I think so," I say, biting my lip. "But I couldn't take the phone off her, she needs to be able to contact me. I read her the riot act, told her how stupid she was being literally exposing herself, then grounded her for the weekend when she refused to listen. Owen is apparently the love of her life."

"Has he sent her a dick pic?"

My eyes go theatrically wide. "God, I hope not."

What is it with teenagers nowadays? Even now I wouldn't think very highly of being a recipient of a picture of a man's cock. In my experience, it's nothing unless it's connected to a man who knows what to do with it.

"Mary, you got that disposition done?" a male voice interrupts.

A bit guiltily, I stand, clasping the file to me. "Here's the hard copy, Art. I've already filed it by email."

"I knew I could depend on you." As he speaks, I notice Art looks tired and relieved as I've confirmed I've completed my work. "Need to speak to you on Monday, we've got a new client who I want to discuss."

"Sure."

Once I've offered my agreement, Art waves his hand.

"Have a good weekend, ladies. And," he pauses and winks, "don't get too drunk tonight."

Terra snorts. "You're invited too."

As a boss, I probably couldn't do better. Art respects people who work hard, and you know where you are with him. Do your best and he'll have your back, slack off, and he'll come down hard. Sometimes he joins us for after-work drinks, and isn't shy on opening his wallet, but most times he doesn't.

"Not tonight. It's my wife's birthday tomorrow, and she's got something planned. But you lot have fun."

The clock's ticked around to clocking-off time, so I take my leave of my friends, wishing I was going out for a drink with them, or having a celebration to look forward to like Art. Instead, I'm going home for a weekend of babysitting my seventeen-year-old daughter who's behaving more like a petulant child.

A drive through rush hour traffic is never my idea of a good time. Stuck in an unmoving traffic jam, I notice a line of motorcycles lane splitting, quite legally, between the cars. As they pass, I notice their cuts bear the same insignia as the biker who I'd met all those weeks back. Idly, I wonder whether he's one of them. If so, right now, I envy the way their journey, at least, is unimpeded. I hadn't recognised his distinctive bike, though I had looked out for it.

When I at last get home, I'm weary. All I want to do is collapse on the sofa having poured a welcome glass of wine.

"You're late," a disembodied voice calls out. "What's for dinner? I'm starved."

At least she's home, I tell myself, having half feared to return to an empty house.

"There's nothing to eat here." A cupboard door slams, followed by the bang of the fridge, tells me her mood hasn't improved.

"Order pizza, or Chinese. Whatever you want." I'm a bad,

bad mom. I can't even feed my daughter. "Tomorrow, we'll go food shopping, maybe cook something together?"

"Count me out. And I want pizza." The sounds of footsteps stomping down the hall to her bedroom, and another door slamming shut, signals this conversation is over.

I stand, head bowed, dreading the weekend ahead.

CHAPTER SEVEN

Grumbler

Church is church. Business is discussed and decided in under an hour.

"Just one bit of other business from me." Lost taps his fingers on the table. "Drummer's getting impatient. It's been almost three months now, and there's still no sign of Stormy."

"What the fuck is Utah doing with all the computer power they've got? I thought they could 'get into Fort Knox.'" Token looks disgusted.

"They're not fuckin' trying, or they know where he is," I offer, thinking it highly likely.

"That's Drummer's thinking," Prez agrees. He grimaces. "He's worried Snatcher knows more than he's letting on and has got Stormy out working alone again."

The VP shakes his head. "Road's a good man. He wouldn't let that shit fly."

"Maybe Pip and Snatcher are doing shit in secret without it being brought out into the open," Salem proposes. "It wouldn't be the first fuckin' time."

Growls go around. Our chapter understands the dangers of

that only too well. Snake and my predecessor, Poke, had plotted secretly against the club, enlisting seven other brothers to help them. I wonder if Drummer thinks something like that's going on in Utah.

"So what's Drummer proposing?"

Lost's lips press together. "He's given Snatcher two more weeks to find him. After that, he'll be enlisting the help of the Wretched Soulz and all friendly clubs to watch out for him."

"The man must be somewhere."

Reboot gets a slap around the back of his head from Deuce. "Kind of obvious."

"He could be dead." Niran frowns. "Man riding on his own is always at risk."

"Unless he's at the bottom of a ravine, there'd be reports of a death or hospitalisation."

"He should be six feet under," I grumble in my normal way. I'll never forgive the man for taking the shot that killed Alder. A sideways glance at Lost shows me he feels the same way.

"Any particular reason you're telling us this?" The VP looks to his right. "Apart from keeping our eyes open in the unlikely event he comes San Diego's way?"

Salem snorts. "Yeah, like he's going to turn up and ask us to do custom work on his bike. He's more likely to be on the other end of the country or even overseas if the man's got any sense."

Lost isn't the normal battle-scarred badass who runs an outlaw motorcycle club. He still has an aura of the businessman he previously was, but he shouldn't be underestimated. When the chips are down and his family, whether brothers or his old lady, are threatened, he's as hard as they come, and not afraid to get his hands dirty. His face darkens now.

"If Drummer's suspicions are right and he makes good on

his threat to disband the Utah chapter, they may not go down without a fight. We may be asked to cross states and be ready to ride at his side."

"If it comes to that, we'll be ready," I assure him. Not that I'd like to take out any man who wears a Satan's Devils' patch, but if they're setting themselves against the mother chapter, they'd better be prepared to take all chapters on as well.

Lost gives me a chin lift and notes the serious expressions all around. "I'm hoping that won't be the outcome, but just wanted to give a heads-up in case. Right." He lifts the gavel and bangs it. "Church is over for tonight."

As brothers get up, snippets of conversation reach my ears. More than one comment is made about *fuckin' Stormy* and what they'll do if he comes into our hands. Pennywise and Salem are more focused on the possible parallels between Snake and Snatcher, if Drummer's worst assumptions prove correct. For a moment, I sit, wondering about Satan's Devils pitching themselves against other club members. I sincerely hope the matter resolves before it comes to that. I'd prefer to think Stormy's disappearance is that he's dead and his body just hasn't been found as yet.

"You wanted to talk to me?" Token slips into the seat Scribe has just vacated.

"Yeah." After that one word, I realise I still haven't come up with an excuse of why I'm looking for a woman. As Token raises an eyebrow, I continue, "I want to find someone's address." I don't have to give him a reason, do I?

"Sure. Who?" Token pulls his laptop to him.

"Mary Styles. I think that's her name. She's got a daughter, Alicia Styles."

"Husband?"

I shake my head. "Not in the picture."

"Hmm." Token eyes me carefully. "You think she may have reverted to her maiden name?"

"No fuckin' clue, Brother. The husband's dead, so maybe unlikely."

"But you're certain of the daughter's?"

I nod. "Yes." Well I think I am. *Do models use pseudonyms?*

"Do you know how old she is?"

"Seventeen." I remember Mary telling me.

"I'll start with the daughter. She should be at high school unless she's dropped out."

It sounds a good plan. From what I remember of Mary, I doubt she'd let her daughter leave school without her diploma. Though I could be wrong, of course.

Token's brow is creased. "I assume I'm looking in San Diego?"

"Start there." She could live anywhere nearby, but the city is the place to start.

"Okay, leave it with me, Brother." His head tilts to the side, and I wait for him to ask me the reason, but it seems he's not curious enough to ask. Whatever question was on his lips remains unspoken.

As he gets up to leave, I realise all my worrying about an interrogation was for nothing. Token walks purposefully to the door with a wave of his hand, totally focused on the task he's been handed.

It's Friday night, business is done, so it's time for partying now. In years past, I'd like nothing more than to fuddle my head with copious beers and sink my cock into any available pussy. It wasn't unknown for me to have more than one girl in a night, and often more than one together. Now, I don't bother thinking about it. I can't be sure if it's my cock that's stopped working or if girls young enough to be my granddaughter don't cut it for me anymore, or maybe it's the fear I'd not be able to perform as expected from a biker.

When Smoker was alive, I'd normally gravitate to him,

drink and shoot the shit. But now he's gone, it's our party nights when I most miss him. Lost is only a few years younger than me, but he's got his old lady, and rightly spends most of his time with her. Bones, now he's on the brink of getting old like me, but when I emerge into the clubroom, I see he's got his arm around Eva, and I doubt he'd leave the promise of sex for a few hours conversing with me.

I don't have it in me to envy him, just mentally wish him well to enjoy it while he still can.

With one less appetite to feed, I make my way to the bar. "Whisky," I demand when I get there.

Curtis jumps to attention and soon there's a shot glass in front of me.

"Grumbler? Want me to deal you in?"

A smile appears on my face. Yeah, a game of poker would suit me just fine. Picking up my glass, I take it over to join Brakes, Pennywise and Snips. A few hours later, I've a nice mound of notes piling up beside me.

"I'm out," Snips says, his eyes narrowing. "You've fuckin' cleaned me out, Grumbler. What about you, Brakes?" When he gets no answer, he asks again, "Brakes?"

"What? Oh, I was..." He doesn't need to complete his sentence.

As one, the three of us turn to see what's caught his attention. It's Kink. He's got two pets tonight. Both naked, both wearing collars, and they're crawling through the clubroom while he holds two leashes and wields a whip as though he's driving a chariot.

"They're wearing tails," Pennywise notes, unnecessarily.

"Pony play," Brakes says, knowledgeably.

"Each to their own," Snips notes, rubbing at his jaw, reminding me I need to mention to Lost that a visit to the dentist is necessary.

A hand lands on my shoulder. Dragging my eyes away

from the procession I'd been avidly watching—well, it might not arouse me, but it sure is entertaining—I glance around and see Token. He's holding a note in his hand which he passes to me. "Only one Alicia Styles of that age in a local high school. Here's her address."

I don't bother asking how he got it, knowing there'll be more than one high school database he hacked into tonight. Luckily, the nosy fuckers at the table with me are still intent on Kink's latest pets, and not on Token or me. I don't think they've even noticed he's arrived. Brakes is unashamedly stroking his dick through his jeans.

"Thanks, Brother."

"Anything you need help with?" Token offers.

I stand, slipping the piece of paper into my pocket, and slap his back. "Nah, I got this."

Walking away from the table, I notice the hours have flown past. It's far too late to pay Mary a visit tonight. A biker turning up at this late hour would not go down well, and anyway, I've had a few too many whiskies to ride. Deciding I'll go and see if I've got the correct address first thing in the morning, I take myself off to bed, noticing as I get to the foot of the stairs that Niran's surrounded by a bevy of girls—not unusual. He's tall and striking looking, and while he's got a prosthetic leg, he's still gets a lot of interest from the simpering hangarounds wanting to find out if the rumours about black cocks have any truth in them. While he's candid about the reason he's a magnet for the girls, he's never told me, and I've never asked whether they've got their facts right.

Presumably, the whisky's relaxed me and as soon as my head hits the pillow, I'm out like a light.

It's another day of cloudless blue skies when I awake. I go through my morning preparations, throwing on the nearest clean t-shirt to hand, then, after making myself a quick break-fast, head out to my bike. I wheel it out of the parking spot in between the other bikes, then taking a rag out of my saddlebag, wipe off the dust that's settled overnight. It's early, most of the other brothers were partying late, making me remember I'm the oldest one now, so no one else is about. Suits me fine. And though I had a few whiskies last night, I didn't overindulge so I've escaped the hangover as well.

I've already checked out the address I'm headed for. Having lived in San Diego all my life, I know the locale and don't need to have my GPS as a guide. After standing back for a second to admire the sun glinting off my beloved Harley, I swing my leg over the seat and settle in for the short ride. Maybe later when I return, I'll see if Niran wants to head out on a longer run. That's if he's recovered from last night. I grin. *Enjoy being young while you can, Brother.*

I'm glad I'm on the bike as the traffic is already building. Even so, it takes me an hour to cover the distance that a few years ago would only have taken me half of that. Idly I wonder whether Mary's a San Diego native, or a newcomer like so many are. Not that anything about her really interests me, it's any knowledge she's got about the damn photographer that's my object today.

The house is small, the front yard well maintained, though the flowers look a little neglected and dry. I park on the road, take the key out of my bike, then head up to the front door. As I approach, still wondering whether Token has the most recent address or the correct woman in question, that this is the right house to find Alicia Styles is confirmed by the sounds coming from inside.

"I'm not going anywhere!" a shrill young voice cries.

"Alicia! I'm not leaving you here. You're coming to help."

"I'm not wasting my Saturday walking around a grocery store. You can't make me."

"I know I can't make you." I hear the resignation in Mary's voice. "I'm not leaving you here on your own."

"I'm not a fucking baby."

"Don't swear!" There's a pause, then, "I know you're not." It's said in a reasonable tone, and I admire her patience. "Please, I could do with your help."

There's silence. Then. "Alicia, no. You're grounded. You're not going—"

In front of me the door is flung open, and the girl who I last saw modelling by my bike comes running out, in her haste, crashing right into me. She's a small tender thing and I barely bend. She though, well, she looks as shocked as I am to find a girl in my arms.

"Who…? What…? What the hell are *you* doing here?"

"Alicia, get back inside."

Mary's got a look of relief on her face as the escape of her daughter has been stopped. It overcomes her curiosity at seeing me here. The girl who's smartly removed herself from our inappropriate closeness by taking a step back, looks past me as if calculating her chances of making a run for it.

"Don't even think about it," I growl, using my best sergeant-at-arms voice, the one that pulls my brothers up short.

It seems to work on her as well, as with one last glance at freedom, she turns, pushes past her mom, and disappears into the house.

I stare after her. "You got a back door?"

"Locked." Mary pats her pocket letting me know the key's in there. Then she sighs. "But the windows aren't. Though I hope she isn't that desperate."

"She got somewhere she needs to be?"

"Just as far as she can get from me." Mary slumps against the doorframe as though needing it to hold her up. "I've grounded her."

I could ask what she's done, or not done I suppose, to deserve that, but that's not why I've driven through the traffic today. I think that the conflict between mother and daughter is the reason Mary's not immediately asked the reason for my visit either. Deciding I've better things to be doing than dealing with two fighting females, I come right out with it.

"Alicia get her modelling fee?"

Mary tilts her head to the side, and her brow creases. It takes a moment for the penny to drop. "Oh, from the photo shoot. No, nothing came of that. Obviously no photos were sold. Not from that shoot, nor the other she did."

I notice the way her mouth twists in distaste but push her reaction to one side of my brain.

I'd expected to find Devon Starr had fleeced me because I was an ignorant biker, and because it was my bike that had modelled and not myself. But now I find it wasn't only me he'd tried to scam out of money. A picture is worth a thousand words, they say, so instead of using words, I get out my phone, and call up the photo of the cover of the book Patsy had shown to me. I turn it so Mary can see the screen.

She reaches out to take it from me and I let her. After she's studied it, I swipe to the next photo which has the model details inside. Her eyes widen, and she raises them to me.

I nod, letting her know what she's thinking is right. Devon Starr has sold at least one of the photos he'd taken and neither paid me nor her daughter.

"The rat," she states firmly. "That rat bastard. He's not said a word."

CHAPTER EIGHT

Mary

I called him the worst thing I could say out loud, but in my head I'm not as ladylike. I'm not so annoyed on my own behalf, but on my daughter's. Alicia, so young and innocent of the ways of the world, is going to have her illusions shattered. For a moment, I wonder whether I could lie and pay her the money myself. But while I work, I'm paying a mortgage and bringing up a daughter on my own, and my car needs work done. I can't find two hundred dollars out of thin air.

Perhaps the biker in front of me is mistaken.

"When was the book published?"

"Recently. I contacted the author. She bought the rights to the photo a few weeks back. Paid in full."

I bite my lip and look back at the phone I'm still holding. "Maybe he takes time to contact his models."

The biker, whose name I'm struggling to remember, shrugs. "I'd like to ask him to find out."

"I've got his number…"

Another rise and fall of his shoulders. "I like discussing money face-to-face."

I eye the sergeant-at-arms patch on his cut and wonder if money talks with him normally involve fists. It wouldn't surprise me from the little I know about bikers.

"Do you, or your daughter, have an address for him?"

"No…" I start, then stop. "Alicia did another shoot with him, but it was in a rented studio space." Again, my teeth worry my lip.

"Can we ask her if she's got any more information?"

"I was with her the whole time." I'm not being difficult, I just don't know how I can help. Obviously the biker wants his agreed payment. I realise I want justice for my daughter and find out where hers is as well. Thinking again, it's possible Alicia might know more, she's gotten very friendly with the first model, Owen.

With my head still bent, I look up through my eyelashes, eyeing him shrewdly. I don't get any threatening vibe and am certain he's not here to rob me. "Look, why don't you come in and we can ask her." And there'll be someone with me when Alicia realises she's been had. Maybe it would make it easier on her if she knows she's not the only one. But who, exactly, am I inviting into my home? Am I right to be sure he's not going to hurt me? I accuse Alicia of being naïve, am I as well? Oh damn it, I've nothing to steal. I raise my head. "Please come in…?"

"Grumbler," he supplies.

Stupidly I hold out my hand. "Mary."

"*I* remember," he says with a quick grin and, leaning in, he takes my hand and holds it lightly in his much larger paw, but he lets it go almost immediately.

Flustered for some reason, I step to one side, and wave him past me, while simultaneously calling out, "Alicia, come here a moment."

There's silence. I roll my eyes. "Sorry, look, take a seat, I'll go get her."

Instead of sitting, he remains standing. He shakes his head, opens his mouth and bellows, "Alicia, get out here. Your mom wants to speak to you."

Resisting the urge to cover my ears, I grin at him, observing, "That should work."

It does. Seconds later, I hear a door banging open, then wince as it's slammed shut. Then my daughter appears.

"What the fuck does she want me for?"

"Ask in a pleasanter tone and you might get an answer." Grumbler pulls himself to his full height and glares at Alicia.

Raised for the past seven years without a father's influence, Alicia isn't used to a man's stern tone. Her mouth opens and closes as she swallows down her retort, correctly surmising the way she normally speaks to me won't work on him. But knowing her as I do, I'm not surprised when she goes the other way instead, turning her eyes on me, and asking in sweet dulcet tones, "Dear Mother, what can I do for you?"

Grumbler snorts a laugh. "You are trouble, aren't you?"

He doesn't know the half of it. But a corner of Alicia's mouth turns up, and some of her anger leaves her.

The biker reaches for his phone which I'm embarrassed to find I'm still holding, having moved it into my left hand when I'd shaken his. He unlocks it again, then turns it toward her.

Now her jaw drops, and a huge grin covers her face. "Mom! Have you seen this? I'm on the cover of a freaking book. Look." She turns the phone to face me. "Look, Mom, I'm on the cover. Can you believe it?" She actually jumps up and down on the spot, then stops and turns to Grumbler. "Can you send this to my phone, my number is—"

Before she can give him the digits, I put my hand on her arm. "Sit, Alicia. We need to talk." I hate to burst her bubble and think how I can emphasise the positives. Yes, one of the photos she had taken was chosen to be on a book, that's the big thing, isn't it? That the photographer scammed her out of the money may not be so important to her.

"It's great news." Grumbler takes the single chair while I sit next to my daughter on the small two-seater couch. He winks at her. "It's a great shot of my bike."

Alicia jumps up. "Can I see it again?"

He passes his phone over to her. "Send it to yourself," he suggests. As she presses a few keys and does so, he sits forward, his legs parted, and his hands clasped together.

I appreciate that he's given her a moment to digest that it's really her on the cover of a published book, and not immediately jumping in with unpleasantries. I know what she's going to want to do next, so standing, I take Grumbler's phone from her, give it back, then stop her when she starts taking her own device out of the pocket of her jean shorts. If I don't, she'll be messaging all her friends and posting about it on Facebook before she's given us a chance to talk.

"Alicia, sit down." It's my *I want a grown-up conversation* voice.

She hesitates for a moment, then looks at Grumbler who's now frowning again, then back at the serious look on my face. "What's going on?"

Grumbler starts before I can. "Devon Starr agreed to pay me a fee for using my bike. He hasn't. He didn't tell me the photo was sold, and I only found out when one of our ol' ladies was reading the book and recognised my Harley."

"One of your old ladies?" Alicia giggles. "*This* book? Old ladies don't read these types of romances."

Grumbler shakes his head, while I reprimand her gently. "Doesn't matter how old you are if it's a good book." I'm still trying to deal with the thought his club seems full of elderly women. Do they clean and cook?

"Not that type of ol' lady," Grumbler starts, but doesn't go on to explain how there can be different types. "Thing is, Starr should have contacted me and arranged payment."

It's my daughter's turn to shrug. "That doesn't mean anything. He's not paid me yet either."

Grumbler just stares at her. I watch as she meets his eyes, then, knowing my girl may be naïve but she's far from stupid, I wait for the penny to drop. It doesn't take long.

"You don't think he's going to, do you? Have you spoken to him?"

"Not yet," he admits. "Thing is, I prefer looking a man in the face, so I'm trying to locate him."

I narrow my eyes. "How did you find my address?"

For a second, he looks sheepish. "We've got a computer guy, he can find anyone."

I'm not sure I like the sound of that. But case in point, "So why hasn't he found Devon?"

I'm intrigued when Grumbler looks completely sheepish. "I didn't ask."

My brow furrows. "You didn't ask? Yet you asked him to find us."

He glances down at his hands. "Yeah, well. I didn't tell my brothers that Devon had used my bike."

I snort in an unladylike manner. He's embarrassed. It's then I realise this rough tough biker isn't as intimidating as he seems. He doesn't want to get teased. I was right to believe I had nothing to worry from him.

"I thought I'd come speak to you first." His eyes plead with me to let the matter drop.

"Why don't we just call him?" Alicia's eyebrows draw down. "That's easiest, isn't it? Ask him for the money?"

"I think it's worth a try." I know Grumbler doesn't, but the man can either refuse or say yes. I don't know how quickly photographers are supposed to pay up, and it's possible he's got cash flow problems or some such other excuse. It could be the payment is delayed and will be coming soon.

Grumbler takes a breath, holds it, then lets it out with a deep resigned sigh. "Okay." He had put his phone away, but now he takes it out again.

"No," I say quickly. "Let me do it." I'm wary Grumbler could easily put the photographer's back up. If he refuses to pay, he might threaten him.

Grumbler stares at me, then he nods, and says with a small chuckle, "You think I might threaten his pretty white teeth?"

I grin back. Apparently, I'm transparent.

"Here, use my phone. I added his number in my contacts," Alicia suggests. "Put it on speaker."

I glance at Grumbler who mimes zipping his mouth and waves his hand. I interpret he doesn't want Devon to know that he's here.

Taking my daughter's phone, I call up his name, then press the green key. Alicia leans over, clicking the speaker as if I didn't know how a phone works. I put it down on the couch between us.

"Devon Starr."

"Hi, it's Mary Styles here. My daughter, Alicia, modelled for you a couple of times."

There's a pause, then a cautious, "Oh yes. Of course. Now what can I do for you? Does she want more work?"

"She's here with me now, actually. You're on speaker."

"Hi, Alicia. You alright?"

"I'm good, Devon." She's using a respectful tone, as though she's slightly in awe of the photographer, the man who, in her eyes, maybe holds the key to a modelling career.

"Devon, we've just found out that one of the photos of Alicia was sold. One from the shoot with the motorcycle and your model, Owen."

"Was it?" Another pause. "I'm afraid I don't know offhand. I'll have to check. Sometimes my assistant deals with that."

I've never seen an assistant. I see Grumbler raising his eyebrows.

"It was sold about..." Grumbler holds up five fingers, "about five weeks back. The book is already published."

Devon doesn't speak for a few seconds. "What book?"

Alicia shows me the photo. "*Death Ride*, by Fara Weir."

"Ah, yes. I remember now. Well, I'll be able to pay your modelling fee once I've had the final payment from the author. She asked to pay in instalments. Often authors do."

"How long was the instalment plan?"

"Six months. It's standard practice."

I see Grumbler shaking his head violently. His face has gone red, and his hands have formed fists. He mouths *she paid in full*. Oh yes, he had told me.

I'm not sure whether I should call Devon out or just leave it. I decide, for now, to do the latter. "So Alicia can expect her money in five months' time?" I remember one has already gone past.

"Of course," Devon replies chirpily. "I'll be in contact if I have any more work for Alicia."

Biting my tongue to stop myself telling him to forget it, I say goodbye and end the call.

"He's a fuckin' liar," Grumbler, well, grumbles.

"Why?" Alicia seems brighter. She's still expecting her money.

"Because," Grumbler gentles his voice, "the author told me she paid in full. All this crap about instalment plans is rubbish."

Alicia picks up her phone again and stares at the picture. She seems torn between the pleasure of having her photo on an actual book cover and worrying about getting her due payment. But then, she doesn't have the money worries she will when she's an adult. If she needs anything, the Bank of Mom pays for it.

When she next speaks, it seems the pleasure at her new fame wins out. "Can we buy the paperback, Mom?"

I sigh. "Of course we can."

She grins and pulls herself to the edge of the couch seat. "I'm going to go tell everyone."

"Alicia. Before you do that, I've some questions for you," Grumbler barks.

Alicia had been about to stand. She now flops back down, her expression sulky that her plans have been disrupted. "What?"

"Have you got Owen's number?" At her nod, Grumbler continues, "Can you give it to me, please?"

Having Grumbler's from texting herself the image, she taps at a few keys. Grumbler nods his thanks. He must have felt his phone vibrate.

"Can I go now?"

"Just one more minute. Have you any idea where Devon lives? He ever mention that to you?"

Alicia's head moves slowly side to side. "I have no idea. Is that all?"

She's bouncing with excitement to share her news with her friends. I cast a glance at Grumbler who seems to realise she has no more information to give. "Yes, you can go."

As she disappears into her room to do exactly that, I lower my head into my hands. "She's never going to get her money," I mumble.

"She will," a gruff voice confirms. "I'll make sure of it."

CHAPTER NINE

Grumbler

he will. I'll make sure of it.

As I drive away from the neat little suburban house, I wonder how I'm going to make good on the rash promise I'd just made. Though there's probably less doubt that I will than how I'll go about it. That will need a bit of thought.

I'll need Token's help, that's for sure, and though I got away with it last time, if I ask him to find someone else, then he's bound to start asking questions. I suppose it's because his business is digging for information, it's obvious he's got to be a nosy fucker. Following trails, adding the dots together is what he's does best.

I could ask him to keep it a secret, but once he knows what my vanity over my bike got me into, he's not going to be able to keep that quiet. Nor that my baby is on the cover of a romance novel. Christ, why did I ever get involved with this?

Because I'm proud of my ride and wanted to show it off. Pride cometh before a fall and all that. Well, maybe I should have thought about that before setting myself up to be made a fool.

On the other hand, perhaps I don't have to involve anyone else. I've got Owen's number, I can just call him. He might have the information I want. I don't need my brothers. I'm more than a match for this Devon fucker. As soon as I track him down, I'll confront him, and if he doesn't pass the dollars over, I'll take payment in blood. His. Nah, I don't need anyone's help for that.

There's no time like the present.

Pulling off the road, I park up and take my phone out of my cut. Perhaps if Owen can give me the fucker's location, I can get this done and dusted before I go back to the club. I call up the text Alicia sent, and press on the highlighted number.

The phone rings, once, twice. By the fifth time, I'm about to give up, but then it's answered.

"It's Owen."

"Hi Owen. It's Grumbler. We met at a photo shoot a few weeks back. You posed with my motorcycle."

"Ah… Grumbler." His voice sounds flat.

"Yeah. One of the photos was used on a book cover. You know that?"

There's silence, then, "Alicia just called me and told me that."

They're so fucking friendly he was the first she'd called? Well, I suppose that's for her and her mom to sort out. I hadn't taken to him that's for certain.

Suddenly I wish I'd asked him to meet rather than rashly giving him a call. It's hard to interpret anything when you can't see a man's face.

"Did you know before?"

"Er, no."

Is that the truth? Or the answer he thinks he should give?

"Alicia told me that author was paying in instalments. She'll get her money in good time, but it's great news about the cover. Always good for models to get their names known. She and I might get more work from it."

She'll get her money in good time. Funny phrasing.

"Did you get paid, Owen?" I ask.

When he again replies 'no', there's something in his tone that makes me wish more than ever we were doing this so I could look him in the eye, as the idea comes to me that Devon might have paid him, but not us. But on the phone, I can't push it, else I risk him hanging up.

"You work with Devon Starr a lot?"

"Some, yeah. I model for him on occasion. He likes my face."

I'd like to rearrange your fuckin' face, you smarmy little bastard.

I hadn't thought much of the egotistical dick the day of the photograph shoot, and it seems I haven't changed my opinion.

"I'd like to see him, you got his address?"

"Why?"

Thinking fast, I reply, "I'd like to talk to him about perhaps using my bike again." *Over my dead body,* I add in my head.

"Ah, well. I've got his number. You can give him a call to discuss that."

He won't be giving me the address even if he knows it unless I was right in his face and using my own brand of persuasion.

"You got another shoot arranged?" If he has, there'll be an extra participant.

"No. Not that I know of."

I take in a deep breath and try to keep my voice calm. "Would you do me a favour, Owen? If Devon contacts you, will you let me know when and where the shoot is?"

There's a pause, then, "Sure. I can do that."

But the undertone suggests that's the last thing he'll be doing. I end the call, more frustrated than when I started. Of course, I can't prove anything, but I reckon Owen and Devon are cut from the same cloth. I start to wonder how many other models they're scamming. If they cut me and Alicia out of it, more money for them both.

Damn. That was no help at all. Now I've got one other person to find and beat the truth out of. Starting my engine again, pulling away and kicking up through the gears, frustration goes through me. I've no option but to involve Token.

I park my bike in its space back at the clubhouse and walk inside.

"Uh-uh. What's got your panties all twisted up?" Salem grins as I walk past.

"You okay, Brother?" Niran queries. "Want to talk?"

Salem gets my finger, Niran a raise of my chin and a dismissive shake of my head.

"Anyone seen fuckin' Toke?" I call out grumpily to no one in particular.

"I'm here," the man in question replies, his voice sounding oddly muffled, which is explained as he exits the kitchen holding a loaded biscuit, half of which appears to be in his mouth. "You find that bitch you were after?"

Pennywise's jaw drops. "Grumbler's got a woman?" He mimics fainting, clutching at the back of a chair to hold himself up. "Never thought I'd see the fuckin' day."

"Who is she?" Bones asks. "Some hottie?"

I've had enough of this. "Shut the fuck up!" They all get my sergeant-at-arms scowl. "I ain't got a woman, okay? Never have. Never fuckin' will."

Token takes pity on me. "Come on, Brother. Let's go sort out what you need."

I stomp after the computer guru, angry with him for opening his mouth. Fuck, if they were like that about me finding one woman, what are they going to say when they know what I did with my bike?

Token steps into his office leaving the door open. I close it behind me as I enter, then stand with my back against it and my arms folded.

"This is between us," I start. "No need to involve the club. It's a private fuckin' matter." I scowl at him. When he raises his chin, I continue, "A month or so back, I was offered cash for my bike to be used as a prop in a photo shoot."

"Ha ha! You didn't fall for that, did you?" Token laughs like a loon. "I can just picture you telling the guy to get lost. You leave him with all his teeth?" He chuckles again, then gets sight of the expression on my face. "Er, you did cut him loose, didn't you?"

I just stare.

Token backtracks fast. "It's a nice-looking ride." His eyes narrow. "Is there good money in that?"

"The deal is, you get paid if any of the pictures get sold."

He nods as though that makes sense. "And have they? Been sold?"

"One has."

Token beams and slaps his hand on the desk. "Well, that's fuckin' ace, Brother. Congrats. What's it going to be used for? One of the motorcycle rags? Advertising poster? The Harley mag? Jeez. This is great. How much did you get? The brothers are going to be hyped about this. I know we give you shit about all you do on that bike, but the results have been amazing. Glad someone appreciated it." He stares at my face, then his smile slowly falls away. "It's not good?"

"I found the picture was sold when it appeared on the cover of one of the books the prez's ol' lady reads."

"You… Patsy?" Token's brows draw down into a V and then he snorts. "She reads fuckin' mommy porn."

Porn? No wonder Lost walks around with a smile on his face. I sigh, there's nothing else for it. Through gritted teeth, I admit everything. "My bike was used as a prop with two young models, and it's appeared as a cover for a romance book. I only found out when Patsy told me. Neither I nor the female model have been paid, and the photographer's come up with a shit story as to the reason why we haven't gotten the dollars we were owed."

Token bends himself in half. "You-you…" he stammers out. "You and a model? Christ, Brother. No wonder you wanted me to track her down."

"What? Me and the model?" Approaching him, I slam both palms on his desk. "The model is only fuckin' seventeen."

"Yeah, bit young for you, I suppose." Token looks confused.

"I didn't want to find the model. I wanted to find her fuckin' mother." I roll my eyes. I don't want him to think I've been harassing an underage girl. "But that's a dead end. I found out she's not been paid either, and the photographer is holding onto our cash for no good fuckin' reason."

Now his mouth thins. "So when are we going to shake down this photographer?"

I lean forward. "When I can fuckin' find him."

"Ah." It looks like a light bulb has been switched on. "Okay. Why the fuck didn't you ask me to look for him in the first place? I presume you know his name?" When I nod, his brow creases, then he bellows with laughter again. "You didn't want to admit what you'd been doing. Christ, Brother, this is priceless." He chortles, leaning over and holding his belly.

"I need you to find Devon Starr," I tell him, speaking as clearly as I can with a clenched jaw, while wondering whether I should have just taken a hit on the money.

Token types the name onto his keyboard then eyes the screen. He waves me to a seat which indicates this is going to take a moment.

I sit, resting my ankle on my opposite knee, and clasping

my hands, tap at my chin. I allow Token the time and space to think.

"Hmm. I got a website," he says after a few moments.

"He's got Facebook and Instagram too."

Token's mouth purses. He tries one thing, then another. "We seem to have a man who doesn't want to be found. A man who clearly doesn't pay his debts. You don't make this easy, do you?" He lowers his head, his fingers massaging his temples. After a moment, he looks up. "You got a copy of the photo that was used?"

"I've got a pic of the cover on my phone."

"Give me your phone."

Unlocking it, I select the photo and pass it over. Token presses a few keys, then hands it back. He's all seriousness now, his joking manner gone. He's obviously emailed the photo to himself and now he's intent on what he's doing. After a moment, he turns around his screen. "I did a reverse image search. There's been more than one photo sold. Your bike is on five covers, not one. They must be popular shots."

"Why would all the authors use the same picture?"

"Look closer. It's not the same shot, but only fractionally different. Technically, the photos are unique. That's how photographers make their money."

I grunt. Seems Alicia and I have been cheated out of a thousand dollars apiece. When I get my hands on Devon Starr, I'm going to kill him.

"These are published books," Token remarks. "Or books up for pre-order or have had their covers released, whatever that means. There could be more."

"Fuck it." I exhale the words.

Token's staring at me. "You've been taken for a ride, Brother."

"Find him, Toke." My words are growled. "You don't mess with me and get away with it."

"Oh, I will," Token promises, leaving me in no doubt he'll leave no stone unturned to find the fucker. "Mess with one of us, you mess with us all. You don't try to get one over on a member of the Satan's Devils MC."

I spend the next few minutes giving him the little information I've got. Owen Leesom's name, and the phone numbers. Then I leave him to do what he does best—finding information.

CHAPTER TEN

Mary

"**D**o you think Grumbler will get me the money I'm owed?"

Drying the plate I'm holding in my hand, I stare out of the window as I think how to answer. While I don't know anything about the man, something tells me that he'll do what he can to get Alicia's money to her. Of course, if he finds the photographer, there's nothing to say he wouldn't get her money as well and keep it for himself, but I don't get the vibe that he'd do that. Honest is not something I'd thought would be my first impression of a biker, but with him, I definitely felt that.

"If he can find Devon, I think he'll get it for you."

"Should we ring him again? Devon, I mean?"

We could, but I doubt we'd get an honest answer. All we'd do is get his back up and put him on his guard. "Let's leave it to Grumbler."

"Well I hope he doesn't take too long. I've seen a pair of shoes I want. Unless," she waits until I put the plate away, then places her hand on my arm, "you could lend me the money?" She looks up and bats her eyelids.

"How much?" I ask, automatically.

"One hundred and fifty dollars."

Did I say my daughter has expensive tastes? Tastes I don't give in to. "Nope."

It seems she hadn't expected me to fork out that much, as she lets it go. "What's for dinner?"

It's Sunday, one of the only days I get time to cook. "Pot roast," I tell her, almost triumphantly. See? I can be a real mom at times.

"Cool. Do you want any help?"

Now I raise my eyebrow suspiciously. "What do you want?"

She gives a theatrical shrug. "Nothing, why?"

Shaking my head, I respond, "Because, Alicia, daughter dearest, an offer from you to peel vegetables always comes with strings attached. Why don't you just cut to the chase and tell me what you want?"

Her lips purse. She looks down at her hands and picks at her fingernails. It's a moment before she speaks. "Marisa has asked if I'd like to go over to her place tonight."

After Grumbler had left yesterday, Alicia had been so amped up by the news she was able to share with her friends, she'd actually forgotten she was on lockdown for the weekend. With a proportionate lifting of her mood to the extent that we'd watched a movie together last night—a romantic comedy which had made us both laugh. But I'd grounded her for the two days and I'm not backing down. I'm not looking forward to reminding her of that.

I decide on a compromise. "Why don't you ask Marisa to come here?"

"Because she's got an Xbox, and she wants to show me a new game she's got."

I narrow my eyes, shrewdly. "You don't like games." It's the reason she hasn't got the same game box as her friend.

"Not normally, but this one sounds good, Mom. Please, can I go?"

Just as I'm about to say no, her phone rings. Her eyes narrow as she looks at the screen, then cautiously answers it.

"Hello?... Oh, hi… Yes, she's here…" She holds the phone out to me. "It's Grumbler."

My eyes widen, then I realise he might be ringing with an update about Alicia's money. I didn't expect him to get results so fast. "Hi. It's Mary."

"Grumbler here."

Even if Alicia hadn't already warned me who it was, I'd recognise that gravelly voice anywhere. "Have you got news?"

"Yes and no." It's an enigmatic reply, and I wait for him to elaborate. "I suppose it might be good news that the fucker's sold four more photos which we haven't gotten paid for."

I glance at my daughter, thinking again how photogenic she is and that it must be her that's selling the photos. Then realise I'm biased. It could be Grumbler's motorcycle.

"The bad news," he continues, "is that the fucker doesn't want to be found. We'll find him but haven't done so as yet. Personally, I'd like to have a look at his financials, see if we can find how many pictures he sells, and whether he's got outgoing transactions showing he's paying his model fees."

"But he must be, surely. This could be a one-off, that he's short of cash flow. And, isn't that illegal? How can you check his bank account?"

Grumbler chuckles softly. "You're right. We won't be able to do that, not until we find him. But someone as evasive as him is probably scamming lots of people."

"He wouldn't get away with it. Surely models would see their pictures on books?"

"You a reader, Mary?"

"I read a bit. Lee Childs is one of my favourite authors. Stephen King too."

"I've been talking to Patsy, our prez's old lady. She's told me about Indie books. You heard of them?"

"Sure. But I like to stick to the big names."

"You're missing out according to Patsy. But the thing is, Indie authors don't have their books in stores in the main, some don't even publish paperbacks. You won't see their books in airports. The only people who'd see the cover are people who read that genre, in this case it's something called MC romance." If you could hear someone rolling their eyes, that's what his voice sounds like.

"MC romance?"

"Motorcycle club romance."

"And your prez's mom reads it?"

"She's his woman, not his mom." Grumbler barks a laugh. "His ol' lady." Ah. The penny drops. I chuckle. "So you wouldn't have seen it, Alicia's probably too young for that type of book—they have sex and filth in them. I certainly wouldn't read them, and I doubt Owen's in the market for them either."

"What you're saying is there's a limited pool of readers, so the chances are good the photographer can get away with it."

"You fuckin' got it, doll." *Doll?* Where did that come from? I let it pass. "Anyway, just wanted to update you on the covers. I thought Alicia might do with another fix of fame. Might give you a break."

Alicia has wandered off while he's been talking. I prop myself up against the counter. "You're not wrong there. Your call saved me from having to remind her she's grounded and can't go out tonight. If you tell me the titles of the books, she might forget to be annoyed if she's got something else to tell all her friends about."

"Can't say I've any experience of kids, let alone teenagers, but I've dealt with more than enough prospects in my time. Doesn't sound much different, except for the mood swings, perhaps. They are all youngsters who think they know it all and won't be guided."

Again, he makes me chuckle. "Got any tips?"

He snorts loudly. "Well, telling her she won't get her patch probably won't work, and my second go-to if that doesn't get results is using my fists, so I think you're on your own there."

"You sound like you're quite the violent man, Grumbler." It's something I wouldn't say to his face.

He takes it as though I meant it as a compliment. "I'm the sergeant-at-arms, Mary. That means I need to make club members stick to the rules as I'm responsible for the safety of the club. If someone steps out of line, they need to be educated, and if it's a situation where words aren't going to do the trick, then the point needs to be driven home some other way. Wouldn't be in the role I am if I weren't prepared to back up what I say with action." I ponder that, but it's so far removed from my existence, it makes me shiver. If someone does something wrong where I work, they get a reprimand. If it's serious, they might get suspended or fired. I try to picture Art using his fists and know he's incapable.

"Mary." All mirth has gone from Grumbler's voice. "I have never, ever hit a woman, or a man who didn't deserve it."

I'm driven to ask. "What if a woman deserves it?"

"I've never had a woman to call mine, but if I did, and she did something way out of line, I'd cut her out of my life. I'd never raise my fists to her. That answer your question, doll?"

I suppose that it does.

"I'm being called, I have to go. I'll text Alicia the book titles and authors, and I'll catch up with you when there's news. Oh and get my number from Alicia and text me with yours. I'd prefer to call you direct."

"I will. Thanks, Grumbler."

He stays on the line. "Mary, um, if Alicia's being a pain and you want to vent, I'm happy to give you sergeant-at-arms tips for dealing with it." Now he's chuckling again. "You'll have my number. Don't be afraid to use it."

I end the call and return the device to Alicia. As predicted, her face lights up when she hears she's on more covers. The phone pings with a text as soon as I've handed it to her. Leaving her in her room, I return to the kitchen while musing over what a strange conversation that had been.

Taking a cut of beef out of the fridge, I begin to prepare dinner. Working on automatic pilot, thoughts go through my head. When I'd lost Dave, I thought my world had come to an end, but I had to go on. I had Alicia to care for. At ten, she'd been devastated by the sudden loss of the only man in her life and focusing on easing her pain had helped me deal with my own.

The first couple of years had been hard. Who would have expected a forty-year-old, seemingly healthy and fit man to be struck down by a brain aneurysm? One day he was there; the next, he was gone. Without Alicia, I don't think I could have survived.

My life wasn't exceptional. I'd gotten a degree and had made the most of my time in college. I hadn't been a virgin when I'd met Dave, but then, neither had he. It wasn't something either of us had expected. But once I'd met him, all my previous lovers had faded in comparison. Dave and I had just fit, both mentally and sexually.

I'd been twenty-seven when I'd met the love of my life, coincidentally the same age as he. We'd married within a year, then waited another couple to start a family. It hadn't taken me long to fall pregnant, and Alicia had been enough to make our family complete. We'd had a good marriage. Of course there'd been disagreements along the way, but we'd always made up and found some middle ground. I'd had no thought in my head other than we were going to grow old together. We'd had plans, dreams. All shattered when that massive bleed on the brain took him away from me.

My bed had felt empty with no one to cuddle me, no one to share my triumphs, or steady me again when I'd butt heads with my daughter and no one to take the burden from me. Sex? Well, yes. I missed that as well. Though we'd settled to being intimate on a weekly schedule rather than the spontaneity of the earlier days of our relationship, it was enough to satisfy me.

But most of all, I missed his company. Missed having someone to talk to. If I had a bad or good day at work, if Alicia had scored highly on a test, or, if she was challenging me, there was no one with whom I could share. Oh, I had friends, good friends too. Women who'd be there for me, who'd come around when I was at my lowest point, bringing a bottle of wine to pull me out of my misery, but it wasn't the same.

Encouraged by said friends, Terra and Kristen, I eventually dipped my toe into the dating pool again. But I'd never found anyone to fill the hole Dave left in my life or come anywhere close to it.

Having Alicia in my life is a blessing, or so I remind myself, but her existence had definitely turned off a few men.

It's been a year since I last dated. I thought I'd made a good choice—he was a banker, good-looking, clever and kind. The type who'd send me flowers and chocolate. I'd felt spoiled by his attention. If it had just been me, we might even have made a go of it. After a few dates, I'd been confident enough to introduce him to my daughter. What a disaster that had been.

A childless man, being confronted with a then sixteen-year-old girl who was comparing him to the image of the father she carried in her head was something he couldn't cope with. Of course, all her defiant behaviour caused by her perfectly normal hormonal mood swings were down to bad parenting by me. Something, on the few occasions they'd met, he'd tried to correct.

Raising a teenager is give and take, and of paramount importance is her safety. I've learned to pick which battles to fight. He'd want to take on every one. Alicia had hated him.

We'd parted ways.

In all, there had been three failed attempts at dating since Dave had been gone. None could hold a candle to him. What I'd never found was a man who'd shown any understanding of what a teenage girl could be like. In fact, one man had refused to even meet her. He'd thought I could be his booty call without him getting involved in my life. I made sure it hadn't gotten as far as that.

The gruff tattooed biker who'd never had kids of his own had shown more understanding in one phone call than any of the men from my failed relationships.

Not that I've got any interest in Grumbler. It's hard to imagine a man who lives in a sphere so far removed from mine. Anyway, once he's located the photographer and got Alicia's money for her, our paths will divide and never cross again.

While I've been in my reverie, I've finished the pot roast. I place it in the oven just as Alicia comes out of her room.

I watch her approach, seeing her do a little dance on the spot. "Everyone's so excited for me. I'm going to be famous. I'm a real model, Mom."

"I wouldn't go as far as that." I let her down gently. "It does mean, as long as the photographer pays up, that you've made a thousand dollars. That's good going, girl."

She's in such a good mood, I'm immediately suspicious. "You can't go out tonight," I remind her, thinking she might have thought I'd forgotten.

She tosses back her hair. "I don't want to anyway. I've still got people to tell, and I'm waiting for replies on my Facebook post. They're going to be sooo jealous." Her tongue licks her lips as though she can almost taste her success. "I might ring Devon to see if he wants to photograph me again."

"No," I say quickly, knowing that's the last thing we should be doing, letting on that we've found him out. "Don't do that. What's the point if he's not going to pay you?"

"But someone might spot me."

"Let Grumbler try to find out more first."

She grimaces. "Oh, alright. But Mom, I'm going to be a model! Maybe go to Hollywood?"

I don't think that's how this business runs. But our fight's been put on hold for now, so I'll count that as a win.

It's such a plus that Alicia's mood is on the positive side that I don't want to send her back the other way, so I avoid returning to the subject that I know I ought to raise, knowing even if I do, it's doubtful any of my warnings would sink in.

I'm worried she's still got Owen's contact details on her phone when I'd have preferred for her to delete them.

When I'd grounded her, I admit I'd blown my top, explaining in detail what could happen if she shared half-naked photos of herself. I hope that I'd gotten through to her with the explanation that while she felt she could trust him now, if their friendship ended acrimoniously, things might be different.

I don't believe Alicia has done more than exchange texts and messages with the guy who I believe is far too old for her. She hasn't had much of a chance. Like any mom, I try to keep track of where she is at any time. She's well aware I can use the location feature on her phone to locate her. It's a fair bet she'll always have the device with her, it's never not in her hand or close by.

It's not that I don't trust her, but I was once, though she might find it hard to believe, a teenager myself. I'd used every trick in the book to do what I'd wanted, even if that meant telling my parents what I thought was a white lie. Well, what they didn't know, wouldn't hurt them, would it? Alicia probably feels the same way.

Like Kristen, I'd made my own mistakes, though maybe not as dire as I suspect hers are.

Unlike my parents, I have technology I can use to track my daughter, and therefore, it's so much harder for her to disappear off the radar.

I hope my lecture sunk in, but if it hasn't, I'll be watching her like a hawk. Any unusual request to meet a friend somewhere or at a time that rings a warning bell, well, I've already decided to check that by ringing said parent of the person she's due to visit. And if I do check up on her phone location when she's out, who can blame me for that.

Alicia can't tell Owen's a player, but I can. I didn't need to meet him more than once to know he's cocky and far too sure of himself. He didn't try to hide he thought he was God's gift to women. A man like that would only want Alicia for one thing.

The request for a sext from her? He's pushing his chances, seeing how far he can go. The fact she was willing will only encourage him, whether or not the picture was actually sent.

CHAPTER ELEVEN

Grumbler

"Pimped your ride out again?"

"Hey. You going to model with it this time?"

I walk into church ignoring the comments coming from one side and another. Everyone knows now. As Niran had pointed out, had I told them what I was up to from the beginning, they would have probably slapped me on the back and wished me good luck. It was because I'd tried to hide it that they were getting so much fun out of it now.

Honestly, I've been giving the bird to so many people this week, I'm starting to worry I'll get repetitive strain injury. I was hoping that I'd have found the photographer, taught him he shouldn't mess with a biker, and be done with all this by now. But Friday's come around, and Token has repeated that Devon Starr is a man who doesn't want to be found.

He's done what he does best, and I've contacted authors. I'd tried to call him again, only to find his number is no longer in use. I think we may have made him suspicious when Mary rang him last weekend, or maybe it was my subsequent call to Owen.

Mary, I've spoken to her a couple more times. Strangely,

our conversations veered off the subject of models and photographs, and I've discovered more about her and her life, finding much to admire about her seeing as she works a full-time job as well as bringing up her child. Alicia, well, she's a handful, but I hadn't lied when I compared her to some of the prospects I'd seen during my time. Those that joined when they were eighteen had been know-it-all brats who needed to have common sense knocked into them.

Our phone calls had all lasted some time. Even when we got onto a topic where are views didn't coincide, I'd enjoyed having an adult discussion with her, without coming to verbal blows. In truth though, most of her thinking aligns with mine. I can't remember when I last really talked to a woman and enjoyed it for what it was. I'm a grumpy old fucker who's lived and played in the company of men for years, but I find talking to her surprisingly refreshing.

I take my seat, knowing I'm going to be the butt of more jokes when I call up the other business I need to discuss.

Lost kicks it off. Salem gives a report about how the custom workshop is doing. It's unsurprising that with the extra space, Salem's been able to take on more jobs.

"Connor's doing well," Salem finishes up. "He's picking up a lot and putting his college education into action."

"He need a stint at the auto-shop?" Pennywise, who still manages our main shop in town, asks. "Get some of the basics down?"

"It wouldn't hurt," Salem agrees.

Blaze is next to raise his hand. "Had a local paper want to do a piece about the tattoo shop. Apparently, we had some good recommendations for our work."

"I hate to bring up something not so good." Deuce gets our attention with his words. "There are a few bikers that have been coming to the bar. I've seen little baggies changing hands."

"Dealing?" Lost asks, sharply.

Deuce sighs. "Yeah."

"We don't want their types around," I say sharply. There are good reasons why we don't deal in drugs and don't want that business conducted on our premises. Not to mention, it might bring us to the attention of the cops. While we're not the ones doing it, we'll find it hard to defend ourselves. Feds are always looking for a reason to take an MC down.

"What d'you need, Brother?" Prez asks.

"Couple of brothers coming to help me sort them out." Deuce responds quickly, as though he's already thought about it.

"Who are the bikers?" I ask. "Another club?"

"They're not flying colours."

It still doesn't rule it out. We don't hide that the bar is owned by the Satan's Devils MC. The clientele we attract are often weekend warriors who like chewing the ear off anyone who'd listen to them talk about their rides, or members of the public feeling tough for taking a walk on the wild side. Local friendly clubs, including members of the dominant—the Wretched Soulz—are welcome as long as they behave themselves. But we're always aware we might attract a criminal element.

"I'll go," I offer.

"Me too."

I give the enforcer a chin lift.

"I'll be there." I'm unsurprised when Niran offers.

"Anymore?" the prez asks. "If we're going to nip this in the bud, we want to make sure we're not outnumbered."

The VP raises his hand. "I'll be there." After cracking his knuckles together, he adds, grinning, "Been a while since I knocked a few heads together."

"Put like that, count me in," Kink offers.

Scribe leans forward and points to him. "No naked pets."

For some reason, that cracks us up.

Lost bangs the gavel, as much calling for quiet as anything else. "Sorted."

Brakes reports the strip club hasn't any problems, and his suggestion that we might want to go along the following weekend to see a new dancer is met with unanimous support.

Bones, after sniffing loudly, says the finances are fine, and then, at last, we're onto other business.

Token stares at me. I clear my throat, and then I start. "You all know that my bike was used in a photoshoot."

"And that you're missing out on at least a grand," Token puts in, staring around the table, letting the brothers know how serious this is.

Brakes, one of the brothers who's given me the most shit this week, widens his eyes. Up to now he'd thought it too much of a hoot to pay attention to the details. "So you did what, stood and watched someone take pictures of your bike and that earned you a fuckin' grand."

Token supports me again. "They're the ones we know of. More photos could have been sold, but the covers haven't been revealed as yet. So yeah, Grumbler pimping his ride earned himself at least a thousand bucks, maybe more."

Bones snorts. "Well, there you go. Grumbler wasn't as crazy as we assumed."

"Er, any chance I could get in on this gig? Mine's a good ride."

"Best get the prospects to give it a shine first, Snips." Keeper laughs.

I rap my knuckles on the table. "Sorry to disappoint you assholes, but you seem to have missed me saying the fuckin' photographer has disappeared, and unless he's found, I won't be getting shit for," I raise my hands and use air quotes, "'pimping my ride.'"

"How we going to find this fucker?" Salem looks disgusted

on my behalf. "You don't steal from a Satan's Devil and get away with it."

Prez has been closely following the conversation. He looks down the table at Token. "You couldn't find him?"

"Nah. I couldn't track his phone as he's clearly ditched it. I suspect Devon Starr might not be his real name, as he's not registered with any of the utilities. He's like a ghost. He appeared, took photos and went."

"You sure he's local? Could be he just flew in for the day."

"First, Alicia, the female model, had another photo shoot with him about three weeks ago. Second, I've spoken again to Owen Leesom, the male model that day." I pause to wipe my hand over my brow, considering what to say. "My gut feel is that he knows a fuckload more than what's coming out of his mouth. I asked him if Devon was local, and he jumped too fast to say he didn't know where he was located."

"Can we find this Owen?"

Token nods at Lost. "That we can as long as he doesn't ditch his phone. And as long as he isn't using a made-up name."

Lost stares at the table for a moment, then raises his head. "I know authors use pseudonyms, but photographers and models as well?"

"I'd say it's possible." Pennywise rubs at his nose. "Maybe because they want a memorable name, or just want to keep their sideline away from their normal life." He pauses and nods toward me. "If Patsy didn't read those mommy porn novels, you'd never have known your photo had been used."

Lost bristles at the reference to the suggestion his old lady reads porn but lets the comment pass by. "So, we could be looking for people who don't exist. What the fuck do we do now?"

"Those studios he rents. That kid modelled again for him, I

think you said?" When I nod, Salem continues, "What name were they rented in, and how did he pay?"

Token sighs. "Devon Starr and cash."

Lost raps his fingers against the table. "For a business-man, he certainly is elusive. You've reached a dead end, Toke?"

Token hates to be beaten. Give him a problem, and he'll solve it. But this is like looking for a fucking needle in the proverbial haystack. He rests his hands on the table and turns them palm upwards.

"If Token is stumped, what about asking Utah?" As all eyes go to Blaze, faces form expressions which aren't particu-larly friendly. The tattoo artist shrugs. "They seem to be tech-nical geniuses with shit at their fingertips far more than you have, Token. Why not ask them for help?"

Lost grimaces, but in the way that he does, he takes a moment to think. "If we trusted them, then yes. But I don't. We know Stormy was a loose cannon, but what do we know of the rest of them? Snatcher's still got a way to go to prove he can run his club right. And don't forget, it's this week the clock runs out on Stormy."

He's going to be out bad for certain. Justice, as far as I'm concerned, will be served. From the murmurs around the table, it's not just me who thinks it.

Dart raises his chin. "One reason they stayed under the radar was for precisely this reason. If they're to be believed, they focus their power on righting wrongs, big things, like stopping or rescuing people from kidnappings. They don't want their computer power to be tied up in smaller shit."

"It's a fuckin' big thing to me," I grumble. "I'm out at least a thousand big ones."

"I hear you, Brother." The VP's eyes soften. "But it's not in their league."

"Perhaps if they did apply themselves to helping us out,

maybe we'd see them as Devils," Dusty states, tugging at his ear.

I raise my chin toward Prez. "If they're willing to help, might go some way toward mending bridges. I, for one, would like to see what they're made of. Must admit it would be hard to take out a man wearing a Satan's Devils' patch, but if they don't come to our assistance, then maybe they don't have the right to call themselves Satan's Devils." And then I wouldn't have so much hesitation pulling the trigger.

Lost is again quiet, then he leans forward. "Point well made, sergeant-at-arms. I'll run it past Drummer. I presume you've spoken to Mouse?" He stares at Token for his answer.

"Yeah, and he can't offer anything more. We've nothing to go on other than a description and a fake name."

"Well, all I can suggest Grumbler is you keep in touch with the model's mother, see if Alicia is contacted again."

Nodding, as that will be no problem, I offer something else as well. "Alicia and Owen are friendly. I'll have a chat with her, see if she can press him on where Devon can be found."

"It is her money at stake as well." Lost stares at me.

"You mentioned the girl and Owen are friendly." Token's brow is creasing. "Can you get her to set up a meeting with him?"

"Yeah, if they get together, get us the details, Brother." Pennywise stops and picks something out of his teeth. "We can be gate crashers."

Now that's an idea. I've got a niggling feeling that whatever scam the photographer is running, Owen is also in it up to his neck. The problem is, Alicia might be a handful, but I don't want to see her being used again. Not by Devon as an unpaid model, or us as bait for a trap.

"Can we table that for now until we've exhausted other avenues?" I grimace, rubbing at my face. "She's only seventeen and I can't reason with her as though she's an adult. Any whiff of a setup, and I think her misplaced loyalties will be with him.”

“Fuckin’ teenagers,” Dart inputs.

“You’ll have one soon enough,” Deuce points out to him.

“Tell me about it,” the VP moans. “Tyler’s nine going on fifteen.”

He loves that kid, but I don’t envy what he’s got ahead.

“I’ll keep doing what I can.” Token shrugs. “Something may turn up.”

Church goes the way church normally does with others offering suggestions, but none of them have any merit. Being a man of action, I hate hanging around waiting for something to surface, but until we get more information, that, it seems, is going to be my lot.

When Lost ends the meeting, I follow everyone else into the clubroom. Lost and Dart hang around for a short time, then they leave to go back to their respective homes. I take a beer and stand at the bar looking around. For some reason, there’s a restlessness inside me, a feeling I’ve not really felt before. As the night goes on and I drink my beers slowly, I watch everyone else getting drunk. The club girls are kept busy, some brothers taking them off to their rooms, others staying right where they are. The sight of a brother getting sucked off or getting it on with a sweet butt doesn’t affect me at all, bringing neither emotion of disgust nor envy. I could have any of the girls with just a crook of my finger, I just choose not to.

Bones tells a few jokes, and I chuckle at the punchline, but my heart really isn’t in it. I miss having Smoker to talk to. Thinking back, he and I had spent most of the party nights together, a practice that went back quite a while. He’d had a dry sense of humour, and together we’d sit on the sidelines looking on, reminiscing about the old days, and how the brothers now don’t know how to have fun. Sometimes Smoker would give a running commentary and assessment on someone's performance. A murmured comment of *well he didn't last long* would have me giving a belly laugh.

I'm not here for sex, and while there's a poker game going on, I'm not in the mood to play.

Like last week, I make my way up the stairway to bed knowing no one will miss me, or probably even realise I'm gone. That my knee cracks on the first step and the other leg I injured in my crash aches as I ascend only reminds me again that I'm getting old.

What would I do were I unable to ride anymore? It's a chilling thought. The answer is simple. *I'd have nothing.*

CHAPTER TWELVE

Mary

Unlike the weekdays when Alicia's at school and I'm at work, my daughter and I treat the weekend very differently. I allow myself the luxury of an extra half hour to sleep, then get up to do the chores I've not had time for during the last five days. Proving learning is far harder than applying the stuff you've learned, Alicia gets a few hours of extra sleep, and may, if I'm lucky, emerge from her bedroom shortly before noon.

Oh what it's like to be seventeen.

Not that I'd go back there. Part of a mom's job is making sure your child doesn't make the same mistakes that you made, and boy did I make some. Looking back on those days when I thought I knew everything makes me shudder now. I'd gotten away with the risks that I'd taken, now I want to make sure she avoids making them at all.

As far as I know, she's still a virgin. Me? I'd given it away shortly before my seventeenth birthday, using it as currency to attract the attention of a boy. Sure, I'd got his eyes on me, but our fumbling and totally forgettable experience hadn't been worth him sticking around. It hadn't been special, romantic or particularly enjoyable, and had left me feeling used, and with an understanding of the phrase, another notch on a bed post—or behind the bleachers in my case.

I want more than that for her. I'm not a prude. Were she in a stable relationship, I'd rather she waited, but if she was sure, I'd make sure she was protected. One thing I've never regretted was having her at the start of my fourth decade, or those years with Dave when we enjoyed being a couple. When I finally became a mother, I could concentrate on her and not worry about stuff on which I was missing out.

One day, if it's her choice, I'd love to have a grandchild, but not for a few good years yet.

As I separate the whites and colours for the laundry, I consider the last week. I got one of my wishes, though it hadn't been Alicia deleting the contact details as I'd requested. Instead, it appears Devon has changed his number. Despite her wishes, Alicia won't be modelling anymore, unless another photographer approaches, and after this experience, I sincerely hope not. I'm both relieved and pleased in equal measure. One war avoided, though I'm sure there's going to be many more ahead.

Owen? Well, I've asked her to delete his contact as well. She's tried to assure me he's just a friend, but I doubt that.

While I didn't condone it, I could understand how Alicia had had her head turned, and why she was willing to throw herself at the first attractive male who'd shown an interest in her. It's how I lost my virginity after all. When in that situation, what has a girl got but her body to offer as currency? Yes, I'd been one of the stupid ones, thinking I could turn the eye of one of the boys all the others had lusted over by giving him the thing all males of his age wanted. I'd had to live with the regret, knowing my first time hadn't been special at all, and it had only been that he had one decent bone in his body and had kept my indiscretion to himself that I hadn't earned a bad reputation at school. I knew other girls who hadn't been so lucky.

I hadn't wanted that for Alicia, had tried to instil in her a knowledge of her own self-worth and self-respect. That I might have failed had become clear when I'd caught her sending that photo to Owen.

Sure, Owen was hot, otherwise he wouldn't have been a model, and Alicia wouldn't have had her head turned if he were not. But what did she know about him, other than he was good looking? What kind of personality has he got? What was it he wanted? I suspect nothing more than the thrill of the chase and ultimate deflowering, or, could I be misjudging him? I think not. I can only hope some of what I've said to Alicia has sunk in.

I put the first load of clothes into the wash and switch on the machine. My phone pings with a text.

Grumbler: Got questions. Can I come over?

Well, why not? I'm doing nothing. I glance around. Everything's fairly tidy, though the floor could do with vacuuming. I laugh at myself. I doubt Grumbler's the type of man who'd notice. I suspect he'd be like my husband who'd walk in, kick off his shoes, or motorcycle boots in Grumbler's case, leave them by the door, and not care how the house was looking.

Mary: Sure

If he's got questions that probably means he's gotten no closer to finding Devon Starr than he had been during our telephone conversations this week.

I decide the house is in good enough shape to welcome a biker, but that doesn't stop me from picking up a duster and flicking away a few cobwebs I could see. Then mentally I give my wrist a slap. *What do I care about Grumbler's reaction to my housekeeping or lack of?* I go to put a pot of coffee on instead.

I don't even tidy myself. I'm wearing a t-shirt and capri

pants, the comfy ones I wear around the house, my face unadorned with makeup, and the only jewellery I have on, my wedding band, now worn on my right hand.

It catches my attention for a moment. It had been three years ago when I'd taken the plunge, moving the ring that showed I was taken. Dave would always have his place in my heart, no one could remove him. But it had been the final acceptance I wasn't married any more, I had no husband to lean on or come home to. It had been Kristen who'd pointed it out.

"If you ever want to find another man, Mary, no one is going to be interested if you show you're still taken. If there is another Mr Right out there for you, he won't come along while you're committed to a ghost."

She'd made me think. I'd reasoned however much I thought Dave was the love of my life, I had possibly four more decades, the second half of my own life, left to live. Did I really want to be alone for the rest of it? Eventually Alicia would leave and make her own path as she rightly should. So, I'd moved the ring to my right hand, unable to leave it off completely.

A loud roar of a motorcycle engine sounds, then abruptly stops. Looking out of the front window, I see Grumbler throwing his leg off the saddle and getting off. I watch as he bends, rubbing his thigh, then starts to make his way past my car that he's parked behind. I notice him favouring one of his legs, limping slightly as he had before.

I'm opening the door just as he reaches it.

"Hi."

"Hey."

We've spoken on the phone a few times, our conversation always flowing easily. Yet here, face-to-face, it feels awkward. I struggle to say anything, so settle for, "Do you want a coffee?"

He's a biker. Should I have offered beer?

"Coffee sounds fine." He raises his chin, and when I back up, enters the house, closing the door behind him.

I go into my kitchen, sensing he's following me. Once I've checked how he likes it, *black with two sugars,* I make him a cup, then, pouring creamer and leaving out the sugar, prepare one for myself.

He takes the cup I hold toward him. Putting it down on the countertop, he turns and leans his back against it, folding his arms over his chest. Not for the first time, I notice the mass of tattoos he has.

I've never thought about tattoos before. Dave didn't have any, and not many of my friends have them. Kristin has a pretty flower tattooed on her ankle, but that's about it. Now I realise they're intriguing, not off-putting, and I'd love to learn whether there was a meaning to each one.

I try to pull my mind away from the marks on his skin. "So, no news, I take it?"

"Asshole's one damn fucker to try and find." He gives me the confirmation, his eyes narrowed. "Need to try and smoke him out."

"You said you had questions? What more have you got to ask me?" Frowning, I add, "I don't think there's anything else I can tell you."

He half turns, picks up his coffee, blows on it to cool it, and takes a sip. "Not you, Alicia."

"She's told you everything." I bristle slightly, thinking he's accusing her of holding something back.

"She's in touch with Owen, isn't she?"

Reluctantly I nod. "Sadly, I think she is, though I've tried to warn her against him."

Grumbler's eyebrow rises, and he smirks. "You suspect he's not got the character to match his pretty face?"

Huffing, I respond, "I'm worried that bad boy image he's projecting might be exactly what he is inside."

"I can't argue with that. A pretend bad boy, at least. Club's got plenty of the real ones."

I wrap my hands around my coffee. "I need to know he'll respect a seventeen-year-old girl, and I don't get a good vibe about that." I don't mention the sext. It's too embarrassing.

"Can't blame you there, doll. You're a good mom. Too many kids don't have them." He goes silent and blows on his coffee. "Here's the thing. The club wants to catch up with Owen and question him. If she can set up a meeting, or get him to come here, we'll know where he is. We'll come get him, take him back to the club and get our questions answered."

"I don't like that." My eyebrows knit. "I suspect you won't take no for an answer. And if Owen's, as you suggested, in cahoots with Devon, he's not going to come willingly." One glance at Grumbler's face shows that I'm right. "I don't want Alicia faced with any unpleasantness."

Grumbler's looking at me carefully, then he shakes his head. "Of course, you're fuckin' right. I don't want you to see that either." His face has fallen, and his jaw clenches. His eyes become shuttered and I assume he's trying to think of something else.

My mind, too, is racing. "You got any good-looking young men in your club?"

His eyes snap open as if I've startled him. "Good looking? How the fuck would I know?" He chuckles, then stops. "You want me to set you up with a boy toy?" His jaw clenches momentarily, then relaxes. "Or find someone who might take Alicia's fancy to get her mind off Owen? Hate to say this, doll, but bikers aren't likely to want a relationship. A quick fuck, yeah. More? No. She'd get no romance from any of us."

"Not for me or Alicia. For Devon." I roll my eyes, while

noting his obvious view of women. *Just objects to be fucked.* It takes me back to my schooldays and the loss of my virginity.

"Devon?" His eyes widen again. "Didn't get the vibe he was gay."

I bat at his arm. "Remember Devon wanted Owen to sit on your bike, and his reaction when you wouldn't let him? It was priceless seeing your reaction to him wanting to borrow your cut." I grin, as I recall it. "He was clearly disappointed. I've been looking at MC novels." I might have bought one, but I don't admit that. Neither have I started reading it yet. "Most have just a shirtless man on the front, or a couple, or a man wearing a cut on a motorcycle. I just wondered whether you have anyone suitable in your club, and whether Devon might be tempted out of hiding if he was offered the opportunity to photograph one."

Grumbler puts his coffee down and holds up his hands. "None of my brothers would go for that. It's one thing my bike appearing on a cover no one, well, apart from Lost's old lady, would recognise. But a face and cut? Out of the question."

"They don't need to actually do it. Just make the offer."

He stills. His eyes meet mine and hold them. Then he tosses back his head and guffaws. "Christ, woman. You've got a damn head on your shoulders. You read it right, and that's exactly what he wants." Then his face grows serious. "It would work if he still thinks I'm just an ignorant biker. But he's changed his phone number. If that's because I made him suspicious, then he's going to steer well clear of the Devils."

"But you didn't speak to him. I did. As far as he knows, you are an ignorant biker." I wink to soften my words. "You weren't the one chasing payment."

"Fuck. You're right." Then, again, his face falls. "But I spoke to Owen."

I know, he'd told me. "You think he might be working with

Devon, them skimming everyone else. But you don't know it. Isn't it worth a try?"

Leaning back his head, he closes his eyes briefly. Just when I think he's about to dismiss my idea, he takes his phone out of his pocket. I suspect he's going to text or make a call, and start to turn away to give him privacy, but he calls my attention back. Instead, he's pulled up some photos and is scanning through them. "Got some pics here. Most are ones I've taken when the assholes have been fooling around, but you can get an idea. You're a better judge than me. Any of them look likely? That's Pennywise and Salem right there." I cock an eyebrow at the strange names. He chuckles as he explains, "Our old prez was going through a Stephen King phase."

"They're not bad. But if Owen's an example of what he's after, maybe someone younger?"

"Hmm. Not sure. Ah, yeah. Look. There's Keeper and Deuce."

They've got characterful faces, but not my taste. The next picture makes me shake my head. Poor guy doesn't have a complete set of teeth and those he has are crooked. He's certainly not photogenic. Niran's black, which doesn't exclude him, but again, older.

"What about him?" I point to one who's got shaggy shoulder-length blond hair, a short beard, and the main selling point, piercing blue eyes which are staring straight at the camera. I disregard whoever it is making devil horns above his head.

"Dusty? He's thirty."

"He looks younger."

Grumbler stares at the photo as though he'd never tried to see his brothers as a woman would before. "You think young girls would go for him?"

"Young or old. Remember, many readers are older. He," I tap the phone, "has a kind of universal appeal."

Grumbler's expression shows he can't quite see it, but his words suggest he's accepted my endorsement. "So we've got our victim. Now, how are we going to contact Devon?"

I'm kind of proud he's asking my advice. "We ask Alicia to suggest it to Owen. She speaks to him."

"Instead of getting the mouse to enter the lion's den, we send the lion to meet the mouse. I like it." Grumbler's nodding with approval. "I like the way you think, woman."

And I like a man who doesn't have to come up with all the ideas. I've enjoyed talking this out with Grumbler and impressed that he's taking my advice.

"Will Dusty go along with it?"

"Doll, I'm the sergeant-at-arms, and he's my brother, but in this case, I know there'll be no need for persuasion. He'll jump at the chance. I only have to ask."

It must be nice to have that security of knowing you have men behind you who'd do whatever you needed.

I hear a door open and close. It would appear Alicia has emerged from her room at last. Realising she won't know we have a visitor, I hastily excuse myself to go check she's decent before she emerges.

CHAPTER THIRTEEN

Grumbler

Well I'll be fucked. Mary's come up with a fucking good idea. If Devon falls for it, Dusty can lead us right to where he'll be shooting his shots. That woman has a good head on her shoulders.

I can't recall taking advice from a bitch before, not that I'd summarily dismiss it had it been offered on the grounds they lacked a part of anatomy unique to males. Prior to my chats with Mary, conversations with women normally revolved around what sexual position they preferred. I think I've had more discussions with Mary over the past week than I've had with any female in the past thirty years. When she'd been at the end of the phone, it had been as easy as though I was talking to one of my brothers, only the lack of swear words coming from her mouth had reminded me that I wasn't.

Now that I'm in her presence again, I'm reminded how far removed she is from any of them. Especially now, as I watch her walk away to go greet her daughter, finding my eyes lingering on her until she disappears. She has a fine figure for a woman. I suspect she's late thirties or possibly even hit forty from what I can see. Her face, while still youthful, has lines of maturity etched on it.

Her eyes, I love her eyes. They look large in her face, and so expressive. But, however attractive I'm starting to find her, she's off-limits, far too young for me.

Rinsing my empty coffee cup, I place it in the sink, then wander into the living room. There's a picture on the side table I hadn't noticed last time I was here. I go and pick it up. It's a lovely snap of Mary and a man, his arms are around her and both are grinning. She's younger in it, so it's not recent. I wonder who the man is. Obviously a lover, a brother wouldn't have that heat in his eyes as he looks at her. Her husband, I deduce.

"That's me and Dave." Mary's soft voice sounds from behind me as she gives me the confirmation. "It was taken shortly before he died."

I wonder whether she's still grieving and suspect she is. I've recently lost Smoker, and hell, I miss the bugger. I'll continue hearing his voice in my head for some time to come, I suspect, but that's nothing to losing someone you shared your dreams with.

"Alicia's just making herself decent. I've told her you're here and want to talk to her."

It's down to me then, but I need her advice. "How do I play this?"

Mary grimaces. "Tell her exactly what you want her to tell Owen," she half whispers. "She's got no reason to know she's not passing on a genuine request."

I get her meaning and agree one hundred percent. I don't know how good an actress Alicia is, so she may not be able to pull it off if she knows she's spinning a line.

"Morning, Grumbler."

"Good afternoon, kid." I grin, not a stranger to people sleeping in on the mornings after a heavy night, though I doubt Alicia spent last night fucking and drinking. "You good?"

"Great."

"You seen Devon lately?" I know she hasn't told her mom she has, but it's worth a try.

"No. Owen hasn't either."

"You've spoken to him again?" Mary butts in, her annoyance showing.

I try and signal with my eyes that she should be careful. On this occasion, we actually want her to speak to him.

Alicia ignores her mom. "Is that your motorcycle outside?"

I raise my chin.

"Cool. I thought I recognised it."

"It's a shame you haven't spoken to Devon," I tell her, trying to inject disappointment into my voice.

"You want your money," she states.

"Sure, that would be nice, but one of my brothers is interested in modelling for him."

She turns and gives me an appraising look, and I know she's putting me into the grandfather age bracket. It dawns on me, any blood brother of mine would be deemed to be too old too. Again I get out my phone, pulling up Dusty's photo again. "That's him. And that's his bike."

Her eyes expand. While I know Dusty's far too old for her, or at least, that's what I hope he'd think, she's obviously seeing something her mom had and that I'd missed. "That's your *brother?*"

"My MC brother, another member. We're like family," I explain.

"I'd love to model with him," she sighs, dreamily. I have to signal to Mary with my eyes once again. Especially when Alicia adds, "Could you introduce me to your *brothers*? Have they all got motorbikes? Do you think Dusty would give me a ride?"

Now that I've got to shut down fast. "Well, you see, Alicia. A man's ride is something special to him. Some men don't mind, but to most, there's only one woman they'd take on the back of their bike, and that's one who's special and who is going to become their ol' lady."

Her head tilts to one side. "Old lady? You said that the last time you were here."

Mary indicates a seat, and I take the hint, leaning back and crossing my legs at the ankles. "Old lady's a term we use for what you'd call a wife. A woman you're going to commit to."

Alicia sits on the couch opposite. "Have you got an old lady?"

"No, never have, never will." Knowing the kid would understand, I add, "I'm too old." That she doesn't refute it, confirms that I am. My time has passed, I accept it.

"I don't think I want to get married," Alicia says, quite seriously.

"You've got plenty of time," Mary interjects. "You might if you meet the right man."

"Not every man's like Daddy."

She's right there, I think to myself. It seems like Mary caught herself a good one, but so many are cheaters or abusers. Must be hard navigating your way through all that.

"If you don't want to get married, you don't. You find your happy on your own, then good for you. You don't have to abide by society's expectations." Fuck knows I don't myself. And I might be old, but I'm not old-fashioned. In the same way I don't think I need a woman, I don't think women need a man to complete them.

"You want to stay for lunch, Grumbler? I was just going to make something for us."

Why not? I've got nothing else planned for today. "Sure."

That's how I end up spending another couple of hours in the company of the two women. A couple of times I act as referee when I find they have some opposing views, but suspect Alicia is just arguing for the sake of it. It doesn't faze me. I've seen enough of that between brothers over the years. In all, I find it relaxing. It's been a while since I was entertained in anyone's home. Well to be honest, the feeling of being a guest soon disappears.

Mary and Alicia's home is comfortable. Tidy and clean enough, but with dust visible on some of the surfaces, a couple of cobwebs on the walls, and a floor which could do with a quick encounter with a vacuum settled me more than a spotless home. The type of place I could kick off my boots and make myself comfortable—or keep them on, and no one would complain about it. A house spotless and tidy would set me on edge.

"What does your club do?" Alicia asks.

I notice Mary's eyes flick to me in concern, as if she's got suspicions she doesn't want confirmed.

"Well, Alicia, let's see. Like most MCs we run an autoshop. The custom work we do has become so successful, we've split that part off. That's now run out of a spare hangar up at our compound."

"Hangar?"

I explain, "The compound is on an abandoned airfield. One hangar has been converted to a clubroom and living space."

"Sounds cool. Are there any planes there?"

I chuckle. "Not anymore. The runways are all broken up with weeds growing through."

"Is that all your club does? Work on bikes?"

"And cars, trucks. Anything mechanical really. Not the big stuff though. But no, that's not all. Not long back we bought the shop next door to the garage and set it up to sell biker apparel. That's become a place where civilian bikers like to shoot the shit and hang out. Keeper gets the credit for coming up with that one. Blaze runs our tattoo parlour, Deuce our bar, and Brakes our strip club. All the brothers work at one place or another."

"Do they each own the businesses?"

"Club owns them," I answer Mary. "We all get an equal take."

Her brow furrows. "But what if someone's not pulling their weight? Do they still get paid the same?"

"If someone's not doing their share, well, that's where I come in," I wink at her, "aided by Salem the enforcer."

"It sounds like a commune," she observes.

"Kind of," I agree.

"What do all the names mean?" Alicia asks. "You haven't mentioned anyone with a normal one."

"Names are given when you patch in—that's become a full member. Sometimes, like Salem and Pennywise, it's the prez's fancy. Sometimes it's because of something you look like or do."

"Do you grumble a lot?" the kid queries.

I snort but try to wear an innocent expression. "I apparently have been known to." Christ knows how I originally picked up that name. I swear I've grown into it and didn't start out that way.

"Tell us about some of the others," Alicia asks.

"Well, I can't explain them all, kid. Names are personal. But for those I can—take Reboot, for example. Whenever our computer guy had a problem, Reboot would tell him to switch whatever device it was off and back on. Token got so fed up with him, he suggested the handle."

"What about Dusty?"

The memory makes me smile. "See, we were out on a ride one day, we were going to a hog roast at one of the friendly clubs up near Los Angeles. We wanted to impress, you know?" Alicia nods as though she does. "All of our rides were fuckin' perfect, gleaming chrome, polished tanks. There was a car pulled up at the side of the road with the hood up. A man was leaning into it fiddling with the engine, while a girl in very short shorts and legs up to her ass was leaning against the door looking bored, long blond hair streaming out behind her. Dusty swears she locked eyes with him as he passed. Trouble was, he couldn't stop looking at her. Had his eyes on the rearview when he hit a pothole in the road. He swerved onto the shoulder, and though he managed to stop upright, it was with one wheel half on, half off the pavement. Beside him was a short drop." I bark a laugh.

"It was like watching a car crash in slow motion. Of course, all of us had pulled up to make sure he was alright. Seemed he was until he tried to get the bike back on the road. He lost his balance and he and his bike ended up in a mud hole. Well, we got both out, checked there was no damage, but he was a fuckin' sight. I swear he had mud where mud has no business being. Anyway, the day was warm and soon the mud dried. So we turned up, a dozen of us on bikes which were gleaming, and then there was him. Our hosts took one look at him and said, 'You're a bit dusty', and well, it stuck. We never let him forget it, and he was Dusty from that moment on."

"You're cruel." She giggles. "What about Token?"

"Hard Token. You ever use a hotel key card to get into your room?" When she nods, I continue, "That's a hard token, a security device."

"Tell me some more."

I frown. "Well there's Scribe. He's always on about writing a book, but if he is, we've never seen it. Then there's Kink—"

Mary shoots Alicia a *that's enough* look and gets my attention by lifting her fingers. "All your businesses sound legit."

I chuckle again. "They are, and I assure you, we're not into money laundering. The cops and feds keep too close an eye on us for us to be doing something illegal." The killing and burying bodies I think it's best I keep to myself.

"Why have you got the reputation you have? I assumed you were involved with gun running or drugs?"

"Not saying we never were, but we got out of the drug trade when Drummer, he's the prez of our mother chapter in Tucson, took the helm. Gun running too. There's too much risk of a brother dying or ending up in jail with that sort of business. No one currently in the club wants to touch either of those."

"Currently?"

"Yeah. We had a clean out a few years back. Nine men left the club because they wanted to take it in the wrong direction." Two were dead at the hands of the mother chapter prez. One died during the mutiny and six sent out bad. One of those met his end fairly recently. How Shark died brought memories of Smoker's death back into my mind. I'd forgotten his absence for a few hours. Now I realise how much I would have enjoyed talking to him about Mary and Alicia, and that there was no one else I'd trust enough to confide in.

Mary has noted my look of pain. "One of them you were close to?"

She thinks I'm sad about the men who'd betrayed the club which is far from the fucking truth. But, was I close to any of them? All of them, if she wants the truth. Until the plots were revealed, I'd have given my life for any of theirs. That's why the betrayal had hit us so hard. "Nah, not them," I correct. "I was just thinking of my friend who died a couple of months back. Cancer." I don't think she needs to know about the bullet which had advanced his natural death by a few months.

Alicia seems to have lost interest. "You don't seem very exciting, not like *Sons of Anarchy*."

"And when have you watched that?" Mary asks sharply.

"At Marisa's. But only a couple of episodes, I got bored. It was all burning bodies alive and stuff."

Mary's already large eyes widen.

"You can't believe the fictional stuff," I tell her. "But MCs are about men who love riding bikes, and who want to live outside citizen laws. We share a bond together. Hurt one of us, and we all bleed."

Mary gives me a look of understanding. Yeah, that's why I know without asking, Dusty will jump at the chance to help out.

We finish eating. I help clear up, feeling like part of a family. When I leave, it's with Alicia's promise she'll try and advance Dusty's presumed desire for a modelling career the next time she speaks to Owen.

When Mary sees me out, she stands by the door before opening it. "It's been interesting. I've enjoyed talking with you, Grumbler."

I realise I've enjoyed myself as well.

"Offer still stands, doll. You need to vent about Alicia, feel free to call me."

"She can be difficult."

I laugh. "We were all young once. You might not believe this, but there was a time when I thought I knew it all."

She shoots me a look that suggests I probably still do, and if she voiced that, then I wouldn't be able to argue with her.

I glance toward my bike, then back at her. "Make sure she just contacts Owen by phone, okay? I've got bad feelings about the fucker. Maybe not justified, but my gut has been proved right more than once. I don't..." I pause. I'm in no position to give her parenting advice. "I suggest she doesn't spend time with him alone."

Mary's eyes harden. For a second, I fear I've overstepped the line, but I'm to be proven wrong.

"I couldn't agree more, Grumbler. While between adults like us, a four-year difference is nothing at all, at her age, Owen's got a wealth of experience she's still got to learn. Now I've just got to explain that to her."

I raise my chin, then at last, head to my bike. *There's a hell of a lot more than four years between us, doll. Try twenty or so. I'm old enough to be your father.*

What's odd, I ponder as I head for the club, is why I find that thought troublesome.

CHAPTER FOURTEEN

Grumbler

"Found something I don't like, Grumbler." Token's mouth purses after he gives me those words.

It was he who called me into his office. Emitting a low growl, I prompt him, "Well don't fuckin' keep it to yourself, Brother."

Token nods thoughtfully. "Let me give you some background first. I've been searching the web for books which uses one of Devon's photos on the cover. He has a website, *Starring Roles*. He boasts he's sold over six hundred photos."

"Since when?" I might not be good at reading, but mental math is no problem for me. Even at three hundred dollars a time, Devon's made himself a cool one hundred and eight thousand dollars.

"The website's been running a couple of years." Token seems to know where my mind is going. "That's not all profit, remember, he'll have to rent out studio space."

"It's not a bad return for taking some shots and putting them on his website."

"There'll be editing time, arranging models. For all the

photo's he's shot, there will be some that will have wasted his time."

I raise my chin, acknowledging the point. "But if he's not paying models, he could double his return?"

"Yeah. I doubt he'd get away with doing it all the time, but perhaps often enough."

Even half the time would make it a tidy little income.

"There's worse," Token adds, his brow creasing. "We know Devon Starr isn't his real name, or any derivative of it." I nod, knowing that full well. "So," Token continues, "I did some digging into the images which carried his website watermark. I came up with something, a photo that I think got into the wrong file, but it led me to some other images."

Now he turns the monitor around to face me. I stare at them for a moment. After I've taken in the subject matter, I say, "Fuck."

"Still could be totally innocent. I mean, you get images like this in *Playboy*. Every young kid's spank bank fodder."

I think I should warn Mary to keep Alicia well away from Devon Starr were he to surface and ask her daughter to model again. She'd be distraught were her daughter be pressured into modelling with no clothes, and in darn near indecent positions.

"For these pics, he goes by the name of Ad Wilson."

"Why use a different name if he's building a legit business?"

"Could be nothing," Token admits. "Or could be a way to scam more models."

I tap my hand against his desk for a moment. "Any recent activity on his *Starring Roles* site?"

"Yes. New photos uploaded yesterday." He turns the monitor back, and taps at some keys, then, again, it's facing me.

Like on his main website, there are hundreds of pictures of my bike, well, in its supporting role of course. I note

Alicia's beaming smile, and also the way she's looking at Owen. Christ, either that girl's an actor, or she genuinely thinks the sun shines out of his ass. A little warning bell rings. If she truthfully has feelings for him, she won't like that we're trying to draw him out. *But she doesn't know.* She thinks Dusty's sudden yearning to become a model is genuine.

"He's selling photos under both names?"

"I suspect he wants some legit ones to draw people in. I'll keep digging," Token tells me. "I've got feelers out for both of his identities on the dark web." He puts his hand to his forehead and raps on it. "Got a bad feeling about this, Grumbler. But fuck it, I don't know why."

"You think it goes deeper than scamming his models?"

"When there's a bad smell, there's usually something rotting."

I lift my chin. Maybe it's because in our life we've grown to be suspicious, but I tend to agree.

It's obvious Token's got nothing more for me now. "You get your shovel working," I tell him as I stand. "Meanwhile, I've got to go fix a car."

He grimaces, knowing I much prefer working with bikes, but I'll do what I need to.

"Hey, you going on the ride this weekend?"

That's an easy one to answer. "That I am. I'm looking forward to it."

Setting off for our auto-shop, I put a good day's work in, replacing a clutch, then doing a full service. It's par for the course, and the next few days continue in the same pattern as I've become used to.

During the day, I work. In the evenings I have a drink, play cards or pool, or just shoot the shit with the brothers. The only change is that I keep looking at my phone, seeing if I've missed a call from Mary. I tell myself, I only want to know if our plan has worked. That she's not called means Alicia's not contacted Owen as yet.

I'd told her to call me if things got tough with her daughter. Yeah, as if I'm anyone who can give kid-raising advice. All I know is that I once was one and probably behaved a hundred times worse.

Why should a woman like Mary want to discuss her daughter with me? Or maybe, things are going well, and Alicia is behaving.

Friday's church is the normal affair with other business mostly confined to discussions about and final arrangements being made for our beach ride out the next day. We end on a high note with brothers upbeat and assing around about the things they'll be getting up to, earning a reprimand from the prez, reminding us we'll be on a public beach. Yeah, like Devils would worry about that.

I leave the meeting with a grin on my face and collect my phone from the box. After getting a drink, I nod when I'm invited into a game. I'm staring at the cards I'm holding, trying not to frown at the hand I've been dealt and wondering what call to make, when my phone vibrates.

Taking it out of my pocket, I answer, "Grumbler here."

"It's Mary."

"Hi, doll. How you doing?" Raising my arm, I signal Pennywise to cover my hand, then I stand and walk to the door of the clubroom. "Hold on, I'm just going somewhere I can hear myself think."

"Is there a party?"

"Yeah. I was in a card game."

"Sorry to interrupt."

"Don't apologise. I was losing." I chuckle to let her know I really don't mind. "How's your week been?"

"Surprisingly good. Alicia's been doing her schoolwork

without being told. Of course, it's all because she wanted to stay at her friend's tonight."

"And did she get her way?"

I imagine her rolling her eyes. "Of course."

"You check this friend out?"

"I don't have to. It's Marisa. They've been friends for years. It's quite usual for her to be here, or Alicia at hers. I often joke she's my second daughter."

She's alone. Does she want company? What am I thinking? Fit woman like her is probably not lacking friends of her own. It doesn't stop me asking, "So what are you up to with time on your hands?"

"I'm just about to put a movie on, oh, and I'll open a bottle of wine."

A car pulls up, and out steps three giggling girls. They cross over the parking lot toward me, give me a cursory dismissive glance and also a wide berth as they walk into the clubroom. They'll be making a beeline for Dusty once inside, I'm certain. He's always a draw with the young hangarounds who come up from town.

As the noise of the party increases then diminishes when the door is opened and closed, I find myself envying Mary's more peaceful evening. I must be getting old, as flopping on a couch to watch a movie seems quite inviting just now.

But I haven't been invited.

"Got a good weekend planned?" I ask.

"Not really. Weekends are when I catch up with all my chores. But I'm going for a drink with my co-workers tomorrow night. They're dragging me out on the town."

Looking for a man. Perhaps she'll find one. I suppress the urge to growl a warning about being careful who she picks up. Good-looking women are fair pickings.

"What about you, Grumbler? How will you be passing the time?"

"The club is going for a ride out along the coast, we'll stop off and have a barbeque," I find myself telling her.

"That sounds fun." The way she says it sounds like she means it. It makes me wonder about asking her if she'd like to come.

What am I thinking? These thoughts have no right being in my head, but it doesn't stop me asking, "You ever been on a bike, Mary?"

"No."

"There's nothing like feeling the pavement beneath your wheels, the wind in your hair, the sun on your face, feeling you're one with the elements," I muse. "Instead of watching the scenery go by, you're part of it."

"Are you trying to sell it to me, Grumbler?" She chuckles.

Am I? Of course not. "Never had a woman on the back of my bike." I say it half in warning. I'm not going to start now. If Mary was riding behind me, I might get ideas that I shouldn't, not with the huge age difference between us, and it would be all one-sided. She'd not see anything in a grumpy old man.

"I just wanted to check in. Let you know Owen hasn't yet made contact."

"I'm glad you did." An idea hits me. "You checked Alicia's where she said she'd be?"

Mary snorts. "I should be annoyed you're questioning my daughter's truthfulness or criticising my parenting skills. Thing is, though, I've been checking her phone. It's been at Marisa's all evening."

"And young girls are surgically affixed to their phones."

She laughs. "You've got it. Well, I'll let you get back to your party."

The sound level has increased, and she must be able to hear it in the background. Loud music and watching my brothers' dicks plough various holes? Or spend a quiet evening in with a woman and a movie. If I was given the choice, I know what I'd choose now. But it hasn't been offered, and if it were, it would be wrong to accept.

"Yeah. I left Pennywise playing my shit hand of cards. Need to see whether he's recovered any of my losses." I doubt it. He's not a magician.

"Don't lose too much. And we'll speak soon. As soon as Owen makes contact, I'll let you know."

"Dusty's ready and waiting."

With that, I end the call, never being one for lengthy good-byes. Re-entering the clubroom, I see that Dusty is far from ready, not with his pants down around his ankles, and his dick disappearing into the crotch of one of the girls who'd just entered. Two things are obvious—one, she hasn't wasted time, and two, that the pool table is out of action for now.

The card game has ended, and not well if the look on Pennywise's face is anything to go by.

"Couldn't do shit with those cards you left me with."

Sighing, I take out my wallet. "How much am I down?"

Pennywise's expression changes. "Put your wallet away, old man. Might have lost that hand but recouped your losses in the next."

I grin. "And they didn't want to keep playing with you at the table?"

It seems they didn't. I don't blame them. Pennywise is the closest we've got to a card shark—on a good day that is. He's not unbeatable, but tonight he's done me a favour.

I slap him on the back and when he turns around and eyes the room, I do as well. The tables have been pushed back, and bodies, mainly female, are writhing on the makeshift dance floor. Twerking, sticking their asses out, all in the hopes of snagging one of the, to them, desirable men. Cindy is twirling around the stripper pole, going through her routine. It's not just the music that's gotten louder. To make themselves heard, men are raising their voices adding to the cacophony of sound.

For years this has been my life and I've been more than happy with it. Only a few months back, Smoker and I would be in the midst of it. Is it just because my friend has gone that I'm seeing things differently now? How can I feel alone when I'm in a crowd?

It's strange, but I feel out of place—an onlooker looking in from the outside.

Disturbed by my thoughts, I retreat to my room.

The good thing is, having become used to the noise levels in the clubhouse, they don't keep me awake. I have, for me, an early night, waking early and refreshed.

There is something to be said for avoiding party night—I start my weekend without a hangover, my thoughts on the ride this coming afternoon. I'm hungry as hell though, so I take a quick shower, dress fast, then proceed downstairs. At this time on a Saturday, the club girls will probably be sleeping off the effects of last night, so I'll have to cook something for myself. Doesn't bother me. I'm not helpless.

I've got bacon sizzling when Wrangler walks in. The prospect licks his lips and sniffs dramatically. We don't starve prospects, though I'm sure not cooking for him as well. He can make his own when I've finished at the stove.

"Strange that you're up, Grumbler."

"Strange?" I half turn. "Just because I've got better things to do than stay in bed all day?"

"Got any extra?" Niran walks in, pushing past the prospect, his hands wiping over the short dark hair on his head.

"Sure," I tell him with a grin toward Wrangler. Watching members eat is all part of the hazing prospects have to go through. "Eggs?"

"Yeah. Thanks."

Wrangler shakes his head. "I said strange because a bitch was trying to get onto the compound just now using your name."

"A bitch?"

"Yeah. Young kid. She was at the gate, crying and shit. I sent her away. She was just probably using a name that she'd heard, figured she was going to land being a baby daddy on you or something. But it wouldn't be you. You don't like them young."

Someone was asking for me? "She give a name?" I pause with the spatula held in the air.

"Liz?" Wrangler's eyes crease. "Allie? Oh yeah, that was it. Alicia."

"*Alicia?*"

"Trouble?" Niran's standing at attention.

"How did she get here?" I reach into my cut for my phone.

"Uber or Lyft or something. I don't know." Wrangler looks confused.

"Cab took her away?" Christ, I hope she's gone home. Why the fuck had she come to see me?

"Nah, it had left. She's walking into town."

Walking? It's fucking three miles to the city, another three to get to her momma's house.

Turning off the burners, I start to move fast. "You can forget your fuckin' patch!" I yell at Wrangler, pushing his shoulder hard as I rush past.

"Why? What the fuck, Grumbler?"

His voice fades behind me as I rush out of the clubhouse and jump onto my bike. Starting it, I'm not surprised to hear another come to life with a roar behind me. I haven't had to say a word, Niran knows me, and knows I wouldn't take off unless there was trouble. And when trouble surfaces, brothers have your back.

Connor, presumably having taken over from Wrangler, is manning the gate. He has it open before we reach it. Once on the road, I continue down the track until we reach the highway, then head into town. I don't go fast, my eyes scanning the kerbside in case, heaven forbid, Alicia's been struck by a car.

I can't believe that prospect just kicked her out without even bothering to check with me. When it comes to voting him in, he's not getting my vote.

CHAPTER FIFTEEN

Grumbler

One thing I'll say, young girls walk fast. It's almost ten minutes before I spy a shape that looks like her, and drawing closer, recognise the long blond hair hanging down her back. Overtaking, I pull up just in front of her.

Not knowing what's happening or why, Niran brings his bike to a halt behind.

"Alicia. What the fuck?"

I'm off my bike and hurrying over to her. *Oh fuck.* Her face is red, her eyes and nose look raw, and tears are still falling. She tries to wipe them away on a tissue which is already crumpled and soggy.

I gentle my voice. "Alicia, baby. What's happened? You need your mom?" I might never have had a female riding behind me, don't even have a pillion seat on my bike, but I'll just squash myself up to make this work. This is an emergency and I don't hesitate. "Get on my bike, I'll take you to her."

Her eyes widen, "No, please." Her voice breaks. "I-can't, I can't speak to her. Not now."

I'm rapidly thinking. Alicia came to me, and she's not ready to speak to her mom. "Has something happened?"

My question starts the tears falling again. As Alicia drops her head, wracking sobs shaking her body, Niran comes up alongside me, suggesting quietly, "I think we should get her back to the clubhouse. Get Lost here with Patsy."

I still think she needs to go home to her mom. But the club-house is nearer, and in the state the kid's in, with her needing to hang onto me on the bike, a shorter journey might be safer. Once there, I can call Mary, and get her to come collect her.

Gently I put my hand on her shoulder. "Come with me. We'll go back to the clubhouse. See if we can get whatever it is sorted."

"It can't be sorted," she wails. Then, she clutches at my cut. "It will never be right, Grumbler."

A feeling of dread grows in me. "Someone hurt you?"

I already know I'm right, and her nod confirms it. I feel sick and hope the worst I'm thinking isn't the truth. That I'm not the only one thinking it is confirmed when Niran again speaks into my ear, so quietly, she wouldn't be able to hear it.

"Eva might be needed."

Eva's a nurse. He's right, she might. She'll come running if we ask her.

"Come on." I encourage her forward with my arm. "Get on the bike, darlin'. I'll go slow. No need to be afraid. You just hang onto me."

She's like putty now, obeying when I tell her what to do. It's going to be hell for me getting on with a passenger already sitting and taking up part of my seat, but she's upset and inex-perienced, so I'll have to manage it. I pull out the rear pegs and put her feet on them. "Just keep them there, okay? And hang onto me. Mind the exhaust, it's hot and you could burn yourself."

When she's situated where I want her, I try to ease my

uncooperative leg over the seat, thankful to Niran steadying the bike for me. I raise my chin to him when I've got it upright and balanced, and kick up the stand. Alicia's so slight, I barely notice the extra weight there.

Then, knowing I owe it to Mary to take care of my passenger, I ease out, doing a U-turn over the meridian, and head back the short distance to the clubhouse.

Alicia's hands clutch at me as though holding a lifeline. At first, I think it's because she's scared of the bike, but when we reach our destination, she's still holding tightly onto me. Niran comes over.

"Alicia, isn't it?" he queries in his deep voice. "Slide off the bike, honey, so Grumbler can park it."

Gently, I try to loosen the death grip she's got around my waist. "Just stay with Niran for a moment, baby," I encourage her.

It takes a minute, but then her hands loosen. Sensing she doesn't want him to touch her, Niran steps back, and lets her slide off. Once I'm alone on the bike, I paddle walk it backwards, park, and dismount.

As soon as I'm off the bike, she flings herself into my arms, sobs coming again.

"Come on, let's go find you some tissues and mop those tears up. Then you can tell me what happened."

She's pliant as I move her around so I can put my arm around her and lead her into the clubhouse.

"Why's Wrangler so worried about losing his patch… oh." Salem's voice cuts off abruptly.

"Here are tissues." Niran presents me with a box.

A bit uncertain what to do next, I take one, then a couple more and hand them to her. Walking her over to a couch, hoping it'd dried off from being in use last night, I press on her shoulders. When she sits, I crouch in front of her.

"I'll call your mom."

"No. Please, no." She looks horrified and scared.

My eyes flick to Niran, then Salem for help, but they've not yet procreated, and clearly, like me, have no idea how to handle her.

"I'll call Eva," Niran suggests.

Well, that's a start. Get a woman here to talk to her. In the meantime, what do I do? Eva lives in Escondido and will take a while to get here.

"She want a soda or something?" Salem suggests, trying to be helpful, but Alicia shakes her head.

I reach up my hand and catch a tear that's escaping. "Who hurt you, sweetheart?" That's the information I need—someone to focus my suppressed rage on.

"Man put his hands where he shouldn't?" Salem growls loudly, making her jump and me to shush him.

Alicia sobs, and just when I think she's not going to confirm anything, she gives a little nod.

"Who?" the enforcer snarls just as I'm about to ask the question.

"It wasn't what you're thinking," she cries out. "It was my fault."

"No." Now it's me who's growling. "If a man has done something you didn't want, there's no way you're to blame."

Her red eyes come to meet mine, then she looks away. "I've been so stupid, Grumbler."

My eyes narrow, but I try to keep my anger in check. "Why don't you tell me what happened, Alicia, and let me be the judge of that?"

Her head drops again, and I don't think she's going to say anything. Niran and Salem take places behind the couch, and I don't think she knows they're still listening.

Wrangler appears, his footsteps hesitant. As if trying to make up for his error of judgement earlier, he holds a bottle of water at arm's length. I take it, shooting him a look that tells him it will take a whole lot more before I even think of forgiving him. The jerk of my head tells him to make himself scarce. As he does, I unscrew the top, and hold it out to her.

Discarding another used tissue on top of the growing pile beside her, she takes a much-needed drink of water to rehydrate.

"I was supposed to be a Marisa's last night," she starts, in a soft, quivering voice. "I left my phone there, so that's where Mom would think I was."

That explains why Mary's not blowing up my phone trying to find her. While she should be grounded for trying to deceive her mother, that discussion's for later.

"Where were you?" It's a battle to keep my voice level.

"With Owen."

That motherfucker. I should have fucking guessed. Swallowing rapidly in an attempt to remain calm, I ask the question to which I believe I already have the answer. "He the one who hurt you?"

"Yes, no."

Salem makes a cutting motion across his throat. It tells me two things. One, Owen is soon going to be six feet under, and secondly, to go easy on her.

"Tell me everything, Alicia. You went to his place?" If yes, we know where to find him.

"No." Her lips press together. "I didn't tell Mom, but I've been talking to him for weeks—ever since the day of the shoot, with your bike, Grumbler."

I nod, showing I remember. It's another thing she's been lying to her mom about. Oh, I know Mary knew they'd been in contact, but not that they seem to have become more than friends.

"Last weekend. You thought I was in bed when you were talking to Mom, but I wasn't. I was listening. I heard you planning to trick him, so I told him all about it. How Dusty wasn't really a model, and you were setting him up."

Jesus. Closing my eyes, I roll back my head. We knew she wouldn't go along with it had we admitted what we were doing, hence we thought we'd been clever. I'd never dreamed she'd been eavesdropping.

Swallowing a couple of times, I look back down. "What was his reaction?"

"He told me what a wonderful person I was to tell him. He said I was beautiful inside and out. He told me he was falling in love with me and wanted to take our relationship further."

"You met him again before last night?"

She sniffs, then nods. "Marisa's been covering for me."

Perhaps Marisa should have a visit from us—another thing to leave until later. I don't tell Alicia how stupid she's been, that's a job for her mom. But judging by her condition, she's already regretting it enough herself.

"So, last night?" I prompt her, while mentally sitting on my hands to stop myself from shaking the truth out of her. I have to remember, right now, I'm not the sergeant-at-arms.

"I was going to… I'd decided…" She goes bright red and buys herself time while noisily blowing her nose. "Owen rented a hotel room. It was a lovely place. Upscale, better than where Mom and I had stayed before."

"Where?"

She names the hotel. From behind her, Salem nods, either to show he's heard of it, or has just noted it.

"He was amazing, Grumbler. He'd laid out stuff to eat, all my favourite food—buffalo wings, fries. He had beer, I had soda. There were flowers too. Flowers for his special girl. For my first time, it couldn't have been better."

"But you changed your mind? Said no and he ignored you?"

She adamantly shakes her head. "No. He couldn't have

been more considerate. He… took his time. He made sure I enjoyed it. It wasn't like being with a fumbling boy my age. He knew what to do." She bites her lip.

"Sweetheart. I don't understand." I open my palms, shrugging my hands in confusion. Then it dawns on me. "He dumped you and said goodbye?"

"Huh," she scoffs. "I wish he had. That would have been better."

"Alicia. Help me out here, please? What did he do? Or didn't. Did he use a condom?"

Her eyes go wide, and she flushes red. "Of course. But Grumbler…" She throws herself forward and into my arms. "I didn't know." Her voice weakens and trails off. "I didn't know." The tone of her voice again becomes stronger and rises. "This morning he told me. He filmed it. He filmed everything, Grumbler. He called it *Deflowering of a Virgin*. He said if I led you to him, then he'd show it to my mom. He'd make sure everyone at school saw it. I was to give you a message. Leave him and Devon alone."

"Motherfucker!" Niran roars.

"How did he film it? On his phone?" Salem fires the question at her while I just hold the girl who's sobbing again.

"He had proper cameras set up, but I hadn't seen them. He'd disguised them."

"He showed you?"

"Yes, to prove he could carry out his threat."

Salem's jaw clenches.

I struggle, barely able to suppress my rage. "But you came to me, anyway, sweetheart?"

"He also said, he'd kill you if he saw you again, and I couldn't have him do that."

An idle threat, that kid couldn't better me. But she'd come straight to warn me. I didn't realise I meant anything to Alicia. "Why do you care about me, Alicia? And you shouldn't worry, I'm more than capable of looking after myself."

"I don't have a dad. Mom's dated, I know that, but she's only brought one person home to meet me, and he was horrible. Now you're coming to the house, and I thought…"

"Hey, sweetheart. There's nothing between me and your mom. I'm no father figure. I'm old enough to be your grandfather. You can knock that idea on the head. Your mom's much too young for me."

"Mom? Young? She's old. She was thirty when she had me."

My head shouldn't automatically start doing the arithmetic. I shouldn't be working out whether a surprisingly short, as it turns out, ten-year age difference was too much. Women, I decide, must grow old far more gracefully than men do. I'd never have taken her for that old. Still, I've got ten extra years of living under my belt, an extra one hundred and twenty months. Nope, can't consider it. I'm still too old and too jaded.

"Alicia, there's nothing between your mom and me, other than we've hit it off as friends. I'm ten years older."

"So? Owen's seven years older than me."

I still. "Owen's twenty-one."

"That's what he told me at first, but then he told me his real age. He just looks young."

"And fuckin' plays on it." Salem is incensed.

"Hey, Grumbler. You need me?" A female voice sounds by my shoulder. Glancing up, I see Eva.

"Yeah." Once again, I have to peel Alicia away from me. "Alicia, this is Eva. Eva, this is Alicia. Alicia's had a hard time of it. Could you take her under your wing for a while? You hungry, sweetheart?" I say the last to the girl in my arms, hopeful, but not optimistic.

"You going to help me, Grumbler? I'm so scared. What if he shows that video to everyone?"

That's an easy question to answer. "Yes."

"And not tell my mom?" This one is far harder.

That I can't promise. Mary's got to know everything. "She has to be told, Alicia. But one thing I promise you, she won't be angry, okay? I'll be there when you speak to her."

"I've ruined my life," she wails. "Just like she told me."

"Listen to me, Alicia. I know you feel fuckin' bad right now, and there's not much I can say to help you, but I promise you this—Owen won't be sharing that video with anyone. I'll make sure of it."

Alicia stares at me for a moment, and I wonder what she's seeing. I'm a rough around the edges biker, yet she's come to me. That means something. Now I'll do all that I can to protect her, and I wonder how she knows that.

"I'm hungry," she admits, finally. "I didn't want breakfast, but I could eat now." My reassurance that I'll help her seems to have taken some of the burden from her. She eyes up Eva, seeing not the club girl we're used to, but the proficient nurse who gives patients confidence all the time. She starts to stand, then looks back down toward me. "I wish you'd reconsider dating Mom."

With one eyebrow arched in my direction, Eva puts a friendly arm around Alicia and leads her away in the direction of the kitchen.

I'm still crouched on the ground. Niran, friend that he is, comes around the sofa and reaches down a hand, helping me to my feet. I nod my thanks at him.

Salem jerks his head toward a table in the corner of the clubhouse. He, Niran and I make our way over.

CHAPTER SIXTEEN

Grumbler

"Leaving aside you've been seeing a woman and not told us," Salem starts, "this fucker is dead."

"Token might be able to find out details about him from the database at the hotel. It's not a cheap place, and I doubt he'd have used cash to buy the room. He'd have had to have left an address at least."

Hopefully Owen won't think Alicia's got friends with database hacking skills. But a thought occurs to me. "He'll have been careful. There's always a chance she'd have gone to the cops."

"After that threat?" Salem's eyes have hardened. "Who'd want a porn video of themselves being circulated around?"

Niran taps his chin. "I can't see how he'd have gone to all that trouble just to ensure he's got a hold over the Satan's Devils MC. Not when surely it's easier to give Grumbler the money he's owed."

Salem's eyes flick toward him. "That's my feeling too. Sure, he got his rocks off, used a poor kid, but I think he was more intent on making a fuckin' porn movie, and she's got the starring role."

I'd been so disgusted listening to Alicia's ordeal, that I hadn't realised the implications. "You think he's going to sell it?" My brothers' expressions show me that's exactly what they think.

"We've got to get hold of the video and destroy it."

"No doubt about that. We've got to get Token onto it."

I nod. Jeez. I've no responsibility for that kid, she's nothing to me. I don't have a relationship with her mother beyond friendship. Yet, her story is hers and should remain private. But unless I bring more of my brothers in and share details she won't want sharing, I won't be able to do shit to get this situation right. I feel for the poor girl. The most I can do is ensure this isn't a mistake that will haunt her forever.

There's something else I need to do as well. "I'll need to speak to Mary, her mother. I better go see her." It's not something to drop on her over the phone.

"Want to leave it to me to update Token, while you have that conversation with the mom?"

It's going to take me a moment to decide how to approach it. Maybe I should take Alicia home and have it out there. But Niran can definitely get started on the technical side of things. Now it's not just finding Owen and Devon because I've been cheated, the stakes have become sky high. Who knows who'll get access to that film of Alicia? Her future could lie in the balance as it could be a school friend, or a potential employer.

"You think Owen's working alone, or with Devon?"

"I don't know what to fuckin' think." I wipe my hands over my face. "Who does this, Niran? Who fuckin' does this? Who takes advantage of an underage kid and fuckin' films it?" I pause for a beat, but don't expect an answer. "There's more to it, I feel it. Devon doesn't want to be found, that's for certain. And it's not just because he owes me a few dollars. What if he's into something far more lucrative? Porn. He used Alicia to kill two birds with one stone. He gets a film that some twisted fuckers would pay to watch and gets what he believes is a hold over us to stop us from locating him."

"I think you're right. I hate to say it, but it's the only thing that makes sense."

"He's fuckin' dead. He just doesn't know it."

"Be careful, Brother. There's one hell of a lot of money in the porn business. They might even have eyes on the kid's house. She was supposed to keep us out of it, remember?"

The enforcer has got a good point. Maybe rushing to Mary's place the morning after would signal Alicia had come running to me.

I'm still reeling from how she trusts me. I hadn't expected that.

I am trustworthy, well, my brothers have faith both in my ability to protect them and my desire to do so. But it's not the first thing civilians think when they see me. All they see is my cut and think *criminal*.

Niran's not one to waste time. Having a purpose, he stands and goes off to find Token. Salem stays for a moment, his eyes resting on me.

"That was hard hearing, Brother."

I grimace. "I'm still trying to process it. How the fuck do I tell Mary?"

Pursing his lips, he tells me, "I'm still not sure if it was rape or consensual."

"She was raped, even if the sex was consensual. She didn't consent to being filmed, or to be used in that way."

"We should film cutting his dick off." Salem gives a chilling grin.

I like that idea. "Put that on the dark web to put off would-be rapists."

But pleasurable thoughts of what we'll be doing to Owen once we get our hands on him must be put on the back burner for now. I can't put off contacting Mary any longer.

Pushing my hands on the table, I ease myself up. "I've got a call to make." Having excused myself, I go outside.

The sun is shining, the air warm but not unbearable as it would be in the heat of summer. It's too bright and cheery for the conversation I'm about to have.

My phone feels heavy as I hold it, waiting for the call to be answered.

"Hey, Grumbler. How are you?"

"Mary, I need you to listen to me."

"You've got news?" Her voice sounds eager.

"Not of the type you expect." I draw in a deep breath. "Alicia's with me, at the compound." Knowing Salem was right, and a Devil rushing to Mary would be suspicious, I'd decided for her to visit us instead. "I need you to come here. I'll give you directions."

There's a stunned silence, then, "Is she hurt? Why is she there? Is she okay? What the hell, Grumbler? You took her there?"

"Mary, she came to me this morning."

"Came to you? Why?"

"Please, just come. She's not hurt," I say fast. Well, I don't think she is, or not physically. "We'll talk when you get here."

"You tell me now, Grumbler. If something's wrong with my daughter, I need to know."

I bow my head. I'd known this wouldn't be easy. "She came to me because she's scared she'll disappoint you, Mary. Please, I can't discuss this over the phone. Please, just come."

Another silence shows she's not happy.

"You know I'm imagining the worst, don't you?"

The worst. Yes, other than death, that's probably how to describe it. "Please," I plead again.

Begging seems to have worked when she asks next, "Where are you?"

I explain how to get here then end the call. Leaning back

against the wall of the converted hangar, I close my eyes, allowing the heat of the sun to rest on my face, thinking back to how everything started. If I hadn't gone to have that tattoo done that day, if Devon hadn't had his eye caught by my bike, if I hadn't been so proud of my handiwork and wanted to show it off, maybe I wouldn't be involved in this predicament now. But that would mean I'd never have met Alicia and her mother, and if things had played out the same way, they wouldn't have the Satan's Devils on their side.

Would I have done anything differently had I known? Fuck no.

"Alicia wanted to find you." Eva's voice startles me out of my reverie.

Opening my eyes and pushing away from the wall, I see Alicia standing in front of me.

"You need me, honey, come find me." When Eva makes her offer, Alicia gives her a small smile, then her eyes switch to me.

Her face is blank, as if trying to read what I'm thinking.

"Come sit with me." I jerk my head toward the picnic bench in the shade of a tree, just a short distance away from the clubhouse.

She follows me, her gaze now moving from me to take in the scenery instead. Here, above the city, it's a beautiful view out to the Coronado Bridge and beyond that, the Pacific.

I breathe in deeply, then warn her, "Your mom's on her way."

Her head snaps back to me. "What? Why? I can't..."

Reaching over the bench, I take her hand, squeezing it gently. "She has to know, sweetheart. And you need her on your side. It's one hell of a secret to keep if you don't tell her."

"She'll be so angry." Alicia's face falls. I don't think I've ever seen anyone looking so distressed.

"It's not you she'll be angry with."

"You can't say that." There's a bite in her voice. "You don't know her. I've gone against everything she's ever said."

"The only thing you can be blamed for is lying to her. Nothing else is down to you, okay?"

"She won't see it that way."

Pulling my hand back, I prop both elbows on the table. Resting my chin on my clasped hands, I regard her. "Adults are full of *do this*, *do that*, *don't do the other*, aren't they?"

The slight rise and fall of her chin show me she agrees, even if she doesn't know where I'm going with this.

"You know why? It's because most of the time we've been there, done that, and have learned from our mistakes. We're not wiser, we don't have a manual we've adhered to, we just have had experiences that have taught us about life. Your mom lays down rules not to curtail your freedom, but to keep you safe."

"I should have listened to her."

"Of course you should. But you're a teenager, and you're programmed to rebel. Won't be the first time a girl's head gets turned by a pretty boy, and it won't be the last. The shame of it is, you picked the wrong one. Or, the wrong one picked you for none of the right reasons." I stare at her until she meets my eyes. "My mom told me not to hang around with the guys that she had bad feelings about. I thought she was being fuckin' stupid and just didn't want me to have fun. Turns out she was right."

Alicia frowns. "What happened?"

"I ended up having to choose between heading straight down to the recruiting office or doing time."

"You served?"

"I did my time." Got out as soon as possible. It wasn't having to be part of a team that bothered me, nor some of the shit that I saw. It was having a regimented routine which fucked with what I saw as my free spirit. It suits some people.

Niran, for example, would have been in for life were it not for the loss of his leg. Still, it was better than going to prison, and that's the only cop I've ever been thankful to.

"Have you ever been in prison?"

I wink at her. "Nah, never got caught again." I haven't been inside, but some of the shit I've done for the club would have put me away for life. I've made a joke of my totally serious answer.

The sound of a motorcycle coming through the gate reaches my ears and I identify it immediately. It's Lost. Shading my eyes with my hand, I see he's brought Patsy. That could work to my benefit. I've no doubt there'll be another distraught woman once Mary finds out what's happened, and Patsy's a calming influence. Considering the shit she went through with her family, she might know what to say more than I. Wasn't six months back and she was burying her son Connor—though he's very much alive and our prospect now.

Lost parks, notices me, pats his old lady on the shoulder then comes across. He's sharp, and I know he doesn't miss that Alicia is young, underage, and has obviously recently cried. He gives her a critical once over, then narrows his eyes.

"Everything okay?"

"Prez, meet Alicia. Alicia, this is our prez, Lost. Alicia needs a little help from us. Salem will fill you in, he's inside."

In my usual man-of-few-words way, I let him know a couple of things with that statement. Firstly, that what she's here for is going to become club business, and secondly, that I don't want it discussed in front of her. She's going to have more than enough on her plate when her mother turns up.

With one last appraising look toward Alicia, he raises his chin, then disappears inside.

"He's your prez?" When I nod, she continues, "He doesn't look particularly scary."

Emitting a soft chuckle, I agree. "He's not. But don't

underestimate him. If something needs doing, he gets it done." Whether that's keeping our businesses running, or dispatching men to meet Satan.

Though the day is warm, Alicia suddenly shivers as though a cloud has come over the sun. Her hand moves to her forehead, then down to her cheek as an errant tear slips from her eye.

I don't know what to say to take the pain away and wish Mary would get here soon and relieve me of the burden. What do I know about parenting? Or how to comfort a young girl? Or even a woman, come to that. Apart from the club girls and one-night stands, I've never had a woman I needed to understand. What words could I use to repair the devastation in this kid's life? All I can do is promise to kill the man who misled and deceived her.

"I promise, Alicia. That film will be destroyed. You won't have it hanging over your head."

Hurt eyes meet mine. "He used me. He made me believe I was special. I thought I loved him, Grumbler. I thought I was the one."

She's not the first and won't be the last—not by a long shot. But those wouldn't be comforting words.

I've never been with a virgin, never wanted the responsibility of initiating a woman, and certainly not a young girl. It's not something I've particularly prized or thought special. To a man, getting your first time over and done without embarrassing yourself is probably more to the point. To a girl? Done right, it means the whole world. Though the hearts and flowers version is not, in reality, one that I've heard.

The sound of a car approaching reaches my ears. My phone vibrates, and I take it out.

"Yeah. Let her in," I say into the device, then, ending the call, raise my eyes. "Your mom's here."

"Oh God." Alicia drops her head into her hands. "I can't, Grumbler. I just can't."

"You want me to speak to her first?"

Grateful, but tearful eyes meet mine, and the accompanying nod and silent plea confirms, for no fault of my own, I'm about to break a woman's heart.

CHAPTER SEVENTEEN

Mary

Knowing how teenage girls sleep late, I hadn't been expecting Alicia home before noon. I had checked her phone when I'd woken, of course, to find her where I expected, still at Marisa's.

Having a morning of peace stretching ahead, I'd made a start on my normal task for a Saturday—the housework that I'd neglected to do all week. I'd been in the process of cleaning the bathroom when Grumbler had called.

My mouth had dropped open when I'd listened to what he had to say, or more, what he hadn't. Alicia had tracked him down to his compound, but he wouldn't explain why over the phone.

The traffic in San Diego was infuriating—every car, every traffic light seemed to exist just to impede my progress. I forced myself to drive carefully. It wouldn't help Alicia if I crashed or was pulled over, and it wouldn't get me to her any sooner.

Questions raced through my head. Why had she gone to him of all people? If she had a problem, why hadn't she come to me instead? If she's hurt, why go to Grumbler? Surely, her mom would always be best.

At last my GPS tells me I'm in the general area, and I follow Grumbler's instructions, turning off on a side road that appears to lead into nowhere, until a gate appears ahead. There's a man who's standing by it. He's wearing a leather vest like Grumbler's, though when, after asking what I wanted, he turns to make a phone call, instead of the club patches, the one on his back simply reads *Prospect*.

I bang my palms against the steering wheel as I wait for permission to enter, then, as the gates open at last, I drive through as the prospect had instructed. As soon as I near what must be the clubhouse itself, I spy Alicia and Grumbler seated at a picnic table.

I pull the car up, apply the brake and cut the engine. Opening the door, I see my daughter is seated with shoulders hunched. An immediate appraisal from a distance, I can see no visible injuries.

As I start to approach her, Grumbler stands and walks toward me, halting my progress. He holds up one hand in my direction and says back over his shoulder, "Give us a moment, kid. Go inside and find Eva."

Alicia jumps up, one quick glance is my direction, then with head down, she scuttles away.

"Alicia?" I call, but she ignores me. "What the hell, Grumbler?" I round on the man in front of me now. "What's she done? What's happened?" There was guilt in that one look she sent me. My mom's instinct knows she's done something that I won't like. "Let me go to her." *And who the hell is Eva?*

"Sit." Grumbler's tone has my eyes snapping to him. It's an instruction voiced in a way I can't ignore. "You're not going to like this, and you need time to process how to approach it with her. If you go after her now, you'll do more harm than good."

"I'm her mother," I point out.

"Yeah." His tone softens, and his hands wipe over his face. He looks drawn, and I wonder how much of it is down to Alicia. "Sit down and listen to me, Mary, please?"

"Has she brought trouble here?" I ask him, finally doing as he says, sitting down at the picnic bench. I don't know what I expected from a biker compound, but it wasn't that it would be in such a scenic position as this.

"Trouble we'll take on gladly." He answers my question in a growl.

His face is so serious, my worries multiply. "Just tell me, Grumbler."

Reaching into his pocket, Grumbler extracts a pack of cigarettes. He taps one out, and proceeds to light it. When I frown, he excuses himself.

"I don't smoke much. Only when I'm bored or stressed." He doesn't have to explain which he is now. Taking a drag and blowing smoke out, angling his head so it doesn't come my way, he sighs. "Alicia wasn't at her friend's last night. She left her phone there in case you checked."

My eyes widen. "The little—"

"Mary!" Grumbler's voice is sharp. "There's a lot more to come. Swallow your anger and just let me tell you."

"Where was she?"

"With Owen." Now I start to stand, but Grumbler snakes out his hand, his strong long fingers reaching around my wrist and imprisoning it. "Sit down, Mary."

I huff, as it seems I have no choice but to do as he says. Then I proceed to listen to one of the most painful things I've heard in my life.

At some point Grumbler releases my hand, stubs out his cigarette, and is my side of the bench. I'm sobbing in his arms without realising how I got there.

He rocks me for a few minutes, as I try to come to terms with what my baby girl has gone through.

"She needs her mom, babe. She needs you to be strong."

"How could she have been so stupid?"

He moves slightly, creating a small gap between us and holding me by the elbows. Staring intently into my eyes, he gives it to me straight. "Was she stupid? Owen, a twenty-four-year-old man for fuck's sake, created the perfect date, the perfect setup to convince her he was the man she could give her body to. A hotel room, her favourite food, flowers… How was she to know the whole thing was a setup?" He pauses a moment, raising a hand to brush back a strand of my hair. "He made it a young girl's dream. How was she to know what a lyin' motherfucker he was? How does a girl her age know how the world works?"

Through gritted teeth, I try to explain, "If she'd listened to me—"

"What? You'd have warned her she might end up in a porn video?"

That pulls me up. The thought would never have occurred to me. "She tried to send him a topless photo. I caught her and thought I'd put a stop to that. I explained how once that kind of photo is shared, there's no pulling it back."

"Which is probably why she knows the significance of how much damage that film could do to her life. A double whammy, as Owen's betrayal also hurt."

How can I repair the damage that's been done? My daughter's no longer a virgin, and though it was her choice, she chose to lose it to the wrong man. She's not unique, but I know it will play on her mind for the rest of her life. Though I doubt many men nowadays are virgins and would be hypocrites to expect a woman to be when they were not, she's lost her chance of giving it to someone who meant something to her. But at the time, she thought she had.

Hadn't I been thinking about how I wasted mine only recently? Your first time is something you never forget, however much you wish you could. But I'd never had to contend with it being filmed, and that film circulated around. The thought makes me shudder.

"Grumbler. You've got to back off. It doesn't matter about Alicia's money, and I'll pay you what Devon was supposed to pay—"

"Don't want your money!" Grumbler roars. "Fuck, woman, do you think I give a damn about that now?" He pinches the bridge of his nose then looks straight at me once more. "Do you really think they'd have gone to all that trouble just to stop a douche canoe like me asking for what he's owed? Fuck, no. They've got a film, and films like that make money. Your best bet is for us to stay involved, so we can shut that shit down. I promise you, Mary. We'll get it destroyed."

"But you can't even find Devon. How can you find the film?"

"We don't need to find him to discover the footage, just his trail on the web."

I'm not at all sure it's as easy as that. There's a growing fear in my overactive mind, of people giving Alicia snide glances as they've watched her with Owen, getting their jollies at the cost of my daughter.

"Hey, babe. We've got this. We're not going to let it do any permanent harm. If I know my prez, this will become the club's number one priority."

I move my head side to side, completely incredulous. "But why should you or your club help? We're nothing to you."

"You are now."

My eyebrows draw down. "I don't understand."

He takes hold of my hand and squeezes it gently. "Your girl came to me, Mary. That means a lot. I'm not going to let her down. And you? Well, I want to be there for you, make your world as right again as it can be."

"Are you saying you want a relationship with me?" I yank back my hand and my voice has gone squeaky.

"Nah." He looks me right in the eye. "I'm far too old for you, and I've never had any desire to take an old lady of my own. We can be friends, though, can't we? And friends support each other."

In my eyes he's not too old, but for now, my focus is Alicia. "Can I see my daughter now?"

An assessing look comes my way. "You got your anger under control, 'cause that's what she expects from you? You've got the power to hurt her badly."

I almost snap he should leave the parenting advice to someone who knows what they're talking about, but deep down I know he's right. Alicia's lesson's been taught already. My focus is on helping her move forward.

After analysing the expression on my face and finding it satisfies him, he stands and holds out his hand to me. I take it to get to my feet but release it immediately. Then, side by side, we head into the clubhouse.

It's full of men clad in leather but looking past and around them, I can see a bar stretches down one side of what is a clubroom. Tables and chairs are scattered around, and at the opposite end to the door is a small stage and stripper pole. I should have expected that, I suppose. *And here is where my daughter's come to ask for sanctuary?* I've got to get her home.

The men, mostly tall, intimidate me. When they catch my eye, their expressions are friendly, but it's the sheer number and the aura of masculinity which makes me pull my back and shoulders straighter.

"You see Eva?" Grumbler asks a man who looks particularly scary.

"Yeah. She and Patsy went upstairs with the kid. Think they're in Prez's room."

Grumbler raises his chin in thanks, then, placing his hand in the small of my back, starts to guide me across to a staircase which leads up.

"Grumbler?" a voice calls out. "Today's ride is off."

Absorbing the information with just a grunt, Grumbler encourages me up the stairs. Once at the top, he leads me down a hallway with doors leading off to either side and stops at one at the end and knocks.

The door is opened. A woman, who doesn't look much older than I am, opens it.

"Mom?" A small voice addressing me serves as my introduction.

"Mary?" At my nod, the woman continues, "I'm Patsy, I'm the prez's old lady. Er…"

"I know what an old lady is," I confirm.

"Come in." She holds the door ajar. "We'll take it from here," she addresses the man behind me.

My daughter is on the bed, another woman is sitting next to her. Alicia's eying me warily, her teeth worrying her lip.

"This is Eva," Patsy informs me, waving her hand at the other woman. "She's a nurse."

"A nurse?"

"I'm not here in my professional capacity," Eva explains hurriedly. "I, well, I have a lot to do with the club. Grumbler called me in as he thought I could help."

I just want to talk to my daughter. I step forward and hold out my hand. "Come on, Alicia. Let's go home."

Patsy steps between me and her. "We think it might be best for you both to stay here—at least for now."

My brow furrows. "Why?"

Patsy's hand rubs at her temples before continuing, "I know a thing or two about bad men, which might be making me overcautious. But according to your girl, the photographer behind this knows her details, her home address as that's how he was going to get the modelling fee to her."

I go still, thinking, yes, he does. Didn't see anything wrong with it when I signed the modelling release for her.

"But surely," I lower my voice considerably, "he's got what he wanted. There's no reason to come after her."

Patsy takes my arm and leads me to the furthest corner of what is actually a large room, twin aspects, one half set up as a bedroom, and the other as a living area. "You want this film found and destroyed, don't you?"

Of course I do. My nod tells her so.

"Alicia had a message to keep the Devils out of it. But as far as I can see it, they're your only hope."

"The threat was that they'd make her life miserable—distribute the film on social media."

Patsy shakes her head. "More likely it will be via some porn network, but who knows what twisted assholes would watch it."

"Then we'll go to the police." Yes, that's what I should be doing.

Patsy tilts her head in consideration. "They could go after him for statutory rape due to her age, but it's the photographer that's behind this, I'm sure of it. The man who did that to her was working for someone. Alicia was very specific his message was 'they', and that the Devils should steer clear of the man she modelled for."

"The boys will be having a meeting if I'm any judge. Why don't you stay around until they've decided what they're going to do?" Eva, approaching, asks. She leans in close. "Alicia is scared shitless of what you're going to say. I know how kids and parents can butt heads when they're alone. Why don't you hang around here for a while? We can be a buffer for both of you."

Undecided, I leave the woman and go to my daughter. Sitting beside her, I don't use words, I just hold out my arms. When she falls into them, I hug her close giving her the comfort only a mom can. When she sobs, I ignore her tears dampening my top, and just smooth her hair.

"I'm sorry, Mom. I'm sorry."

I continue my stroking action, a tactile reassurance. She might have gone against everything I warned her to be careful of, might have lied as I'd never have let her go out last night if I'd known the truth, but it's only disappointment that I feel, heavily tinged with my failings to keep my daughter safe. It's her who's hurt, and her who'll have to carry the burden.

Her tears slowly begin to dry. I try to tilt her head up so I can look into her face, but she turns away and won't meet my eye.

"Eva and I are going to get some dinner on for tonight. I like to make sure the guys have edible food at least once in a while." Patsy winks at Eva, sharing a private joke. "Why don't you and Alicia come down to help? Many hands make light work as they say."

I'm not sure about entering that crowded clubroom again.

"I'll check that the men are in church." Eva seems to read my mind. She does so by sending a text and instantly getting a response. "Yeah. Tits says they're in a meeting."

Tits?

I open my mouth to query the strange name, when I hear a barely suppressed giggle from my side. In that moment, I realise anything that can make Alicia smile today is worthwhile, even though I'm not certain I want to meet a woman of that name. Mind you, I'm projecting it's a woman at this point. I suppose it could be a big-chested man.

"Church!"

It seems that Salem has updated Lost as I hoped. After his shouted instruction, the prez is storming into the meeting room with his face as black as thunder. He might not have kids of his own, but has taken on two, admittedly older, already being in their twenties, who came with his old lady. Patsy's daughter is expecting their first grandchild in three months' time, and Lost couldn't be prouder if it were going to be of his blood. We've all been subjected to the ultrasound picture. His regard for Connor has to be more tempered as the just turned twenty-three-year-old is our prospect now, and Prez can't afford to show any favours. Point is, Lost may not have sired kids, but I've always suspected it was something he'd wanted though his path led down another route.

As they enter, brothers move to their chairs fast, indicating it wasn't only the prez Salem had updated.

Lost kicks off the meeting without wasting time. "It will come as no surprise that the ride out today is cancelled." He pauses, waiting for objections, but none come. I hadn't expected any, club business comes first. I've made Alicia mine, and thereby, by extension theirs. "You all know why we're here? Anyone need updating?"

If Alicia were my daughter, would it upset me that everyone already knows what's happened to her? Maybe I'd be embarrassed on her behalf, but the outcome would be the same. I need my brothers' support to put her world, as far as it can be, back to rights. As no one looks puzzled or raises their hands to request more information, I'm pleased we don't have to go back over the details. Hearing them was hard, explaining what had gone down to Mary worse. I don't want to go through it again. I raise my chin to Salem who lifts then dips his jaw.

"No blame attaches to her. The kid was duped by a man who turns out to be seven years' older. A practised liar by the sounds of it." Niran, having heard the story first-hand, puts up a defence in case anyone was still on the fence.

"Is he working alone or with somebody?" Bones asks.

"He must be working for Devon Starr," Salem interjects. "It's the only thing that makes sense."

"Or, he's working with him as a model, but the porno business is his own initiative," Brakes states.

"We need info. My suspicion is that this Owen fucker wasn't working alone, but we need more to go on before discounting that he was." Prez looks pointedly at Token.

Token shrugs. "I got into the hotel's database. A room for Owen Leesom was reserved and paid for by a Brandon West. Either there's a third man in play, or that's Owen's real handle, or maybe even Devon's. I'm trying to track back on the credit card details, but those databases are tough to crack."

"Getting help on that, Brother?"

Token nods at the VP. "Mouse has asked Cara to look into it, but her family is having political problems right now. They can't afford an international incident. She's hoping to get her activity cleared, but it might not be in time."

Cara's a hacking expert but is married into a ruling Arab family. As such, her illegal activities have to be kept under the radar.

Lost grimaces. "Finding Owen is one thing. As far as I can see, finding that video and destroying it comes top of the agenda. I know we all want our pound of flesh but stopping that before it starts circulating has to take priority. Grumbler's kid does not deserve to have her reputation destroyed by one fuckin' mistake."

"I'm just one fuckin' man, Prez." Token moans, putting his head in his hands.

I feel for him and know he's trying his best. It's time that's against him. I've no doubt in his abilities to track everything down, but can he do it fast enough, that's the question.

"I was coming to that." Prez stares at him. "I think it's time we called in reinforcements."

"The brothers who can get into Fort Knox?" I breathe out. As my eyes meet those of my prez, I know how much that will cost him. I'd rather we left it to the experts we know, Token, Mouse, Cad in Colorado and Keys from Vegas, but they haven't got the computing power of Utah. My objections are that I don't trust that chapter, but are they valid, and should they take priority over Alicia's future?

"I know I objected last time when it was helping us find one man, but this has escalated, and I think we should involve them." Dart rubs at his nose. "They've got the ability. This isn't passing off a task that we can do easily. We're up against time on this one, and they've got more than one Token."

Prez nods. "My view is that we split the investigation. Token can concentrate on finding Owen and Devon. They're local, and up to us to deal with. Alicia's problem is a different issue. Once a video like that gets posted, it can go viral."

Reboot's holding up his hand. "I might not be in Token's

league, but I know my way around a computer. If he wants help, I'll work with him."

"If you can avoid switching everything on and off, I'd be grateful, Brother."

Bones sniffs loudly. "Any help you need dissecting the financials, send shit my way."

Token gives a chin lift toward the treasurer.

"Soon as you've got a name and location, give it to me," Salem growls.

My eyes shoot a laser beam at him. He's doing nothing without me, that's for certain.

Lost raps the table. "No need to waste time. Salem, you get a team together, ready to head out. It's a case of when, not if, we find them. Leave no stone fuckin' unturned, you got that?"

"I'll be with you." They're not leaving me out. The way Salem's eyes go up and then down show my words were unnecessary.

"First, I want you with me, Grumbler, when I put the call into Snatcher." Prez's words explain why he hadn't immediately named me. "You can present a personal perspective that maybe I can't."

"Going to bring Drummer in on the call?" Dart narrows his eyes. "I think he should know what we're asking. He may be interested in Utah's reaction and whether they're going to play nice with another chapter."

Prez considers it, then nods. "Yeah, I already warned him we might need assistance. He'll want to hear what Snatcher has to say. We can have a three-way." Then his eyes narrow at the man who's just laughed. "And you, Kink. We've got visitors in the clubroom, one who's underage. You keep your fuckin' pets out of sight, you hear me?"

"Or suitably clothed," I warn him. "And that doesn't mean fuckin' collars and leashes."

For an answer, Kink just winks at me. I hope he'll keep everything PG.

Salem waggles his hand. "We start lifting rocks, I'm not sure what we'll find under them. I suggest we need the woman and the kid to stay on the compound. Just for a few days, until we find out what we're dealing with. Alicia was told not to involve Grumbler, and thereby us. If they find out, they might want retribution."

"You really think they'd hurt them?" Deuce asks.

"Could be," Kink, now serious, answers. "The video may just have been to silence Alicia, but why? To cover up a scam to cheat models? That doesn't make sense, it's too elaborate. Our supposition the video will be used whatever they say is far more likely. And that brings more problems. The porn business is serious fuckin' money. Alicia is not only a victim, but a key witness. Would they take the risk she might go to the cops? Someone might decide she's better out of the way. Permanently."

Prez nods. "I've already given the heads-up to Patsy. She'll be trying to persuade them to stay, and it might take your help, Grumbler, to get them to see sense. They can stay in my room, it's bigger." He waits for me to acknowledge his suggestion, then he bangs the gavel. "We know what we need to do. Find that motherfucker and erase those images. Grumbler? You're with me. My office. Now."

I waste no time getting to my feet and following him to his office conveniently located next door. Once inside, he rounds the desk taking his normal seat, and I pull up a spare chair just as he places his phone in the middle of the desk. He taps at a few keys.

"You got Drummer."

"Got a situation here, Drum. Need to ask a favour of Utah. Got an urgent situation to deal with and need their expert help. Thought you'd want to be aware."

Drummer doesn't hesitate. It's a sign of the regard in which he holds Lost. "Sounds urgent. Get Snatcher on the call. You don't want to go over everything twice."

Lost is fast, clearly used to making multiple connections on his device while it would take me time, and probably a visit to Token to know what to do.

The phone rings once, twice and then a couple more, and just when I think we're going to need to call back, it's answered.

"Snatcher here."

"Snatch. Lost here. Drummer's on the call too."

There's a brief silence from the Utah end, followed by a cautious, "Yeah?"

"I got a problem, Snatcher. Needs your expertise on it if you've got the time."

Snatcher sighs as if Lost's call was what he was worried about all along—a frivolous request taking them away from the important work that they do. "We're quite busy, but let me know what you need, and I'll see what we can do."

Now I'm glad Lost got the mother chapter prez involved, when Drummer jumps in. "If this isn't up your street, then I'll see what Mouse can do." His voice is decidedly chilly.

"Mouse is already helping us, Drummer. He needs Cara's help, but she's not been given the go ahead."

A sigh from Snatcher comes down the line. "Give it to me."

Lost does. He leaves out the history about how I got involved, something I'm grateful for, but the gist of his summary involves a dodgy photographer, a model who's older than he's led people to believe, both with fake identities, and a film of an underage girl which has no business being distributed for perverts to watch.

"Names that you know, aliases or not, that will do for a start." Snatcher's interest is obviously caught.

Lost rattles off all that we know.

"This something Utah can help with?" Drummer's voice sounds tight. Even the headlines that Lost had given make hard hearing.

"Yes," Snatcher confirms fast. "Only thing that worries me is what rabbit hole we might be falling into. This isn't something that's started overnight. It sounds too practised to me. Might end up a full-on job for us, but if there's an illegal porn trade going on, I promise you we'll put a stop to it." He thinks for a moment. "I'll get Honor and Duty trying to track down your suspects, and Swift can start delving into where that video might have ended up."

"Token's already trying to find Owen, or this Brandon, whatever his handle is."

"He'll have to break into a credit card database. We can probably get the results faster. It's our bread and butter, Lost."

I'd like to defend my brother, but I know Utah's probably more skilled in this type of work.

"Get your members to call Token to get an update on where he is. I'll square it with him." Lost sees the benefit as I do.

I lean forward. "Need to get this video off the web before it starts circulating. I don't want Alicia's life ruined by one mistake."

Snatcher comes back quickly. "You get that hotel room checked out?"

I go cold. It hadn't occurred to me.

I hear his sigh down the line. "Might mean Honor flying down there, but we'll see if the room is still empty, and if it is, book it out for a few days so we can do our investigation. If it's been let out, there's probably not much point. The equipment will have been removed, but there might be clues we can trace. They could have gotten the video out via the hotel's network."

This is why we needed the experts. Utah appears to think more like cops, whereas we're men of action.

"Honor would be welcome at the clubhouse," Lost confirms.

"Well, we'll check the hotel records and see whether he can help. Grumbler?"

"Yeah?" I answer Snatcher.

"We'll deal with the tape, but this might be the tip of the iceberg. You come across Owen or Devon before we do, don't do anything too drastic. Break arms, legs, but nothing to stop them talking. Not until we're satisfied we don't know anything else. Then," Snatcher pauses for effect, "after that, you can fuckin' castrate them."

"Well, I think that's about it, isn't it?" Drummer's amusement comes down the line. But then he adds seriously, "Sounds like you know what you're doing Snatcher. Any word from Stormy?"

There's another audible sigh. "I'm starting to think he has to be dead, Drummer." He pauses. "Fuckin' embarrassing we can't find him, but we've no leads to follow. He's disappeared off the face of the earth." He sounds legit in my view. It can't be easy to admit to being a failure. But I can't see his face, and he could be lying—hard to tell over a phone line.

"We'll talk next week, Snatcher. And Lost? Keep me updated. You need any help from here? You got it. I fuckin' hate child molesters and this comes under that heading. Grumbler? You take care of your ol' lady."

"She's not my—"

But Lost ends the call before I can finish. Seeing the look on my face, he slaps me on my back. "You might want to think about that. Can't recommend enough what it's like to have an ol' lady."

I've seen enough of Mary to know if I was in the market for a woman as a permanent fixture in my life, she would do nicely, but there's one obstacle I can't get over—she's too young for me. It's not just a matter of the ten-year difference, she's from a different generation.

She's youthful, energetic, while my bones creak. I don't want to burden someone with the pains of my old age which can only get worse, not better.

Lost's already gone before I come back to myself.

What do I do now? No point going to talk to Token, Lost will already be updating him. I suppose I should go and update Mary with as much as I'm able to about what's going on. Sift through what I can and can't tell her and somehow persuade her to stay on the compound.

Dragging my hands down my face, I wonder how the fuck I can do that. Hopefully Patsy will have already persuaded her. I'd picked up on Mary's discomfort as soon as we'd stepped into the clubhouse and read that she'd want to get away fast.

I can't tell my brothers to mind their language and behave around her, this is their home. But hopefully they'll have the sense to step carefully, especially after what happened to Alicia last night.

Leaving Lost's office, I shut the door behind me.

"Where…" I start to ask about Mary, but Pennywise catches my eye.

"Kitchen," he informs me, guessing the person I seek.

Raising my chin, I go in that direction, but come to an abrupt halt before I enter, hearing some of the conversation emanating from within.

"My first time was awful."

CHAPTER NINETEEN

Mary

The clubroom, as promised, is empty of men when I tentatively follow Patsy and Eva down the staircase. Both Alicia and I trail in their wake as they lead us to a kitchen. It's big, almost industrial.

The name *Tits* is still going around my head, and I'm still wondering who and what gender the owner is. It seems I'm soon to find out.

Apart from the appliances, some of which look relatively new, and a table able to seat about ten people comfortably sat in the middle of the room, my attention is caught by three women who Eva immediately pushes away from the stove, leaning over as though to check what's cooking.

"It's for one of my casseroles. It's going to be good." A woman in her mid-twenties is frying up something on the stovetop. "Look, I'm doing it properly, browning off the meat first." It's not her cookery skills nor what she's cooking that attracts my eyes. It's her clothing, or lack of. Her top can only be described as a bra, and her shorts, well, they're little more than panties.

Eva and Patsy exchange glances and then start to quiz the woman about what's she's actually got going on.

"Cindy knows what she's doing." Another scantily clad woman is peeling potatoes at the table. I can't see what she's wearing, or not, to cover her hips, but her top is a miniscule tank. She's big boobed, too much so to go braless in my view, but she is.

"Thanks, Tits." The woman I now know is Cindy, glares at the other women. "At least someone has faith in me."

The third, who's at least got her belly covered, if not her complete ass, as she's wearing a clingy dress that appears to have trouble confining her breasts, also offers support. "Come on, Eva. It was only the once she gave us food poisoning."

"How was I to know you had to cook chicken that long?" Cindy turns, waving a spatula. "I know now, alright? And anyway, tonight's beef. Some people eat that raw, you know." She ends with a dismissive sniff.

Patsy chuckles, and I swing around, wondering how the older woman can put up with half-naked women in the kitchen. For one thing, if that fat splashed out the pan, it could do serious damage to Cindy's naked midriff.

"We'll just supervise, Eva. Seems like Cindy's got it all under control." Patsy turns to me. "These are Cindy, Tits and Pearl." She points to each one in turn. "Along with Eva, they're our club girls."

Club girls?

Alicia, who's been standing quiet by my side, asks me quietly, "What are club girls?"

Seeing what they're wearing, or not as the case may be, it's fairly obvious. I don't want it spelled out in front of my daughter. Eva though, she seems so normal, and is dressed conservatively. *Surely, she's not one as well?*

"We cook, clean and keep house for the men," Eva starts, giving the others a warning look, but she's too late.

Simultaneously, Tits speaks up, "We're here to service the men. In exchange, we get board and lodging, and a bit extra in our pockets each week."

"We service the men's rooms is what she meant to say." Eva casts a worried eye toward me as she tries to give what they do an innocent slant. But neither I, nor my daughter is stupid.

I'm not sure if the look I'm wearing is more of shock or disgust as I reflect upon just what services these women offer. *Does Grumbler partake?* My jaw clenches as I say tightly, "Thanks, Patsy, but I think we'll leave now." What hit me hardest was how this sensible woman who introduced herself as a nurse is not embarrassed to own herself as one of their number.

Is Patsy the same? I hope not. She did introduce herself as Lost's old lady, but maybe the men here like to share? Whatever, I have to get my daughter out of here.

It's Alicia who tries to dissuade me. "Mom, look, Owen and Devon know where we live. I'm scared, Mom. What if they come for me? What if Owen wants to… use me again? He could blackmail me with that video. What would I do?" Her eyes again water, and I have to admit I'm scared of that too. What could two defenceless women do against two determined men?

I don't even own a gun. For the first time in my life, I think I ought to look into buying one. But could I shoot a man? Send a bullet tearing into flesh? If he was coming to hurt my daughter, the answer is a resounding yes. That thought makes me frown. There's nothing I won't do to protect Alicia.

The desire is there, but not the ability. If I insist on taking her home, could I chance Owen wanting more? Even if he didn't use physical violence, as Alicia had said, he could use the threat of distributing that video to God knows who.

"We'll go to the cops," I decide. It's the only sensible decision.

Alicia looks at me, her eyes wide. She steps closer, and keeping her voice low, hisses, "That's not your decision. Oh, you can take me there, but I'm not going to say anything. First, that would make matters worse with Owen, and second, I'm not listening to cops telling me I was asking for it. That I went knowing what was going to happen. He didn't rape me, Mom."

Patsy interjects, also quietly into my ear, "How could she prove videoing it wasn't previously agreed to? Cops might say she only withdrew her agreement after she'd spoken to you, or perhaps, just came to have regrets. If Owen maintained it was only for his own private viewing, he's committed no crime."

"Statutory rape," I tell Patsy, equally softly.

Patsy breathes in deeply. "You really want to force Alicia to go through that?"

Do I? Surely that's the right way to go about it, to give the problem to people who know how to deal with it and get justice for my daughter. Grumbler would say I already have.

"I'm not going to the cops," Alicia whispers again, with fresh tears glistening. "I wouldn't trust Owen if I got the law after him."

She's made a good point. I didn't trust him and that was before he'd violated my daughter.

Are we safer to stay on the compound? Are my sensibilities of being alongside women who are open about the fact they are whores clouding my judgement over what's best for my daughter?

Am I being an old fogey? If they were dressed in everyday clothes, would I have looked at them twice? Am I too judgemental? They seem friendly enough, and if they're not ashamed of their lifestyle, who am I to judge? *I'm worried about them influencing Alicia.*

Do I doubt my parenting skills so much? Alicia's not going to change her life's ambition to becoming a club girl just from being around them. I brought her up to respect herself better than that.

Perhaps, a niggling doubt assails me, I'm more concerned that these women have, and will, warm Grumbler's bed. But why should that concern me, it's not as if I'd want to be there instead?

"You're overthinking it." Patsy again speaks into my ear, her tone amused. "I can see from the expressions going over your face. Don't think I don't know how you're feeling, I came here with my son not that long ago. Some club girls can be real bitches. I've heard that from the women in other clubs, but the four we have here are pleasant enough, as long as they don't think you're going to poach one of the men and take him off the market. Believe you me, they won't see you as a threat. In the same way as they didn't think that of me."

"Because I'm old?" I admit, whispering back.

"Hate to say it, yes. And you've caught the eye of Grumbler, who I'm pretty certain doesn't take advantage of the services they provide. Not that I've seen in the months that I've been here."

My heart lifts more than it should to know Grumbler hasn't, at least recently, been with the girls. But he's a man, doesn't mean he hasn't. To be honest, my stomach twists at the thought. With the exception of Eva, these girls aren't much older than Alicia.

In honesty, I think worse of the men than I do these women. What do Tits, Pearl, Cindy and Eva get out of it? Nothing but heartbreak I'm sure. I really can't understand Eva, who's pretty, intelligent and has a good profession.

Alicia takes her eyes off me at last, and goes to sit next to Tits, offering to help with her task. Cindy hands her an extra peeler, and soon she gets down to her chore, something I would have problems getting her to help with.

"You sleep with the men in the club?" Alicia asks.

I swallow rapidly, wishing she'd kept quiet.

"Uh-huh." Tits eyes come to me warily, cautious as to how much to share.

"Don't you feel… used?" Alicia asks, her voice husky.

Tits puts a peeled potato aside, and her eyes steady on my daughter. "Oh, sweetie, no. We use the men as much as they use us. We have fun, they have fun. Nothing more than that."

"This life wouldn't suit everyone." Eva too sits down at the table and links her hands together. "I'm not looking for a man, so that's why I'm here. I love the MC atmosphere, it's like being part of a family. The brothers are good to us."

"What about you, Alicia? You got a boyfriend?" Cindy asks. My eyes widen, wishing she'd kept her mouth shut.

"I thought I had," Alicia cries out, then cries for real, tears which had dried beginning to fall once again. Before I can get to her, Eva puts her arm around her. Her warning glance at the back of the woman at the stove goes unnoticed.

Cindy pauses cooking again and swings around fast. "What did he do? Dump you? Who do we have to kill?"

She looks so serious, I think she'd do it, even if the spatula she's holding right now is her only weapon.

Patsy tugs at my arm. "What happened to Alicia is nothing for her to be ashamed of. She's the victim, that's the only way of looking at it. Keeping it a dirty secret will only make it worse. I'm not saying tell everyone, but the women here all have their own stories. Of anyone, they'll understand."

As her words sink in, I realise it's true, Alicia has nothing to be ashamed of. She can mourn the loss of something that she'd thought she'd held precious and had given up to the right man, though in that, she was sorely mistaken. But to her there's no blame, only that perhaps someone older would have seen through his lies. Though who would have expected to become the star of a porn show?

"Alicia?" Eva's softly comforting hug has at least helped her get herself back into some semblance of control. When her eyes come to my face, I ask her permission. "Can I tell them?"

She glances at Tits who's eyeing her with sympathy, having realised something's seriously wrong.

"There's nothing you can tell us that would shock us," Pearl speaks from the other side of the room. "And before your story starts, we're on your side, sweetie."

At Alicia's small nod, I begin with just the highlights. "Alicia met a man, he pretended to be twenty-one. Turns out he was twenty-four, and you can guess why he lied. He was a model, so again, you can imagine how he looks. They met on a modelling shoot."

Tits pushes aside the potatoes and puts her full attention on me. Her eyes have narrowed as though she thinks she's got an inkling about how this story ends. Cindy turns off the burner and moves the pan away from the heat.

I continue the story as they listen without interrupting. A few nod as they realise how Alicia was deceived. It's when I add the part about it being filmed that their mouths drop open in shock.

Pearl is the first to speak. "So that explains why they're all in church on a Saturday afternoon, and the ride out has been cancelled. Don't worry, kid. They'll get the film deleted and will be plotting that bastard's slow and painful death. I promise you that. You've got nothing to worry about."

"I don't want him to die," Alicia wails.

"Well, they'll cut off his dick so he can never do anything like that again," Tits offers in a way that presumably is supposed to be comforting.

Cindy walks over and places her hand on Alicia's shoulder.

"Apart from the filming, for which I agree that fucker needs to die, your first time sounds okay, huh? Unlike mine."

"How was it?" Tits asks conversationally.

"Fumbling under the bleachers with the school jock. Pretty cliché. Put me off sex for a whole week."

If hers was cliché, so was mine. It sounds almost identical. Perhaps I had something in common with her after all, though the lesson it had taught me lasted a much longer time.

"Mine was with a man who was older, experienced, and married, though he hadn't admitted that at the time. At least he knew what he was doing. I thought it was going to be a happily ever after." Tits stares dreamily into the distance, then shakes herself. "I suppose I was lucky he was unavailable. As it turns out, I never want to be tied down. What about you, Eva?"

"Virgin until I met my ex, and so was he. We were young, neither of us knew what we were doing. Oh, we had the mechanics right, we had to have done as we produced the kid. But I wondered what all the fuss was about. Took our divorce and my experimenting after to discover what sex should be. Then I found out… with a biker." She fans her face dramatically, and the women all chuckle together. "The rest is history."

As they're talking, I'm watching Alicia. Her face turns to each as they're speaking.

"Sex is a biological function," Eva continues. "Society tells us the first time is something to be treasured. I've known many men," she grins and then waves her hand at the snorts of the club girls in a pipe down gesture, "but never men who are particularly intent on taking a virgin. Well, not unless they'd behave like they've got the experience which is a contradiction in terms."

Alicia's looking at her carefully. "You say it won't matter? It won't affect me if I meet the right man?"

"Honey, if you're worried about that, then he wouldn't be

the right man, anyway. Unless you're looking for a religious nut. If you meet someone who prizes virginity, to be honest, if I were you, I'd run a mile. Live your life, enjoy it. In my view, God gave us sex, and it's up to us to make the most of it."

I kind of agree with her view of sex and sexuality.

"My first time was awful."

CHAPTER TWENTY

Grumbler

Entering the kitchen, I sum up the situation immediately. The fucking sweet butts are hovering around Alicia, clearly making her uncomfortable. And those words? The last thing the poor kid should endure is hearing about the sexual exploits of the club whores.

I take a determined step forward, my face showing my rage, when Mary's hand lands on my arm, holding me back. When she puts her finger to her lips, she lets me know she wants me to remain silent.

What the fuck?

I didn't even want Mary to meet the club girls. I had thought Patsy would have the sense to keep her and Alicia upstairs. But no, here she was, right in the thick of what is to us quite natural—girls we provide for so they in turn, can provide for us. A situation that men in an MC find quite acceptable, but one which fills most citizens with horror.

"Go on," Eva encourages Pearl, while I want to scream she's to keep her fucking mouth shut.

"I was eighteen and legal, believe it or not." Pearl pushes

away from her place against the counter and pulls out a chair. Once she's plonked her ass on it, she continues, "I'd been friends with Frank since we were about ten and he moved in next door. As we got older, we'd called ourselves boyfriend and girlfriend. It was a Romeo and Juliet situation though, our parents never got on. Our dads clashed, and our moms snubbed each other in sympathy. So Frank and I had to sneak around. But he was 'it' for me, I knew it."

Her eyes glaze slightly as she thinks back. "I think part of it was the danger. Keeping our relationship hidden made it exciting, though we spoke many times about how we wished we could date in the open. Date," she repeats the word with a shake of her head, "that's what we were doing—keeping things innocent—hand holding, a few kisses, never taking it further. Saving ourselves for the marriage that we knew we were heading for."

"What happened?" Tits prompts, realising like me that there was not going to be a happy ending.

"I thought Frank was ready to wait. But one day I went looking for him at school and found him behind the bike sheds. He was fondling a cheerleader's tits, and she, well, she had her hand down his trousers."

"I hope you dumped his ass," Cindy states.

Pearl shrugs. "Nope, I wasn't as sensible as that. I went in all guns blazing and slapped her face. Then I asked Frank what he thought he was doing." The hurt is so plain on her face that even a hardened biker like me can see it. I realise I've just accepted Pearl had come to the club, and we'd never bothered to learn her history. Of course Token had investigated her, but satisfied she wasn't a plant by our enemies, that was all we needed to know. Oh, and that she knew how to fuck.

"What did he say?" It's Alicia's soft voice that encourages her this time.

"He fumbled his words. Said two things, one that he had sexual needs and I wasn't prepared to do anything about them, and then came up with an excuse that he didn't want to come to me as a virgin. That he needed to get in some practice first with a girl who didn't mean anything. Of course, I couldn't see the real him, all I saw was the moon and stars and that he was my everything. I'd do anything not to lose him. He promised me that this was the first time he'd given into his urges, that he could no longer live with his frustration."

She stops, shakes her head, then resumes, "My parents were going out that evening, so I invited him over. One thing he'd told me was true, he hadn't yet lost his virginity. He hadn't a clue. His eagerness made him rough, and his hands were all over me. Talk about not knowing where a G-spot was, he didn't know there was one to find, or even how to get a girl off. No, he just inserted item A into slot B, painfully as he hadn't prepared me. But that didn't matter, as he came almost before he was in completely. But I forgave him. I loved him, see? And knew in time it would get better."

"Did it?"

Pearl turns toward Alicia. "Didn't get a chance to find out. You've got a great mom, kid. See how supportive she is?" She jerks her head toward Mary. "Mom had gotten a headache, and my parents came home early. They caught us in my bed."

"No." Eva's hand covers her mouth. "She stopped you from seeing him?"

"Oh yes," Pearl confirms. "Dad hit him, hard. Frank's mouth was bleeding. Me, he left to my mom, and she slapped me across the face." She touches a small white scar on her cheek which I had noticed but never questioned. "Her ring caught me here," she explains, now unnecessarily, her gesture had told us all we needed to know. "Then she grabbed hold of me and pulled me naked out of bed. She allowed me at least to pull on some clothes, then, in just what I was wearing, she threw me out of the house."

"Pearl, no." Even Tits is shocked.

Pearl raises and dips her head. "I tried to go back of course. I pleaded and begged. Maybe if it had been someone else, I'd have gotten away with it. But I'd fucked the son of their enemy, and they no longer had a home for me."

"What did Frank do?"

She snorts. "Ran home with his tail between his legs. I spent the night on a park bench, then went back to try to see him the next day. He told me in no uncertain terms I was to stay away from him. He was lucky, our parents didn't speak, and he didn't want his folks to find out."

"What did you do?" I notice Alicia's sent a sneaky look toward her mom, as if realising how lucky she is to have her.

Pearl grimaces. "What could I do? I needed to eat. When I got too hungry, I accepted twenty dollars to give a man a blow job. Finished my education on the streets, but it wasn't one that led to a GED. Fucked my way from Los Angeles to here, and then finally, *thank fuck*, joined the MC." She takes hold of Eva's hand, and when she looks up, she even sends a smile toward me. "I finally found my family."

Her gratitude cuts me to the bone. Why had we never known her story? She might be comfortable here, but what happens when she loses her looks and her firm body? Will we throw her out on the streets?

Patsy's one step ahead of me. "Yeah, Pearl. We're your family. This is your home now—for as long as you want it to be."

I'm glad the prez's old lady has made the decision. Now I don't even have to propose that the Satan's Devils will give Pearl a home for life, Patsy will clear it with Lost.

Alicia's staring down at her hands. Various expressions

appear then disappear on her face, then she raises her head. "Seems like the mythical magical first time doesn't exist."

It's her mom who steps forward. "Honey, it really doesn't. And it's the twenty-first century. Men don't give that much weight to virginity. Not that," she adds fast, "I condone what Owen did. Not in any way."

"Thank you." Alicia looks directly at Pearl, then at the other women. "Thank you for telling me your stories. It helps."

Sure, it helps, but only a little. I can see that from her face. Sounds like the others have all shared similar stories, about what bastards men can be. We cheat and lie our way into women's beds. While I hope I've not done so myself, I couldn't say one hundred percent that I hadn't, especially when I was younger. As I stare at the girl, I realise if I had my way, I'd make sure from here on out she's kept safe from predators, and any potential boyfriend is vetted very carefully.

But, I pull myself up, I've no place in her life. Unless I cultivate this friendship with her mother and stay linked to her in some way, which is unlikely. For now, though, all I can do is mitigate the current threat, then our paths will probably go different ways.

Tits has started on the potatoes again, Alicia picking up her own peeler. Cindy's turned the heat up under her pans, and I see revelation time is over.

"Mary?" I ask, quietly. "Can I have a word?"

She checks in on her daughter. "Honey? I'm just going to talk to Grumbler. You okay here?"

At her daughter's nod, Mary in turn raises her chin toward me, and as I turn to leave the kitchen, she follows me. Heading for the far table on the other side of the room, I pull out a chair for her, then take the adjacent one for myself.

"Did you know?" she asks when she's seated. "Did you know Pearl's story?"

With a sigh, I admit, "I did not."

I wait for her to berate me, to point out how we take advantage of damaged girls, but she surprises me.

"She's happy here. They all are." A little shake of her head, then she says, "I can't understand it myself, but I suppose it's better than being on the streets."

"We don't force the girls to stay, or to do what they don't want."

"But if they said no? If they refused to have sex with you?"

I chuckle softly. "Been a long time since I've been with the club girls, doll. It would be like fuckin' my granddaughter. But yeah, you're right. If they kept refusing, they'd be out." I try to put it in words she'll understand. "What would happen at your job if you refused to do what you were paid for?"

"I don't have to fuck the boss."

I lean in closer. "Look around you, Mary. Look at Dusty over there, and Pennywise and Salem playing pool. The girls fuckin' fight over who's going with them. And even if they haven't got the looks, the others are popular too. Bikers know how to fuck, babe. We go at it hard just like everything we do, giving it everything we've got. And unlike Pearl's boyfriend, we don't need a road map to find a G-spot."

Is it my imagination, or does a flush come over her face?

And fuck, I didn't expect the question which next comes out of her mouth which has formed a small smile. "You keep saying we, does that include you?"

Is she tempted?

"It did, babe. Haven't fucked for a long time now."

Her face seems to fall, but whatever she's really asking, I don't want to mislead her. Then I frown as a stirring in my long dead cock causes me to shift position.

I've got to get this conversation back on track and do what I need to do—update her. "We're pulling in the big guns now, babe, to locate and destroy all copies of the video that was made."

That gets her attention off my sex life, or lack thereof. "The big guns? Have you gone to the cops?"

"Nah. One of our chapters is full of technical experts. They've got the resources to go far deeper than Token." I level my stare at her. "They'll succeed, Mary. I've no doubt of that."

Her expressions says she's not convinced. But then, she doesn't know me or my brothers, or the lengths we'll go to, to set things right.

She's biting her lip. "I want to go home, but Patsy said I shouldn't."

"She's right," I don't hesitate in telling her. "Not going to keep you here against your will," I pinch the brow of my nose, "but here you'll both be safe."

"But you're no closer to finding Owen or Devon."

"Babe," I growl. "If you think you can face them down alone, then you've got another fuckin' think coming. There's a risk that Owen wants more from Alicia, if only to make sure she's keeping quiet. If you go home, you'll be unprotected."

"But for how long?" she queries, shaking her head. "I've got work and Alicia's got school. We can't stay at the compound. All the stuff we need is at our house. We've got no clothes here, only what we're wearing. How long until you find them and put a stop to this? You've already spent weeks searching, and nothing's come up."

I can't tell her we're hoping to get a lead when Utah hacks into the credit card database. There are some things she's better off not knowing, but she's right in that I can't give her a timeframe.

"When I first met the club girls, I wanted to get into my car and drive. But I stayed and got to know them. They're good people."

They probably were, to her. I know enough about women not to tell her this, but they'd have scratched out her eyes if she were younger. But seeing as Alicia's too young, and

Mary herself too old, they'd retracted their claws and acted human.

"But thinking about staying just brought up problems. I thought about going to stay with a friend. Kristen or Terra would be happy to have us."

Sounds like a good solution, so why don't I like it? *Because I'm a control freak, always have been.* I was voted the sergeant-at-arms because it suits me to be in charge of everything and I've never run from responsibility.

"I dismissed that idea too," she continues, to my relief. Sounds like she's staying. But it seems I've been premature in my assumption. "So it's back to plan A. Alicia and I will go home this evening."

"No—"

"Let me finish, Grumbler?" Her gaze lowers and when she looks at me again, it's through her eyelashes. Even her voice sounds shy when she asks, "I'd like you to come home with us?" The next words come out in a rush. "I know it's an imposition, but if Owen or Devon put in an appearance, you'll be there to deal with them."

Fuck. She's come up with a solution. While I don't want to put her or Alicia in danger, it's only a small risk that Owen or Devon would turn up. But if they did, and I was there to intercept them, it saves the club tracking them down.

My mind starts working at light speed. "I'll come back and stay. As you say, we can't fix a timescale, so if I can't be with you, another brother will. I'll get a prospect to escort Alicia to and from school."

Her face lights up. She leans toward me, places her palms either side of my face and plants a kiss straight on my lips. Just a peck, but fuck it surprises me. But I don't get a chance to think about it.

"Grumbler, thank you so much." She grins widely. "I almost want Owen to visit now. He'll be no match for you."

"I fuckin' hope he comes to us too." I tap the table, knowing I need to get Lost in on this. "I'll need to run this by Prez. I'll take you back to Alicia."

Mary glances behind her, then turns back to me. "She's only in the kitchen over there, I don't need an escort."

Her way, however, is blocked by the bodies of my brothers. Maybe it was meeting the club girls, maybe it's just that she's recovered her balance from the shock she received earlier, but Mary seems to be feeling more confident in the clubhouse.

I raise my chin at her. "I'll come find you when I've squared it with Lost. He'll be fine with it," I hastily reassure her. "I just need to warn him what we're doing."

With a little nod, she stands, and confidently walks through the clubroom, nimbly evading Pennywise striding from the bar carrying two beers over to the pool table.

Lost is in his office as I expected and looks up as I enter. Quickly, I run Mary's proposal past him.

When I finish, he sits back, linking his hands behind his head. "That's a fuckin' good idea, Grumbler." His eyes narrow slightly. "You need backup, or are you okay on your own?"

I'd briefly thought about having someone there with me and had dismissed it. "If Owen and Devon turn up, I won't have a problem taking either of them on, or both of them together. I'll go back with Mary in her car, so in the unlikely event they've got eyes on her place, they won't see me arriving."

"You want the prospect to come in a cage when he's going to take the kid to school?"

Now this is our prez. He thinks of everything. "Yeah." I don't want Alicia on the back of any man's bike, not even a prospect's. "Can you organise Wrangler or Curtis?"

"Why not Connor? He's closer to her in age."

And he's a good-looking fucker. "His age is exactly why I don't want him."

Lost tosses back his head and chuckles loudly. "I'll feel sorry for the kid if you and Mary become an item."

Now it's my turn to bark out a laugh. "Not fuckin' going to happen, Lost. We're just friends."

He shakes his head, adding knowingly, "That's how it starts, Brother."

CHAPTER TWENTY-ONE

Mary

"Alicia? Can I have a word?"

"Yeah, Mom." She gets to her feet.

Patsy waves to a door leading out of the kitchen. "Picnic benches out back if you want to get some fresh air."

Giving her a grateful nod, I indicate to my daughter that we'll go that way. Once outside, I take a seat, then point with my hand. "You can see the Coronado Bridge from here."

She glances that way for a second, then loses interest fast and looks back. Her brow is furrowed. "What did you want to talk to me about?"

"How are you feeling? Really feeling I mean. Don't tell me 'fine' as I won't believe it."

She presses her lips together. "Like my world's been shattered. I trusted him, Mom."

It's the first time we've had a chance to talk one-on-one about what's happened to her, and her opening gambit makes me want to cry. I fight back my tears, knowing my own sadness and disappointment won't help her.

"I know you did."

"What was your first time like?" A quick glance spared for the scenery, then her eyes come back to me.

"A disappointment." I swallow and tell her the truth. "I was the starry-eyed girl who made it easy for the most wanted guy in school. Then, having got what he wanted, he made sure he was never alone with me again."

"Why, Mom? Why are men like that, always taking advantage?"

"Not all men are. But yeah, the bad apples seem to be attracted by good girls."

She ponders that for a moment. Her brow creases again. "That video—"

I cover her hand with my own, squeezing it. "There's another chapter of the Satan's Devils who are technical experts. They are going to track that video down and destroy it. I believe Grumbler when he says they can do it."

"Grumbler's a good man," she agrees. "I like him, Mom."

I ask the question that I'd had since I first arrived. "Why did you come to him, and not to me?"

She looks down to where my hand is still holding hers. "I didn't want to be shouted at. I knew I deserved it, Mom. I didn't know where to go. I couldn't admit what a fool I'd been to you, or my friends. I had no one else to go to. I don't really know why, but I thought of him."

"How on earth did you know where to find him?"

"I didn't, but the Uber driver knew where the compound was." Which was lucky. I doubt many people could find it. I'd needed Grumbler's instructions. Alicia continues, "Apparently, he used to be a pizza delivery guy and had been here before."

Seeing cooking wasn't the club girls' primary role, I can imagine they get takeout quite a lot.

"I don't mind staying here, Mom. I think talking to the women helped."

I'm glad it helped, but I'm not sure I want my girl to be influenced by them. "We're not going to stay here—"

"Mom! How can we go home? What if Owen comes around? What if he threatens me? Threatens you? What—"

It's my turn to interrupt. Jumping in fast, I explain, "We won't be alone, Alicia. Grumbler's coming back with us, and a prospect will come and take you to school and pick you up. We'll be hoping Owen does come around so Grumbler can sort him out."

"Grumbler isn't young, Mom. Do you really think he could take on Owen? And what if Devon comes too?"

"Grumbler's the sergeant-at-arms, Alicia. I'm sure he'll know what to do." I have faith in Grumbler, even if she doesn't.

"But I want to stay here." She's pouting now.

"All our stuff is at home. On Monday, you have to go to school."

Her face falls, she looks scared. "I don't want to go. Can't you tell them I'm sick?"

"No. I won't lie for you, Alicia. Oh, and don't forget, we need to collect your phone from Marisa."

Her head sinks lower at my subtle, but not actually intentional, reference to how she lied.

"You two good?" Grumbler appears out of nowhere, and I've never been so glad to see anyone.

"I think so, yes. I was just telling Alicia we're headed home."

"Not going to stay and eat what the club girls were cooking?" Grumbler winks.

I chuckle. "It didn't look all that appetising." Though Cindy was trying hard.

Alicia rolls her eyes. "We'll go home and Mom will order takeout. It's all she ever does."

Not quite true. Though in some ways I'm glad my daughter

is regaining some spirit, if it's only to rebel. She's coming back to herself.

"Your mom works," Grumbler states firmly. "And what about you, Alicia? You cook? You put something on the table for when your mom returns from her job?"

Her wide-eyed expression makes me smile, though I try to hide it. No, Alicia's not gotten to that stage yet. Probably because I've always tried to be the perfect mother, providing for her, even if it's just takeaway food.

Alicia turns and gives him an appraising look. "You're going to be on her side, aren't you? If you come stay with us."

"Your mom's side?" He glances at me shrewdly. "I'm not coming to take sides, I'm just going to be there to keep you safe. But," he holds up his hand when Alicia snorts in disbelief, "if there's any side to come down on, I'll land on the side of common sense."

"Would you have stopped me going to see Owen?"

Grumbler stares at her. "Would your mom have, had you told her?"

"Well, yeah," Alicia replies as if he's dumb.

"And she would have done that, why? To stop you from having fun?"

"Well, yeah," she repeats.

Grumbler slowly shakes his head as though he's disappointed in her. "Really?"

Alicia thinks for a moment. "She'd have said I don't know enough about him."

I bite my tongue because she's absolutely right. I wish she'd have talked to me. It wasn't that she'd raced off to give her virginity to the first man who'd turned her head, I'm the last person who could criticise that, it was that she hadn't known him, and certainly not realised he wasn't to be trusted. Not that I hadn't made the same mistake myself, but I'd wanted to pass on what I'd learned from it.

"I can teach you a bit about checking people out," Grumbler offers. "Take this Owen. He said he was twenty-one which was wrong, and his name might not even be Owen for a start. What you needed to do was check out his driver's licence, that would have given you those details."

"But I trusted him."

"A man earns trust. His actions always speak louder. Any asshole can open his mouth and promise you the earth. It's when he gives it to you, you can take that to the bank. Words mean fuck all."

"His actions were fine." Alicia's not contradicting Grumbler. By the way her lips are pressing together, she's going back over the events in her mind. "He was perfect. He opened my car door, led me into the hotel. The hotel was much posher than I expected." She glances up quickly. "I'd expected a cheap motel—just somewhere with a bed."

"Did you know he had money?"

She shrugs. "I didn't ask. I assumed he'd done more modelling gigs."

Grumbler rubs his hand over his face. "Apart from checking him out before you went out with him alone, kid, I don't know what more you could have done. Someone older might have seen some red flags, but honestly, no blame can be attached to you."

"Thank you." Alicia moves closer to him, and interpreting what she wants him to do, he adjusts his position allowing her to snuggle under his arm. "I feel so stupid. If I ever have a boyfriend again, will you check him out?"

Grumbler chuckles softly. "That I'll be more than happy to do, and, sweetheart, it's a matter of when, not if. Your chance hasn't come and gone, you know? I can also teach you some methods of self-defence. Or at least, how to kick a man's balls. Owen deserves some pain for what he put you through."

"Can you teach me self-defence, too?"

"Why, sure, Mary." He nods approvingly. "It's a good skill to know. Now, the arrangements are I'm riding home in your car. That way no motorcycle will be seen at the house."

"Wouldn't that be a deterrent?" I ask.

"It would, but after the message Alicia gave me, it might make them start distributing that video. Until we know it's been taken down and destroyed, we don't want to do anything to rock the boat. Once Alicia's reputation is safe, then that's the time to draw them out."

We walk back into the clubhouse via the kitchen. Alicia gets hugs from all the club girls who seem genuinely sympathetic to her ordeal, and sad to see her go. Then Grumbler gets back slaps from all the leather-clad men.

"I'll be there on Monday with a cage to take the kid to school." A man, wearing a vest which says prospect on the back, calls out. In recognition, Grumbler raises his hand.

"A cage?" Alicia hisses in consternation. "I'm not a freaking dog."

The man who'd spoken overhears and bellows a laugh. But it's left to Grumbler to explain. "It's what we call a car, kid. Bikers don't like being caged in."

A few others stop to have a quick word with Grumbler on the way out, more than one offering their help unasked.

"Prez." Grumbler nods as a man approaches him.

His title made me expect someone who looked rough, scarred perhaps if I were to tell the truth. But in different clothes, the man could pass as a businessman.

"Mary, this is Lost, our prez. Prez, Mary."

Lost nods. "Nice to meet you."

I wonder if I should say something about him agreeing for his club to help, but he doesn't seem to expect it. He raises his chin at Grumbler, then walks on.

Finally we emerge into the warmth of the late summer evening.

I'm half expecting Grumbler to want to drive when we reach my car. Dave always wanted to take the wheel, but to my surprise, he waves me into the driver's seat, and tells Alicia to sit by my side. Then he folds his body into the rear seat, and settles in for what, for him, will be an uncomfortable ride.

"Park in your garage," he instructs. "That way no one will see me in the car." He looks approvingly at the blacked-out rear windows.

I can see by glancing in the rearview mirror that Grumbler doesn't relax at all during the journey. He's constantly looking from one side to the other, and also behind us, then peering out in front. His vigilance makes me feel safe.

We reach home without incident. When I've parked and the garage door has slid itself closed, thanks to the remote in my car, Grumbler opens the rear door, reaching back inside for his pack he brought with him, then indicates the door to the kitchen.

"Stay here while I check it out."

"There'll be no one there." Alicia rolls her eyes.

"Hey," he turns. "Look, ladies, I'm here as your own personal bodyguard. Enjoy the service, okay?"

He winks at me, then disappears inside my house.

Within moments—it's not big after all—he's back.

"All clear."

Impatient, Alicia pushes past, then stops and looks at me. "What are we going to eat?"

"Guest's choice?" I turn my head toward Grumbler and raise my eyebrow.

"Ain't no fuckin' guest," Grumbler chuckles. "And I'm easy."

"Pizza!" Alicia fist bumps the air.

"Gets my vote." He nods approvingly.

"I'm going to be outnumbered, I can tell."

But as I follow them into the living area, setting my keys

down in the place for them, and my purse by the side of the couch, I smile to myself. This is how it would have been if Dave hadn't died. The three of us, together. Would he have guessed Alicia had lied? That she'd had a liaison with a man last night? Would he have rung Marisa's parents to check? Or have relied like I so stupidly had, on a technical gadget?

Dave's not here. There's no point wondering whether he'd have been a better parent than myself. He'd only been Alicia's hands-on dad for ten of her years, and a ten-year-old was far easier to deal with than a teenage girl.

The doorbell rings. I go cold, especially when Grumbler holds up a hand and goes to his saddle bag he'd brought in with him and draws out a gun. He positions himself by the side of the door, then jerks his chin, a sign that I should check it out.

Tension leaves me in a rush when I see through the peephole who it is, and immediately open up. "Hi, Marisa."

"Er, hi, Mary. Is Alicia here?" She peers around me.

"Alicia? It's Marisa," I yell over my shoulder.

"Um, tell her I'll call her later. I'm just about to jump in the shower," comes a disembodied voice.

Marisa's face falls while mine grows tight, summing up the situation immediately. She wanted to get the dirt on what happened last night, and understandably, Alicia hasn't had time to get her story straight. It's up to her to decide how much to tell her friends.

"Alicia left her phone when she left earlier." I notice Marisa avoids giving me a time she left. Morning, noon or afternoon, earlier could mean anything. She hands me Alicia's phone with just one more statement. "Tell her to call me later."

As she skips back down the path toward her mom waiting in the car, Grumbler chuckles beside me.

"And that's how you do it."

"Do what?" I turn, puzzled.

"No embellishment. Giving you no reason to call her out in a lie. She doesn't know what time Alicia returned home, so she didn't give details."

I'm not so sure I admire the girl's ability to cover a lie, but then I don't think the same way as the man by my side.

Alicia appears, her eyes wide. She looks to me, then to the closed door. "I can't do it, Mom," she whispers. "I can't talk to her. She'll want to know how the date went."

I open my mouth, but Grumbler gets in first. "You trust her to keep her trap shut?"

"She can't," I say firmly. "Whatever Alicia thinks, this is too juicy. Marisa might let something drop, and the whole school would find out she was almost a porn star."

"Mom! Marisa wouldn't do that."

"Kid, you fucked up. You know that." Grumbler acts as if I hadn't said a word. "You trusted the wrong guy. I agree with your mom, certain things you keep to yourself. You're certainly not unique at being taken in by an expert, but that should teach you to be more careful now. You can give a version of events you're comfortable with, and which, if it gets around, could be a public service."

Alicia moves closer, her brow creased. "Lie?"

"Tell Marisa he strung you a line. That you left when you found out he was older than he appeared, and he wasn't such a nice guy. You can admit you're embarrassed and too upset to talk to her."

"But where was I last night?"

"Just tell her you were upset and hurting," Grumbler says determinedly. "Not wanting to admit it had all gone wrong, which was why you hadn't contacted her. Let her make her own assumptions that you came home to lick your wounds. Maybe by telling her you narrowly escaped making a mistake, it might make Marisa think twice about getting her head turned by a pretty face." He pauses, then adds, "You know I'm in the motorcycle club lifestyle. It's in my nature to be cautious, and trust comes hard. You never give people ammunition that can come back and hurt you. Give a version of events that isn't exactly a lie, but not the whole truth."

He glances at me. I study him for a moment, then turn back to my daughter. "This is one time when you've got to think as an adult, sweetie."

"I can't keep this bottled up inside."

"Of course, you can't," Grumbler agrees. "I suggest your mom arranges professional help. While we can tell you until the cows come home that you're not to blame, you're carrying too much shit in your head. Talking to someone will be able to put this into focus, and it will be a safe environment where you can talk without fear of any of the salacious details getting out."

Why I hadn't immediately thought of it I'm not sure, but Grumbler is right. She needs someone safe to speak to, someone she knows won't judge her.

CHAPTER TWENTY-TWO

Grumbler

What am I doing?

I'm not a family man and have always prided myself that I stayed away from drama. Never getting close to a woman meant never having to mop up tears or provide a shoulder in comfort. Now I seem to have become embroiled in the type of events you'd watch on a soap opera.

Strangely, it doesn't make me want to run a mile. Instead, I want to put my arms around both women and tell them what happened was neither of their faults. Mary hasn't been a bad parent, she's done everything right and tried to guide her child. But like every teenager, Alicia has a rebellious streak, an idea she knows better than the adults around her. Striking out on one's own path is part of growing up, it's just a fucking shame she chose a direction that was wrong for her.

The risk of Owen coming calling has been minimised by them not going to the cops and not openly involving us. Any investigation by Token or Utah will firmly be done under the radar, so my presence here is probably overly cautious. But I can't deny there's a possibility of having duped Alicia so successfully last night, he might come back to get more mileage out of her.

I'm not an angel, of course I've watched porn. But I've never had any inclination to watch anything that wasn't readily available, knowing there were some you could find if you wanted to that catered to deviant interests. While not particularly liking knowing paedophilia and even snuff movies were out there if you knew where to look for it, I never saw myself as having any role to play in stopping it. Where would I start? I'm not a one-man crusader, even if I'm a man with healthy desires and a natural abhorrence to any with extreme perverse interests. But the knowledge it exists makes me worried for Alicia.

Although the sex last night had been consensual, filming it had not. She's underage, and that's probably how it would be marketed. The thought of how she'd been used makes me so angry, I hope Owen will appear. I can almost taste his fear and surprise when he finds me waiting for him. In my mind's eye, I can already see him strung up in our brig, and Salem going to town on him.

All my brothers are of my way of thinking—none of us would allow a woman to come to harm. Kink may have peculiar tastes, but he's so hung up on obtaining consent, no one could ever doubt what he puts his pets through has all been discussed and agreed to prior.

I sit on the couch, ruminating, running everything through in my head. Owen needs to be found and stopped, and Devon, while his part in the proceedings isn't completely clear, there's got to be someone behind the male model. The discreet cameras Alicia had described, and their positioning suggests they were placed by someone who knew exactly what they were doing. Would Owen know where to start with distribution? I doubt it, which means even if it's not Devon, then someone else is behind him. It's my job to find out who. Am I missing anything?

I trust my brothers to be doing the investigating while I'm here to provide protection. While I'd rather be doing something more positive right now, being here in case Owen makes contact again is just as important.

It's in my role of protector that I cautiously approach the door when there's another loud knock on it.

Mary appears, but I wave her back, looking through the peephole. When I see it's a guy carrying pizza boxes. I open the door, take the delivery, exchanging the boxes for some dollar bills, adding a hefty tip in the process.

"You didn't need to do that," Mary admonishes, taking the pizzas from me as I replace my wallet in my cut.

I wave off her objection. When my stomach, sensing food, growls, she shakes her head and stops arguing, going to the kitchenette and taking some plates from a cupboard.

Unlike the evening when I ate here before, the conversation doesn't flow easily. Alicia, predictably, is quiet. She eats mechanically without enjoyment, and my gut twists for her. Mary, too, seems lost for words. After we've eaten and Alicia's taken the plates into the kitchen, she returns, stifling a yawn.

"I'm going to my room, Mom."

"If you need me…"

"I know where you are." Alicia permits her mom to hug her and place a kiss on her forehead.

To my surprise, Alicia comes over and puts her arms around me, resting her cheek against my chest for a moment.

"Thank you, Grumbler. I don't know what I would have done without you today."

I hold her close and then release her. When she disappears down the hallway, I say softly, "She's a good girl."

Mary's tight smile toward me confirms she knows it. "I doubt she got much sleep last night. She must be tired."

I doubt she'll get a good one tonight. Things like that tend to go around and around your head not allowing you to switch off. But I don't point out the obvious to Mary.

"I was going to suggest you take her room, but…"

But she needs her familiar things around her to take the first step to restoring the balance in her life again.

"I'll be fine here." I indicate the tiny two-seater sofa.

"Don't be silly, Grumbler. You take my bed and I'll sleep out here."

It's still early, we don't have to finalise the arrangements right now, but it doesn't stop me smirking at her. "What is it about me being here as your protection that you don't understand?" I point to the door. "Point of entry, darlin'. I'll be out here as your first line of defence."

She grimaces. "You really think there's a chance he'll come around?"

I shake my head in answer. "No, I don't. But we can't take the chance I'm wrong."

"Want a beer?"

"Sure." I take a seat on the couch, feeling that it dips one side more than the other, presumably the favourite seat in the house. It adds to the fact I'm facing an uncomfortable night for sure. My old bones are going to be complaining in the morning.

Carrying a bottle and a glass of white wine, Mary returns and takes the chair. She picks up the remote and points it toward the television.

"Er…?"

"Put anything on." I'm easy. It will just be background noise while I listen to the thoughts in my head.

She clicks on Netflix and pulls up a series. Despite my intentions, it catches my interest, and I settle in to watch. Mary replenishes my beer halfway through the episode.

"Your prez and his old lady surprised me," Mary says

conversationally, when the action on the screen stalls. "Lost wasn't what I expected as an MC prez."

"Our last prez was more what you'd think of. Rough, ugly looking bastard with a snake tattoo winding around his neck. Lost came to the helm three years ago. He's a good man and has got all our interests at heart. He's got what it takes to command respect without demanding it, you know?"

"A natural leader?"

She's summed it up well. "Yeah."

"I always expected it to be young men who were in a MC. Youngsters tearing around on motorcycles and getting into trouble."

"Us old-uns can do that well enough." I chuckle.

"You're not old, Grumbler."

"Babe, I'm staring sixty in the face. I'm fifty-seven."

"You don't look it." She sends me a glance that can only be described as appraising.

"You look pretty good for your years," I say, holding my bottle toward her in salute. "I thought you were a decade or so younger when we first met."

She smiles at the compliment. "I work hard at it," she explains. "My anti-wrinkle cream works miracles."

Perhaps I could do with some of that myself, though I suspect it's too late. The wind and sun have weathered my skin beyond the point of any hope of return.

"Am I a bad mom?"

The question comes out of left field, and for a second, I'm stuck for an adequate response. "No, you're not."

"I worry Alicia hasn't a dad—someone else who could be there to help direct her down the right path."

"And you think she'd listen to him any more than she would to you?" I lean forward, putting my beer down on the coffee table. "Kids will be kids, Mary, and adults walk behind them to clear up the mess. This situation is looking dire right now, I know, but we'll sort it. We'll make sure there'll be no repercussions. Sure, Alicia's head is fucked up right now, but not many people are lucky enough to have a first time that means much. What about you, Mary? Were you a virgin when you married?

"I was twenty-seven, Grumbler. So hardly. How old were you when you lost yours?"

I grin widely, knowing I'm going to shock her, but I'm not going to lie. "I was twelve."

"Twelve?" she squeaks.

"In my defence, the girl was sixteen and thought I was older. I was tall for my age." Sometimes I wonder whether starting early has caused my lack of interest in recent years. Maybe I literally only had so many fucks to give.

Though, casting a sideways glance toward Mary, seeing her giggling like a young girl, makes my dick twitch for the second time today. No one has sparked my interest in ages. But she's got baggage, she comes with a kid, and I'm not a family man. I tell my dick there's no fucking chance and force it to behave once again.

I turn my attention back to safer things, the television. She's got me hooked on this fucking series. When the episode finishes, we watch another, and then put one more on. By then, I see her eyes starting to droop, and I stifle a yawn.

"Go to bed, doll."

Her hand covers her mouth, hiding hers which I guess also gapes open. "Why don't you come with me? I've got a king-sized bed, and you won't be comfortable out here."

"I'll manage," I say, gruffly.

"No, you won't. Come with me." She stands and holds out her hand. "We'll keep the door open so if anyone does come, you'll hear as well from there as here."

"Mary," I tell her, a little harshly, "you can't ask a strange man to share your bed."

"Huh. You're not a stranger. A stranger wouldn't have helped Alicia the way you have. And what's so darn dangerous about a bed? It's not as if you're going to jump my bones, you've already said you don't fuck."

Christ. *What's she doing to me?* When I'd told her that, it had been the truth.

"I haven't fucked because the girls in the club are too young and I'm not a perv. But you…" Narrowing my eyes, I lewdly view her from her head to her toes, "Your age doesn't put you out of bounds."

She puts her hands on her hips and subjects me to the same intense inspection. Unfortunately, my dick likes the scrutiny and my tight jeans do nothing to hide my bulge.

Then she looks up to the ceiling. Raising her fist she shakes it. "Why me, Lord? Why tonight when I'm really not in the mood? Now you choose to present me with a hot guy?"

She thinks I'm hot? I file that away but dismiss it. Of course she's not up for anything of the sort right now. It hits me, she's been through far too much in the past twelve hours. From my call to her to come to the compound, from having to deal with the knowledge of what happened to her girl and having to cope with the aftermath. She's emotionally drained and being pawed at by me wouldn't help her.

Turning and eyeing the couch one more time, I come to a decision. "I'll come to bed, but I'll sleep fully clothed above the covers. If you need me to hold you, babe, I will."

It's almost a shy look she now gives me. "Would you think any the worse of me if I said, I'd like that?"

"Of course, I wouldn't."

CHAPTER TWENTY-THREE

Grumbler

It's true I'm more comfortable lying next to Mary than I would have been on the couch, but that hasn't translated into making falling asleep any easier.

Once we'd come to bed, her in full pyjamas, lying under the covers, and me fully clothed—the only things I'd removed were my cut and boots—on top, despite our attire we both felt awkward. I'd felt unable to fold her into my arms, and she made no move to come to me.

I lay on my back with my hands behind my head, half of me wondering what I'm doing here and trying to avoid thinking about the woman tossing and turning by my side.

When I hear a sob escape, I can no longer ignore her.

"Hey." Rolling over, I pull her against me, her back to my front. My thumb moves to her face and wipes away a tear rolling from her eye. "Hush, babe. It's going to be okay."

"I want to kill him," she quietly wails. "I've never wanted to hurt anyone in my life, but him? I wish he were dead."

She'll be getting her wish if I have my way. "His days are numbered. Can't have a fucker like that walking around a free man."

"Do-do you think he's done that before? Conned a young girl?"

I nod, though in the darkness she can't see that. "I do. Maybe worse. I'm certain this wasn't the first time he'd set someone up. Alicia didn't suspect a thing. He's had practice, I can almost guarantee it."

"She wasn't on the lookout for someone like him."

"You've kept her from the evil in the world, babe. That's your job as a mom. Can't see what more you could have done."

"I hate him."

"What's done is done," I tell her. "There's no point revisiting what could have been done to prevent it. Now we deal with shit and get to the point where you and Alicia can move on."

I find I'm stroking her face. She relaxes into my touch. "You're wise, aren't you?"

"Hate to say it, babe, but I've seen the ugliness that exists. Far too much of it. All you can do is learn from your mistakes and then make sure you don't make them again."

"I can't believe you make mistakes."

Oh I do, I reassure her in my head. Big ones. Perhaps the biggest of them all was trusting Snake. Maybe if I tell her some of what went down, it will take her mind off her daughter. "I mentioned our old prez. Well, he was called Snake because of his tattoo, but in the end, he was a real snake. When the previous prez, Bird died, Snake had been his number two, our VP. He moved to the head of the table, and none of us saw any reason not to vote him in. Actually, that's not true. I think a lot of us were slightly uneasy, but what we didn't do was canvass opinion. I didn't care much for the man, but could I follow him? Did I respect him as a leader? Fuck yeah. So I kept my doubts to myself."

"What happened?" Her shaking has stopped, and I hope her tears too.

"Snake seemed to settle into his role, and he made Lost his VP. Now Lost, as you observed, isn't the kind of man you'd particularly associate with an MC. But he'd been with us over a decade and had proved he fit in. What he brought was business acumen, and Snake left the day-to-day running of the club to him."

"What does an MC prez do?"

"Basically everything Lost was doing, making sure our businesses are prosperous and that we get paid, looking out for the members in the club, being aware of any threats coming our way and preparing us for them."

"How long was Snake your prez?"

"Two years." Two fucking years. "Turns out Snake wasn't looking out for the club at all. He wanted to get us into shit the majority of us wanted to steer clear of. He convinced eight others to go along with him. The club had divided itself into two factions, none of the current members were aware of it."

"What happened?"

"You haven't met Alex, and I don't think Dart as yet. Dart is Lost's VP. Well, he originally was from Tucson. He came to San Diego following Alex, who he eventually made his. That's their story to tell if they ever want to speak of it, but it was the catalyst, and everything came to a head. I hadn't a clue, babe. That was my mistake. I couldn't see what was happening under my fucking nose. I looked up to Snake, to Poke, the previous sergeant-at-arms. I never suspected they were going to betray the Satan's Devils, but then it came out."

"What did you do to the men who betrayed you?" She goes still. "Did you kill them?"

"Fuck no." I can be honest here. Snake and Poke lost their lives at the hands of the mother chapter prez, Drummer. "We sent them out bad. Kicked them out of the club."

"Men you once trusted."

"Yeah. I should have dug deeper. Should have checked with Pennywise and Salem, Bones and Snips too. I should have talked to my best friend, Smoker, but I thought only I owned my doubts. I kept my mouth shut, and Snake took the chair. Fuckin' stupid, eh? But the point is, I don't dwell on it now. No fuckin' point. But if I ever have more doubts, ever get a feeling in my gut, I act on it."

"Your club must respect you if they made you sergeant-at-arms."

"Respect? I suppose. I think I'm just good at telling people what to do." I chuckle, mostly to myself.

"You like to take charge."

Oh fuck, my dick has perked up again. See, in certain circumstances that's exactly what I'd like to do. Give Mary a few orders to follow? Fuck yeah.

Luckily, she's oblivious and yawns loudly.

"Go to sleep, babe. I'm here."

It seems like forever, but before long, she does. Unlikely as it might seem, being in a strange bed and doing something for the first time in my life, holding a woman I haven't fucked, I also drop off.

I'm startled awake by the vibration of my phone.

Seeing Mary's still sleeping, I slide it out of my cut, accept the call, but don't answer until I've pulled the bedroom door closed.

"What you got?"

"Utah came through for us."

"Yeah?" I answer Lost. "They didn't waste time."

"We've got a location on Owen. You want to give him a Sunday morning wake-up call? Salem and I are getting ready to head out. Niran is already on his way to you."

I grin into the phone. Lost knows I wouldn't want to miss out on this. My palms are already itching in anticipation of being around the fucker's neck and throttling the life out of him.

"Any news on the video?"

"They're still digging. Snatcher complained they've all been up all night watching porn." When I chuckle, he continues, "We'll find out more when we speak to that asshole."

And that is very true. By the time Salem and I have finished with him, he'll go to the grave with none of his secrets intact.

"Where and when?"

He gives me an address out La Jolla way and tells me to leave when Niran arrives.

Which is exactly what I plan to do.

I hadn't wanted to wake Mary, and looking at the time, see it's only six am. But neither do I want her to wake and find a big Black motherfucker sitting in her living room. I decide I've got time to wake her with some coffee. I go put it on, finding the sugar and creamer too.

When my own is cooling on the side, I walk back into her room. I sit on her side of the bed, placing the cup on the bedside table.

One eye opens, then two. Then both snap to my face and her nose does this delightful little twitch.

"Is that coffee I smell?"

"Sure is, babe. An apology for you. It's early as fuck, but I've got to head out. Niran's coming to stay with you. Just wanted you to know so you didn't get a shock and think I've changed colour overnight."

She brushes my explanation of a replacement away. "You got a lead?"

When I nod, she starts pushing back the sheet. "I'm coming with you."

I reach out my hand, holding her back. "Nah, babe. This

isn't for you. You've got Alicia here. Your job is being here for her."

Her lips press together. She frowns, then twin spots of red appear on her cheeks, but I refuse to be moved. When our unspoken conversation ends with her realising I'm right, she takes a deep breath, and then says the words I didn't expect to hear from her mouth.

"Make him hurt, Grumbler. Alicia's going to live with the shame all her life. Ending him cleanly won't do."

I lean in, planting a kiss to her forehead. "Easy to make that promise to you. One thing though, don't tell Alicia we've found him. I don't think she'd approve."

"I'm not stupid," she huffs. "I wish I was coming with you."

There's a light tap on the front door. "Gotta run." Before I can leave, she sits up and pulls my head to hers, and rubs her lips against mine. As we've no time, as a kiss, it will have to do.

As I stand, I press my finger to her mouth. "If I had my way, we'd continue this later. You think on if that's what you want to do."

I go out into the living room, pausing for a moment. Those few words had emerged without me thinking about them. If I do follow through, Mary wouldn't be a one-night stand. Is it possible, when I'd written myself off as too old, that I might actually be setting myself up to have an old lady by my side, not only that, but a kid too?

Shaking my head in disbelief, I now hurry and pull open the door.

Niran hands me his bike key. "Take my ride." He winks. "Though I know it's a step down for you."

I shove him back. "Ha ha. By the way, she's expecting you." I start to take a step forward, then turn around. "And while she may not look it, she's far too old for you."

His shrewd look shows me I should have kept my mouth shut. "Don't tell me Grumbler's got himself a woman. Huh! Never thought I'd see the fuckin' day. Your bike know you're stepping out on her?"

Of course, what can I do but show him my finger on the way out.

Unimpeded by traffic this time of a day, I reach my destination in just under half an hour.

Stepping off Niran's bike, a sportier model than mine, I slide the pack of cigarettes out of my cut and walk up to Lost and Salem. Cupping my hand around the flame, I touch the lighter to the tip, then put the Zippo away.

"Whatcha got?"

Lost jerks his head, indicating the direction behind him. "House is just on the next street. Thought you and I could head around the back while Salem rides straight up to the front door."

"There's a driveway? And rear access?"

Lost nods. "Salem's been playing with one of the toys Dart snagged while we were in Utah."

"The drone?"

Another rise and dip of his head. "Looks good, Brother. We," he indicates Salem and himself, "reckon the asshole will make a run for it as soon as he hears the bike. If not then, when he opens the door and sees the Satan's Devils' cut. Can almost guarantee he'll head for the hills and straight into our waiting arms."

I grin, liking the sound of that. "What if he's not alone?"

"Leave that to me," Salem growls. "Utah says he's not married, and no kids they can find. Anyone there is likely to be a girl or boyfriend, perhaps."

"You armed?" I check.

Salem beats his chest. "Wearing Kevlar too."

"Oh yeah." Lost turns around and goes to something strapped onto his bike. "Didn't forget you, Brother."

Taking the offered body armour, I soon have it on under my cut. "We ready then?" I'm impatient to find Owen.

"One last thing." Lost calls me back. "If there's no one home, we'll see if we can get in via the back door. Token's on standby should he have a security system we need to crack, so keep your eyes open."

I don't want to waste any more time, but quickly I run over the plan in my head. Can't see any holes in it. It's a male model we're taking down, not a crime syndicate king. I don't expect him to have a security detail.

"Utah turn up any military training?"

"None." I'm not surprised Lost has already checked. "Ready?"

You bet I am.

Salem gives Prez and I time to get into position, then, we, quite nimbly in my view given both of us are in our fifties, vault over the, okay, low fence, and approach the back of the house carefully. It's not large, and I can easily hear the roar of Salem's engine as he arrives.

I also hear a door inside opening.

Seconds later the back door flies open and out runs a man trying to simultaneously run and pull up his pants. *It's Owen.*

"Not so fast, *kid.*" My meaty paw lands on the collar of his t-shirt, twisting it hard so it painfully pulls against his neck. His hands come up to try to loosen it.

"You're strangling me, man," he rasps out, his words only just intelligible.

Lost is beside me, pulling Owen's hands down and expertly zip tying them behind him.

"Prospect is on his way with the truck." Salem appears, his eyes full of mirth as he watches Owen, now unable to ease the pressure against his neck, going red in the face, helpless to get away. "Better loosen your grip, Brother. Before he expires."

If he passes out, he'll be easier to transport that way.

Owen's eyes are rolling up in his head. I realise I need him alive, not dead, so withdraw my hand. When I do so, he collapses to the ground, but weak and with his hands secured, he falls forward, screeching as his head meets the concrete.

"Jeez, all that from a little bump on the head." Salem kicks the prone man. "He's going to be fun."

Knowing the next step is for Owen to come to his senses and start screaming, I sacrifice my bandana, stuffing it into his mouth.

"Ok," Lost looks up from his phone, "Wrangler's approaching the back gate now."

None too gently, Salem jerks the guy up by his tied together hands.

"Oomph." It's about all Owen manages to say.

Getting an uncooperative man into the truck isn't a new occurrence for us, and as expected, it goes like clockwork. Wrangler's not fazed driving the secured man back to the compound. When he pulls away, Lost and I follow him on our bikes, Salem catching us up when we've only gone a short distance.

As we near the compound, my sense of anticipation begins to rise. At last we're going to get some answers.

CHAPTER TWENTY-FOUR

Grumbler

Parking my bike in its usual place, I fire off a quick text to Niran. While I update him—we've got Owen in our hands—I ask him to stay put. Devon's still out there. If the pair are working together and Owen's disappeared, the photographer may start asking questions.

The truck doesn't stop by our clubhouse but continues around to the rear of the second hangar and the entrance to the brig. Salem heads off on foot, whistling to himself and in no particular hurry. Knowing he'll be making sure Owen is secured, Prez and I continue into the clubroom where we're greeted by the smell of bacon cooking.

"Hungry?"

"I could eat." I grin at Prez. While I'm anxious to get started, experience tells me leaving Owen waiting in anticipation will help soften him up, and, of course, questioning is best done on a full stomach.

Even if we didn't know exactly where we were headed, our noses would be sufficient to guide our way.

Pennywise looks up as soon as we walk in. "It go okay?"

"Piece of fuckin' cake," Prez replies, kicking out a chair.

"Want everything, Prez?" Tits waves a plate his way.

"Sure," Lost agrees, patting his stomach.

"Only one egg," Patsy calls out as she walks in. She strides over to Lost, reaches down and gives him a kiss. "Don't want you getting more love handles."

"You love my love handles." Lost eyes soften as he looks at his old lady, pulling her down onto his lap. "Tell you what, you can share mine."

Patsy giggles like a fuckin' kid, which clearly appeals to Lost, as breakfast forgotten for a moment, he leans his head down and proceeds to make a meal of her lips.

Brakes rolls his eyes. "Is that allowed at breakfast?" he asks primly.

I shake my head, accepting my own loaded plate from the sweet butt.

Deuce wanders in, yawning widely, Keeper following shortly after. Both look like they've just rolled out of bed.

"What time d'you call this on a fuckin' Sunday?" Snips asks, also appearing and making a beeline for the coffee jug.

"Fun time," Kink, who's already eating, offers. He winks toward me. I suppress the urge to look under the table. It wouldn't be the first time he's had a naked pet sitting beside him.

"Why are you all up so early?" Patsy queries.

Silence descends. "Club business, babe," her old man reminds her.

Undeterred, she chews then swallows a piece of bacon Lost has just passed to her, and then, with narrowed eyes, looks around the table. "If it's got anything to do with that kid, Alicia, make it hurt."

"MC lifestyle rubbing off on you?" I chuckle, mopping up some egg.

"Women should mind their own business." But Dusty's got a huge grin on his face.

Patsy looks around, presumably checking her son isn't within eyesight, then gives Dusty the finger. The unfamiliar gesture makes us crack up.

The heavy stomp of boots announces the arrival of the enforcer. I raise an eyebrow.

"Wrangler and Curtis." He gives me the answer to my unspoken question as to who is looking after our 'guest'.

I give a chin lift.

"Where's Toke?" I ask Prez.

"Speaking to Utah. I think they've all pulled an all-nighter."

"Any progress on the video?"

"None so far."

That's not what I want to hear. Every minute that video is still out there is a minute too long as far as I'm concerned. Still, one side of my mouth turns up. It won't be too long, and Owen will be telling me everything he knows. Maybe he'll have all the answers.

With that thought, I place my silverware down and take my empty plate over to Tits. I help myself to a coffee, then lean back against the countertop.

"Are we ready to get this show on the road?" I ask generally.

My response is a clattering of metal on plates as brothers hastily finish their meals. It seems we're all eager to get started.

"I want a piece of him," Deuce states as he comes alongside, picking his way along the path that leads to the second hangar. "I've got a sister not far off Alicia's age."

I didn't know that. "You see her regular?"

"Nah. She lives with my mom. I stayed with my dad. Kinda lost touch. Not that staying with the old man did much for me. He kicked me out when my stepmom had her child."

Sad, but it's the way things so often are. Many members

come from broken families, and that's why the MC has become home.

A hefty slap on my back sends me reeling. "Ready for this?" Salem's looking pumped.

"Asshole," I hiss at him. The forward motion had had me stomping down hard on my not so good leg.

Unrepentant, he grins widely. "At least that asshole Stormy's not around to spoil my fun this time." He might sound confident, but still he shades his eyes, and looks around as if Stormy might be hiding unseen, ready to show off his sniper skills as he had with Alder.

As I straighten, I glance behind catching Lost's eye, noticing his jaw is clenched. It will be a long time, if ever, before he forgives Stormy. While we're all pretty certain any risk to his old lady died with Alder, it would be nice to have heard it from the man himself.

When we reach the soundproofed room at the end of the hangar, the brothers stand back so I, as the brother who'd suffered the most injury, can have the honour of being the first inside, well, the first, that is, besides the two prospects.

Owen never succeeded in pulling his pants all the way up, and no one, it appears, was inclined to help him. With the result, he's strung up to an overhead beam with them precariously perched on his thighs. Having had insufficient time to pull on underwear, as soon as I walk in, I get an eyeful of his flaccid dick hanging down. Thinking of exactly where that dick had been on Friday night makes me see red.

I act on impulse, approaching him before I can have a second thought and punch him right in his junk.

Salem's derisive snort, which tells me he'd planned to do that himself, is quickly drowned out as Owen takes in air, then lets out an ear-piercing scream and comically tries to bend his body to bring some relief to the pain in his balls which, already, are swelling to twice their size. His face is red, and his mouth opens and shuts. Under the t-shirt that clings to his sweat-dampened body, the muscles of his stomach visibly roll.

"Stand back, he's going to hurl."

Noting Pennywise's warning, I, and my brothers, all give him a wide berth. Luckily, it's not projectile, but bile dribbles out of his mouth, further moistening his shirt.

It takes a few minutes before he recovers his breath, and, once again, opens his eyes. They fall on me, his tormentor. "What have I ever done to you, man? I didn't deserve that."

Does he think I don't know?

"Well, let me see." I pull at one of my fingers. "First, you and Devon Starr conned me out of money."

"I don't know nothing about that."

I leave his double negative response and continue counting off his crimes. "And then, you conned Alicia into giving up something worth so much more."

His eyes crease with cunning. "Alicia's my girlfriend."

"Oh, Owen. You can do better than that." I sigh deeply as though disappointed. "Alicia's told me," I indicate all the men standing around, "us, exactly what you did to her."

"I did nothing she didn't want!"

As I lurch forward, Salem tugs me off balance, holding me back. His strong arms hold me while I fight him.

"You'll get your fuckin' turn," he hisses, his words bringing me back to myself.

When he feels me relax, he jerks his chin to the side. I move in the direction he indicated, allowing him to stand front and centre.

For a moment, he just eyes Owen. "Grumbler here has skin in the game. I don't. So here's your chance, Owen. Tell me what I want to know, and I'll keep Grumbler away."

Salem's just stringing him along. While I'd rather be the man making Owen hurt, he knows what he's doing. My punch to his junk will pale in comparison once the enforcer brings his toys into play.

"What…" Owen starts in a squeaky voice. "What do you want to know?" The sweat is pouring off his face, and only some of it is from fear, most from the throbbing going on in his groin. I've no sympathy, it's less than he deserves.

"First," Salem snaps, "who's got the video?"

It's plain as day that he wants to dodge its existence, but sensibly he decides there's no point in a denial. He filmed their interaction, our words have shown we know it.

"I don't know, man," Owen cries. "I just get paid to play my role. And Alicia enjoyed it. Some women—" His words cut off. But he's said enough for us to pick up on it.

"So, not your first rodeo?" Salem asks, taking a step closer. "You've starred in these films before?"

"Yeah, but there's no harm in it."

"No?" Salem asks, deceptively quiet. "You get paid, Owen?"

"Of course." His face suggests he doesn't think much of the suggestion that he's doing it for nothing.

"Do the girls?"

"No." His head, as much as it can move, tilts to the side, and his eyes crease in confusion.

"So what do they get out of it?" Salem advances another step.

"My cock," Owen states, well, cockily.

The comment enrages me. Lost puts his hand on my arm and whispers hastily into my ear, "That man and his cock will soon be parted."

I allow myself to be held back. It's only that thought that keeps me rooted here.

A knife appears in Salem's hand and almost quicker than the eye can follow the blade slams down into Owen's thigh. He lets out another piercing scream which seems to go on forever.

"Your fuckin' cock?" Salem spits at him. "They get more than that, don't they? They also get threats of the video being widely distributed if they go to the cops and don't keep their mouths shut."

"I'm bleeding, man," Owen wails. "I think you hit an artery. Do something, or I'm going to die."

"You're not going to die from that little cut. But you might if you don't tell me what I want to know." Salem growls, his voice, cold and menacing, a tone only he can achieve. I try, but while Salem can make people wet their pants with the timbre he uses, I have to use a bodily threat as well.

"Please, let me go. I'm just a model. I don't have anything to do with any cameras or distributing the videos." Owen starts to beg. "It wasn't my choice, man. I was told to do it. All I did was follow instructions." He looks around, trying to find a face that's sympathetic. Of course, he doesn't find one. Then his eyes land on mine. It appears my scowl and bunched hands must be working, as a dribble of urine trickles down from his swollen balls.

Dart coughs, getting Salem's attention. The enforcer gives way as Dart steps up and takes his place. When he wants to, in his own way, the VP can look scary. "How are the videos distributed, who deals with that?"

"I don't know the mechanics. There's a website."

"Can you tell us which one it is?" Dart proceeds to push.

"I don't know," Owen cries out. I'm guessing he's recovered enough intelligence to know that non-information isn't going to save him.

"You don't know?" Dart gives a menacing growl of his own. "You don't know a fuckin' lot, do you, Owen?"

"I know I can't afford the subscription!" he yells out, then risks a glance at Dart to see whether he's satisfied him or not.

Whether it has or not, the answer gives me no satisfaction. I turn and raise my eyes at Token who raises his chin to show he's noted the response, and his frown suggests it's going to make it harder to find. This isn't a site which someone can stumble on by accident.

The VP shrugs and, stepping back, hands the lead over to Salem again.

"I'll buy you're just a foot soldier doing what you're told. So, who's pulling your fuckin' strings, Owen?"

Owen's eyes flick around, taking in my brothers who are all looking on. It seems he can find no one to appeal to. As if it's possible, he slumps even more against the chains. "Devon Starr."

My eyes go quickly to the prez and VP, knowing it's good having it confirmed.

"Anyone else?"

Owen's head moves in a negative motion. "Not that I know. He could be working with someone I suppose."

"Who's Brandon West?" Token barks.

Salem raises the knife.

"That's me. That's my name."

One mystery solved at least. Salem glances at me. I raise my chin to say I think in that he's being truthful. When the enforcer turns back to Owen/Brandon again, he continues the questioning.

"So, where do we find our friend Devon? Do you know his real name?"

"That is his real name—" Another scream shuts off his lie as Salem's knife finds a target in Owen's side. He can tell as well as the rest of us when he's being sold a lie.

Another dribble of urine, and the man is openly crying now. "He'll kill me." He tries to breathe through the pain, struggling to find an answer before Salem can stab him again. "He also goes by Ad Wilson."

"Tell us something we don't know," Salem suggests, flashing the blade once more.

"Carson Frome." Owen's eyes look wild. "That's all I know. That could be another alias. How the hell do I know?"

"You got contact details and a location for him?"

When it looks like Owen needs more encouragement, Salem turns to me, holding out the knife. "You want to do the honours? Maybe Owen here will talk when he sees his dick separated from his balls."

Do I want to touch the perverts swollen appendage? Fuck no, but if that's what it takes, I'll do it.

I take the bloodied knife and talk as I approach. "You know what Alicia is to me, Owen?" I wait for his wild eyes to come to mine. "She's fuckin' family. Do you think I'm going to let Friday night go unpunished? Do you think I'd have a moment's hesitation in castrating you?"

"I know where he lives!" Owen screams, louder than he's done before, making me stuff my finger in my ear then pull it out and shake it. "He's got a property, whether it's his or rented I don't know, but that's the only location I know for him." Now he looks crafty. "Let me down and I can take you there."

Salem tilts his head as if he's considering it. "I'll let Grumbler here slice off your dick. One of our girls is a nurse. She can stop it haemorrhaging, then you can take us where we need to go. Course, you won't be able to give a fuck anymore."

Well fuck. Torturing anyone takes its toll on the soul, which is why, moments like these cause a burst of chortles and laughter far more than the comment deserves. Even I can't stop my lips turning up or prevent a deep chuckle coming out of my mouth.

There's more than one thing to grin about in Salem's statement. Eva might be great for sewing us up when we cut our hands open accidentally while working on a bike or car, but I think sewing a gaping hole where a dick used to be is beyond even her. The thought of watching her face were we to ask her makes me smile, and my own expression must convey something like anticipated pleasure as Owen opens his mouth.

"I'll tell you! I'll tell you!" he screeches like a little girl and then spits out an address.

My eyes widen. It's in a decent neighbourhood and most of the houses there are worth a bundle of millions. Must be even more money in this porn business than I'd thought.

"Do you want to draw this out?" Lost leans in close. "I'd rather we tracked that photographer down, now we've got a possible address."

I eye Owen thoughtfully. I'm at one with Lost, but I'm a suspicious bastard. "Leave him here, keep a prospect on him. If he's fed us a heap of shit, then we'll let Salem loose again."

CHAPTER TWENTY-FIVE

Mary

I take a sip of the coffee Grumbler had thoughtfully brought me, prepared just how I like it. I'm touched that he remembered, more than that, how he had to be observant to put in just the amount of sugar and creamer that I like.

I hear male voices, and then the closing of the front door, followed by the roar of a motorcycle engine. Guess, Grumbler has gone. My powers of deduction tell me he's probably borrowed the bike the unknown man has ridden in on.

Slightly concerned about the stranger who might be making himself comfortable in my living room, I delay getting out of bed. But my mind is racing, half due to the early caffeine consumption, and half because I'm sure where Grumbler has gone will provide some answers about what I hope isn't, but dread is, Alicia's unwilling entry into the porn industry.

Normally, if I have a guest in the house, I'd make myself as presentable as necessary, then go and see to his comforts. Today is weird, as I've no idea who's waiting for me outside my bedroom door. The only comfort is that Grumbler must trust him.

Oh God. Grumbler. Covering my face with my hands, I remember I all but told him I fancied him last night. Like a gentleman, he hadn't taken advantage. He wouldn't have gotten far. After the day I'd had, I was in no mood for a man. But when things have settled down and our problems have been resolved—and somehow Grumbler has given me the confidence that that day will come—would I want to explore something with him?

I prop myself on my pillows, pulling up my knees, wrapping my arms around them and resting my chin on my hands. Since Dave died, I've never found a man who I feel as comfortable with as Grumbler, which is crazy. I've never been one for the bad boy types, and that Grumbler is one is undeniable. Maybe I've been looking in the wrong direction all this time? *Perhaps I should grasp this chance with both hands?*

Grumbler is a good man, otherwise, he wouldn't be helping me. At first, sure, there was something in it for him, he contacted me to get the money he was owed. But when he found Alicia was also being conned, he began to fight for her as well.

Alicia's only got a dim memory of having a father in her life. I thought I was doing well on my own, but perhaps after how badly she messed up two nights ago, there's room for improvement. It was, after all, Grumbler who Alicia had run to, wanting to avoid telling me. Of course, I'm angry she lied, but as to everything else? It was only a matter of when and not if. I just wished she'd waited a little longer and had found someone worthy of her.

I suspect, were I to conduct a poll, the vast majority of women wouldn't have stayed with the man they lost their virginity too, and again, for a high proportion, losing it wouldn't have been like the often happy circumstances read about in books. It's a rite of passage, something we all go through. For my part, the best first time is with the man you give your heart to. I might barely remember the details of the first time I went with a boy, but Dave? I can still remember every touch, every moment. Or maybe I'm glamorising it in my mind. I knew right then I loved him and had found the partner of my dreams.

Not that Dave hadn't had faults, he was a man after all. But any mistakes he'd made weren't intentional. It had taken time for us to learn to live with each other, neither of us having been in a committed relationship before and everything different, right down to what food to buy at the store. But we were happy, the divorce word never came up. Any plans made were about growing old together, though life had had other ideas.

Grumbler's older.

He is, by ten years.

What am I considering with him? A few romps in the sack until we see how unsuited we are? If that's the case, maybe we should just stay friends and not add in any benefits. But what if we found we could be more? Would this age difference mean I risked losing another man that I may give my heart to too soon once again?

One thing losing Dave had taught me was, life was to be seized and lived. That future assumed so enticingly close, but just out of reach, may never come to pass after all. Sure, Grumbler might one day be stricken by the ailments of an older man, but he was just as likely to come off his bike, and I could be knocked down crossing the street.

Ten years at Alicia's age is a lifetime, it doesn't seem so much at mine.

Hearing the stomping of motorcycle boots, I interpret they're crossing the living area to the kitchenette. I should be out there providing for my unknown guest. I feel awkward not knowing who is in my house, though the knowledge that Grumbler arranged for someone to be here is comforting.

Having raised the spectre of Owen or Devon visiting, I wouldn't want Alicia and I to be alone.

Forcing myself out of bed, I collect some clean clothes and go into the bathroom. Not sure what the day's going to hold, I shave my underarms and legs, and neaten up my lady garden. Rolling my eyes as I tell myself, *knowing I'm fresh and nice under my clothes helps me feel good. I'm doing it for no other reason, oh no.*

I dry my shoulder-length hair, take the time to straighten it, then immediately pull it up into a messy bun. Staring at my naked face, I decide against putting makeup on. *Might be a mistake, Mary. Might be a hot biker out there.*

Yeah, but my hot biker's just gone. Having seen me at my worst, and normally without adorning my face, if he can be attracted to tear-reddened eyes and blotchy skin, it must be the inner woman who attracts him.

At last I feel presentable enough to start my day. I tiptoe for some unknown reason, to the door to my bedroom, open it and, after a breath to fortify myself, step out.

I expected a younger version of Grumbler, which in a way is what I got. I hadn't expected him to be Black. Not that it mattered to me at all, Grumbler had vouched for him, but it was him who seemed a little uneasy, turning around fast as he heard my bedroom door shut.

"Ma'am. I'm Niran. Grumbler sent me. He asked me to watch out for you and your daughter in case anyone turned up." He holds up his hands in a non-threatening manner.

I realise it's not only me who's uncomfortable about him being in my house, and it's down to me to make him relax. I give him a warm smile. "The name's Mary," I say fast. "I know who you are. Grumbler warned me when he had to leave. It's very kind of you to give up your time on a Sunday to stay here with us." Suddenly I feel remiss for not emerging earlier. He'd just been hanging around without anything to do. "I'm just about to get some breakfast on, can I get some for you too?"

"I helped myself to coffee."

"That's alright. I won't call the cops." My delivery is so dry, it takes him a moment.

His eyes snap to mine, then when he sees my laughter lines softening my face, he chuckles. "Well, I hoped it wouldn't be a capital offence."

"I'm sorry." I grimace. "I should have come out earlier."

"You knew there was a strange man in your house." He understands immediately. "Ma'am, *Mary,* you're Grumbler's friend, and hence, one of mine. And if the offer's still open, me having admitted to my crime," he winks, "I'd love some breakfast."

"Have you been friends with Grumbler a long time?" I call over my shoulder as I round the countertop and then bend to open the fridge. I take out bacon and eggs, then, thinking about the size of the man who's going to be eating, look again and add ham.

"Three years now since I joined the MC. Of course, I was just a prospect for the first twelve months, so didn't have a lot to do with the members then, except jump at every order barked at me." His easy grin shows he didn't mind. "'Bout the closest I got to Grumbler was when I had to clean his bike. He used to stand over me, pointing out specks of dirt I couldn't even find."

I chuckle, that sounds like Grumbler. "He sure does like his bike."

Niran snorts. "We call it his ol' lady, 'cause he's never had one of the flesh and blood kind. Swear if he could, he'd take that motorcycle to bed with him."

"Carry on." I stand, placing the food on the countertop. I waggle my hands. "Spill all Grumbler's kinky shit."

"Kinky?"

"Like wanting to sleep with his bike." I wink at him.

Niran barks another laugh, putting up his hand to smother it. "You're a feisty one. Grumbler's going to have his hands full with you. Or is it hands full of you? I'm sure he'd prefer that to his bike." He waggles his eyebrows suggestively.

I blush red. "We're just friends."

Niran gives me a strange look. He waits for a moment while I get things cooking on the stove. "You asked how long I've known Grumbler?" He props his butt on a stool and leans his arms on the countertop. "As a prospect, I had great respect for the man, for all of the members. Part of the initiation process is giving them that, no matter the shit task they give to test you."

"So you have to do everything they say?" My brow creases.

"Sure. You have to prove trust and loyalty." Niran waits for a beat while I digest that. "Grumbler's the sergeant-at-arms. He was voted in as an officer just before I joined. At first, I thought he was the way he was to prove he should have that role. Then I realised, behaving like a sergeant major, rallying the troops was just the way he is. He doesn't have patience for anyone doing anything half-hearted, and he didn't earn his road name for nothing."

Grumbler? Sure, I'd wondered whether there was more of a story behind his name than the headline he'd told me. Thinking back, he'd been anything but grumpy with me and he'd shown no impatience with Alicia.

But Niran hasn't finished. "You know he laid his bike down a while back?"

"You mean his crash?"

"Yeah. He smashed his leg up pretty bad. Thought for a while he might end up copying me." At my quizzical gaze,

Niran stands, walks around the counter and pulls up the leg of his jeans, revealing a prosthetic to me.

"Oh." It's inadequate. But what do I do? Express sympathy? I'd never have guessed if he hadn't shown me.

"Fuckin' accident ended my military career. I didn't even fuckin' get it during one of my tours. It happened stateside when I was home on leave." His eyes roll in a *would you believe it* fashion.

"You came off your bike too?" I always knew they were dangerous.

"Nope. Sure I was on my bike, but a fuckin' woman knocked me off it, then managed to drive over my leg to make sure she did a proper job." Niran gives a little shake of his head, showing he'll accept no commiseration. What's done is done. "Grumbler was luckier than me. At least he's still got his flesh and blood one, though he might have just as much metal as a prosthetic." He chuckles, softly. "Point I'm getting to is, for a while he was laid up. I offered to help him out. Maybe I was sympathetic when it was suggested he'd lose his leg, maybe it's my service that led me to step up, but when Grumbler agreed and started passing off some of his tasks as a sergeant-at-arms, Prez agreed I could support him. Well, as time went on, I got to know the man, and the more I came to know him, the more I found to admire. He's a good fuckin' man, Mary." His eyes come to mine as if he's telling me something important. "He's resumed his role now, but I still help him out." Another chortle comes from him. "The brothers say that between us they've got a two-legged sergeant-at-arms."

"That's cruel," I tell him, dishing up the cooked food and sliding a plate toward him.

Niran's eyes meet mine. "You either spend this life regretting what passed or move on and deal with it. Losing my leg lost me my career, but I found something to compensate and, in many ways, something better. I not only found a team, I found a home. There's no point bottling regret up, that's not how you deal with it."

A shuffling of feet has me looking past him. Alicia's come out of her bedroom, and in her bare feet, neither of us had heard her. From the look on her face, she's obviously been there a while.

"Want breakfast?" Anticipating a yes, I push my plate toward her, and turn to start cooking more for myself.

She steps forward, tilting her head and looking up to Niran. He's a tall man. Even seated on the stool, he towers above her. "You're a friend of Grumbler?"

"I am."

She takes my knife and fork and starts in on the food while I turn back to the stove. "Where's Grumbler gone?"

"I'm not sure," Niran replies, carefully.

"Has he gotten the video taken down yet?" Her eyes look hopeful.

"Again, I can't tell you. But he'll be doing all he can so that video is completely destroyed." Niran's tone leaves no room for doubt and seems to reassure her.

"I spoke to Marisa last night, Mom." She looks straight into my eyes. "I told her Owen just wanted to make a notch on his bed with me. I didn't tell her about the filming."

It's up to my daughter to know what to tell her friend. Sure, she hadn't shown good judgement with Owen, but Marisa's been her bestie for years. "And?" I ask cautiously.

She shrugs. "She said the amazing first time was over glamorised. That it never happened that way in reality. She said most boys preferred girls who know the score." Picking up a piece of bacon, she chews on it.

I think she showed good judgement. If Marisa knows and hasn't criticised her, maybe she'll be feeling better about herself. That she hasn't mentioned the video is good. Hopefully that means if the footage can be found and destroyed, no one need ever know about it.

I notice Niran's eyes are focused on my face. In that instance, I believe he's read my mind and is trying to tell me to have faith.

<hr>

CHAPTER TWENTY-SIX

<hr>

Grumbler

Bypassing Niran's bike which had been sufficient to get me from A to B, I go to my own ride, patting the seat before swinging my leg over it. Niran's rides well enough, but there's nothing like being on your own where you're truly one with the machine. Not that this ride is for enjoyment, but at the end of this jaunt, I hope there'll be something to put a smile on my face.

Glancing up at the sky, I see clouds threatening, so I pull my waterproof jacket out of my saddlebag and slip it on. When it rains, it rains like it means it. I'm not surprised that my brothers around me are doing the same.

Lost waves his hand over his head. Behind him, I slip into position beside the VP. Salem's behind us, with Bones and Token then Pennywise bringing up the rear. Behind the bikes, Connor is driving the truck. The whole club had wanted to come, but Lost had kept it to a small group. Well, how many did it take to bring in one man? Besides, too many bikes turning up might bring us unwanted attention.

I punch down into first, then into gear, musing I still find it strange to ride close to the head of the pack like this. Before

Snake and Poke betrayed the club, I never expected to rise through the ranks. Still, here I am, and, it appears, my brothers have faith in me. I suspect the self-doubt I used to see in Lost eyes is mirrored in mine, and for the same reasons. If we could be so duped, let a mutiny be planned without even sniffing a whiff that something wrong was brewing, how could we be trusted to lead an MC?

Perhaps, like Lost, it makes me try harder.

Before we left, Lost had instructed we use our Bluetooth headsets, when normally most of us prefer to ride without constantly hearing brothers yammering in our ears. But today, when we're going to plan our approach off the cuff, it makes sense to be able to react immediately.

From the map Token had pulled up, it looks like the house is set in its own grounds. We'll park a ways out, send up the drone, and then analyse what we can see. Christ, how things have changed. In the old days when I first joined the MC, we had radio headsets to use if necessary, but often the signal didn't come clearly, and they had next to no range. Drones? Never even heard the word. We'd roll up and cope with whatever is there, our information limited to how many cars were on the drive.

Now we can get copious amounts of information before we go inside. We even have the ability to look through windows.

After a few miles, Lost waves his hand in a downward gesture and points to the side. We pull up. Connor parks the truck behind us and soon has the drone out and ready, while Token calls up the app on his phone. Within moments, our little friend is flying high, ignoring the rain and zooming off to our target's house. We all crowd around the tech expert trying to get a look at what's on his phone. Unable to see clearly, I slide my reading glasses out of my cut, feeling less embarrassed when Lost does the same. He's only given in and started wearing them recently, under the influence of Patsy of course.

It's just one more sign our bodies are aging faster than our minds.

Mentally, I'm as sharp as I ever was, I muse, as the footage sent back from the drone comes into view more clearly. I note the house sits in the midst of a well-manicured and expansive yard. It's a fucking mansion. Fancy, well maintained. Somehow, I don't think Devon would dirty his own hands with the upkeep, he didn't come across as that sort. Then again, when I met him, he hadn't come across as a particularly affluent man. There's a garage with the door closed, and no vehicles in sight to suggest there's anyone inside.

"Wish we had a drone with an infrared camera," the VP remarks. "He could be at home, or not. No way of knowing."

Lost considers for a moment, his head bowed and his fingers pinching the brow of his nose. "It's quiet, but he might be there. We'll proceed as though there's someone home, and if not, well, we stake it out. Either way, we're close to him now."

"We pick the locks then," Dart observes. "No outward sign that someone is waiting."

Token is fiddling with the controls and after a short while, the drone returns. Picking it up and putting it under his arm, he raises his chin. "I'm gonna need to get in the truck for a moment. See what info I can call up on the security system he has. I'll try and disable it remotely."

Token disappears. I shift impatiently while I'm waiting. To pass the time, I take a few steps away from the others and light a cigarette. By the time it's burned down to the filter and I'm stubbing it out on my boot, carefully pocketing the evidence, Token walks back to our group.

"I think that's it," he informs us. "But just in case, I'll have my jammer at hand." I note he's carrying a small device.

Dart and Lost have been re-examining the drone footage saved on Token's phone. Lost comes to a decision. "We'll go in the truck," he starts. "Connor will pull up outside the front. Salem, Dart and Pennywise—when we stop, you get out via the back doors and make your way around the back of the house. There's some shrubbery you can use for cover. Once you're clear, I'll take one of the boxes of spares in the van, and pretend I'm making a delivery. If he comes to the front door, we'll take him. If not, Token will get us in. All clear?"

All fucking clear. Chins are raised in acknowledgement.

"I've got my lock picking shit. Just give me the heads-up and I'll get us in from the rear." Salem pats his pocket.

"If we can, we'll just come back and open the door," the VP states.

Taking off our cuts, we squeeze into the cage, the enforcer and the others getting into the cargo bay. Lost indicates that Connor should move to the rear passenger seat so if Devon's at home, he'll only see Lost driving the truck. Connor takes the middle seat, I sit one side, and Token the other. It's not particularly comfortable, but there's only a short way to go.

When Lost pulls away, it's hard to keep my leg from bouncing in anticipation. I'm so close, I can almost smell Devon's blood on my hands. If I get my hands on his scrawny neck, it will take a lot to persuade me to loosen them. Owen might have been the one to seduce Alicia, but it was at Devon's command.

My body stills as we drive up the street. There's a man out washing his car, but he doesn't give the truck more than a cursory look. Devon's house is further along. Most of the houses have privacy fencing or shrubbery, so luckily, we can approach virtually unseen. Lost makes as though he's turning the truck with two results. One, is that the truck is out of sight of the road, the other is that the back doors are close to the camouflage that the three who'll be heading to the rear can use.

When the engine stops, Lost gives the prospect his instructions over his shoulder. "Wait here until we're inside. Then get back to the bikes and wait." Prez then gets out and goes to the back door of the truck, whistling as he walks unhurried.

The building is more impressive when seen in the flesh and not on a smartphone screen. Rage rises within me, thinking how Devon's built his empire on ill-gotten gains. My thousand dollars pales into insignificance.

Token whispers as though he can read my mind. "He didn't get this from cheating models."

Lost has got the rear doors open now and is reaching inside taking out a box then replacing it as though checking for the right package. This gives Salem, Pennywise and Dart time to ease out and begin to sidle around the boundary, using what shrubs they can to reach the back of the house unseen.

When they're out of sight, the prez steps up to the front door of the house, package in hand. He rings the doorbell, then respectfully steps back and waits. It doesn't matter if Devon looks out of the peephole, he'll have never seen Lost before.

I'm holding my breath as I wait for the man who I haven't seen for weeks open the door. But as time stretches out, it's obvious no one's coming.

Prez turns, waves his hand, and Token exits the truck and goes to join him. I, too, ease myself out, and then wait as Token works his magic, knowing if the alarm system goes off, we'll have to make a quick getaway.

My concern was for nothing, it all goes to plan. Token has the door open in seconds, then steps inside. Again I stop breathing, wondering if alarm bells are going to blare out. But luck, or rather Token's skills, are on our side. It's only seconds later that Lost is turning and beckoning for me to join them.

Leaning back into the truck, I instruct Connor, "Go kid."

"We're in," he tells Salem using the Bluetooth connection. Then to us, Lost instructs, "Check this fuckin' place is empty."

The three of us fan out. There's no hiding place in the large open plan living area, and in the kitchen, the coffee pot feels cold to the touch, as does the stove. Seems like Devon is an early riser and has long left.

I then check out the study, carefully looking for any sign of a panic room, but I find nothing. By the time I've inspected the bathroom and half bath on this floor, I'm content I missed no one.

Returning to the living area, I find Lost, and then watch Token come down the stairs. "No one's home," he announces.

"Grumbler's coming to let you in."

I dip my chin but pause before going to open the door for the others. "There's a computer in the study," I inform Token, who looks like a kid on Christmas day.

"Now we might get fuckin' somewhere," he states, grinning.

It takes a matter of seconds to open the back door, and let Dart, Salem and Pennywise in. When I return to the study, it's in time to see Token opening a small bag he brought into the house. I assumed it was just carrying the jammer, but it appears to hold other stuff as well. One item he brings out is his laptop.

Having booted up the PC, I'd be stumped at the login password, but Token's hands fly over the laptop keys, and plugs a small device into one of the USB slots. Within moments, the home screen awakens.

"Bingo," Token announces. "I'm in."

With his fingers flying fast, Token goes through the files on the PC. He talks as he works. "Okay, as I suspected. There are pictures from his photo shoots all in various galleries. They look kosher to me."

Apart from the little fact his models don't get paid, of course.

Dart leans in to look. He's alone, Pennywise and Salem

have taken up position close to the front door to warn us of any approach.

"Contracts for photo usage and model release forms are all here," Token continues. "No videos though. They must be buried under some secure levels. Possibly not even held locally." Token tries again, following searches on the PC, tracing fuck knows what.

He sighs, shakes his head, clenches his jaw, but the PC won't give up any secrets. "Jesus H Christ. It's got to be here somewhere. Maybe it's obvious…" Token clicks on a program, and video editing software appears. "Jackpot," he says softly, his eyes intent on the screen.

"Alicia?" I try to see over his shoulder. It's not footage of her and Owen. It's far, far worse.

"Fucker must still be editing this. He hasn't deleted it from the PC yet." Token touches another key, and the video starts playing.

"I want my mommy," the child, who's little more than a toddler, wails.

The man with her laughs. "Your mommy doesn't want you, kid. But now you've got a new daddy. Call me daddy, yeah?"

The toddler does nothing but cry.

"Daddy's going to give you a bath. You want to get all clean, don't you?" The man roughly overpowers the little girl and despite her protests and wriggling, removes her clothes. "You've got to be nice to your new daddy."

"He's dead. So fuckin' dead," Lost pronounces. He covers his eyes with his hands, then, manfully, looks back.

Me? I turn away, my stomach revolting.

"Oh God, no." I don't need to, can't look at this. Token's commentary is bad enough. "He's got his dick out. He's—"

"You really need to watch that, Token?" the VP sounds in the same amount of distress as me.

Token clicks a key and minimises the window. "I feel I

have to man, but you don't." He puts headphones on. "Leave me be, okay?"

Lost places a hand on his shoulder, and Dart and I follow him away.

Out of sight of the PC, Prez shudders. "I want to bleach my eyeballs just from the little I've seen."

"We need to shut him down," the VP states. "Christ knows where he got that kid from. Surely, someone, somewhere is missing her."

"Could be the parents are involved," I suggest. "Twisted fucks selling their daughter."

"But we know Devon doesn't like to pay," Lost points out.

Suddenly, I hear a chair moving so fast it falls over. Token rushes past, and I hear him being violently ill in the bathroom I'd inspected earlier. Hardening my resolve, I stride back to the PC, but all it's showing is an innocuous scenic image.

When Token returns, the back of his hand wiping his mouth, he informs us in a harsh, disbelieving whisper, "He raped her. She was… she was hurt bad, Prez."

Jesus. I stop breathing. Then when my lungs can do without air no longer, I inhale, and say, my voice almost unrecognisable, "That kid?" I don't need his confirmation. It leads me to say the words I don't often utter, "We've got to get the cops involved."

Prez, white as a fucking sheet, considers for a moment. "I think we go one better." He pulls his phone out of his cut, selects a number then calls it.

"Snatcher? I think we've got one for you." He explains what we've found in gory details that I hope never to remember while only too well aware it's going to haunt my nightmares for nights.

Lost updates the Utah prez on what we've just found, adding, "Token thinks it's recent footage he's editing. Can't find anything else. Maybe he only keeps it locally until the final product is done. Yeah, I'll pass you over." He hands the phone to Token.

"Brother? Yeah. Here's what I got." Returning to the computer, Token gives Snatcher the location, and the computer's IP address and various other technical details which go over my head. He finishes up with, "Yeah, Swift, you've got remote access."

"Swift?" I ask.

"Yeah, Snatcher pulled her in to discuss the technical shit."

"You called her brother," Dart remarks.

Token shrugs. "Don't know what else to call her. Sister doesn't work. From the little she said, she knows her fuckin' shit, and Utah has the resources." He grimaces and waves his hand toward the PC. "This shit must stop. Fuck, Lost." His eyes fill with distress. "I've never seen anything like this. That kid…"

I won't be the only one having nightmares, that's for sure.

I stomp to the window. I thought I was looking for Devon because he hadn't paid me what I was due. Then, it was to avenge Alicia and that fucking asshole Owen who'd filmed her and destroy what in comparison to what we just found was a fairly innocuous video. Now we've fallen in deeper and have found kiddie porn of the worse possible type. Have we reached the depths of his depravity now, or is there more to discover? One thing I'm grateful for, I didn't have to watch it play out. Did the kid even survive? From what Token said, maybe not unless they got her medical attention. *Motherfucker!*

What sick fuck gets their kicks watching shit like that? What even sicker fuck gets a kid to call him daddy while he's molesting her?

My hands bunch at my sides. They are all dead.

"Now we know how Devon affords this house," Lost states grimly. "Nothing remotely legal about that footage. Now it makes sense there's a subscription service somewhere where equally sick fuckers pay a fortune to watch it."

I kick at a table so hard, the leg splinters. "We wait for him to come home," I growl. "This is that fucker's last day of living."

"I want to take that PC back to the compound," Token exclaims.

Prez's narrowed eyes show he's not convinced. "Are you likely to find anything more?"

Token purses his lips. "I might."

"Utah's got access," I remind him.

"It's not a good idea, Token." Prez fixes him with his eyes. "We still might have to get the cops or the feds involved in this. What are they going to say if the most incriminating piece of evidence is removed?"

Token tugs at the latex gloves he had used on the keyboard. His shrug shows he's conceded the point. "I'll give myself remote access too. If Swift turns nothing up, I'll take another look." He cheers up and goes to sit in front of the screen again.

Prez calls out for Salem to join us, then leads him, me and Dart into the kitchen. He props himself up against the countertop and folds his arms. "Fuck knows when Devon could come home. Maybe soon, maybe tonight. Maybe he's gone filming outside the state. I think we should get back to the compound. We'll leave Pennywise and Connor here."

I'm happy with that. All I know is that I want some fresh air. Something to clear my head of what I've just seen. It was like all the evil in the world coalesced into a short half hour of film. No matter how many times I shower, I don't think I'll ever feel clean.

CHAPTER TWENTY-SEVEN

Grumbler

Back at the compound, Prez calls everyone into church and quickly gives an update on what we found in Devon's house. The mood grows steadily darker, sombre as he speaks.

Sure we're all men, and none of us could deny having jerked ourselves off sitting in front of a television screen watching porn stars getting it on in front of our eyes. Hell, most nights, we're subject to a live show in the clubroom.

As far as I'm aware, anything I've watched before has been consensual. I'd even once met an actress who starred in a few of my favourite spank bank shows, describing herself as on the path to a successful showbiz career. From her I knew some of the porn stars could make their fortunes and be revered wherever they go. Though also, that many more would be spat out and left adrift, at least when their looks faded, or their outlook on sex became jaded, and they just couldn't pretend to perform for the camera anymore.

I have never, ever, watched anything depraved, shying away from anything non-consensual or bestial. Sure, I knew it was there, just never wanted to go looking. As for kids? Hell to the no. Looking around the table, I note the men I ride with seem to be of the same view.

"Caught Snake playing with his dongle in front of some questionable shit once." Bones looks around. "But even he wouldn't sink that low."

"Kids, man, that's twisted." Keeper looks pale. "You think Owen knows?"

"I think I fuckin' want to ask him," I growl. "Perhaps give him more of an incentive to come clean about anything else he might have knowledge about."

"If he knows anything else, I'll make sure he doesn't keep it to himself." Salem catches my eye. "Now we know what we know, we can dig deeper."

Deuce snorts. "He's not going to admit to any kiddie fiddling. He has to know that's his death warrant for sure."

Token looks toward Deuce, then it seems like a light bulb's gone off. "I reckon he's got to know more about the site and the login details. Vain fucker like that would want to know how good his ass was looking."

Token might be right, but I'm not so certain. Something like that would be a tightly guarded secret. Would Devon trust Owen with something that could put him inside for a very long time?

"If he does, I'll find out," Salem promises. "Knew there was a reason we left him breathing."

"Grumbler? Get Wrangler to go take Niran's place watching your woman. He'll want to be in on this. I don't want her and the girl unprotected while Devon's on the loose."

I agree one hundred percent, but I brought his ride back to the compound. "Niran will need to ride the prospect's bike," I tell Lost, to a chorus of sniggers. Yeah, Wrangler's ride is a work in progress to put it politely. It needs a full paint job to get the tank and fenders to match, and that's just for starters.

Prez, himself, gives a quick grin, then grows serious.

"He'll take a moment to get here. He can catch up on the proceedings when he arrives." He takes in a deep breath as though he's mentally preparing himself. "Okay. No point wasting time. Let's go talk to the fucker again."

To say Owen looks sorry for himself is an understatement. Curtis, now the only prospect guarding him—he certainly doesn't need more—is idly flicking through a bike parts book as the strung-up man seems to give off almost constant low-level groans. His limp dick still offends me just as much as it had earlier on today, but I can't summon up one ounce of sympathy, particularly now we've got evidence of some other games he might like to play.

He doesn't even seem to be aware that we've walked in on him.

Salem jerks his chin toward me, and I walk up and kick one of Owen's legs from under him. The chains rattle and pull at his arms as he tries to find purchase with his feet again. When he gets his balance, he opens red raw eyes and squints at me.

"Please… please. Let me go."

"Not yet." I phrase my words so he can find a glimmer of hope in them, even though I know the only release he's going to find is death. The answers to my questions will determine the level of pain that will entail.

Pulling over a wooden chair, I rest my foot on the seat and fold my arms over the back. "Tell me again about the kind of home movies you star in Owen?"

"Some soft porn. Some like with Alicia."

Shaking my head, I let him know I'm not satisfied. "Not a fuckin' chance of releasing you unless you give me more, Owen."

"We've got Devon's PC," Token puts in, winking out of Owen's sight.

It wouldn't do any harm stringing Owen along. If he knows

nothing is stored there, he'll be admitting to being deeper embroiled in this mess than he's hitherto indicated.

Owen, if possible, pales. "There were girls, drunk, strung up and off their asses." When I give him a gimme more gesture, he admits, "GBH was used, I'm pretty certain of that."

"And you fucked them, even though they were probably unwilling?"

"Unwilling, unresponsive." Owen actually shudders. "Once, he got me to fuck a dead girl."

Jesus H Christ. "Dead? He kill her?"

"No, man. No. I'd never condone murder. She was homeless, died on the streets of an overdose, and Devon happened to find her."

That he could get it up for an unresponsive woman is one thing. But a woman not even breathing? Cold, presumably to the touch?

"Fuck, man." Niran, who must have arrived at some point during the proceedings, can't restrain himself. "How the fuck could you do that?"

"It was like a blow-up doll, you know, it didn't mean anything. I got in, got off, job done. I got paid, man. Good fuckin' money, especially for something unusual like that."

"And what else?" I suddenly thunder. "What fuckin' else, Owen? What age were the girls?"

"Alicia's age or older. She was one of my youngest."

"You sure of that?" Salem's voice sounds beside me. He's tossing his knife from hand to hand.

"You watch your movies when they're finished?"

Owen closes his eyes then opens them again. "Sometimes."

"Online? Or do you work with Devon to edit them?"

"Devon never lets anyone help with that. But he does great work, splicing and editing. What he produces is top notch."

"So you watch online," Token speaks from beside me. Then he snaps, "Website details, your login and password."

Owen doesn't say a word. Not until Salem grabs a foot and expertly slices off his little toe, then, for a moment, all he can do is scream. When he gets his breath back, he says "I only know Devon's personal site. Not where they end up after he finishes them." *It's something to start with at least,* I think as he churns out the details Token was after.

"I'm in," Token says after a while. "Hold on while I send these details to Utah. They can investigate the back end."

Bones is looking over Token's shoulder, avidly scanning the screen. "Christ, it looks like Owen here was doing his own investigation of the back end in this one."

"Whatcha got?" Lost walks closer.

"From a quick scan, Prez, shit that needs to be kept underground. But whether the other stuff is on here or not, fuck knows. I can't tell immediately."

"There another level you need a password for?"

Owen looks confused by the question, so I expand, "Underage girls, little kids."

He shakes his head. "There's nothing like that. Devon wouldn't…"

Devon's a man who either kills or conveniently finds a dead girl and makes her a posthumous star in a movie. I'd say there wasn't much Devon wouldn't do.

"Come on, fucker," Salem taunts him. "I'll cut off another toe then keep going until you tell. Pretty fucking hard walking without any toes I'm told."

"If there is something, I wouldn't know," Owen screams.

Prez cocks his eyebrow at me, as I shake my head and run my hand over my face. Damn it, but it seems the fucker's telling the truth. One thing I've learned is that he's scared of pain. He also has no doubt Salem will carry out his threat.

I decide to change tack. "Devon wasn't at his house. Have you any idea where he might go? Any particular haunts or locations he uses? Studios he might rent?"

Owen has tears rolling down his face. "I'd tell you if I knew. You're going to hurt me whether or not I keep my mouth closed. Devon chooses different locations. As far as I know, he doesn't go to the same place twice unless it's for a normal shoot, like the ones for book covers. Sometimes he rents out an Airbnb or a private house. He's filmed me in one of the big beach houses before. Or hotels, like where I went with…" He's wise and doesn't mention her name.

Lost hasn't done any of the questioning, leaving it to Salem and me. Now he steps forward with an unreadable expression on his face. He tilts his head to the side as he examines Owen for a moment.

"The shoots for book covers…Why does Devon bother with that?"

Owen's chin drops down to his chest. "He has a legitimate business."

In other words, it's his own cover, and the shit in the internal pages wouldn't make for happy reading, or not for someone not twisted.

Lost takes over again. His normally affable face now a mask of anger. "What do you feel when you're fuckin' an unresponsive woman? What did you feel when you took Alicia knowing full well she hadn't given consent to be filmed? How does it make you feel, Owen?"

Owen's eyes crack open a fraction more as he stares at the prez. "It's a job, man. Where else could I earn money like that?"

"What do you think it's like, Owen? To wake knowing you've been violated but no idea by whom?"

"I don't know," Owen wails. "They can't remember so what's the harm in it?"

Lost's attention is on me now, his voice when he speaks is low. "Is there anything else you want to know? Is there a reason for keeping this piece of shit around any longer?"

He can't help with more information. I think we've already wrung out of him everything he has to give. He can't help us find Devon, and about the more deviant side of the business, he doesn't seem to know. Not sure I completely trust him. Would he have owned up if he'd abused little kids? On balance, I'm sick of the man and want him out of Alicia's life, permanently. I don't want to risk freeing him and have her come across him walking around without a care in the world. One thing he hasn't expressed has been guilt.

After these thoughts go through my head, I give Lost his answer, "No."

Prez raises and dips his chin, signals to Salem to stay back, then draws nearer to the strung-up man.

"I gave you a chance to show remorse, but it's clear you have none. Your disrespect for women isn't going to be fixed. You'll just go on and on before you are stopped. So I'm going to stop you now. But I'm feeling generous, so you can choose which way to go. I can send you to Satan minus your dick and you'll take your chances as to how long it will take before you bleed out, or, I'll end you with a bullet to your head."

"You can't. You can't do that." Owen screams and a burst of urine comes out of his recently threatened cock. "I won't touch another woman. I beg you. Let me go!" The level of his screams rise and start a headache behind my temples.

Lost may not look like your typical MC prez—more like a jovial grandfather at times—but he should never be underestimated. His old lady's been good for him, given him the confidence to believe in himself, and right now, I read there's no doubt in his head as to how this should end. And that's with Owen dead, one way or another. I know he's serious, Owen does not.

"Just let me go, man. I won't say anything about the Satan's Devils. I'll say I was jumped and beaten. Just let me go. I can't tell you anymore."

"I'm quite aware you can't tell me anymore, Owen, which is why I'm giving you the choice. Little head or big one?"

Lost's delivery is so dry, it makes me smile and a couple of brothers laugh.

Owen's eyes flick around the room as though seeking someone who'll have sympathy for him, but of course, nobody has.

Salem sighs heavily and starts pulling on a pair of latex gloves. "Guess I'll make the decision for him." He takes out his knife and steps forward, reaching for Owen's dick. Right now it's shrunk so much there's little to get hold of. It certainly doesn't look worthy of a porn star's appendage.

Owen can tell he's serious as he screams out one word, "Head."

In what looks like a choreographed movement, Salem steps back and Lost waves me forward. I slide my gun out of my cut and press the barrel against Owen's forehead. For a brief second, I see him hope I'm still just using threats and that my weapon isn't loaded, then he gets a good look at the expression in my eyes.

"Oh fuck no, fuck no, no no no."

I pull the trigger with the same amount of remorse Owen had shown for his victims. Zero.

As the echo of the gunshot fades, Lost points to Curtis. "Get started on clean-up, I'll get someone to—"

"I'll help," Keeper offers.

"Me too," Niran chimes in almost simultaneously.

The pair look at each other and shrug. Well, prospecting's not so far in their rearview that they've forgotten about this shit.

Brothers start making their way to the door, more than one pausing to spit on the corpse. Before any can actually exit, Lost's phone rings. Eyeing the caller ID, he holds up his hand causing all forward movement to cease.

"Snatcher?... Uh-huh... Yeah... What? No. We don't need fuckin' help... We're perfectly... Oh. Yeah. That makes sense... You want what?... Yeah... Shit. Yeah, I understand. I'll clear it this end, brother... See them tomorrow."

All eyes are on him. Lost sighs and shakes his head. "Snatcher's got news he doesn't want to discuss over the phone, not even on a secure line, and fuck knows, between us and him, we can sew that up tight." Prez's jaw looks tense. "Bolt and Swift are coming tomorrow. Need all of you in church first thing. Oh, and we're to keep an eye out for Devon, but not pull him in. If he returns to his house, he's to be watched, if he leaves, followed."

"What the fuck?" My hands are itching to get on that fuckin' bastard, especially now I know the shit he's into. Such instruction goes against the grain.

Prez ignores my interruption. "Niran, Curtis. You want to go on a stakeout tonight?"

"Yeah, 'cause we'll be hidden by the dark. We'll blend in." Niran shows there's no animosity behind his comment by his wide grin.

"As long as you don't smile, Brother." Blaze can't help getting his dig in.

Lost slices his hand through the air, and the ribaldry stops. "No. Not because of the fuckin' colour of your skin, but because we don't want Devon to know Satan's Devils are after him, and he probably doesn't expect us to have Black members." His eyes fall on Niran, then he looks at the prospect. "And, because, you've both got the skills needed. You've done surveillance before when you served."

Curtis had been a member of the military police. He'll know what to do, and Niran? Well, he was a Marine.

"I'll get Pennywise and Connor out of the house. They can make sure it looks untouched. Token..."

"I'll sort the alarm out, get it reset." Token doesn't look happy as he answers the prez, but he'll do what he has to.

There's a moment when we all continue to watch Lost, but as he seems to have said all he needs to, most start to wander out. Dart steps up, frowning, and I, hanging around, overhear.

"Swift? How's that going to go down, Prez?"

Lost shrugs. "She's a member, she'll get due respect."

But as he says it, I wonder if it's going to be that easy. Sounds like tomorrow we'll have a woman sitting around the table in church, and I, for one, am not sure how I'll take it.

"Grumbler?" Lost notices I'm still there.

"You need me, Prez?"

His eyes soften. "Nah. Not until the morning. Sounds like there's nothing more we can do until then."

It's probably a good move not to send me to watch out for Devon. I'd find it hard to follow instructions just to follow him and keep my hands to myself.

CHAPTER TWENTY-EIGHT

Grumbler

I killed men when I served, but they were the enemy, nameless targets I pointed my gun at following orders. Did they deserve it? Well, it was either them or us- so clearly, they did.

When I first joined the MC, it was far more violent than it is nowadays, and we had to fight for our turf, again, a case of survival depending on who shot first.

For the past three years I've been sergeant-at-arms, willing to kill for the safety of the club or, as in this case, justice. Poke, for years, had acted as executioner for Snake. I'd watched on as he killed in cold blood, ending lives almost on a whim. I'd accepted that if there was a need, I could be like him, though I wouldn't approach the task with anything like pleasure.

I'd felt nothing when Shark had died a few months back, tortured first of course. He'd been one of the members who'd followed Snake and who had turned up working for Alder of all things. It was the whole club dispatching Shark to meet Satan, everyone wanting to get their punches in. Lost had fired the bullet, but in my view, Shark was probably dead by then.

Today was the first time I personally took the life of a man in our brig. Not coldly, fuck, I was irate with rage. I out of everyone had the most reason to want him dead, but it still gets to a man, ending a life of someone who can't fight back. I've no doubt I was right to do it, nor that my reasons were just. But there's still an unease inside me. Maybe the smell of cordite sent me right back to dark days when I was serving my country.

There's one thing I know. *I'd do the same thing again and again.*

Does the fact that my hands are now shaking make me weak? Fuck no. Dart had confided when he was drunk one night that the scary-ass motherfucker of an enforcer, Blade, from Tucson, always threw up after he'd done some torturing. It's a natural reaction and won't last long. I should be celebrating that the earth's rid of scum like Owen, not trying to justify why it had been at my hand.

In some ways, I feel cheated. I'd expected his death would wipe the slate clean for Alicia, but it's an empty resolution where she's concerned. First, she must never know about it, more importantly, second, even if she did, it wouldn't negate the fact that it happened and that he'd deceived her and robbed her of her innocence. Then there's the fact that the film of her is still out there, and someone could be watching it right now. A willing young girl? That could be on any porn channel, not even one hidden on the dark web. That's what I've got to make right for her. What I can't stomach most is that I can't throttle the truth out of Devon tonight. That's what's making me vibrate with anger.

I dispatched Owen to meet Satan, but he was only a substitute for the man I want worse. That fucking video Token had found—it was beyond sickening. Trouble is, try as I might, I can't get it out of my mind.

Kids should be kept safe, cherished, not abused, and certainly not to satisfy the depraved appetites of twisted men. I shake my head trying to clear it, but the little I'd seen replays in my head on a loop. *How did Token watch the whole thing?* I might not know how he stomached it, but I'm grateful he did. Even hearing about how it ended had broken me.

Now I'm told I have to wait for retribution until tomorrow. It's too fucking long to wait.

Exiting the brig, I take a moment to breathe in the fresh air and decide how to make the time pass. As the remainder of the brothers walk around me, some slap my back as if I deserve praise for taking that final shot. Truth is, any of them would have done it.

Knowing Owen wasn't around to corrupt anymore young girls hasn't brought the anticipated relief. It's Devon I've got my sights set on now, and I'll be fucked if Bolt and that member without a dick from Utah are going to swoop in and take him out of my hands. They've got a habit of doing that.

"You okay, Brother?" Prez has stopped by my side.

I glance toward him. "I'll be fuckin' fine just so long as Utah doesn't pull a Stormy on us again. That fucker's mine."

Prez purses his lips, then nods. "Already thought of that, sergeant-at-arms. I'll be calling Drummer later and giving him a heads-up. Working with us is one thing, taking the kill shot for us, something else. It's a question of trust, Brother. Utah lost ours when Stormy took out Alder, lost Demon's too when he finished Major for them. It caused them to lose the trust of Red and of Drummer as we're all one fuckin' club. If Snatcher hasn't learned that lesson, then he won't have a fuckin' chapter to lead."

What Lost has said makes sense. That he's worried that has any possibility of being the outcome fuels my rage. "I suppose Stormy hasn't shown his face yet?"

"Not as far as we've been told."

I raise my eyebrows at Lost. "You really think he's back and Snatcher's protecting him?"

Lost shakes his head vigorously and snorts. "I'm seeing conspiracies all over the place now, Brother. Utah hit us hard."

He's right. They had. As he pats my shoulder and walks off to the clubhouse, I gaze after him. San Diego is no stranger to underhand plots—we'd had Snake and his betrayal to deal with. While Utah hadn't betrayed the club as such, they'd kept so many secrets, I'm not sure even now whether they're all out in the open. Perhaps meeting two of them tomorrow will shed some light on whether I can really trust my northern brothers, or, whatever I should refer to Swift as.

"Beer?"

I swing around, not realising Salem was following me. I consider it for a moment. Yes, I could use a drink, but the club-house will be full of brothers talking about Owen and his revelations, going around in circles without solving shit. Rather than reliving the last few hours, some space might clear my head.

"Not sure my heart's in it right now," I tell the enforcer.

When he replies, "I know what you mean," I realise this is the man who had been prepared to slice off a man's dick and let him bleed to death. His job, but it doesn't mean he enjoys doing it. But I'm only partly on the money as he continues, "Christ, the whole fuckin' business makes me feel sick, Brother."

I rest a sympathetic hand on his shoulder, and for his sake, and mine, I change the subject. "So, how do you feel about meeting Utah's enforcer?" I can't help the roll of my eyes.

"Yeah, what about that?" Salem gives a quick grin. "Think I might need to see what she's made of."

Good luck with that. From what Dart had said, even Blade, the fearsome enforcer from Tucson, hadn't seemed to want to push his chances. It might prove entertaining to watch Salem go up against her. I'm reserving judgement as to who my money would be on.

I slide my bike key out of my cut and bounce it in my hand. "I'm going for a ride. Need to get some breeze on my face."

"Yeah?" Salem gives a snort. "As if I don't know where you're going."

Unable to tell him he's wrong, I ignore his comment instead. Mary's good for me. Somehow being in her presence soothes my soul, and I'll be damned if I don't need some calming down now.

"I'll expect Wrangler back soon." Salem salutes me with a smirk and walks off.

Fuck but it's good to be back riding my baby. She, too, tends to have the effect of calming me. I frown as I approach, seeing the rain marks on the tank. Since the prospects had been tied up on other duties, she hasn't had a proper polish to clean her up. Taking a rag, I do my best to get the worst off, contemplating only for a moment whether to stay here with her and do a proper job, or, to do what my heart is telling me, and go see Mary.

Mary's like a magnet drawing me, and I've no idea why. No woman has ever affected me like her. Is she still in the friendzone, or would I like to explore deeper? Maybe, possibly. For the first time in ages, my dick says it's ready. Just thinking of her has me adjusting myself in my pants.

But what about her? She's a respectable lady. What would she want with a biker like me? A short ride on the wild side? I can't see anything else between us working out.

Maybe I should stay away. Wrangler's on his way to being patched in. Apart from his slipup with Alicia, which I won't let him forget, I trust him and will give him my vote. Knowing a man learns from his mistakes, I doubt anyone would be better to leave protecting the women. I don't *need* to go.

I realise as my leg seems to work of its own accord, stepping astride my bike, it's not a need, but it is a want. If I can't spend the night choking the truth out of Devon, the only way to settle the unease inside me is to go see *her*. There's no point fighting it.

The rain's long gone, and the late afternoon sun is warming when it lands on my face. The sky has become an endless sea of blue once again—a perfect time of day for riding. With my bandana around my face, my shades on, I slip on my riding gloves and place my helmet on my head. For a moment, as I tighten the strap, I wish for the days when I could feel the wind blowing my hair as I ride. Then, if I hadn't been wearing a lid when I'd come off my bike, it might not have been my leg that had taken the brunt of it. I could have crushed my skull.

Starting the engine, I point my bike toward the gate. It opens automatically thanks to the remote attached to my girl. Then, I head south toward the city.

The air becomes cooler as I grow closer to the ocean. I make my way through the traffic, steering clear of the touristy zones, like the zoo and SeaWorld as I'm nearing Mary's house. The nearer I get, the more my anticipation grows at seeing her again.

I'd slept with this woman last night. I'd like to sleep with her again, this time without clothes coming between us. There, I've admitted it at last. Not that it's likely to happen. She's got a kid in the house.

I park my bike in the driveway, sighing when I see no other vehicle here. *Damn.* I'd forgotten Niran had had to make do with the prospect's ride. Well, there's no way in hell I'll let the prospect ride my bike. I take out my phone and place a quick call, and of course, my answer is an affirmative.

The door opens, and Wrangler is standing there. "Grumbler." He raises his chin respectfully.

"I'm taking over from you," I tell him, noticing the gleam in his eyes as he views my baby behind me. "No fuckin' way," I growl. "Connor's going to swing by and pick you up."

"I ain't riding bitch…"

"With the fuckin' truck." As I pass him to enter the house, I slap him around the back of his head. Quite hard.

The fucker just laughs. *Must be losing my touch.*

I realise Mary's standing right behind him, her hand over her mouth as though she's trying not to laugh.

Immediately, I want to take her in my arms, nuzzle my face against her hair, and just take comfort from her. Which is weird, I'm the protector. It should be me comforting her.

"You look tired, Grumbler." Her eyes soften. "Long day?"

For a response, I simply nod.

"Come in. You look like you could do with a beer. Alicia's watching some junk on TV, just ignore her."

"Hey, Grumbler." Alicia turns as she hears her name. "I'm learning all about MCs."

What the fuck? My eyes narrow. "Whatcha watching?" I step over to the sofa and stare at the television, the characters recognisable immediately. It's fuckin' *Sons of Anarchy.*

"Aren't you too young to watch this?" Now I half turn toward Mary.

"Pah." Alicia waves her hand in dismissal. "I'll be eighteen in three months."

I suppose she's not going to change much in twelve weeks. Mary shrugs, then goes off, presumably to get my beer. "You get her into this?" I growl at the prospect.

Wrangler doesn't look contrite. "She asked me to find something about MCs."

Thinking I'll be speaking to him later, I go and sit on the chair opposite the couch, and half turn so I can watch the television. "This isn't how we roll, sweetheart." But my eyes narrow as I view the president of the fictional club, recalling in later episodes he meets his comeuppance. Maybe a bit too close to us and Snake, a prez leading a club in the wrong direction.

"What's different?"

Now that's a question, and I hesitate to reply. I can't tell her we never do the shit they're into, because during my lifetime with the Satan's Devils, I've seen and done most of it. Gun deals with the mafia are well in the past, but sure, I'd had a hand in it. The difference is, it never was a daily occurrence. MC life is about earning enough to survive and living with like-minded brothers while you're doing it. A daily routine, sometimes broken by bursts of activity where we mete out our own form of justice. The last three years have been quiet, and while it might be that I'm getting old, that's how I like it. I struggle for something to give her, words which don't show us in a bad light.

After a moment, I dredge something up. "You already know we run a number of businesses. That's how we earn our money. We're not into guns or drugs, and we don't run around shooting people just for the sake of it. We also don't openly carry, not in California." I struggle to come up with the differences.

"Sounds boring." Just like that, I'm dismissed, her attention caught by the screen once again.

Mary's hand lands on my shoulder, lingering there for a moment, then she passes me a beer. Taking it, I thank her.

"Want another, Wrangler?"

I glare at the man who shouldn't have been partaking of her hospitality. Seeing my expression, he shakes his head. "Nah, my ride should be here in a moment."

There's a shoot-'em-up battle going on. For a few minutes our attention is held by the scene playing out in front of us. Despite myself, I become as vested in the outcome as anyone else.

CHAPTER TWENTY-NINE

Mary

Wrangler was good company for Alicia. He's a good-looking guy, and I'd seen the way my daughter had been looking at him, but also noticed how he was around her. Respectful and keeping his distance. Friendly enough, but not encouraging anything. To be honest, if his presence helped take her mind off what had happened on Friday, I wasn't too upset about it. Just as long as Wrangler knew her teenage attraction didn't mean anything.

Alicia, who I normally have to prompt to be a host, couldn't do enough for him, offering to get him a beer, and even making a sandwich when his stomach had growled. I actually didn't mind the television programme she was watching. Sure, technically she's too young, but I'm not naïve enough to know this won't be the first time she's watched something with an adult rating.

More often than expected, my own eyes are drawn to the screen, wondering if this really is the kind of life Grumbler is immersed in. I'm particularly intrigued by the fictional sergeant-at-arms, even though my Grumbler is nothing like him. *My Grumbler?* The claim in my head surprises me.

Realising I couldn't sit around all day binge-watching a series, I leave them to it, and get on with the chores I'd neglected all week, and then again when I spent yesterday trying to help Alicia come to terms with what had happened. I'm just walking in with a basket of laundry, grimacing slightly when I see a sex scene going on, but having to admire the way the buttocks of the male star flex. I come to an abrupt halt.

"Do you like your girlfriends to be virgins?"

While he hadn't noticed me, I see Wrangler's eyebrows rise so high they almost meet his hairline. I'm about to step in and call this inappropriate conversation to a halt, when Wrangler's face forms a more normal expression.

"An honest answer?" When my daughter nods, he complies. "No. Never been with one, never had a yearning to. Oh, if the girl was right, I probably wouldn't mind if she was, but I'd much rather be with women who know the score." He leans forward, clasping his hands between his knees. "Look, I know what went down with Owen, and I won't say anything other than he was one-hundred-percent wrong, misleading you the way he did. But if a virgin expects a dinner, flowers, and an expensive hotel room, then most guys would probably run a mile."

"The girl wouldn't be worth it?" Alicia challenges him.

"Put it this way, I prefer my women less high maintenance." He softens his words with a wink.

Glancing at my daughter, I can see her calculating what that might mean. I put the laundry in the washer, then return to the living room, sitting on the couch beside her.

"What have I missed?" I say, brightly, turning my attention to the television. My action and words having the desired effect of bringing that particular conversation to a close.

I make some lunch, start the preparation for dinner, doing enough for three even though Wrangler can't commit to staying. The pair finish one season, then start another.

It's late afternoon when I hear the loud sound of a motor-cycle coming up the road. It seems my ears are attuned to the sound as I'm certain it signals Grumbler is about to arrive.

Wrangler goes to open the door, gesturing me back, even though I'm sure he knows who's going to be outside.

I want to laugh as I get an insight into how Grumbler got his name—the way he treats the young prospect so at odds with how gentle he is with me and Alicia. It doesn't worry me, I know it's just a way of testing Wrangler knows his place.

I stay back, listening, while he and Alicia discuss the programme she's gotten engrossed in. I think he's being careful as he's waiting for Wrangler to leave.

I'm right. As soon as the door closes behind the prospect, Grumbler gets to his feet. His eyes are on mine when he addresses my daughter.

"Got to talk to your mom, okay?"

Alicia waves her hand dismissively.

I retreat to the kitchen area, Grumbler following me.

"Any progress?" I ask quietly.

He leans back against the countertop and bows his head, then raises his eyes which I realise look weary. "You don't need to worry about Owen anymore."

Maybe it's just what we've been watching on television, but I gasp in a breath. "What have you done, Grumbler?" My voice sounds tense. Was it only this morning I told him to kill a man? That was just my mother's anger talking. I don't really want a man dead. Hurt, maybe, in jail, certainly. But not breathing? I hold my breath, hoping Grumbler hadn't taken my words at face value.

His expression hardens a little, then he shakes his head. "All you need know is that Alicia will never be seeing him again."

I jump to the only explanation I think I can accept. "He's left San Diego?"

Grumbler breathes in deeply. "Yeah."

How does he know he'll stay away? "You can't promise that. He could come back."

"He won't, baby. Believe me."

Again, the question occurs to me, what has he done? "Did you hurt him?"

Grumbler pushes away from the countertop, crowding me. I take a step back, and his chest pushes up against mine. His face is as fierce as I've ever seen it, and I realise I'm being addressed by the sergeant-at-arms. The strange thing is, it doesn't scare me.

"What he did to Alicia was the tip of the iceberg, Mary." His mouth opens and closes, then he shakes his head, as if there's more he wants to tell me.

"What do you mean?"

Grumbler rolls back his head on his shoulders, his mouth opens, then closes. When he speaks, his voice is hard. "It's club business, and you won't be told anything of it for your own safety."

"Again, what do you mean?" I bristle that he's not sharing details with me.

He sighs deeply. "If he's reported missing, if somehow Alicia's linked to him, it's best you answer with a clear conscience. That way you can't hold back anything you might know. You'll just have to accept you'll never know what's happened to him."

"You expect the cops to turn up?"

"Highly unlikely, but someone might crawl out of the woodwork to raise questions. Alicia did model with him. She might be asked what she knows."

That worries me. "What if she tells them about… Well, Friday?"

"That could have given him a good reason to get out of Dodge. It was statutory rape, however willing she was."

Pleading eyes meet mine. "Please don't ask me more, babe."

As he steps back, I take hold of his hands, turning them over carefully. Grumbler cocks an eyebrow at me. There's more, I can feel it. Things he won't tell me, things he won't share. Suddenly, I realise, I probably don't want to hear them.

"You're a good man, Grumbler. I get what you're saying, and I don't want to know. I'll just take your assurance that we'll never see him again. If he's done the same or worse with other girls before…" I pause and look up questioningly. When Grumbler gives a reluctant nod, I carry on. "I'm just glad he's gone. We can move on and pick up the pieces of our lives."

A smile curves his lips. "You're perfect, Mary. You know that?"

"Huh," I refute. "You barely know me."

"And that's something I'd like to rectify."

I regard him quizzically. "Will you ever let me get to know you? Or will everything be club business?"

"I'll tell you anything else, babe. All you got to do is ask."

He's clearly waiting so seriously for me to question him about his past. Lines are etched deep around his face, and whatever he's done today has affected him. I grin.

"Here's one for you. Do you like roast beef? And will you stay for dinner, not because you're protecting me, but because you want to stay?"

"I can't separate the two, Mary. Will never be able to. But yes, I like beef, and I'd love to stay. But," his eyes harden again, "Devon's still out there. While a visit to you seems unlikely, I need to be here to keep you safe."

"Owen wasn't able to tell you where he was? Did he help you trace the video?"

His brow creases as if sifting through what he can and can't say. "No. But we've got guys," his mouth quirks for some reason on that, "coming down from Utah tomorrow.

They're tech experts and if they can't track the video down and destroy it, nobody can."

"What are you two whispering about?"

Intent on Grumbler, I hadn't heard her switch off the television, nor approach.

"This and that," Grumbler says offhandedly. "Like what's causing those delicious aromas coming from the stove."

His observation is a signal that dinner is ready. I plate up, and we sit and eat. Instead of the back-and-forth conversation we'd had when Grumbler ate with us before, tonight we eat mainly in silence with just an odd 'please pass the this or that'. It's not awkward, but more that Grumbler seems a little lost in his head, and I'm wondering just what happened to put him there. Strangely enough, I'm more sympathetic than concerned at what he might have done. A man without a conscience I'd be more concerned about.

Alicia disappears to her room as soon as her plate is clean. Tonight, I don't have the energy to call her back. Instead, it's Grumbler who helps me clear the plates, rinsing them off and stacking them in the dishwasher. Apart from a few pleasantries such as my observation he looks quite comfortable doing this, and his response that he's not quite as helpless as he might seem. We avoid conversation again, instead working together in a companionable silence.

When we're done and the washer's doing its work, we return to the living room.

"That yours?" Grumbler points to an object that's so much part of the furniture it's normally ignored in its place in the corner.

"What? Oh, no. Alicia begged me for it for her birthday one year." I, too, stare at the guitar sitting forlorn and neglected. The only hand that touches it is mine when I dust. "When she found it wasn't easy to learn, she soon became fed up with it."

"Do you mind?" He tilts his head toward the instrument. When I frown, he elaborates, "Can I play it?"

Surprised he'd be interested in something that doesn't have two wheels, I incline my head. "Be my guest."

He stands, collects the guitar, then brings it back to his seat. He strums it once, grimacing when he realises how out of tune it is. "When were the strings last replaced?"

"Er, never?"

"Hmm."

The one thing Alicia had learned was how to tune it. I'd watched as she placed her finger on the fifth fret of one string to tune the next. As Grumbler's brow furrows in concentration, I expect him to do the same thing. Instead, he rests one ear to the body and listens intensely to the sound of each string. After a moment he strums a chord. My eyes widen, as Alicia had never managed to get such a clear tone out of it.

He seems to know what he's doing. I settle back on the couch, wondering whether he can actually play it.

Suddenly the guitar bursts into life. He plays a few riffs, his fingers flying up and down the fret board. It's magical, fascinating, particularly as he seems to lose himself. Suddenly he starts playing an intro that I recognise. It's one of the songs I often play on my phone, loving the original from when I was young, and appreciating the version he's now launched into. His foot starts to beat rhythmic time as he repeats the intro again, then, closing his eyes, he opens his mouth and he begins to sing.

"If I were a carpenter..."

Oh my God! My hand goes to my mouth in shock at his voice. It's no longer the gruff tone of a sergeant-at-arms—still deep, but melodic, almost hypnotic. I hardly dare breathe, not wanting to spoil this moment and remind him I'm there.

But he hasn't forgotten me. When he sings, *"Give me your*

tomorrows," his eyes come to mine, but he doesn't falter for an instant.

That guitar sings. The strings might be old, but the instrument doesn't care it's been sat unused for almost three years, coming to life as though saving itself for this moment. I'm lost, transported somewhere far away as he picks the intricate accompaniment to the incredible melody that's coming out of his mouth.

The volume increases. He throws in a few vocal tricks not unlike Robert Plant himself. It's as though my living room's been transformed, and I'm in the front row of a concert I've paid good money for.

I dare not breathe when the song comes to an end. He glances at me. When I give him a *carry on* gesture, he does. Song after song comes out of his mouth while his fingers keep picking those strings.

He launches into a rendition of *Roll Me Away* and I realise that's who his voice reminds me of, Bob Seger. He's only got a guitar, but somehow, he makes it work, his voice strengthening as he reaches the crescendos, his boot now stomping down hard, forming the percussion to accompany his song. His head moves, his expressive tones belt out the words taking me away, picturing the rider on the road, wishing I was the girl up behind him. *I* wouldn't have gotten too cold, and I'd have never left him.

A movement catches my eye. Looking over his head, I see the music has drawn Alicia out of her room, and she's standing wide-eyed and avidly listening. When he next reaches the end, he ruefully eyes the guitar, the last few chords sounding a little out of tune, not unexpected, given the bashing the instrument has just had.

"Said it needed new strings," he mutters, fiddling with the keys on the machine head, the action drawing my attention to his long and deft fingers once again.

Alicia comes around the couch.

"That's my guitar."

Grumbler looks up, his hand curled around the fret board. "You mind?"

"Hell no." She plonks herself down beside me, making the couch cushions bounce. "I've never heard it played properly before. I didn't even know it could sound like that. Will you teach me?"

He studies her carefully, then casts an eye my way. I know what he's thinking. A promise made by Grumbler is, I suspect, a promise that will be kept. And who knows whether we'll keep seeing each other or go on separate paths. For my part, I know I don't want to see him walk away, even when our issues with Devon are resolved. On his? I've no freaking idea. My shrug stops me from influencing what he next says.

"Sure, if you're serious. But you won't learn in a day." He's addressed her, but his gaze immediately comes back to me—an eyebrow raised in challenge. *Is this his way of saying he's not going to be walking away?* I shiver slightly, knowing it's in anticipation of the excitement a man like Grumbler could bring to my boring life. A bad boy, can I handle that? It might not have been something I anticipated in my life, but I have no doubt I want this. I'm old enough to know what I want and go after it. I won't be a hands-on mom for the rest of my days. All too soon, Alicia will strike out on her own. Why shouldn't I take something for myself?

I have to admit, Grumbler agreeing to give time to my daughter does something to me inside, remembering the man who wanted to ignore her existence and the other who wanted to walk in and take over. It's not as though he hasn't seen the worst of her, he has. He knows what to expect. That he's agreeing to help her and not running for the hills scores many points in my book.

Having been disturbed, to my dismay, he puts the guitar

aside. I swallow my regret. I could have listened to him for hours. That voice? In a womanly way it made me feel alive. The action he used on the strings made me wish it was me he was strumming instead. I feel like I'm experiencing a crush on a rock star more appropriate for someone Alicia's age. My face feels hot and I resist the desire to fan myself.

"Have you been playing long?" my daughter asks. I suspect she's wondering how long it will take to match his proficiency.

"Got my first guitar when I was twelve," he answers.

"You should be in a band."

His mouth quirks at her statement, then he shakes his head. "Bit past it now, but I was, once."

Alicia bounces on her seat. "What band? Would I have heard of you?"

"Nah, we only played local clubs, and that was well before you were born." His eyes glaze as he thinks back, then his mouth twists, as though his memories have turned dark. "We were approached to go into a recording studio. Yeah, we were good." He shudders slightly as he comes back to himself. "But it was a dream, that's all it was."

I'm curious. "What happened? Why didn't you make a record?"

His expression hardens, and just when I think he's going to clam up, he looks at Alicia. "I didn't listen to my mom. She took a dislike to our bass player, but I couldn't see why. He was hip," he pauses, seeing her not understand, "with it. A man, well, a kid really, you'd look up to and admire. He always seemed to have it together. I thought that was what she didn't like. I was eighteen, he was twenty. At that age, two years is like a mile."

Giving a wistful look toward the guitar, he brings his attention back to us. "Mom wanted me to get a proper job. I got by on the shit that we earned playing in the band. It wasn't bad bread for a man my age. One night, after a gig, we were coming out of a club. Rod, the bass player, well, he must have seen something I hadn't. Anyway, he passes me his guitar case, said he had somewhere to be, and would I get it back to the van. I agreed, of course, saw nothing wrong in it. He left. I walked around the back of the club where I was jumped by two cops."

Suspecting I know where this is going, I ask, "What was in the case?"

Grumbler doesn't hesitate. "Coke. More than one man needed, but not enough to seriously deal."

"Did you tell them the case wasn't yours?" Alicia's perched on the edge of her seat, her fingertips at her mouth.

He regards her for a moment. "Didn't matter. I was in possession."

"You were arrested?"

He shakes his head. "One of the cops, he was a friend, a *very* good friend of my mother's, if you get what I mean. He'd been inside watching the show. He knew it wasn't mine as it was a bass guitar. Tried to get me to tell them whose it was, they needed me to say it. But you don't rat on a friend, you know?"

"Did you go to prison?" Alicia's eyes are wide.

"Nah. That's when I was given the choice of a trip to the cells or to the recruiting office. He didn't do that for me, of course, he did it for my mother. Still, he gave me the choice, and I chose the latter."

"And the band? Did they split up?"

Grumbler half smiles. "See? That's when I found what true friends are. Rod hadn't betrayed me, he'd betrayed us all. There wasn't going to be a place for him anymore. Instead of finding two new members, they broke up the band. Fagan continued playing drums, but not with the calibre of bands like ours had been. Jon Boy left to do some sessions down in LA."

Jon Boy, I grin to myself. He's the same age as me, but he's not lost his full handle along the way.

"But you still play?" I ask. It's obvious. You don't pick up a guitar after forty years and remember the skills.

"Sure, but for myself. Got a couple of guitars back at my place."

"At the club?"

"Nah. I got a house. Not somewhere I really go, just when I need space to unwind. That's when I play."

That's what he was doing tonight. The music hadn't been for my benefit, but for his. I'm not complaining.

"Do you ever see the men in the band?"

I nod. "Yeah. A few years back, I bumped into Fagan. He said Jon Boy was local, and we got together to jam. They'd met up with a guy, Kurt, who joined us on bass. I meet up with them from time to time."

Alicia's attention span is limited. Seeing the end to the sharing has passed, she turns to me. "Got anything to eat, Mom?"

"In the cupboard, I'm sure."

When she goes, I stand and go toward Grumbler, placing my hand on his shoulder, saying quietly, "I bet you got all the girls with a voice and talent like that."

He chuckles softly. "That would be telling." His eyes sharpen and seem to pierce me. "What I want to know, is whether I've still got what it takes?"

It's my turn to chuckle, well, it's more of a giggle. "Seems you have, old man. Seems you have." I wink at him.

"Christ woman." He grabs hold of my hand. "It's a fuckin' shame you've got a teenage daughter living here."

Alicia walks back into view carrying a slice of leftover pizza, a large portion of which is in her mouth. With the result, I have to ask her to repeat what she just said.

"I asked if Grumbler's going to sleep in your bed again tonight."

How the hell did she know that he had? I don't deny it. "The couch is far too small for him." I wave to indicate his size. "We're adults. Nothing happened."

She nods. "I noticed he wasn't on the couch when I got up to get some water, but I know there's nothing to worry about. You're far too old, not like Marisa's parents. She has to wear earplugs to bed at night."

My mouth opens and shuts. Worried, I glance at Grumbler but he's staring up at the ceiling, his body vibrating slightly as though he's trying hard not to laugh.

"Anyway, I'm off to bed. Night."

Eventually, Grumbler lowers his chin and his gaze captures mine. Smirking, broadly, he murmurs, "Is it bad that I kinda want to prove her wrong?"

Would Grumbler make me scream? I gaze at his bare arms covered in tattoos, suddenly having the urge to see if he's got them elsewhere. I can tell he's muscular but lean by the way his t-shirt clings. His beard, hell. I'd always wanted Dave to grow one, but he never had. It's not bushy, but short and neatly trimmed. Then there are his eyes. When I'm subjected to the full force of his orbs staring into mine, it's like I'm being pierced by laser beams. I know, without even experiencing it, that sex with Grumbler would be the real deal. He'd be focused on me completely.

Am I woman enough to survive?

"We can't." I'd scar my daughter forever. It's bad enough she knows we've shared the same bed.

CHAPTER THIRTY

Grumbler

oo old are we?

Maybe I am. But not Mary. To me she's a woman in her prime. She makes me feel youthful, almost a teen. The thought of being naked with her makes my cock harden until it feels like a rod of steel, pulsing almost painfully as precum leaks out, making my boxer shorts sticky. I haven't had this strong a reaction to a woman in years.

But her daughter is in the next room. I should let her sleep, just as I had last night. Perhaps it's because I know a sexual release would ease the soul deep ache inside me, wash the horrors of the day away. But not with anyone, only with her. I suspect, losing myself in her would save me. Selfish? Maybe.

How quiet could Mary be?

I'm driven to find out. Driven to see if I can make this woman cover her mouth to smother her screams. I have no doubt she'll be crying out. I have confidence in my skills, and just like playing the guitar, doubt I've forgotten them. Over the years, I've mapped every part of a woman's anatomy, know all the various pleasure points and what buttons to push.

I'd picked up the guitar for myself, using, as I so often

have, music to quiet the demons in my head. I'd played only for me at first, then found I was playing for her instead. It had been impossible to miss the effect it had on her, the way she'd so delightfully flushed when she watched my musician's fingers moving so fast, plucking at those strings in the way I've perfected in more than four decades. I'd suppressed my smirk, but her reaction had taken me back to those long-ago days when I'd been on stage, thrusting my hips, playing my guitar slung low, knowing many of the girls were wishing it was them my fingers were strumming instead. Even as a teen I was never short of someone to warm my bed, or allow me a quickie against a back wall of whatever club we were playing in. Of course, I allowed my fingers to do the work first, only then giving them my dick and finding my own pleasure. A woman, in my book, *always* comes first.

Then I'd seen the horror of life when I had served. I grew up, I had to. Learned there was more to life than following my dreams and getting off, that there was a real world and I had to join it. My guitar lay forgotten, untouched in its case for many years. I joined the MC, prospected, worked my fucking socks off to earn my patch. I threw myself into the life and the brotherhood, and found a new reason for living, my cherished bike. For years, she'd been my sole mistress, but my music still called.

When I bought my house, well, it seemed the adult thing to do and preparation for a time I might not be able to ride, and hence not be in the MC any longer, I got my guitar out of storage. I was rusty at first, but it soon came back, and so did the pleasure I got from playing music.

Alicia said I should be in a band. I'm far too old to strut my stuff on stage now, but about the time the business blew up with Snake in the club, meeting Fagan had come at the right time. Jamming had given me an outlet, a way to escape from the other crap in my head. I still joined them occasionally, just playing for ourselves. Both had tried to make it in the music business for a while, but never made their mark. Money had to be earned, so they went citizen ways. Jon Boy was a carpenter, and a good one. I'd gotten him in to do much-needed work at my house. Fagan? Well he was a truck driver.

My MC brothers have no inkling what I do on those rare evenings I meet up with them, and recently with Kurt, another old-timer who's a fuckin' good bassist. It's a secret I keep for myself. But now I feel my past slamming into my future, knowing I'd like Mary to come see us rehearse, see me play for real on one of my electric guitars and not an acoustic.

When Alicia had asked me to teach her, I knew if I said yes, I'd be making a commitment. She's had too many broken promises for me to add one more. It means, even after we've destroyed the evidence of what Owen had done, and Devon is taken out of the picture, Mary and Alicia will still be in my life.

I find the thought isn't at all unappealing. Though previously I had doubts, maybe I could find time for the right woman in my life. Maybe even have her riding up behind me on my baby. What previously had been a sacrilegious thought, I can see me adding a pillion seat, even a sissy bar to keep Mary safe.

Perhaps she wouldn't want to ride with me?

I suspect that she will. Mary's got a devil streak in her. I don't know how, but I'm sure of that.

Suddenly I realise while I've been lost in my reverie, Mary's been going through her nightly routine, taking out her glass and my empty bottle, checking the windows are locked and that the alarm on the door is set.

She pats me on the shoulder, saying softly, "Come in when you're ready."

I stay where I am, giving her time to get decent. Or at least, how she expects she'll be spending the night. My plan is to get her naked, but I know she's got to be at ease first.

When I think I've given her long enough, I get up from the chair, move the guitar from the place where I left it and settle it safely back on its stand. Then, I switch off the light and proceed to her bedroom, tossing her a wink before I enter her bathroom and do what a man does before going to bed. I take off my t-shirt and toss it onto her hamper, just leaving it there ready for the morning. Then, I replace my cut over my bare shoulders. I might be getting an old man's body, but I work out, particularly since my accident, and know I still look fit. I've learned a thing or two over the years that two things can do it for a woman.

She's already seen the tattoos on my arms so she's not going to freak out at the rest of my ink. Now she'll see them framed in all their glory, and covered by my cut with the sergeant-at-arms patch in pride of place, shows me off nicely.

As a touching finish, I unbutton the top two buttons on my jeans, allowing them to settle on my hips, drawing attention to the defined V I've got going for me. Yeah, I can be a sneaky fucker at times.

Of course, she might just roll over and go to sleep, but I've a sneaking suspicion my looks will do it for me. I'm going to have Mary tonight, fuck that her daughter's sleeping nearby, and she'll just have to be quiet.

I gaze in the mirror, for a moment seeing in my reflection myself as a younger man, then the image morphs slowly into the man I am today. I realise my accident had caused me to accept my mortality. I'm lucky to be alive to ride another day, but the damage to my leg had hit me hard. Having to depend on others when I was laid up in hospital, then at the compound when I was unable to climb stairs by myself, it had made me feel weak and helpless. It had given me insight into the years ahead and had made me feel old.

I don't feel old with Mary. It's as though she's breathed life back into my veins. I don't need Viagra when she's around. She's special, good for me, now I've just got to keep her. Patch her and make her mine.

Really?

I raise my chin at my reflection and ask, *why the hell not?*

Slowly a grin covers my face. You never achieve anything unless you try.

I open the door and enter the room lit only by a bedside lamp on the side of the bed I slept on last night. *My side.* The door closes behind me with an audible click. I wait.

It takes a moment, but slowly she turns. The light illuminates me as though I'm standing in a spotlight. When her eyes take me in, her tongue licks her lips, then her mouth opens forming an O. It closes again and she swallows. Her gaze which had rested on my tattooed chest sinks lower, focusing on the V leading down. Suddenly her examination falters, and her eyes rise to meet mine.

The intensity of my stare makes her swallow again.

"What are you wearing?" I ask, my voice husky and low.

"Er, t-shirt and sleep pants."

Too much. "Take them off, now," I command, using my most dominant tone.

"Oh, er…" She wants to, but she hesitates. "Alicia's in the next room."

"We'll just have to be quiet." If I was in the brig, my captive would know I'm not out to take prisoners.

"Grumbler, I…" She waves her hand, indicating my body. "You're fit as hell, and I'm…"

Words aren't going to cut it. I stalk her, moving forward to the bed. Placing my good knee on it first, I slide my less amenable leg after it, moving up until I'm situated astride her legs.

"Whatever you are, I guarantee, I'm going to like it."

She snorts. "I'm a middle-aged woman. I've had a kid."

Leaning forward I speak into her ear, "I don't fuckin' care."

"The girls at your club, I can't compete."

"No competition, babe. I don't want young in my bed. I should be asking you why you want an old man like me. If, indeed, you do want me?" A flicker of doubt comes into my head.

"You're not old. You're well matured."

I bark a quiet laugh. She's made me sound like a piece of cheese. "Back at ya, babe. You think I'm going to run from the marks life has left on you? Fuck, babe. That's more of a turn-on than any young girl." Reaching forward, I trace the laughter lines around her eyes. "These here? They show me you've lived, and that's all any other marks will show. You're fuckin' beautiful, Mary, inside and out. I want to see all of you. Now." For encouragement, I slide down the sheet.

She bites her lip, then comes to a decision. "Don't say I didn't warn you."

And fuck me, her hands go to her hem and she lifts her shoulder off the bed and pulls that shirt right over her head. I actually admire the strength in her abs that I know it takes to do that. Her old? I only hope I can keep up.

As her tits come into view, I feast my eyes on them. I already knew what to expect as I may have sneaked a few looks at them, albeit they'd been hidden by her clothing. They're not small, not overly large, not perky like a girl's, but teardrop shaped like those of a woman. Soft pillows I can't wait to get my hands on. Her nipples are large, whether naturally, or because they've nourished a kid, I have no idea. Beneath my gaze, they harden.

"Fuckin' gorgeous," I tell her.

Her stomach is rounded, and it tempts me to see more. I place my first fingers and thumbs inside the waistband of her sleep pants and question her with my eyes.

She looks to the side, delightfully shy. I take it as permission, easing her pants down her legs, shuffling backward at the same time. She's wearing pretty panties. For now, I leave those on. When the offending item that hid her from my sight is discarded, I ease back up the bed again, pausing to put my nose against her mound and inhale deeply.

"Fuck, you smell good." I thought my cock was already as hard as it could be. What do I know? It seems not.

"Grumbler!"

"Shush," I admonish her for raising her voice. "We've got to be quiet," I remind her, grinning broadly that I made her forget.

"Are you going to get naked now?"

"Nah." If I let my dick out from its confines, it will act like a heat-seeking missile to get inside her. I know my limitations. I'll only be able to go once tonight. Once I've come, for me it will be game over. I want to stretch this out, make it last. "Right now, this is about you, sweetheart."

I go back to my intense scrutiny of her again, but she shudders, and looking into her face, I see a fleeting indecision come over her.

"Should we be doing this?"

It's easy to read her, easy to see she's worried this is just about sex and relieving her newly found attraction to me, and mine for her. She's wrong, *she's mine*. She doesn't know it yet. I need to convince her. This isn't getting off, scratching a mutual itch. No, I'm going to be making love to her, banishing all other men who've been inside her.

On hands and knees, I move up the bed, hovering with my mouth over hers. Then I lower my head gently letting our lips meet. Softly, I *lovingly* start to move them. She opens for me. I deepen the kiss, resting my weight on one hand and tangling the other into her hair. I control the kiss but am careful not to ravish her.

Fuck but it's good. I've never kissed a woman so carefully before. With the whores a kiss is unexpected, with a civilian it's something they expect. But now, with my mouth, I'm worshipping her, thanking whatever deity might exist for giving me this chance. I won't be letting her go. A man my age doesn't look a gift horse, or woman, in the mouth.

She gives a little moan, pressing her mouth firmer against mine. I tighten my grip in her hair and she moans again. Guess my little vixen likes a man who takes control. Well, I've absolutely no problem with that.

Without breaking our contact, I shift until I can lie on my side, the arm I'm lying on is the one I can leave in her hair. Thanking the deity again that I'm ambidextrous, I move my now free hand, pausing to touch the softness of her breasts, then taking a moment to tease those nipples.

My mouth on hers smothers her moans, for which I'm thankful. God forbid we disturb Alicia tonight. Then, my hand continues its downward journey, reaching under her panties, and easing inside. I flick her clitoris, feel her jump, then continue on, easing my fingers between her folds. She's slick with her own desire. I can easily slip two fingers inside her.

I start to explore, curling my fingers around, knowing I reach the right spot when her eyes open in astonishment. *Hmm, seems no one's found that before.* My left hand is positioned as if playing an upside-down guitar. I press my thumb firmly on her clit, and strum with my fingers.

Hell, she must be turned on, or desperate, or maybe it's my technique, but hell, she tightens, her internal muscles clenching down on my fingers, playing havoc with my dick who's throbbing with jealousy. I press my mouth down more firmly, smothering her cries as her body convulses. Yup. This old man has still got it.

While her body is still wracked with aftershocks, I bring

her down gently, extending her pleasure for as long as I can before she slumps against me.

Only now do I raise my mouth from hers. Staring into her eyes, I see her looking at me in amazement. It was good for her, her body's reaction doesn't lie. I'm not looking for praise, I'm just glad I could give her that. I smile down at her.

"That… That was better than my vibrator."

I snort. Loudly.

"Grumbler, *shush.*"

"Babe, she'll just think I'm snoring."

She stuffs her hand against her mouth, and her body vibrates with laughter. "*Do* you snore?"

"How the fuck would I know?"

A considering look, then she says, "Don't you often sleep with anyone?"

"Maybe I have," I frown, trying to remember. Normally I'm a love-'em-and-go man. I've never been one for intimacy. Mary's changed me. Tonight, even if I wasn't here for her protection, there's nowhere I'd rather be. "Fuck, Mary, with you, it's just different."

She analyses my face for a moment before giving a small nod. Then she smiles. "I'm up for another round. This time, I want you inside me."

"Yeah?" I seem to have a frog in my throat, my voice sounds so husky.

"Yeah."

"I'm clean, babe. Haven't been with anyone after I came off my bike. Got tested for everything in the hospital."

"I'm clean too," she tells me. "I got tested after the last man I was with out of caution and haven't been with anyone since."

I take the fingers that were so recently giving her pleasure and suck her essence from them. She tastes as good as I'd thought, and my dick twitches, giving me it's approval. My fingers, now wet with my saliva, I lightly circle her nipples, then pinch them. She gasps, and her face flushes.

"You like?"

"It seems I do."

I'm cataloguing everything, for once wanting to learn everything about the woman beneath me.

"I'm wet."

Her words make me grin. "Already know that, darlin'."

"I'm ready."

Torn between playing with my new toys or getting down to business, I decide I'll be back here tomorrow and can pay more attention to her breasts than I have tonight. Easing myself off the bed, I slide off my cut and place it neatly on a chair, then I take out my wallet and keys and put them next to the bed. Then, seeing her eyes on me, I unbutton my jeans, and take off them and my boxers in one go, relishing the sight of her eyes almost popping out of her head. What can I say? I'm tall, and my dick is in good proportion to my size.

She's giving me a *come here* gesture, but I need to stay away. Once she gets those hands on me, I'm not going to be able to last, and then I know I won't get it up again. While I hate to disappoint a woman, I ignore her nonverbal pleas, instead picking up my wallet and extracting the condom I know I'll find there. I've never gone unprepared in my life, despite not recently having any expectations of using it.

I make a show of putting it on, rolling it down slowly as though demonstrating my length.

For a second, I wonder whether my less-than-perfect leg is going to prevent me performing at my best, not having fucked since before the accident, but hell, I've got to try it sometime. Mary won't mind, she's not to know how I was before.

Putting my nerves behind me, I approach her as I had earlier, slowly, and with a determined expression in my eyes.

"You've got to be quiet," I remind her.

CHAPTER THIRTY-ONE

Mary

"You've got to be quiet."

As if I needed the reminder. Alicia's *hopefully* asleep in the next room, but I couldn't say no if I wanted to. Already he's made me feel so good, the most powerful orgasm ever, and I want to see what the rest of his body can do. He might be dominant, but also playful. It makes me want to let the lighter side out of me too.

"You think you're going to make me scream?" I tease him.

"I think I already did," he boasts, but quite rightly. "But you ain't seen nothing yet, babe."

"No?" Curving, my lips form a challenging grin.

Already he's lowering himself onto the bed and pushing my legs apart. Masterfully manoeuvring my knees until they're bent and form a cradle for him. He positions my hips just where he wants them, then, unexpectedly leans forward and steals another kiss from my lips. He leaves his mouth there, connecting us, while I feel a pressure down below.

His cock is long, not too thick, but still it's been a while for me, and I appreciate that he's taking it slow. He raises his head for a moment, and his jaw tightens as he pushes inside.

He doesn't neglect checking in. "You doing okay, babe?"

My reassurance is fast, though breathy. "I'm fine. You're big."

He glances down with a quick grin. "Complaining already?"

I'm about to answer, but he thrusts again, moving over that place he found earlier with his fingers. When he sees the look in my eyes, he does it again. Automatically my body pushes downward, allowing him to gain more ground. Although he's not completely seated, he starts pulling out and pushing back in. Each time he does, sensations flood through me. A fleeting thought crosses my mind that even with Dave I never experienced such pleasures before. Intercourse, for me, was more about the closeness, penetrative sex for him more than me. Then I rid my head of the traitorous thought and give way to the sensations provided by the current man in my bed. Dave is long dead, and there's no room for him here.

While ramping up my own arousal to hitherto unattained levels, Grumbler slowly works all of himself in until he's fully seated.

"If you want more, I ain't got it," he whispers into my ear.

"That's enough, I think," I gasp back, thankful that I've taken all of him.

Then he starts to move.

Oh my God. My mind goes blank and I can think of nothing but the feelings he's evoking in me. This man has moves I've never known could exist. I feel alive in ways I never have, my body showing me it's capable of more than I ever expected. My muscles tighten and my skin is covered in a sheen of sweat. Why, I don't know, he's doing all the work.

He's fully invested, swivelling his hips, grabbing one of my legs and holding it, opening me to him even more. Each time he pushes in, he finds that special spot.

My reactions are purely automatic, my body under his sole

control and none of mine anymore. Little shudders wrack through me and to my surprise, I find my breathing stalls as I feel another orgasm come upon me.

"That's right, babe. Come for me. Come all over my fuckin' dick." Grumbler's voice is hoarse, as if he's been holding himself back.

When I have no alternative but to obey, I feel his hand clamp over my mouth. I need it, I can't prevent the scream that comes unbidden, which he had the forethought to muffle. I see stars. Hell, I think I visit another universe for a brief space of time. To come with a man inside me without external stimulation at all? Unheard of. To come so hard? Another freaking first. I hope Grumbler knows this isn't a one-off as I'll want to do that again and again. I doubt I'll ever get tired of it.

I'm vaguely aware he's been grunting, presumably enjoying his own release. It's then I realise I'm having difficulty getting air into my lungs. I lick his hand as my chest heaves, a reminder I'm restricted to only breathing through my nose. He lifts his meaty paw away, allowing me to take in a huge gasp of air. When I open my eyes, he's grinning down at me.

"Fuck, you nearly bit me trying to scream." He shakes out his hand as if proving it.

"I don't scream," I tell him primly, but I can't keep the twinkle out of my eye.

"Woman, you're a fuckin' liar." He bends his head to kiss me, then, to let me catch my breath and, I suspect to get his back as well, he rests his head against my forehead.

Christ, but he got me soaking. I can feel a wet spot slowly cooling beneath me on the bed.

"I'll go get rid of the evidence. I'll be right back."

It's a necessary but not particularly romantic chore. The benefit of condoms, however, is that they make less mess, or less for a woman to clean up. But still, I could do with a wipe, and I'm too sated to leave the bed right now.

"Could you bring me a washcloth back?"

"Sure," he winks, "I'll clean you up."

I'm forty-seven, not a young girl with starry-eyed dreams. Practicalities don't get me embarrassed, I realise, as he slides off the bed. As he stands, a little shakily I'm pleased to note, the reason why I feel so uncomfortable becomes clear.

Grumbler notices the same time as I do and stares down in consternation at his limp dick trying to hide in its broken latex cocoon.

He rolls his head back. "Fuck, babe, I'm sorry."

Natural horror of the consequences run through my head. But there won't be any implications, will there? Sure, I've not started the menopause as yet, but I'm forty-seven for God's sake, and Grumbler's ten years older. Though I have heard men are fertile decades later, women, luckily, are not. No, we're safe. Not a chance.

"Just how long has that condom been in your wallet, Grumbler?" He'd said he hadn't had sex in a while. Unless he came prepared tonight, which I doubt. It was his voice and his masterful demonstration of his guitar playing skills that had gotten my defences down, despite my daughter sleeping next door.

"Not long," he tells me.

I bristle slightly. "Was this your plan all along? To get me into bed?"

"No, no," he refutes fast. "I always have one in my wallet. It's a habit since I was a teen. A boy scout always likes to be prepared."

I doubt he was ever a boy scout, but I let that pass, as suspicion dawns on me. "When did you put it in there, then?"

Grumbler's brow furrows, then his eyes open wide. "I've not fucked since before the accident..." He breaks off, goes to the foil wrapper that's discarded by the side of the bed, picks it up, and gets a pair of glasses out of his cut. He stares down for a moment, then says, "Fuck." His gaze comes to me, and the heel of his hand hits his forehead. "How could I be so fucking stupid? This thing's well out of date."

"It's alright," I start. "I doubt I can get pregnant."

"You sure of that?" he asks.

"It's really unlikely, isn't it?"

He stares for a moment, then chuckles. "With my lifestyle, yes. Probably fried my swimmers years ago with the heat from my engine. Look, I'll just go get cleaned up. I'll bring back a cloth."

He disappears into the bathroom. When he's gone for a few minutes, I suspect he's taking some time to think, as I do myself. *It's impossible, isn't it? But what if it's not? How can I, at my age, have a baby and bring up a kid?* Grumbler wouldn't want a child, that's for sure. Technically, he'd be old enough to be its great-grandfather.

It's ten minutes later as told by my bedside clock when he returns with the promised washcloth and, after cleaning me up, disappears yet again. This time, he's back immediately. He climbs into his side of the bed, lies back, then holds out his arm in invitation.

I hesitate just for a moment, then snuggle into him. He smells wood-smoky—there's a background tinge of cigarette, all wrapped up in the masculine pheromones of sweat and sex. The combination is heady, just because it's him.

"If you're worried there could be an outcome of tonight, there's the morning-after pill. I could go and get it for you."

"You want me to take it, in case?"

Grumbler shifts me until I'm half lying on him. "Been thinking, babe. And not just now. Nah, thoughts have been creeping up on me. I never wanted an old lady, couldn't see the point. Now I know it was just because I hadn't met the right woman as yet. I'd decided earlier that you were mine, and that I was going to claim you."

"You decided, huh?" I should be annoyed, but the way he's said it makes me feel warm and protected instead, and my objections are more for show than genuine.

"I decided. Yes." He's unrepentant.

"Because I let you into my bed?"

He sniggers. "Nope. Plenty of women would do that. But not many would talk to me, or that I'd like it when they did. We've got a good friendship going, babe, from the day we first met. Told myself I came here to find out details on the photographer so I could track him down, when I hadn't even explored other options. If I'm truthful, I jumped at the chance to see you again even if I hadn't admitted that to myself."

He's right. We have been friends. Not for long, but long enough that I know we do click. The way he is with Alicia, had impressed me. He's shown a patience with her that I wouldn't have expected, and I can't forget he was the one she'd run to when she couldn't face me.

"I'm uncertain what you're saying." He said claimed, but what meaning does that have for him?

"That you're my ol' lady. In my world, that's as good as being my wife."

"Did we get married? I don't remember it."

"Funny," he replies. "But yeah, I'd put a ring on your finger, if that's what you need. It's happened fast, but life's too short not to go after what you want. And, I decided that before I came to your bed, darlin'. Before I'd even tried you out." He winks.

I bat at him with my hand. "Before?"

"Before I knew we were more than compatible in bed. Before, well, before my carelessness left us with possible consequences. You asked me if I wanted you to make sure there were no ramifications from tonight? Surprised the heck out of myself when I came down on the side of chance. Might be the lifestyle I lead, living on the edge, but hell, if you're pregnant, it is what it is. Never expected to have kids, never was against the idea either. It just never came up. You pregnant? Well, I'm not sure it's for the best. I've got my best years behind me, and, while I'm too much of a gentleman to mention your age, it would take a toll on your body. So, I think it's for you to make the choice, and I'll be right here by your side whatever you choose. And here for a baby, if one exists."

"It's highly unlikely, Grumbler." A baby? At my age? Grumbler's right. It would take a toll on my body and for a very long time. Having a baby ties you down. "Kids aren't easy, Grumbler. They're hard work. They—"

"Shit, puke, scream, and grow into teenagers. Yeah, I can guess. But if I have to, I reckon I could change a diaper. I'm used to handling shit." He nuzzles the top of my head.

He's leaving the decision to me. I couldn't ask for more. But just how involved would he want to be with a baby? Would I end up on my own when Grumbler found it too hard to deal with? I should be looking forward to the time when any infant in my future was my grandkid, not another child I'd birthed. Could I do it?

"I'd like to sleep on it," I finally decide. "It's a lot to process. If I don't take the pill, I'll need to speak to a doctor, find out what's best."

"If you want, I'll go with you."

"You will?"

"Of fuckin' course." His tone questions how I could think anything else. "I'll be with you, whether there's something to concern us or not. If you're mine, babe, that's it. I'm yours for life."

I still can't believe how I got so lucky. How did I get this big bad biker in my life? Do I want to commit to him? What does that mean?

"Where does this leave Alicia?"

He draws in a breath. "With us, of course. I suppose I'll have to ask her permission if we're going to tie the knot, but I'll find some way to persuade her. Look, babe, I know she's your girl. I can't step in and be her father, but I can be a man in her life. Heard some shit about stepdads, but the man who ended with my mom wasn't so bad. Didn't give a damn at the time, but he did get me out of a fix."

"The cop? What happened to him?"

"They married shortly after I joined up. Got himself killed on active duty while I was in the military."

"Your mom?"

"She found some other sucker to marry her soon after his death. He hated bikers. She took his side, and well, I never saw her again. She was happy in her new life and didn't want me rocking the boat. She died a few years back. I went to the funeral, only to be asked why I'd fuckin' bothered, and that she'd left nothing for me. As if I wanted anything."

"Who the hell said that?"

"Her latest husband and my brother. Well, we've never been close. I think he resented that he still remained in contact with her, while I had moved on. He got caught in the role of dutiful son, and I suspect got roped into paying money to her. If she'd left anything, he was entitled to it."

My heart breaks for him and how it seems like he didn't have a loving family to fall back on. No wonder he thinks so much of his MC. "Sometimes when we've seen the worst, it makes us want to do better ourselves."

"You got that straight, babe. Which is why I won't be introducing myself to Alicia as a stepdad. She wants a relationship, it's up to her."

I yawn, loudly.

"Babe, go to sleep. One thing about problems, they'll still be here tomorrow."

And he, in turn, has got that right.

How is it that men, whatever's on their mind, seem able to go straight to sleep by the time the light is switched off?

The one good thing is—I find as I can't turn the thoughts off in my head—he doesn't snore.

CHAPTER THIRTY-TWO

Grumbler

It was all systems go in the Styles' household when I woke up alone this morning. Despite me normally being a light sleeper, Mary had managed to vacate the bed without me knowing. The sounds reaching me are that of mother and daughter already about and talking.

I grab the clothes I was wearing last night and slide into them. Finally, I put on my cut and replace my phone and my wallet, the latter with its traitorous contents, back in my pocket. Then, finger brushing my short hair, I leave the bedroom.

"Breakfast?" Mary asks, cheerily. "Not that it's much. We make do with toast or cereal in the mornings."

"Toast is fine." My eyes narrow as I see Alicia wearing a cheeky grin and holding out her hand to me.

"What?" I shake my head in confusion, sure that I must have missed something.

"Money," Alicia taps the palm of her hand. "To buy some earplugs."

"Alicia!" Mary's eyes about fill her face having widened so completely.

We'd been quiet, I think. Then I fall back on my Satan's Devils' spiel where we never deny or confirm a thing. "You didn't hear anything." I scoff.

Shrewd teenage eyes look at me, then she giggles. "That's not telling me anything."

But I do take out my wallet, extract a twenty and pass it to her.

"Grumbler," Mary squeaks. "You don't have to give her money."

"I know I don't," I reply, winking at Alicia. "But the kid could do with a treat. Buy some donuts or something." Pausing, I add, "Or, earplugs." I wink at the girl who seems quite cheery this morning. It seems if she'd known we had done the deed, it didn't bother her.

"You like school?" I pull out a stool and perch on it.

"Well, school's alright. I want to catch up with Marisa. I've missed her this weekend."

She wouldn't have missed her if she'd been where she'd said on Friday night, but I keep that to myself. Mary catches my eye, and I suspect she's thinking the very same thing.

A horn beeping outside tells me the prospect I'd summoned has arrived.

"If you're not going to keep your lift waiting, you better get a move on," Mary warns her.

Alicia runs to the window and looks outside, then turns, looking disappointed. "He's got a truck."

As Mary rolls her eyes, I chuckle. It's not difficult to see Alicia was hoping to turn up at school on the back of the prospect's bike.

The next few minutes are taken up with Mary making sure the kid has everything. Turns out she's forgotten half her stuff, and the pair of them rush to locate it. Then, just as she's about to disappear through the door, Alicia runs back to me and gives me an unexpected hug. After an awkward pause, I hug her back.

"I like you for Mom," she whispers in my ear. "So I might invest in earplugs."

I bat her off, trying not to laugh, in case I give the words spoken in confidence away. "Go get some learning, kid."

Then I hear a giggle, followed by a slam of the front door. Now it's just me and Mary.

Watching her go about her morning routine, stacking the dishwasher and wiping down the surfaces, I breathe deeply. I'm in unchartered territory here. *What do you say to a woman you might have made pregnant?* In nearly six decades, I haven't had to face up to anything of its like.

Do I mention it? Avoid the subject?

Mary, too, seems undecided. But when she picks up her purse, grabs the keys from the table by the door, it's clear she doesn't want to say anything.

"I've got to go, Grumbler, else I'll be late."

Taking a last swig of my coffee I stand, go rinse my cup, then pat my pockets to make sure I've got everything. "Me too, babe. But I'll be back tonight. There may be an update about the video."

For a second, I'm not sure if she'll agree. Clearly, she's warring within herself between finding out if that tape isn't going to bite Alicia on the ass and moving into dangerous territory with me.

Then she comes to a decision. "We only have takeout during the week, but if you want to eat with us…?"

While thinking how domesticated it all seems, I nod. "Takeout is fine with me." I don't say the words, *we need to talk,* but my eyes must signal it anyway. I leave her with just one thought. "I'm all in, babe. I mean it." I told her I'd claimed her, but I'm not sure my words have sunk in.

Her eyes meet mine briefly, then, the hustle and bustle of

the morning comes to a close when she leaves the front door unlocked, trusting me to close up behind her. She goes to her car and opens the driver's side door. I've left the stool, followed her out and am now beside her.

"Think you've forgotten something, babe." At her scrunched brow, I add, "Want your lips."

She glances around as if the neighbours are all choosing that moment to peer through the curtains. But I'm not letting her get away without reminding her, she belongs to me. Which I do, thoroughly. Her mouth looks thoroughly ravished when I've finished.

"Good morning," I tell her, as I pat her butt and hold open the car door for her.

She gives me a half-smile, then settles herself in. As I close the door, I realise I'm already looking forward to seeing her again.

Having gone back to quickly lock up, I'm only a minute or so behind her, but turning left instead of the right she'd taken.

My bike backfires as though voicing its objections, though probably down to the mixture being too rich. I pat the tank. *Hey, baby. I'm not replacing you, okay?* That seems to settle her, and the remainder of the ride to the compound goes without further incident.

Unlike yesterday, I'm now riding in Monday morning rush hour. Too many cars and trucks around to get lost in my head. So it's not until I'm nearing the compound that I let thoughts of last night come back to me.

Damn that condom being out of date. Surely any repercussion is beyond unlikely? Nonetheless, I know it's going to take however many days it takes for Mary to get a negative pregnancy test result for me to be able to breathe again.

I promised her I'd be by her side. But in the cold light of day I have to ask myself, *just how hard will that be? A baby for fuck's sake?*

"Hey. You look like a man with the world on his shoulders." Niran's concerned eyes break me out of my reverie as soon as I pull my bike up.

Mentally shaking myself, needing to keep my personal shit to myself, I offer an excuse that will work. "I just fuckin' hope the Utah guys can live up to their advertisement." Personally, I hope they destroy that footage of Alicia. Kid doesn't deserve that. As for the rest of the shit Devon's into, I haven't got words to express how much I need that to stop.

Niran raises his chin. "Utah's landed. Wrangler's on his way to pick them up. Prez thought a sit-down might be useful before they arrive. He wants us in church for a pre-meet."

I can see the sense in that.

"They flying in on their fuckin' private plane?" If nothing else shouts Utah is different, that does.

"Nah, they've flown commercial for some reason." Niran waits while I back my bike into its parking space. His narrowed eyes watch me carefully as I swing my leg over the saddle. Pointing to my leg, he asks, "You put a strain on that last night? You look a bit stiff, old man." He grins. "Might want to ask Eva to give you a massage later."

Something she's done a few times before. She's a nurse. And while she kept well away from my dick, knowing I'd shown no interest in her, it still seems wrong to go back to her now. Maybe I can persuade Mary to give me a rub down when I see her? *Sure, and like that will end with her panties still on.*

Making a note to stop off and buy new condoms later, I don't give him an answer beyond a noncommittal grunt and follow him inside.

Most brothers are already seated around the table when I walk into our meeting room. Those that aren't, don't take long wandering in, some with cups of coffee in their hands. I notice two extra chairs have been placed, ready in anticipation for our visitors. As the brothers enter, they shift toward the top of the table, leaving the spaces empty at the end.

"How the fuck is this going to work?" Brakes asks as he sits down. "We really gonna be comfortable with having a fuckin' bitch in this room?"

"Whether we are or not," the VP replies, eyeing the manager of our strip club carefully, "that's where she's going to be sat."

"Give her a chance," Lost starts, supporting his VP. "See what she's made of before passing judgement. I, for one, liked what I saw."

"I can tell you what she's made of," Bones states firmly. "Breasts and ass, and no dick. That disqualifies her around here."

Prez, normally content to let things ride out, smashes his hand on the table. "Satan's Devils' regs don't disqualify women from being members. Utah was correct on that. Wait, keep your opinions locked up until you meet her. Then, see if you can tell me if a woman with her credentials requested to prospect here, whether or not you'd let her."

"Fuck that!" Dusty snorts. "I'd fuckin' rather turn in my patch."

"And I'd fuckin' take it off you." Lost's hand hits the table again. "Swift has skills which we need to get the sergeant-at-arms' kid off the hook, let alone put a stop to Devon's other business. We'll be fuckin' polite to her. Show any fuckin' disrespect and we risk her heading back to Utah, taking their fuckin' help with her."

"Didn't know you'd adopted a kid, Grumbler?" Pennywise is looking at me shrewdly. "You got an ol' lady now?"

"Stick on topic," I growl.

Salem immediately raises an eyebrow. "If you have, you gotta bring it to the table sooner or later."

I suppose he's right. I throw them a bone. "Looks like the

wind's blowing that way, but it's early days, okay? The enforcer's right, so if you've any objection to her, let me know now." I don't know what I'll do if they have—use my fists to persuade them to my way of thinking, probably.

"Looked into her background when I was trying to trace the photographer, she's good. I'll give my vote." Token makes a supporting statement.

"Didn't see much of her, but I could tell Patsy likes her," Bones puts in.

Kink chuckles. "So we'll be the chapter where fuckin' ol' ladies are *old*. Is that our criteria now?"

"Like you'd worry about fuckin' criteria." Blaze rolls his eyes at him. "If it's warm and willing, you'd give it a try."

"Don't call my fuckin' ol' lady old," Dart snarls.

"Children, children." One side of Lost's mouth is upturned. "If you want to vote now while we're waiting, anyone have any objections to Mary as Grumbler's ol' lady?"

"I haven't got any objections so long as she won't expect to sit around the table with us." Bones gets another dig in at Swift.

Prez raises an eyebrow at the treasurer who has the sense to shut up. Then the voting starts in earnest.

Apart from Patsy, there's not been another old lady voted in in San Diego for years, least none that are still around. Dart's woman, Alex, came as a done deal with him from Tucson.

I hadn't expected any objections, but like most things, the brothers string it out, Snips wanting to hold out until he'd first *met the bitch*. His words, not mine. My growl in his direction and Pennywise's slap around his head, soon has him shutting his mouth.

The newest members, Deuce, Reboot, Keeper and Niran seem almost bored by the vote. Dusty and Bones taking it more seriously, knowing that bringing in any outsider could be a risk. At last, the vote comes around to Salem.

The enforcer raises his hand. "I want to know if Grumbler's fucked her. If he's not as yet, then this might be a waste of our time."

Seriously? I mouth at him.

"Good point that." Pennywise backs up his friend.

"Unless the old man can't get it up," Kink suggests, his eyes filling with sympathy. "You need to get your script for Viagra filled?"

I can take quite a lot, but this hits so close to home that I snap. "Don't need fuckin' Viagra. My dick works great as it happens. It's in good working order." Too good, I think to myself.

Lost wipes his hand over his face and sighs. "Let's do this another way. Any valid objections? No. Right." He bangs the gavel. "You're cleared to give your patch to your ol' lady, Sergeant-at-arms."

I give a sharp nod, wondering how I, a long-confirmed bachelor, who thought I'd be that way when I died, had picked up a woman I wanted to live with for the rest of my life. I'm still wondering if it's a lingering effect of the accident I'd had, when there's a knock at the door and, after Lost calls out permission to enter. It's opened.

All heads point in that direction. Expressions are varied— some welcoming, some not so, some downright curious. It doesn't help when the woman striding in is holding a leash, on the end of which is a black spaniel dog.

"Oh Jeez." Brakes rolls his eyes. "She's brought a fuckin' lap dog."

"Hey, where's your ol' man?" This comes from Dusty. "Road okay with letting you out without him?"

The man who'd entered, who I deduce is Bolt, stiffens and raises an eyebrow at Swift. She reaches down and murmurs something to him, causing a wide grin to appear on his face.

Then, they wait, until Lost directs them to the seats waiting for them.

Swift pulls out her chair and points down to the dog getting settled at her feet. "This is Apollo, well, everyone calls him App. He's my hearing aid dog. You okay with having him here, Prez?" Her brow rises in challenge.

"App?" Scribe queries.

The other newcomer Bolt chuckles. "You know us tech guys. We've got an app for everything. Just so happens Apollo's her hearing app."

"You're fuckin' deaf? Can. You. Hear. Me?" Brakes asks.

Swift rolls her eyes. "Perfectly. As long as you don't all talk over each other. You know, you show your good manners like your mummas taught you."

"Where you from?" Pennywise asks. "Picking up on an accent, here."

"England."

"Well," Bones drawls, "if you enunciate clearly, we might just be able to understand you."

Prez bangs the gavel. He bangs it hard three times to get everyone to settle. "Thank you for coming to *help*." He emphasises the last word with a glare at the San Diego members.

"How's Road settling in?" the VP asks.

"Good." Swift nods at Dart. "Getting up to speed fast. He's on a mission right now, which is why we had to fly commercial. Preacher's taken the plane for that."

"While we're talking about old friends…" Salem's voice is hard. "What about our dear friend, Stormy?"

If I thought Salem's face had gone hard, Swift's becomes even colder. "Dead, if he knows what's good for him. But if you're asking if we've heard anything of him, we have not."

Salem's not going to let it drop. "You're here as fuckin'

experts in technology. What fuckin' good are you, if you can't find one of your own?"

It's Bolt who answers this time. "Yes, we're experts, but so is Stormy. He knows ways of disappearing, reinventing himself so he could never be found." Both of his hands fist on the table in front of him. "Nothing concrete, but my gut feel is he's gotten himself out of the country."

"Fuckin' coward," Pennywise remarks.

Swift actually gives him a chin lift, but Bolt shakes his head. "He'll come back and take his punishment. The way I see it, the man's got issues. Maybe he's putting those to bed first."

I glance at Prez. So far, they're saying nothing more than we knew from the reports he's passed us from Snatcher. But do we believe them? I'm not sure. Could Stormy even now be hidden by the Utah club?

Token looks grim. "To be honest, this is one situation where I had hoped that Stormy could magically take over my PC and give me all the answers. So far, I've got shit, and I don't like it one bit."

He's complaining about the time when he was trying to solve the mystery surrounding Lost's old lady. Someone had planted pop-ups and messages direct to his monitor. At the time, he never knew who sent them and it annoyed him immensely. But truth be told, had Stormy not contacted him, we would never have known Patsy needed protecting.

CHAPTER THIRTY-THREE

Grumbler

I notice Swift doesn't squirm or look embarrassed, she just acknowledges Token's comment, and then looks down the table at the prez.

"We've found out some shit. Shit that you need to hear personally. That's why we're here." She nods at Bolt who reaches into the bag he'd brought in with him.

As he does, all of us stiffen, and a few hands go to rest on guns in their holsters. Trust only goes so far with Utah. The last thing we want is for him to produce an AR-15.

Swift notices and grins. "Easy, he's just getting our laptops. If we wanted to kill you, we wouldn't need weapons."

"Fighting talk," Salem drawls lazily. He points at Swift. "Heard about you. How about you showing me what you got in the ring later?"

Bolt's eyes go to the enforcer sharply, then he shakes his head. "If I were you, I'd take that back, Brother."

Salem bristles. "I can take the both of you on."

Lost bangs the gavel and glares at Salem. "What have you found?" he asks, directing his question to the end of the table, getting us back on track.

Swift grimaces. "Grumbler?" She knows I'm the sergeant-at-arms, so picks me out of the lineup. I raise my chin to show she's got the right man. "What your girl got herself into is a whole heap of stinking dung. Devon Starr, or Ad Wilson or any of his other identities is small fry in a very large and very disgusting pool."

Bolt, who now has his laptop open, takes over. "You all know about hard porn, hell, probably have watched some of that shit. Subscription only channels, but they're there to find if you want in. But underneath that is another level of hell. Token?" Our own tech guy nods when he hears his name. "Your members educated on the deep and dark webs?"

In case we're not, Token reminds us. "Websites on the internet are searchable by easily remembered website addresses. We see the names, the computer directs you to the IP address of the domains. Easily found if you know the right search terms. Underneath that is the deep web where no one can go without knowing the IP address first. That's where your bank, or a company will store their customer or business details." He pauses to make sure we're all following along. "At the bottom is where nefarious activity takes place. It's where contracts are put out which you only want interested parties to answer, or," he nods toward Bolt, "if you want hard-core porn that goes beyond which any normal person would want to watch. It's where the bottom feeders dwell."

"Kink probably knows all about that."

Kink's eyes widen, and his face flushes as his hand hits the tabletop. "I'm kinky, not into that fuckin' shit, Brother." He rounds on Keeper. "Sex clubs of the type I frequent are above-board and of all things, consensual. I suspect what we're hearing about is non-consensual shit, like Owen talked about."

Bolt nods as if Kink's answered correctly, but adds, "And non-consensual will include snuff movies." He pauses for a beat to let that sink in. "You want to see a woman—or man—

killed for your personal gratification, well you'll find it on the dark web."

"That's sick," Dart says, but he doesn't attempt to deny it doesn't exist. "And our photographer is into that shit?"

Swift opens her own laptop and stabs at a few keys. Then, she slides the device down the table. Brothers look at it, then a quizzical look comes onto their faces, then it's passed on. When it reaches me, I do the same. On the screen is a page of pictures of young and pre-teens, both girls and boys. The only thing they have in common is their Hispanic features.

"What are we looking at, Swift?" Lost asks, when I pass it to him.

Swift's lips press together. "We couldn't get back to you earlier, I'm afraid, hence the delay. But in trying to locate your girl's video, we stumbled across a porn site catering to the most deviant of bastards. Rape, mutilation, death. These were some of the victims."

The laptop's been passed on from me, but those images are seared on my brain. "One was an *information wanted* poster."

"Indeed," Swift agrees. "We set up reverse image searches on the clearest pictures we could get from the videos. These were the 'before' pictures if you like. Believe me, you wouldn't want to see the after."

Beside her, Bolt shudders, and I have new respect for the members from Utah who'd presumably forced themselves to watch.

"So who are they?" Prez asks.

Swift doesn't tell us immediately. "As you can imagine, risks are taken when creating these videos. The subscription fee is exorbitant to cover those costs. For someone willing to stoop to that level, the rewards are there to be reaped."

"By someone?" Dart asks. "The photographer?"

"Photographers, models—if you can call them that—and I don't mean the kids. I mean the men, and some women, who are the molesters. Then there's the production factory and distribution. There's good money to be made."

She glances around the table, then continues, "Devon Starr probably wanted to buy in. But to do that, he had to have something he could offer. There are hundreds of thousands of videos on that site, and hundreds of people making videos, some with adults, some with children. But this set, well we think it's how Devon got his way in."

When Swift pauses, Bolt takes over. "The images I've just shown you are unaccompanied children who either made their own way over the border or got separated from their adults once they were here. We believe Devon has a network pushing these underage kids his way. Maybe criminals, maybe even border agents wanting to make good money on the side. Whatever it is, they disappeared when they reached California."

Swift lifts her chin at Bolt again. "What Devon could offer was untraceable victims who no one really cared about."

"I care." Lost's hand slams down onto the table. "I fuckin' care. No kid, from wherever, deserves to be molested like that."

I stand, my chair flying over backward. "Where's Devon now?" I yell down the table. "Give me a location and I'll go take him down."

"Easy, Brother," Swift comes back fast. "That's what we all want. But taking him out isn't enough. We need to shut down whatever pipeline he's got going. It won't just end with one photographer. Now we've found this, we've got a good chance ending this shit. And by that, I mean destroying the porn site and everyone facilitating it."

"We've already got a comprehensive list of all the subscribers." Bolt grins. "When we're ready, we'll leak it to the feds."

"Why Grumbler's kid?" Salem asks as I pick up my chair

and sit back down. "Alicia's ordeal was horrible, but not in the league you're talking about. What did Devon want with her?"

Swift's eyes catch mine. "We got into Owen's text message history. Seems Owen wants to do some extra modelling for Devon. It seems he obliged, apparently. On this occasion, Devon had seen the way Alicia had been looking at Owen and suggested he could use her. He told him to groom her, though those words weren't used exactly. Devon's clever enough to steer clear of saying too much in text. Again, he didn't go into specifics, just told Owen to get him something juicy. Alicia was just one of his auditions."

I go cold. "So it could have been worse?" I ask through gritted teeth.

Swift's eyes meet mine, but she doesn't say a word. I wipe my hand over my face thanking a deity that Owen didn't do more.

"We'd like to talk to Owen," Bolt drops in. "See what else he knows."

There's silence around the table. I'm opening my mouth when Lost admits, "Owen's dead. We didn't want him breathing our air."

Swift closes her eyes and her mouth moves. I think she's counting to ten. When she speaks her voice is even. "We can take the servers down and destroy the videos. We can get the feds onto the subscribers and freeze all the assets of the fuckers running this show. But we can't stop the key players starting this business up again. Not unless we can trace them, and so far, we have no leads." She pauses, and glances around the table. "We need this photographer of yours. He'll have the contacts, or at least some of them."

Bolt takes over. "We need Devon. This is a crime that crosses state lines. The subscribers are nationwide as far as we can tell. We need leads to leak to the feds, and that's not going to go well unless we also hand over Devon."

And there's the punchline. I'm not going to be given the pleasure of killing the man I hate down to the marrow in my bones.

Swift reads the expression on my face. "Grumbler, I know how you're fucking feeling. I want to tear this wanker apart, limb from limb. Would it help if I promised we'd trace the penitentiary he ends up in and get him taken out inside?"

"How can you promise that?" Salem asks. "Depending on what the feds make of his crimes, he could end up anywhere."

Swift seems unconcerned. "We can. We will. He's as good as dead already. But we've got to find him first. And, for that, we need your help."

"I thought you usually flew your lot in when you were on a mission?" Dart is shaking his head. "You normally do the track and trace work yourselves. Why not this time? Why come to us?"

"Because," Lost glances at his VP, "they're trying to prove they're team players. Have I got that right?"

Bolt and Swift look at each other, then Bolt raises his chin. "We wear the same patch," he confirms. "I have to admit, maybe Utah got arrogant, but in the technical area, we are the fuckin' best—no disrespect Token."

Token gives a dismissive wave of his hand. "Heard about your setup, Brother. You've got the computing power I can only dream of. No offence taken."

Swift takes over. "That raid, when," she pauses, gritting her teeth, "Stormy took out Alder." Another beat passes while she waits for the reaction she knows she's going to get. "I don't want to sound condescending, but San Diego can handle themselves. We wouldn't have approached it any differently. So it makes sense. You're here, we'll work with you. As long as you can promise that we take Devon, alive."

"Does he need all his body parts to testify?" Salem asks, flexing his hands and making his knuckles crack.

Swift spares him a glance. "I think we'll find Devon resists arrest."

Salem, clearly speaking her language, gives an evil smile.

"All this because you wanted to pimp your fuckin' ride." Dusty's long hair swings as he shakes his head, his eyes settling on mine.

"If I fuckin' hadn't, we'd have never known what was going on," I retort.

"We'll get your modelling fees out of him before we hand him over," Swift offers with a grin.

"I didn't fuckin' model," I grumble. "He just used my bike."

Prez gives a sigh, then asks, "Had you no idea this was going on?"

"Hadn't come onto our radar," Bolt states. "Hate to say this, but Hispanics coming over the border illegally are just one more statistic. If they get through the border patrols, then they do tend to disappear, even kids."

"The one with the missing poster?" I ask.

"Was supposed to end up with an uncle. Never arrived," Swift says, succinctly.

There's a brief spell of quiet, which is broken by the prez.

"So, where do we go from here? How are we going to take Devon Starr?"

Swift straightens, all business now. "We have a list of locations, studios he uses, places he frequents." I notice Token shaking his head. He's been trying to find info like that with no success. Swift eyes him too. "We use facial recognition software. We were able to pick him up."

"Duty and Honor are trying to track him at base," Bolt explains. "Currently, we know where he's been, but not where he is or where he's going. They're trying to rectify that now."

"When we have some locations, we'll split up into teams. I brought communication devices with me." Swift gives an exasperated sigh. "But your prospect wouldn't let me bring my bag in."

Good on Wrangler. No recording devices in church. Well, not for the likes of them—visiting members who we don't know.

"We're hoping to know enough to make our move tonight," Bolt confirms. "The cover of darkness is always good, and if we catch him with his pants down, or off as the case may be, so much the better."

"Sergeant-at-arms, VP. Will you sort out the teams? Liaise with Bolt and Swift to see how many we're going to need."

"On it," Dart and I answer Prez together.

"Everyone else stick around until you know who your team is, okay? Then you're free to go but stay in communication. We'll meet back here at…?"

"Ten pm," Swift inserts.

It must be getting on for midday now. I'll square things with the VP and the arrangements for tonight, and then I can go see Mary. Talking about tracking Devon down had taken my mind off my own problems. Now I start wondering what thinking she's done herself, and whether she's decided to take precautions. Lost in my head, I follow my brothers out into the clubroom.

Music is playing, and there, dancing gracefully on the pole is Alex, the VP's wife. Swiftly turning my head like all the San Diego brothers, I start to head to the bar.

"She's incredible," Swift breathes out, watching Alex move.

"Fuckin' is," Bolt admires.

"Eyes off my fuckin' ol' lady," Dart snarls, then calls out. "Alex?"

"Just finishing up," she calls back, swirls around one last time, then sinks to the floor, landing perfectly. Of course, all this I see out of the side of my eye.

Swift immediately approaches her.

A wail announces Eva's entrance. She's carrying Dart and Alex's baby, who's what? Fifteen months or so now. The kid spies her parents and wriggles her way out of Eva's arms, and starts weaving drunkenly toward her mother. Then, she spies her dad, and, as fast as her little legs will take her, changes direction.

Dart crouches and holds out his arms. "Who's my clever girl?" he asks, as he sweeps her up. "You been good for Auntie Eva?"

For an answer, she sticks her thumb in her mouth.

Seeing how besotted he is, I have to ask. "You happy being a dad, Dart?"

"Already was one to Tyler." He reminds me of how he's adopted Alex's nine-year-old boy. "And this littl' un's just the icing on the top." He glances at me, seeing I've asked the question seriously. "Wouldn't change it for the world, Brother." He grins, and, though his arms are full, nudges my arm with his elbow. "Why, you thinking of starting a family yourself?" He chuckles as though he's made a good joke.

When I don't join in laughing, or answer immediately, his mirth fades. "Grumbler?"

I lean in. "Broken condom," I tell him.

"You fuckin' what?" Dart's eyes widen.

"Language, Dart!" Somehow Alex hears and admonishes him, then gets back to talking with Swift.

"Christ. This is good." His brow furrows. "How old is Mary?"

"Forty-seven."

He slaps my back. "So you've got nothing to worry about, have you?"

"What's Grumbler worrying about now?" Salem's none too gentle when it's his palm now landing on my cut.

Dart shoots me a look, then betrays me completely. "Grumbler's had a condom misfunction."

Salem snorts. "But you're both too old, surely?"

"Hopefully," I tell him. "Fuckin' hopefully."

"That's it." Alex steps up, taking Isla from her father. "We'll be lucky if the first thing she says doesn't begin with an f."

"She already says, Dada." Dart grins at her. Yeah, Alex is pissed Isla doesn't call her momma as yet. Dart certainly milks that.

"You pregnant?" Pennywise must have overheard—his expression looks like a mixture of shock and amusement.

Why did I open my mouth?

"Impossible," Salem observes. "What's the likelihood of you having a baby?"

Pennywise shakes his head. "Is this a cause for celebration, Brother?"

"Fuckin' no." I round on them. "I shouldn't have said anything. It's highly unlikely. Even if she is, it's got to be risky. I don't know what the fuck I want, but I sure didn't plan on having a baby."

"Keeps you young, old man," Dart observes, wisely.

I'm wondering how to shut this conversation down, when their attention is caught by something behind me. I turn as well. Swift has pulled herself up on the pole and is contorting lithely.

"Now I see what Road sees in her," Pennywise murmurs. "Just watch those muscles work."

"I can still take her," Salem growls.

CHAPTER THIRTY-FOUR

Mary

"So, is he hot?"

I grin at Kristen who's in her normal position, hanging over the partition between our cubicles. For an answer, I pretend to fan myself. To me, Grumbler is indeed good-looking, to someone younger, perhaps not.

During my sleepless hours in the night, I considered how I'd approach this morning. I'd veered from telling my friends what had happened, to keeping everything bottled up. I'd come down on the side of full disclosure. I need someone to talk to, someone to bounce ideas off. It may help me get perspective. Who else could I trust, except for my closest friends? It hadn't been a mistake. While I'd surprised the hell out of them when I'd answered their polite enquiry about my weekend, there had been no censure, just sympathy. Though they had taken a moment to take it all in.

Kristen wants to know all about my biker. Terra focuses on something else. "How's Alicia now? Dreadful thing to happen to a young girl. She must be crushed."

I recall Alicia this morning, she'd seemed eager enough to get back to school. "She seems to have accepted she's joined the club of losing her virginity to someone who wasn't worth it." I grimace. "There's enough of us in it."

"But not all of us were filmed. You sure your boyfriend is going to be able to get that video locked down?" Terra shudders. "I'd hate to think there was a porn film of me out there."

"I have confidence he will," I say. "And Alicia's convinced he'll do what he says."

"Don't you think she should have gone to the cops?"

"She's too embarrassed," I respond to Kristen. "And it was consensual, it wasn't rape. There was nothing untoward until it was filmed, and it's only her word for that. They might think she was making things up to get back at a man who slighted her after he took what he wanted."

"It's the way of the world," Terra confirms. "It would be her words against his, no marks showing force. And, if that film, hopefully, never turns up, no proof she was videoed during the act."

"But she's underage," Kristen protests. "He should be arrested for that."

I shrug. "He should, but she'd have to face him in court, and I wouldn't want to put her through that." I believe Grumbler when he says Owen will never bother us again, even if I don't like to consider why he's so certain.

"As long as Alicia can put it behind her and move on. Maybe learn a lesson not to go behind her mom's back." Terra winks at me.

I smile. "Hopefully she'll now respect that I know what I'm talking about."

"Getting back to your man. When are we going to meet him? Can you get him to come out for a drink with us one night?"

Could I see an after-work get-together with Grumbler in tow? I don't think he'd mind. The problem is, we've still got things to discuss, things that might influence where our fledgling relationship goes.

As Art comes into view, Kristen ducks down and goes back to work. After Art talks to me for a moment about a job he wants done, he disappears again. It's then Terra starts quizzing me in earnest.

"What's on your mind?" she asks, her voice low.

I wonder whether to tell her, but in honesty, she's not only my friend, but is close to my own age. I can't talk to Alicia for obvious reasons. This is one of the things I've warned her about.

Glancing around to make sure Kristen's heads down in her cubicle and no one else is around, I tilt my head and say quietly, "The condom broke."

"What? Alicia's?"

I shake my head. "No, thank God for that. Grumbler's."

Terra snorts loudly. Frantically, I wave her to stay silent. When she's finished chuckling, she tells me, "Well thank goodness you don't have anything to worry about."

"You don't think? I've not gone through menopause."

She shakes her head. "Fertility goes down drastically with age. I have a friend. When she was forty-four she met the man of her dreams, got married, and wanted to start a family. She'd turned forty-five by the time she started trying. It never happened for her, even with fertility treatments."

That's sad, wanting a family and not being able to have one.

I'm not against abortion per se, it's every woman's right to choose. But as far as I go, I'd always felt aborting a foetus was a kick in the teeth in the face of women who'd give their eye teeth to give birth. As long as I was in the position to raise a child, I'd always see it as a blessing. Or so, I'd thought. Now?

"Grumbler suggested the morning-after pill."

"He want you to take it?"

My head moves side to side. "No pressure, just a suggestion." It's a sensible one and a way to make certain.

"Do you want to?"

"I don't know," I wail softly. "I don't know what I want. On one hand, it's ridiculous continuing a pregnancy if, in the unlikely event I am. I'm too old to raise a baby, and I'm nearing the time when Alicia would be off my hands and I'd be able to live my life. Having a baby now ties me down until I'm nearing seventy."

"So take the pill," she says reasonably. She pauses for a moment to answer an email. "Does Grumbler want a kid? Would he support you?"

I smile, remembering his words last night. "He says he would now, but he's nearing sixty, Terra. Will he really want all the shit that goes with bringing a child up?"

"He hasn't other kids?"

"No, never had any. He's never been in a relationship before."

Terra's eyes go comically wide. "And you think he's a good bet as father material?"

She's only said what I've been wondering myself. I simply shrug. "He is good with Alicia."

And good with that guitar of his. I get goosebumps as I remember. *His voice, so deep, so full of emotion when he sings, and those long fingers of his...* I snap myself out of it. *I'm at work.*

"From that faraway look you got just there, I'd say he's got something going for him. Tell me, has he any other hot biker friends in his age group?"

"I don't know." I laugh. "I'll have to ask him."

The volume of our voices has increased.

"A younger one for me, please," Kristen cries out.

Terra and I look at each other and burst out laughing.

Seeing Art approaching again, Terra and I buckle down to

our work. I've been given something complicated, so I lose myself in the ins and outs of zoning restrictions and the like, checking and double-checking facts to make sure what I'll be telling the client is right. Before I know it, it's clocking out time and I can go home. Stretching my arms over my head, I let out a yawn.

Terra nudges me in the ribs. "Ouch."

"Best make that hunk let you sleep tonight. You're not young enough to burn the midnight oil anymore."

"Speak for yourself." I wink at her.

"Don't forget to ask him about any hotties for us!" Kristen calls out when I give her a wave of my hand.

I'm fine until I get to the underground parking lot and sit in the driver's seat of my car. Then everything comes back to me. *Will Grumbler be cross I've not gotten the morning-after pill? Did I make a conscious decision not to get it? Should I stop off on the way home and get it now?*

I stare at the steering wheel in the hope that it might give me some answers.

Surely a baby at my age is not what I want?

How does Grumbler really feel? I wish I could read his mind. But, if I can't read my own, what chance have I got?

At last I switch on the engine, put my car into drive, and head out into the traffic. I go straight home, wondering what time Grumbler will arrive.

Well that's one puzzle easily solved as soon as I park on the drive. He's already here, or at least, that's his bike.

Putting my key in the front door, when it opens, I step inside, coming to a halt at the sight in front of me. Grumbler's crouched down in front of the couch, patiently positioning Alicia's fingers on the fret board of her guitar.

"You've got it. That's C. Now go to G, then back to C."

"It sounds better when you do it."

"Feel that?" Grumbler holds out his fingertips to her. "Feel those callouses? Your fingers have got to harden a bit, then that guitar will be ringing out."

Alicia looks up and sees me. She beams. "Grumbler bought new strings, Mom. Only, when they're new, they stretch at first. It needs tuning a lot."

"Only for the first day or so," Grumbler explains. "Want me to do it again?"

"I got this," Alicia tells him, then slowly proceeds to tune it herself. Experimentally, she goes to try a chord she just learned, then grimaces, and starts her tuning again.

"She's got a good ear," Grumbler tells me. "Now she knows what it's supposed to sound like, she knows when it's wrong."

I place my purse and keys on the side, then frown. "You been here long?" I realise he must have been to have restrung the guitar.

"'Bout half an hour."

"I'll leave you to it." Alicia suddenly jumps up. "Got homework to do."

As she disappears in the direction of her bedroom, I raise my eyebrows. "Who was that, and what have you done with my daughter?"

"Told her to give us five minutes when you got home, babe. Bargained with her with those new strings I got." He picks up the guitar she'd left leaning against the couch and replaces it on its stand.

"How much were they?"

Grumbler's eyes widen. "Fuck, woman. You don't have to pay me back. Her smile was all the payment necessary." He walks forward and takes hold of my hands. He stares down into my face for a moment, then, releasing one of mine, lifts his now free hand up to caress my cheek. "You okay?"

"I didn't get the pill." I wait for his reaction.

He doesn't use words, in fact, he pulls me to him. "You know anything coming of this is very unlikely, don't you?"

"Of course."

"I don't mind letting things ride. See where they take us. But it's easy for me to say, isn't it, babe?"

"I can find out in about ten days, I think." I'm not totally sure. "If I am, I'll need to think about the implications. But, as you say, I'm certain I'm not."

"Been doing some thinking today," he tells me. "Let's just say, I won't be disappointed whichever way this turns out. Hey, babe. Boys voted you in. You're officially my ol' lady. If that's what you want." He adds the last fast.

Do I?

At work it had been back to normality after the fiasco of the weekend and a relationship with a biker seemed so out of place and out of character for me. Now, faced with Grumbler, I know I don't want to turn him down.

He holds out his hand. "Come, I've got a surprise for you."

I half expect him to take me into the bedroom, but instead he leads me outside and indicates his bike. I stare at it for a moment, trying to see what he's pointing out.

"Is that new?" The seat looks different.

"Fitted it for you, babe. Want to go try it out?"

"Me? I...?" My voice squeaks as I try to think of an excuse.

"We won't go far, just around the block. See how you take to it."

"I can't. Alicia..."

He chuckles in that deep sexy way he has. "She can't look after herself for a few minutes?"

He's right. Of course she can. My mouth opens and closes as I try to think of a reason why I can't, dismissing any before I voice them, already hearing his comebacks in my head. Reminding myself he's gone to the bother of putting a passenger seat on his beloved bike just for me, in the end I think, *what can it hurt?* Just a quick ride around the block and then I'll be able to tell him, for me, riding doesn't work.

Suddenly I find what I'm searching for. "I haven't got a helmet."

But this, too, he has an answer for. "Sure you have, I brought a lid for you."

Of course he has.

He prods me in the back. "Go, grab a jacket. Tell Alicia we'll be gone half an hour tops."

I'm Mary. I'm a middle-aged mom. I don't do anything spur of the moment. I think everything through carefully first. Riding a motorcycle is dangerous, everyone knows that. I already know I'm going to hate it. I'll feel vulnerable and at risk without the comforts and safety of a metal cage wrapped around me. I'd chosen my car because of its safety rating.

But seeing the set expression on his face, the raised eyebrow in challenge, I know he won't let this drop.

I grimace, allowing my distaste to show, then capitulate. "Once around the block?"

He visibly relaxes. "Go tell Alicia."

I go first to my bedroom, dragging an old denim jacket out of the back of my closet. It's years' old, and heaven knows why I kept it, but I hope the material is thick enough to afford some protection in case we crash. Then, I change my work pants for a pair of old jeans. Finally, seeing the lack of appropriate footwear, settle for a pair of tennis shoes.

When I get to my daughter's room, I'm ready for an inquisition.

"Alicia. Grumbler and I are just going out. We won't be long."

"Uh-huh."

"He's taking me on his bike."

"Uh-huh."

Her lack of reaction puzzles me, and I take a step inside her room. "You don't mind?"

"Why the hell should I? I've ridden with Grumbler before."

I suddenly wonder how. "He had no passenger seat. How did you ride with him?"

"It wasn't far." She glances at the screen of her laptop and scrunches her eyes. "He edged up on his seat, and I squeezed on behind him. I'm small."

Does the fact he's got me a special seat mean I've got a big ass? I suppose, in comparison with my slim-as-hell daughter, I have.

"I'm busy, Mom. Enjoy your ride."

Why hadn't she objected? If my daughter had begged me not to go on such a dangerous machine, I'd have had reason to refuse him, but the last obstacle has been cleared.

With trepidation, I follow Grumbler out to his ride. Despite my apprehension, I still have to admire it. It absolutely gleams. Even the passenger seat he's added seems to enhance it, the rest at the end, hopefully which will stop me slipping off, has *Live to Ride, Ride to Live*, emblazoned on it.

He hands me a helmet, taking a moment to tighten the straps to his satisfaction, then gives me a pair of sunglasses I hadn't thought to bring. Then, he puts on his own helmet and shades, slipping his hands into gloves.

I watch as he swings his leg over the saddle, looking all at once at one with the machine. When he holds out his hand, I grip it hard as I try to get myself onto the seat. I manage, but I'm sure I'm more awkward than fluent.

"Arms around my waist," he instructs. "Hold me tight. Budge up the seat so I can feel you behind me, babe." He helps by yanking on my hands, making me slide down toward him. "If you need me to stop, tap me on the shoulder. Just go with the flow, lean when I do."

I don't need his instruction. Even with the engine off and us not moving, I'm holding him with a death grip. When he starts the engine and the bike begins to vibrate, I squeal.

He's backed onto my drive, so once he kicks up the stand, making me feel unbalanced, he's only got to put it into gear to start us rolling.

We must be going at a walking pace, but I'm scared. Terrified. My heart is in my mouth. Once we gain a little speed though, the bike feels steadier.

This is Grumbler. He's been riding for years. He had a crash a while back. Is he really safe?

Just once around the block, I can do this.

But Grumbler ignores the turn that would make the circuit short and heads out along the main road.

It's his bike, not us, that attracts attention, I tell myself, as kids lean out of cars and wave, while some adults watch us with disgust on their faces. I try to convince myself it's not that a woman my age has no excuse riding on such a bike.

Grumbler eases his way through the traffic, and for once I'm not stuck waiting in a line of cars but making my way past them. For some gaps I close my eyes, but Grumbler seems to know what he's doing, and despite myself, I begin to relax, admiring instead his competency handling the big two-wheeler. Quicker than I would have made it in my car, we're coming to an open piece of road. When Grumbler opens the throttle and the bike leaps forward with a roar as though excited to show off its stuff, I shriek, and hug Grumbler even tighter.

The vibration of the bike, the feeling of the cooling breeze on my face, the sheer thrill of being part of the countryside makes my nerves slide away. Instead of worrying about the ride, I'm now consumed by thoughts of the man who's in front of me. My hands on his chest loosen slightly as I realise I don't feel in danger. Riding with him, I feel safe.

Safe in a way I haven't had for years.

Dave and I had a good marriage. I'd grown used to having a man by my side. Our household duties were split, not that he wouldn't take a turn at the cooking, but I normally found another job for him instead. *That cupboard's loose. The yard needs cutting.* He'd taken most of the financial burden as his wage was higher than mine, but I had my own bank account, and knew how to manage my money.

When he'd gone, I thought I could manage to get through life, that the devastation of his loss was the overriding emotion. That soon began to be usurped by a sense of how useless I was. Putting together a new bed for Alicia had seen me in frustrated tears, so had dealing with the insurance company who tied me in knots. I'd come through, stronger than before.

I don't *need* a man in my life, but it sure would be nice to have one. One I can depend on.

As I'm beginning to trust Grumbler's handling of the bike and ultimately my life, I realise I'm ready to trust him with something else—my happiness.

It's almost an hour later when we draw back up at my house.

"Around the block? Really?" I dismount, take off my helmet and stand with my hands on my hips.

He smirks widely, completely unabashed. "Told you to tap me on my shoulder if you wanted to stop. You didn't, so..." He shrugs.

"I was scared for my life," I tell him, unable to keep the grin off my face. "Couldn't let go of you long enough to give you the signal."

He snorts. "Yeah, I felt you feeling up my abs." He approaches me, takes the helmet from my hands, and twists one hand in my hair. "Tell me you hated it, babe."

I can't tell him that. Instead, something else comes out of

my mouth. "Yes, to being your old lady. Yes, to playing with fire and seeing how things pan out." His wild side, how he lives on the edge, must be rubbing off on me.

"Fuck, woman. You're perfect." He leans down to rest his forehead against mine. "I'll make sure you don't regret it."

CHAPTER THIRTY-FIVE

Grumbler

I enjoy what I can spend of the evening with Mary and Alicia, not minding we're eating takeout—a common occurrence, but one quite explainable. Mary works.

"Mom always gets takeout," Alicia complains. "Marisa's mom cooks every night."

"You get in earlier than your mom," I observe. "You could get something going for dinner."

Alicia's eyes snap to mine, then slowly a snide grin spreads over her face. "I *love* takeout."

"Were you brought up on home-cooked meals, Grumbler?" Mary asks.

I nod, swallow, then tell them, "Actually I was. Mom knew her way around a kitchen as it happens. But you know what? I fuckin' yearned for takeout."

"Guess we always want what we can't have," Alicia observes.

She's not wrong there.

Right now, I want to stay here and lock the rest of the world out, but I've responsibilities, and fuck knows, I'm eager to deal with them. All too soon, I'm heading for the door. Mary comes with me.

"We're going to have to tell her soon." I jerk my head to Alicia's room where she's disappeared again.

Mary grimaces. "Leave that to me. If what's between us is going to work, she's got to be on board with it. I mean, where are we going to live for a start? I'm hoping being your old lady won't mean you'll just pop by for booty calls." When I widen my eyes and shake my head, she offers, "You could move in here."

"Come and see my place this weekend," I counter. "See if you think that can work. Or, if you want, we could buy something together. Make a fresh start."

"I don't care where we live as long as I have my own room."

Both Mary and I jump so fast, it's comical. Behind Mary, out of immediate view, stands her teenage daughter. She's a fucking ninja.

"Or," I suggest, looking seriously down at Mary. "You could move in with me, and we'll leave Alicia here."

"Can I? Can I have my own place?" The glee with which my inane suggestion is greeted draws one word out of both of our mouths at once.

"No."

"Aww, shucks. Having two parents is going to suck. Later, Grumbler." Alicia disappears back into her room, carrying a bag of chips.

"Guess you won't need to have that chat after all. How the fuck is she still hungry?"

"Growing teenager." Mary rolls her eyes. "You going to be back, later?"

I wish I could. But I've no idea what the night's going to hold. "Probably not, but I'll catch up with you tomorrow, okay? I'll check in with you when I can."

"You're going after Devon, aren't you?" When I stay silent, there's another roll of her eyes. "Just remember, that this time club business is my business. I need to know that video has been destroyed."

Leaning down, I take her lips with mine, trying to imprint her taste on my memory to last me through the next few hours.

"Be careful."

"Always am, babe." I put my lid on my head and pull on my gloves. Part of me wishes I didn't have to leave her but know if I'm going to put her troubles to bed, I've got to go do what has to be done.

In my rearview, as I drive off, I see her waiting at the end of the driveway until I disappear around the corner, as though she wanted to keep me in sight as long as she could.

How the fuck did I get so lucky?

Then, I try to put her out of my head and get my mind back into the game. Tonight will be too serious for me to allow myself to be distracted. I've got to be one-hundred-percent focused on the task ahead. To be anything else would be dangerous.

While it's still an hour or more before we're due to leave, when I arrive back at the compound, it's buzzing. Men are over-spilling out of the clubhouse, some hunkering down by their bikes, making last-minute checks. No one wants a hith-erto unspotted nail in the tyre to cause any accidents or delays tonight.

Prez is standing, a beer in his hand, leaning against the exterior wall, surveying his domain. I feel as much as see his eyes on me as I park my bike and make my way over.

"Sissy bar? Pillion seat? Never thought I'd see the fuckin' day."

I grin. "Yeah, tried it out tonight."

Dart comes over. "That's not all he's tried out." He grins

widely as I mime slitting my throat to keep him from spilling more of my secrets. Thankfully, he keeps quiet.

"Utah got us the locations?" I presume they have, otherwise the brothers wouldn't be getting ready.

"Yeah." Business-like now, the VP pulls a paper out of his cut. "We've got four locations where he might be. Two houses he's known to frequent, a hotel he's been seen at recently, and a studio."

"What about the house we visited? Any chance he'd go back there?"

Prez raises his chin. "We've still got that under surveillance. Curtis is still there. So far, he's not been back, so won't know we've been there."

"Where are the teams headed?"

"I'm heading to the studio. Lost is taking the hotel. You're at one of the houses, and Salem's at the other." Dart points out the address to which I'll be headed, and I program it into my phone.

"What about them?" I jerk my head toward Swift and Bolt, who are in conversation with Pennywise.

"They'll be in the truck and will stay in contact with Utah. If there's any last-minute information which means our plans change, we'll adapt on the fly. If any of us gets a hit, then they'll bring the truck. Wrangler's going with them as the driver as he knows the locale."

"She taking that fuckin' dog?"

He chuckles. "Nah, one of the sweet butts has agreed to look after it. Jeez, Brother. Swift can actually be scary. I think Cindy darn near wet herself when she had to promise not to let him out of her sight."

Yeah. But Cindy's a girl. I doubt Swift's threats would work so well on a man.

While we'd gone over the plans earlier, it doesn't hurt to go through them again. Whistling, I attract the attention of my team and lead them to one side. I've got Niran, who's solid, Kink, who's good once his focus is off sex, and Keeper, still a bit green, but not likely to go off half-cocked.

"We capture," I remind them again. "No shoot-to-kill shots. We want him alive and able to talk."

"Fucker deserves to die." Kink's shaking his head. "Nah," as I go to speak, he holds up a hand, "don't worry about me. I'll play nice."

"Permission to get one punch in," Niran requests, his eyes twinkling, white flashing in the dark of the night.

"Granted." I may get in a few of my own if we end up being the ones to take him in.

As we finish up, Bolt comes around, handing out tiny devices we apparently fit into our ears.

"You'll be on your own channel else it will get too confusing," he informs us. "But once someone's made contact, I'll feed all comms into one."

Having made sure my team is up to speed, I wander around the other groups, listening in on the individual pep talks, and raising my chin when I approve, or cuffing assholes, like Reboot, around the head when they don't seem to be paying attention.

Having done my rounds, I stride back to the prez.

"All good?"

"Seems that way." My eagle eyes span for anything I might have missed.

"Okay." Lost holds out his hand. I grab it, pull him in tight and we exchange back slaps. "Let's get on the road."

"Ready to roll in five!" I make my deep voice boom out, pausing for a moment to make sure everyone's heard.

It seems they have. Men start approaching their bikes and getting ready for the signal to ride.

Lost's team will go first, Dart's behind him, then mine and finally Salem's. The roar of all the bikes heading out sounds thunderous—a wonderful sound in my ears. The noise diminishes as groups start to peel off.

I don't need a map, I know exactly where I'm going. It's not long before I'm signalling to back off on the throttle. I then make other hand signals causing Niran, giving me a salute in passing, with Keeper beside him to head down a street which will bring them up at the rear of the property.

Kink and I carry on to the front, coasting the last few yards with our engines off. We pull up in the street. Looking around, I see some bushes up ahead. When I point them out, that's where we head to and park. Stepping back, I nod in satisfaction —a cursory glance from the road won't reveal our bikes.

Having gone over our plan, I have my skeleton key ready. Token, and/or Utah have confirmed they've already disabled the alarm. I stand at the end of the driveway for a moment. The garage door is closed, there are no lights on in the house. Doesn't mean there's no one home, of course. One of my hands forms a fist and I slap it into the other's open palm.

"We're here." Niran's voice sounds directly into my ear. "There's a back entrance opening onto a yard. It looks like one that will be bolted on the inside. All windows are closed, no lights on and no sign of anyone being inside."

Don't give up yet, I remind myself. I'd hoped to be the one coming across Devon. He could still be inside, but it's starting to look unlikely.

"We'll open the front door first, then come and let you in." I can't get used to just speaking normally and having my voice picked up.

"Copy that," Niran responds.

"Going in now."

Sliding out my skeleton key, I approach the front door.

"You sure you don't want me to try first? I'm an expert at undoing lock," Kink says both from inside my ear, and by my side.

"This isn't a pair of fuckin' handcuffs," I respond.

I'm hoping he'll shut the fuck up. It's not a time to be distracted. I eye the lock then crouch down at ground level, pulling my glasses out of my cut and sliding them on. I jiggle the key around a bit, then hear the snick and feel a satisfying give as the lock disengages. *We're in.*

Once inside, I pause, listening carefully. But there's no sound, not even snores coming down from the floor above. I gesture to Kink, and he sets off in the direction of the rear of the house.

While he's gone, I glance around. This certainly isn't as opulent as the house we made the abortive visit to yesterday. The décor could do with a refresh, and the wooden flooring is scuffed. The kitchen, what I can see of it, is outdated. A crash pad? An escape? This doesn't seem up to dear Devon's tastes.

I've completed my immediate appraisal when Kink, Niran and Keeper appear. I point to Keeper, giving him the sign for *stay the fuck here,* while to the others I point upstairs.

I can tell it's a bust as soon as we reach the top step. It doesn't even seem lived in up here. We each take one of the three rooms. The one I enter hasn't even a bed. I shake my head in disgust and exit the room again.

"Clear," I say, half-heartedly.

"Clear," Salem replies.

"Clear," Kink says.

I pinch the bridge of my nose. "So if he doesn't fuckin' live or even stay here, and it's not fuckin' set up for a studio, what does he use it for?"

"Status report, Sergeant-at-arms." Bolt's voice comes into my ear.

I'd forgotten that while we couldn't hear the other teams, those in the truck are listening in. "We got fuck all."

"He's been tracked there recently." Swift comes on the

line. "His phone was logged there yesterday. Have a good look around, Grumbler. There could be something we're missing."

"How are the other teams getting on?"

"Haven't found him yet. The other house was a bust, the hotel too. No report back from the team at the studio yet."

I think they can cross this one off the list, but then I suppose I best do as I'm told, even if it is by a woman. But hell, maybe it's time I get used to that. No doubt my old lady will try and tell me a thing or two.

Returning downstairs, I see Keeper on his hands and knees. "What the fuck you doing?"

A bit sheepishly, Keeper looks up. "These scuff marks..." he points them out.

"Someone's moved furniture?" Niran suggests, but he, too, sinks to his knees and starts looking. "Grumbler, Keep might have something here." He indicates something. "They're all heading the same way."

Kink starts following the tracks, while the others stand up, both brushing dust off their hands.

"I can't see... Wait." Kink takes out his knife and uses the blade against something. As whatever it is eases up, my eyes widen.

If we hadn't been searching, we'd have never found anything. But what Kink's opening up is a trapdoor of some sort. *A basement?* That wasn't on the plans. We hadn't expected to find that, nor to find a door whose underside is six inches thick with insulation.

Neither did we expect to find what we did behind it.

CHAPTER THIRTY-SIX

Grumbler

I blink once, then twice.

"What you got, Grumbler?" Swift's impatient voice sounds in my ear.

I'm a big scary biker, and these are just kids. Replacing my gun in its holster, I climb the ladder that leads into the hole in the ground—something that must have been dug out for this purpose. Sinking to my haunches I hold out my hands.

"*¿Hablas inglés?*" It's about all the Spanish I've got, so I hope to fuck someone does. There are half a dozen Hispanic children huddled in front of me—four girls, two boys, ranging in age from about five to fifteen if I'm any judge.

A boy, probably only just entering his teens, offers a hesitant, "*Sí.* I speak English a little. Is it safe to go now, mister?"

The question surprises me. "Safe?" I ask. "How did you get here?"

The boy looks at the others and speaks to the oldest girl rapidly in Spanish. She shakes her head.

"Are you bad men? Will you send us back?"

How do I answer? I'll get them out of this hellhole that's for certain, but I've no idea what will happen then. Right now,

I've no intention and no means of getting them back to Mexico. I've made an educated guess that knowing the scam Devon's running, that's where they've come from. I move my head side to side. "No. What's your name, kid?"

"Jorge."

I raise my chin. "Well, Jorge. I need to know how you got here. Can you tell me?"

They seem cautious, but not particularly scared. That seems odd.

"A good man saved us and brought us here. Told us to stay until he told us it was safe to leave. There are bad men searching for us."

It was the devil himself who'd taken them, that I truly believe. Carefully I slide out my phone and show them a picture of the photographer. "Is this the man?"

"*Si.*"

"Status report," Bolt again demands.

Niran, who's descended behind me, turns away and starts mumbling as though to himself. At least he's taken the onus from me.

"You got family in the States? Have any of you?"

"*Si.*" The boy nods his head. "My sister," he indicates the youngest child, "and I are going to our aunts. She lives in San Francisco." He pronounces the name of the city carefully.

"How were you going to get there?"

"I call her," Jorge says, full of confidence. "She'll come get us."

I can make that happen, I think. That's two out of the way. "And the others?"

Another discussion in their native language, then the story comes out. All but the eldest crossed the border with their families but were separated by border control. Their parents taken into detention, but a 'kind' border control agent passed them onto the good man so they wouldn't end up taken prisoner. They're beyond grateful to the man who saved them. Their plans? To hide and wait out until, hopefully, the adults they made the crossing with were set free. *Not going to happen.* I know it's more likely they'll be sent back to Mexico, leaving their kids to fates I hope they can't imagine.

"This man," I tap the photo on the phone. "He bring you here? Does he come back to check on you?"

The boy nods. "He said he'd be back soon when it was safe. He left us with food, but it's gone now."

I eye the pile of candy and chip wrappers, and realise Devon knows shit about children's nutrition. But it's a way to curry favour perhaps by giving them what they enjoy. I also view the pile of empty water containers. A couple of the kids have half-filled bottles by their sides, but there's no more.

Either Devon's due back soon or he seriously underestimated how long what he left them would last.

Behind me, Niran updates Swift with what I've just seen, and she fast comes to the same conclusion as myself.

"Stay there. I'm directing everyone else to you. You okay to head this for now, Grumbler?"

I turn, and like Niran, lower my voice. "One of us will stay with the kids, the others will hide in the house. If Devon's coming back, he won't know we're waiting for him."

"Make sure the front door is locked. Bolt will turn the alarm back on, so he's not set on his guard immediately."

"What about the fuckin' kids?" I ask her.

"Trying to sort that out," Swift confirms in her business-like manner. "They'll be taken care of."

Hopefully by not giving them back to the type of bastard who traded them to Devon. "We got a dirty border control agent," I tell her.

"We're aware."

Those two words speak volumes, and I don't know why, but I'm reassured that dirty apple will be brought down. The problem is, money speaks volumes, and while we can take him and Devon down, someone else will step in, both in the porn business and snatching unaccompanied kids.

This time I address Niran. "Wait here for a moment. I'll send Keeper down to watch out for the kids." For some reason, I don't want to leave them alone for a moment.

"Let me stay," Niran replies. "Devon's got no other fuckin' reason to be here but to open the hatch. I'll be waiting for him. The rest of you can deal with him from the top. You think he'll be coming alone?"

I'm not sure. "He may be bringing transport and may need help in case any of the kids decide to go their own way. Can't rule out he won't be here mob-handed. Might need you up top, Brother." Protecting the kids is a simple job, Keeper should do it.

Niran shakes his head and leans in close to my ear. "Don't like the thought of bullets flying in this confined space. I can handle it better than Keeper."

I hate to admit it, but he's right. As a Marine, Niran is capable of almost anything.

"Jorge?" I wait until I've got the boy's attention. "This is Niran, he's a friend. He's going to stay and keep you company. I'll be back in a bit then we can contact your aunt for you and your sister, and sort something out for the rest of you. Is that okay?"

Jorge studies me for a moment, then puts his hand into his pocket and pulls out a dirty and creased piece of paper, looking like it's been unfolded and folded many times. His hands shake slightly as he hands it to me. "My aunt's number."

Fuck, if that doesn't hit me in the gut. This kid, he's trusting me. But that's what got him into this position isn't it? Trusting the wrong adult. For once, I make a promise, he's picked the right one.

"Give that to me as soon as you can, Grumbler," Swift says

into my ear. "I'll make sure she's contacted and ready for Jorge and his sister to arrive. You got a prospect who doesn't mind a trip to San Francisco?"

"I can make it work." By now, I'm pulling myself up the ladder. Once at the top, Kink and Keeper close the trapdoor behind me, and I reel the number off.

"Got it," Swift confirms, reading it back.

"You need any more men inside?" Bolt's voice comes into my ear. "The others are nearing to your location, but I'll tell them to stay back."

I glance around at who I've got. If directed, Keeper will be fine, and Kink knows the score. "We've got the element of surprise, we'll do alright."

"I've locked the doors," Keeper confirms.

"And the alarm's alarmed," Bolt confirms. "If we get a sighting of activity, we'll give you the heads-up. Otherwise, we'll be looking to you Grumbler to get that motherfucker locked down. Then we'll come in and take him off your hands."

Hopefully they'll take him back to our brig so I can have a conversation with him myself. But that's out of my power now, if they've other plans.

Now, I've got to decide how this will play out. "Kink, station yourself behind the door, let him or them come in before showing yourself. Keeper, get up to the landing on the stairs and keep down low out of sight. Don't show yourself unless things start to go south. I'll get down behind the kitchen counter and will make the frontal approach." That means I'm the one most exposed to a stray bullet, but I was never one to run from a fight. Especially not as sergeant-at-arms, it's my job to keep everyone safe.

"Take fuckin' care, Grumbler." The voice of my prez booms in my ear. "There's still time to get more men to you if you need them."

"Too dangerous, Prez. If I were Devon, I'd be scoping things out, making sure there's nothing suspicious around." Thank fuck we managed to park our bikes out of sight. "He might already be driving around. There's a lot hanging on those kids not being found."

"You need us, we'll be there. Keep the comms open."

As if I could close them.

"Truck turning into the road." This is from Bolt.

"Positions," I instruct, waiting myself until Keeper's taken his vantage position, checking he's where he can see but not be seen, and Kink's waiting with his gun raised ready to fire or use as a threat out of sight behind the door.

It's only then I sink to my haunches beside the countertop. In order to see anything, I'll have to expose myself, but hopefully anyone will be looking at eye level, and not down at their feet.

An engine cuts out in front of the house, and doors quietly close, probably with respect to any neighbours near enough to be disturbed. Then, there's the scraping of a key in the lock and someone steps inside. The alarm is luckily affixed to the wall on the side of the door opposite to where Kink's hiding.

I hold my breath, but the alarm apparently raises no red flags, and spy Devon tapping a number in.

Come on inside and close the door, I mouth.

Devon steps back, allowing two others to walk past him into the room.

"You want to bring the kids up so we can get them into the truck? They going to come quietly?"

"Don't they always?" Devon snorts, kicking the door closed behind them. "They think they've arrived in the goddamn States and will make their fortune. Most of them won't care where we're taking them, two might. They've gone on and on about contacting their fuckin' aunt."

"We'll shut them up, won't we, Bert?" The speaker elbows

the other man, and his answering chuckle sends shivers down my spine.

"You need to rethink your plans." An audible click shows the men that the man who has suddenly appeared behind them is armed.

Of course, one wants to be a hero. I see him sliding a gun out of a shoulder holster ready to fire as he turns, but I've got half a second on him and take him down, luckily before he can get a shot off. My gun's equipped with a silencer, his was not. All we'd need is fuckin' nosy neighbours.

"Don't fuckin' move," I say, as I stand and expose myself. "We've got beads on you both. Take out your weapons *very carefully* and put them on the ground."

The unnamed man left standing obviously wants to live. He takes out his gun and lays it gently on the ground.

"Slide it over here."

At my instruction, he does. Picking it up, I put it into my belt.

Devon, though, he's not moved. "I know you." He narrows his eyes. "You're the asshole with the bike. What do you want?"

Does he know we've found the kids? Watching him very carefully, I notice him nonchalantly glance around, his eyes resting momentarily on the closed, and now invisible again hatch.

"Money you owe me." I string him along.

"And that's worth killing someone?" Devon's eyes open wide. "You could have just asked me, man."

"You're a hard person to track down," I tell him.

I hear a snick and see while we've been talking, Kink's got the thug's hands cuffed behind him. Trust Kink to bring the proper equipment, myself, I just use zip ties.

"On the ground," Kink barks, waiting until the man lies prone. "Keep? Got him covered?"

"Yeah," Keeper replies.

Devon's hand moves toward his jacket.

"Stop," I bark. "Lower your hands."

"Just getting my wallet out. I'll give you your money, then you can leave us alone."

Hmm. Not that I need it, but Alicia might. "Two thousand dollars. You carry that much around?"

He rolls his eyes. With Kink's gun to his head, he takes out his wallet and carefully counts out twenty hundreds. Walking forward, I snatch it out of his hands and place it in my cut.

"We straight now?" He eyes the dead man on the ground but doesn't seem heartbroken over his death.

"I don't think so." I shake my head sadly. "Gone way past that now. Got some folks want to have a conversation with you."

As Devon stiffens at the touch of the barrel of Kink's gun digging into the back of his head, I start searching the man, patting him down. He's got a gun, but other than that he's clean.

"I got more money," he tells me. "Far more than you'd get modelling your fuckin' bike."

"Too late," I reply. "See, when a man's dishonest in the small things, it makes people start to think. You've done shit to me, Devon, shit much more than stealing from me. Owen and Alicia, ring any bells?"

"That had nothing to do with me!" Devon screeches as Kink yanks his arms behind him, another loud snick proving he's come equipped with more than one pair of handcuffs. "That was all Owen. I refused to touch the video he'd made. I'm not into that shit."

"Grumbler?"

"Two trussed and ready for transport. One dead," I answer Bolt.

"On our way."

"Is there anything you want to tell us before my friends come for you?" I ask, well aware there's a hole full of kids right under our feet. Devon doesn't seem to suspect we've found them. What's he going to do? Fess up so we can save them or leave them to die to save his sorry ass.

"Owen tried to get me involved in shit I wouldn't touch." Devon's voice rises louder. "I just take pictures. I'm not interested in videos. It's him you should be after. If you let me loose, I can take you where he hangs out."

But he won't be there. By now, he's six feet under if the prospects have done their job right.

Bolt and Swift appear in the doorway.

"I told the others to go back to the compound as you've got it all handled here. No need for multiple bikes waking up the neighbourhood," Swift informs me. As her eyes fall on the man on the ground, she looks almost impressed. "Take the body out to the truck."

Keeper comes down the stairs and assists Wrangler to drag the body.

"This one's going to go bye-bye for a while." She stabs a syringe in the other thug's neck. His eyes go wide and then he drops to the floor. "Keeps them quiet for transport," she says conversationally.

Something about Swift must warn Devon he's in the presence of no normal woman. It might be the way her eyes are so hard, or that she's regarding him like a specimen in a jar, but he tries to back away, coming up against Kink.

"What are you going to do to me?" he cries.

"Nothing less than you deserve," Swift promises, "which gives me a lot of scope." She winks at me. "Before I put you to sleep like the animal you are, are you sure there's nothing you need to tell us?" She glances around. "This place isn't lived in, so what do you use it for?"

"Meetings! Just meetings!" Devon cries out.

Swift too must realise he'd happily leave the kids starving and crying out for help that never comes, so she smashes her fist into his stomach. "Motherfucker, I wish I was sending you to rot in hell." She raises her hand with the syringe, but then hesitates. "But then, a living death might have you suffering longer." She uses another syringe in the neck of the man who's still hunched over. That punch must have hurt.

I hope she's damaged something vital.

CHAPTER THIRTY-SEVEN

Grumbler

As two limp bodies are dragged out to the truck, Swift approaches me. "Where are the kids?"

I point to the trap door she's all but standing on and point downward. "There."

"Where's the entrance?"

I fight a smile as I tell her again, pointing to the same spot. "There."

Bemused, she drops to her hands and knees. I help her out, raising the loose planks and showing her the hatch. "Are we going to let them out now?"

"Yeah. I told Wrangler to bring the truck straight back."

"What's going to happen to the kids?" I narrow my eyes. Border security did wrong by them once, it doesn't feel right to just hand them back. Whatever the rights and wrongs of allowing illegal immigrants in are, the best these kids could expect would be to be housed potentially in cages and that just feels off.

"I've contacted some social workers who help get kids like this off the streets. They'll get them fostered out until any adults with them get their immigration status sorted. Oh, and she's expecting four, not six. I've called the aunt, and she's beside herself with relief. Jorge and his sister will go straight there."

I suppose that's all we can do.

Bolt comes over, his face bemused as he sees the more than adequate soundproofing on the hatch.

"Fuck." He wipes his hands over his face. "We might never have known they were there. Make that bastard hurt, Swift."

She turns such a cold look on him. It's in that moment I get the first glimpse of Utah's enforcer. "I know ways," she tells him in an icy tone, "that won't leave a fuckin' mark, but which will scar him forever."

If she can, then she'll be good in my books.

Niran's head appears at the top of the ladder. "Didn't hear a fuckin' thing down there. All good?"

"Bad guys gone," I tell him, grinning. "You had it easy."

"Easy? You know how often these fuckin' kids pee?"

I hadn't thought of that and hadn't noticed any receptacle down there. "What do they use?"

"There's a compartment where a bucket is stored. Doesn't do much to reduce the stink, but the kids know what it's for." Niran clambers out. "Come on, kids, you can come out now."

The oldest girl is the first to reach the top, leaning back her hand to help the others. Jorge comes up last after his sister.

"We go see my aunt now?" he asks.

"Yeah, kid. She knows you're here and is waiting for you. Just need to organise someone to drive you there." His little face brightens, and he turns and speaks to his sister, updating her in Spanish.

Then, well, fuck me, the little kid throws herself at my legs and hugs me as well as she can. "Good man. Good man."

Swift meets my eyes and smirks.

Bolt goes toward the front door and picks up a bag he'd left there. He returns and opens it. How they got a hold of the items inside, I can't imagine, but it's filled to the brim with sandwiches, bags of chips and chocolate. He empties it out and hunkers down.

"Why don't we have a picnic while we wait for the transport?" He rises and steps back, waving his hands in invitation.

The older girl says something in her own language. To my surprise, Bolt responds. He seems to be quite fluent. There's a lot of gesturing, and at first her face falls, then she straightens her back and nods.

When I raise my eyebrow toward him, he satisfies my curiosity. "I explained she was going to live with an American family. That has to be better than where she expected to be, which was begging on the streets."

"You can trust these people?" I glare, worried about sending the kids from the frying pan into the fire.

"Emphatically. We've done favours for them before."

Which is the way the world works. I can appreciate that.

A vehicle pulls up outside, and in walks Connor. "Someone want a ride to San Francisco?" He waggles the car keys he holds in his hands.

"Me!" Jorge leaps up and runs toward him, stopping abruptly before getting too close. "Are you taking us to our aunt?"

"Yeah, little man." Connor gets down to his level. "You've got to be good, alright? You and your sister sit in the back and do everything I tell you. There's a blanket on the back seat. If I tell you to get on the floor and cover yourselves with it, are you going to be able to do that?"

Seriously, Jorge translates for his sister, who, after giving Connor's words some thought, nods, but her brow creases as though thinking adults do some foolish things sometimes.

"You tell us, and we'll play the hide and seek game," Jorge says.

"Your English is good, kid," Connor tells him after giving him an admiring look. "Your sister doesn't speak it?"

"She's learning, but it's hard."

He's not wrong there. I'm always grateful I've been born with the English language as my mother tongue. I take off my hat to anyone who conquers it as a foreign language.

"You want me to take them now?" Connor approaches me.

"Sure." I pull out my wallet and take out a hefty amount. "Cash only when you top up the tank, don't let anyone see the kids, and obey all the driving laws."

"I know the risks." Connor raises his chin.

I slap him on the back. "Jorge?" The kid turns. "You be good for Connor, you hear?" The kid fucking salutes me.

Kids. The fleeting thought comes into my head that there's an outside chance I might end up with one of my own. Why is it that those I've met lately have been good kids and not bad? It makes me have thoughts about something I'll probably never have.

The club SUV starts and leaves, then there's another sound.

Niran, Keeper, Kink and I stay in the background as the rest of the kids go with the social worker who Swift and Bolt had arranged. They complete the handover with nothing but the kids changing hands.

"You ready Bolt?" Swift turns to him once it's just us here.

"Yeah." He picks up that bag whose inside seems to be bigger than the outside just like the Tardis and pulls something out, then going to the kitchen, kneels down and opens a cabinet.

"What's he doing?" I ask Swift.

"Setting our signal to leave. You best get going now. You'll want to be away before this place blows."

"You're burning it down?"

She shrugs. "Easier than cleaning the blood up, and I don't want this place being used for this purpose ever again."

I shake my head but am unable to find fault with her proposal. "Come on, Brothers. Let's get to the bikes."

As Niran and Keeper disappear out the back, Kink and I use the front door. Thankfully, we find our bikes just where and how we left them. I never like leaving my baby alone. We're just starting up the road when there's a loud *boom* from behind us. I grin, guessing Bolt rigged a gas explosion in the house. Well, that's Devon's investment gone. Thank fuck.

When we arrive back at the compound, Bolt and Swift aren't far behind. The first thing Swift does when she jumps out of the truck is go find her precious dog.

"You and that dog." I chuckle quietly when I see her retrieve him from the care of a bleary-eyed Cindy.

Without turning, she tells me, "He's changed my life. I couldn't live without him."

Instead of mocking her as I might have done before—I've re-evaluated my feelings for Swift over the past few hours— now, rather than seeing her adoration for the canine as a weakness, I appreciate he has to be a lifeline for her. As I watch her greet her four-legged friend, I wonder for a moment what it's like to be deaf. I'd hate to be so vulnerable, to be unable to hear danger approach. Terrible for anyone, but for those of us who served, maybe worse. We'd had it ingrained in us always to be aware at all times.

"You okay to look after him a bit longer?"

Cindy yawns widely. "If you don't mind me taking him up to bed with me. When you want him, someone will know where to find me." She ruffles App's ears. "He's a sweet little thing, isn't he?"

Swift seems reassured App's in good hands, though her eyes follow Cindy as she leads him to the stairs. Then her back straightens.

"Where will they have taken him?"

She doesn't need to elaborate on who she's talking about.

"To the brig," I answer.

"Brig?"

I chuckle. "Don't ask. Most of us have forgotten why it was called that. Think it was a Navy man back in the day. It's this way."

As I walk beside her, I make an observation. "I'd have expected a girl like you to have a Malinois or some other big and threatening dog."

She glances at me, but sees curiosity, not censure in my face. "If I'd wanted a dog, and before App, I never considered it, I'd probably have gone for something I could train as an attack dog. But hearing dogs tend to be smaller. They don't need to be tall as they would to lead a blind person around. And there are benefits, like being able to take him on the plane."

Bolt catches up. "Like that's easy." He snorts. "There was App, wearing his service dog coat, and though Swift explained, the airline didn't want to carry him. They thought and can you fuckin' believe it…" he pauses to give a shake of his head, "that Swift was the kind of woman who'd take her lap dog on a trip for fun?"

"Is the steward still breathing?"

It's Swift's turn to snort. "Just. But I had to get out my paperwork showing I was deaf to prove it. Fuckin' wanker." She matches her pace to mine, which means she has to slow down, then continues, "I hate flying commercial, but we do when we have to. With Bolt beside me, there wouldn't have been a problem, but if he wasn't, I'd have needed App. The drone of the engines fucks with my hearing aids so I have to turn them down. App would have alerted me to a tannoy announcement, or the flight staff trying to get my attention."

"Tannoy?"

Swift looks up, then down. "Loudspeaker." I swear she says *heathen* under her breath.

My thoughts return to the track they were on before—how awful it must be for a strong woman, or man for that matter, to be rendered helpless.

"We're here." I lead them to the rear of the second hangar and push open the door.

In the middle of the room, lying clearly where someone had thrown him, is the photographer. I want to kick him where it hurts on sight, but we'd made a promise to keep our hands off.

Swift stands, staring at him for a moment. Then she glances around. "You got a board we can lie him on?"

"What, you're going to stretcher him out of here?" Blaze sneers. "Just give me five minutes with him."

All the brothers are here, and all, like me, want to make the man hurt. *But no marks,* Swift had stated.

Bolt, I notice, is leaning back against a workbench which contains some of Salem's tools of the trade. I see him glance at them, but he doesn't draw Swift's attention.

"Board?" Swift asks again, ignoring the comments and objections.

Salem huffs and goes through to the front of the hangar, coming back with something he lies on when getting under a bike. Swift nods in satisfaction.

"Blocks and rope," she requests next.

Interested to see where she's going with this, I place myself next to Bolt. When I raise a quizzical eyebrow at him, he just grins.

The female Satan's Devil is looking around, an evil smile appearing as she spots something. Then, when the items she requested are found, she raises her chin at Salem.

"You want in on this?"

I see Salem hesitate, but Prez leans in and whispers to him.

Salem draws in a breath, then goes to her side. "Whatcha want?"

"Him. On his back. Ropes wrapped around him, tight enough so he can't move. I've got a little surprise planned for when he wakes up."

It's good timing as he starts to stir just as they've got him trussed up tighter than a Thanksgiving turkey.

He actually comes around fast, trying his bindings immediately, but they've rendered him immobile. He's even bound around his head. All he can move are his eyes and mouth, and the latter he starts exercising immediately.

"Who the fuck are you? Let me go. I've done nothing. Let me loose."

"Who am I?" Swift puts herself in his line of sight and adds in a tone so chilling I have no problem in believing her, "I am your greatest nightmare." She considers him for a moment. "You can save yourself a world of hell if you answer my questions. If you don't, I assure you, you'll be begging for death."

Bolt nudges me. "She knows what she's talking about. Hard to believe, but she had torture methods used on her as part of her training. That was meant to make her strong and know what to expect if she was ever captured by someone who didn't abide by the Geneva Convention. Of course, she knows all about the effect." His brow furrows, and he shakes his head. "When she says he'll beg for death, she knows what she's talking about."

"But she passed her training?" Or at least, that's what I was told.

"Sure. She didn't beg. But he will." He jerks his head down toward where Devon is tied up.

I pull my attention back to Swift and listen to what she's saying. "I'm going to ask you some questions, and if you've got an ounce of sense, you're going to answer them."

For a response, Devon presses his lips together.

"I need names of the investors, owners of the network, and anyone connected to the porn business you're a part of."

Devon stays quiet until she kicks him. Not hard, just a reminder he's helpless and tied up.

"I have no idea what you're talking about. I run a photography business. It's legit." His eyes meet mine and he reads something on my face. "Sure, I cut corners when I can get away with it, but I don't know anything about porn."

"So you didn't know about the hole in the ground of the house that you rent was filled with kids? The kids you would have left to starve to death."

"What? No." Devon tries to sound adamant, but there's a flicker of fear in his eyes.

CHAPTER THIRTY-EIGHT

Grumbler

Sparing him only one look of disdain, Swift walks to the back of the hangar to the space I saw her looking at earlier, picks up the water bucket and fills it from the faucet.

She walks back and makes a request. "Use the blocks. Raise his legs. Make sure his head is tilted back." When they do, she bends down as if to check the angle is to her satisfaction, adjusting it until it is.

"Wha-what are you doing?" Devon's eyes are frantically moving left and right.

I start to grin. I'd already suspected, but now I'm certain where she's going with this.

"I need a cloth."

Again, Salem disappears. It seems his step is spritelier now that he, like I, have cottoned on. He reappears with an old t-shirt—one he collects to use as rags on the custom bikes he builds.

"How can I help?" he offers, as he hands it to Swift.

"Hold it over his mouth and nose."

"No. No. What are you doing? You trying to suffocate

me?" Devon's muffled voice sounds. He seems to have no idea of the horror that's really about to be unleashed upon him.

"You going to talk to me?" Swift asks, indicating to Salem to raise the rag.

"I know nothing. You've got the wrong man."

She raises her chin toward Salem, and the rag is replaced. Then, taking the bucket, she begins to pour the water onto his face. He can't escape. Even if he clamps his mouth shut, his nostrils will be filling, causing him to open his mouth to breathe, the only result being to take more water in.

Gagging and spluttering sounds come in vain. Swift seems to know what she's doing, stopping the stream of water after a short time. Salem tilts his head in question. She shakes her head. After Devon's managed to get some air in, she starts pouring again. This time, when she stops, she gestures that Salem can lift the rag.

Niran, making himself useful, goes to top up the bucket and brings it back.

Devon's eyes are streaming. Choking sounds are coming out of his mouth along with other unintelligible noises.

She gives him a moment, then asks. "Are you ready to tell me?"

"You're a fuckin' crazy bitch," he spits out, along with a mouthful of frothy saliva. "Fuck that hurts. My chest…"

"Yeah, yeah. I know all about that. So, are you ready to speak to me?"

It would appear that he's not. So it's the rag once again, and another few applications of water.

The feeling of drowning is making him struggle against his constraints. Even if his movements are involuntary, the body's impulse is to get away. Swift takes a moment to check his bindings.

"We don't want him to break anything," she tells Salem conversationally.

This time, when she removes the cloth, Devon takes longer to recover. When he does, it's with a look of absolute horror on his face. When he can breathe, he howls, "It hurts. It hurts!"

"You've probably got damage to your lungs. You'll get more if you don't speak to me. I need names."

She indicates to Salem again, but Devon screams, "No! I'll tell you. I'll tell you everything."

"Well, I lost that bet." Bolt sighs beside me, taking a small tablet out of his cut. "I had him lasting for another round."

Swift overhears, turns around and winks. "You should know better than to bet against me."

Devon's so terrified that the drowning might start again, that this time his struggles are to get all the names out. By now, I reckon he'd sell his first-born child in order to get free. Name after name comes out of his mouth, as well as words that allow us to piece together a story.

Devon's got a porn addiction of his own, the more deviant the better. Once he accessed the site via a friend's invitation and after having paid an extortionate fee, he began to wonder how he could get some of that money. He'd managed to track down one of the key players and offered to make videos for them. They'd had no need to take on an extra contributor, wanting to keep their operation tight and secure, but like all greedy men, they were interested. If he could bring something new to the party, then he might have an in, and a part of the proceeds.

I feel ill as he told us about coming across a young Hispanic girl who'd made it over the border and was now begging on the streets for money. I almost vomited when he described what had happened to her, while noting Swift calmly indicated Bolt was to write down the new leads, including the model who'd agreed to let his inner devil out to play and abuse her.

Names, deeds, and more names. The only ones he couldn't

give were those of the victims. Some dead, some left mentally and physically damaged and released back onto the streets again. Devon being safe in the knowledge that while they were in the US illegally, they wouldn't cause a fuss.

He disgusts me. I want to see him dead.

"Can't we kill him, Swift?" Kink calls out, starting a rumbling of agreement.

Bolt stands, bows his head, then looks up and addresses us all. "There's nothing that would give me more pleasure than to dispatch this piece of shit to meet Satan. But if we did that, what would happen? Sure, we've got names, but the feds need him alive to testify against them. If we want to break up this porn ring, get all the players taken off the streets, then Devon needs to stay breathing."

"How do you know Devon will talk once we've let him go? He could refuse to co-operate with the feds." It's the VP who poses the reasonable question.

"I've taped every word he's said," Bolt states. "That recording will be in the hands of the feds, suitably edited to take out the screaming. And, of course, we're giving Devon to them without a mark on him, so they know the recording wasn't made under duress."

Clever.

"How will you get him to the feds without exposing us?" Prez asks.

Swift's taken out her phone and is looking at it. "Devil's man, Sean Cooper has touched down in San Diego. He should be here in half an hour." She looks at the man at her feet. "Get him up now. Be careful, he'll probably puke."

I know she knows as much as she does because it happened to *her.* How anyone could put themselves through that is beyond me. I wonder just how much about her training she knew in advance.

While Brakes and Dusty come forward with knives to cut

Devon's bonds, Salem holds out his hand to Swift. When she takes it, he pulls her forward and gives her a back slap. Without hesitation, she returns it with one of her own.

"Fuckin' good work, *Brother.*" Salem accompanies his words with a wink.

Swift laughs and gives a genuine smile, and I see what attracted Road to her. "Yeah, the Utah brothers don't know what to call me either. Sister doesn't work."

A chuckle from Salem, followed by, "Fuckin' immense respect. I didn't believe you could get him to spill all that without leaving a mark."

"Oh, there'll be a mark left," she contradicts. "In here." She taps her head. "Thinking you're dying, not being able to stop it, and then that happening again, fucks with you in here."

"But not with you," I observe.

Swift sets her eyes on me and shrugs. "I'm made of stronger stuff. And, in my case, I could cheat. I *knew* I wasn't going to die. It's just at the time, it wasn't easy to remember it."

As she'd had him tied up over his clothes, though the ropes must have bitten in, there's probably limited bruising under the pants and jacket he is wearing. Also, apart from some dampness around the collar, and a urine stain by his zipper, his clothes are barely wet. As a torture technique, it's impressive.

Freed, Devon rolls onto his knees, then vomits on the floor in front of him. He's incapable of standing, and just stays on his hands and knees, breathing shallowly, making me think his lungs must be screaming.

He's still not recovered by the time Prez takes a call, which involves him giving permission. Shortly after, there's the sound of a vehicle arriving outside the hangar. The back door opens, and Curtis shows the newcomers in.

"Prospect?" Lost calls, then points to the vomit. "Come back and clean that up when we're out of here."

"You got it, Prez," Curtis replies.

The man who's entered has a shock of blond hair, and twinkling eyes. There's also a woman with him. He steps forward.

"Sean Cooper and this is my wife, Nessa."

Bolt's eyes lighten up and he's the first to step forward and greet them. "Nice to meet you in the flesh. You've helped us a time or two. I'm Bolt."

"As have you." Sean pumps his hand enthusiastically. "Nice to put a name to the face."

"This him?" Nessa's eyes are on Devon. She raises them to Swift.

"That's him. You got your instructions?" Utah's enforcer confirms.

"Yeah. Devil's sorted it and the feds are waiting for their package to be delivered. Hey, nice to meet a fellow limey." Ness grins at Swift, and I note she doesn't seem to be intimidated at all by her. "Swift, I presume? We've talked before."

"We have," Swift confirms with a quick grin. "You've got quite the brain for analysis."

The members from Utah and the newcomers put their heads together for a moment, then it all happens fast. Devon's put in handcuffs again—a pair that's appeared out of Sean's pocket. Then they start toward the door, stopped by a call from Kink.

"Hey." He approaches them, his eyes gleaming. "You work for Devil? You know anything about that BDSM club he owns?"

Nessa's eyes drop, but Sean's meet Kink's head on. "Sure do, man. You ever in the UK, give me a call. I can get you set up with an invitation."

Kink looks like all his dreams have come true. "You for real? Club Tiacapan has one hell of a reputation."

"And well deserved, man. Well deserved."

After they disappear, Bolt and Swift escorting Devon out to whatever vehicle the British pair have brought along, Dart shakes his head.

"Really, Kink?"

Kink laughs. "That man's a Dom through and through. It was a safe bet. And that woman? Well, he's collared her for sure. She's submissive to the core."

Swift chooses that point to return. "Submissive to her man, maybe, but don't underestimate Nessa. She's a qualified Close Protection officer, even though neither of them work in the field anymore. They're on Devil's personal team."

"What's Devon's long-term prognosis?" My eyes zero in on Swift.

Without missing a beat, she confirms, "Once he's sent to the pen, he won't last long. Child abusers aren't popular inside." She raises her chin slightly, a narrowed stare speaking volumes. It's so cold it almost makes me shiver, but instead I raise my chin back to her, knowing she's just made me a promise.

Prez walks up. "I don't know about anyone else, but I could use a drink."

"See?" Bolt nudges Swift. "These San Diego boys ain't all heathens."

I chuckle and step beside the prez, noticing Salem has positioned himself next to Swift. They seem to be talking animatedly to each other.

Numerous pairs of boots echo behind us as we walk to the clubhouse, and it's only then I notice the sun is already rising in the sky. It seems a lifetime ago I rolled out of bed answering that summons to church. No wonder I feel so damn tired.

I'm getting too old for this shit.

No, I'm not. Better buckle up. If Mary's pregnant, I'm in for a lot of interrupted nights.

One thing's for certain, if she is, then what we've done

tonight has made the world a slightly safer place to bring up a kid in, if only for a short while.

Once we've got beers in our hands, I corner Bolt. "When can those videos come down?"

"Your daughter's?" I don't correct him. I'm starting to think of her as that now. If I'm claiming her mom, I'm claiming her too. She's part of the package, and hell, I'll be damned if I don't like it.

"Yeah."

Bolt thinks for a moment. "Feds will start casting their net, trying to catch everyone red-handed. Can't afford to give anyone the heads-up. But one video getting corrupted? Doubt anyone will think much of that. And, in the scheme of things, while it was fuckin' terrible to happen to her, it was almost innocent considering some of the other shit on those servers. I'll get Honor and Duty onto it."

I breathe out deeply. "Thank you, Brother."

"Nah, only glad we could help." Bolt raises his bottle to his lips, then takes a long swig. "You know? I've enjoyed seeing how another chapter ticks. I think Swift has too." His eyes soften on his colleague who, now reunited with her dog, is still talking to Salem. "I did wonder how you were going to take to her."

I choose my words carefully, knowing what I want to express, but not exactly how to voice it. In the end I settle for, "Couldn't understand how a woman could wear a Satan's Devils patch, Brother. But she's one in a million, isn't she?"

I seem to have summed her up to his satisfaction.

"That she is, Brother. That she fuckin' is."

CHAPTER THIRTY-NINE

Mary

Nearly two weeks have passed since the Monday that I went to bed worried about where Grumbler was and what he was doing. I don't think I've been as concerned about anyone in my life, easily equalling any unrest felt when Alicia's stayed out late at night. Maybe it's because I lost Dave so unexpectedly that I couldn't stop worrying that I might just as quickly lose the new man in my life.

It would have been so unfair, I'd thought to myself. Just when he'd made me love him, he could disappear from our lives.

When the phone had rung at dawn, waking me from the fitful sleep I'd eventually fallen into, I was beside myself with relief that he was still alive and unharmed.

I was over the moon with his assurances that everything had been sorted out. The video of Alicia would be taken down and destroyed, hopefully in the next twenty-four hours. And better still, Devon's been delivered, without injury, to the feds. I'd been certain the Devils would have killed him and had worried I may end up starting our relationship visiting Grumbler in jail.

While tired, I could dress and go to work feeling more lighthearted than I had for days.

Grumbler had returned that evening with a bag full of clothes. He moved into my room and we hadn't spent any night apart since, which, I had found, was just how I wanted it. The following weekend he'd taken me up to his place—a house nestled against the backdrop of trees and desert. It was neatly maintained, by the prospects he told me, but had an unlived in feel. Casting my eye around with a feminine eye, I could spy cobwebs and dust which must have passed the prospects by.

"How often do you come here?"

"Once every two or three weeks," he replied. "When I want to let loose in music for a while." He found a key on his key ring and opened a cupboard. Three guitars were propped against their stands inside.

Alicia's eyes had opened wide. "Can I play one?"

"Alicia—" I didn't know much about the instrument, but they looked expensive to me. A cut above the cheap one I'd bought for her.

"Go ahead," Grumbler replied, at the same time. Then he turned to me and offered an aside. "Kid knows how to treat them with respect."

While Alicia sat with a guitar held reverently on her lap, I continued nosing around. There are four bedrooms, two with en suites, a family bath and a half bath too. All except one bedroom is empty of furniture, and that one only includes a bed, fancy enough though it is. It looked hand carved, a thing of beauty. I couldn't help having visions of what Grumbler and I could do on that.

"Why did you buy this place if you don't live in it?"

He shrugged. "I bought it up cheap, oh, twenty-five years or so ago, did a lot of the work. It seemed the sensible thing to do. I told myself it was a refuge when I needed time away from my brothers. Turned out, apart from playing my guitar, there's not much I want solitude for. I don't know." He shakes his head. "Told myself I didn't need company, but maybe I was kidding myself. Maybe at the back of my mind was a picture of a woman in my home. That never happened. Never even came close."

It is a family home. It would be utterly stunning given some love. All the basics are here, not much of the decoration I'd want to change. New furniture, maybe use some of mine. Wait. Was I really imagining moving in?

I forced myself to think of the practicalities. "It's further for me to drive to work, and there's Alicia's school to consider. I doubt her bus stops near here."

"Up to you," he'd said. "Whether you could make it work, but Alicia could have her own car. Have a little independence herself."

Living where we do, she doesn't need it. But she did have her learner's permit, and I've allowed her to drive mine. The thought of Alicia driving herself around sent chills through me, but she's getting older. I can't keep her tied down forever.

Mindful of where the house is situated, I had one more question. "What's the fire risk?"

He raised his chin as though glad I'd asked the question. "There's a two-hundred-foot firebreak all around. The prospects keep the shrub cleared back. I've no propane tank, so to answer your question, minimal."

"What do you do for power?"

He gives another grin. "Solar panels on the roof, a few more out back in the yard. And," he pulled me to the rear window, "out there, see?" It's a freaking windmill. Far enough away from the house so it wouldn't be loud. "Power-wise I'm pretty independent. Sun or wind powers my home."

I heard a noise and turned around to see Alicia putting

away the guitar. "If we move here, could we have a dog? And chickens?"

"Whoa." Grumbler laughed. "You'll want us to have our own cow next."

"Maybe a horse?" Alicia asked, quite seriously.

Instead of laughing at her, Grumbler smiled. "There's a riding stable right up the road there. How about you start with having a few lessons?"

It hadn't taken me long to decide an extra half hour onto my journey would be worth it. Alicia had been over the moon to move to what she called the country, but which was only just outside the city limits. Hence, this coming weekend we would be moving.

But first, I've got to get through today.

Two days ago, I'd taken a pregnancy test. I'd nearly fainted when I'd seen the results, showing me, although unlikely, that Grumbler's seed was growing inside me. I'd rushed out, bought another test, and then a third. What are the chances of three false readings?

I'd told Grumbler immediately. So convinced I had nothing to worry about, I'd taken the tests while he wasn't around. Just to confirm what we already knew, that we couldn't possibly be pregnant, but as it turned out, we were.

He'd held me as I cried. Admonished me slightly for not waiting for him to be there. He'd continued to hold me as I incredulously laughed. Him, me and a baby? We'd discussed our options, whether I'd regretted not doing something about it before, whether he did and now blamed me, but Grumbler's the good man I'd believed he was. I knew he'd stand by me in every decision, but would try not to influence me. As he said, it was my body the baby would be renting out for a further eight months. And while he wished he could go through the pain instead, it would be me who'd have to give birth.

He'd convinced me to get a doctor's appointment as soon as I could, and that's where we're heading today.

Part of me hopes the doctor will say it's menopause causing a wrong result, and there's no baby after all. Part of me is terrified that she will say exactly that, or, that I'm too old and a pregnancy is too risky, either to me or the child.

I need Grumbler with me. As he drives, he holds my hand, the tactile support encouraging.

"We're in this together. Whatever happens, Mary, never doubt that."

"You're a good man, Grumbler."

He grunts. I'm not sure what to make of that. But whether or not he believes it, I'm convinced. I'm also sure he'd make a good dad. I only need to watch him with Alicia to see proof of that. He seems to know just how to handle her—when to be firm, or when to jokingly try to coax her out of a snit. He's more inclined to offer her a reward for good behaviour, than want to punish the bad. He even tries to help her with her homework, though, at her age, she's beyond both of us.

In the waiting room, I sit alongside pregnant women, all younger than me by two decades or more. I fidget, wondering if they're wondering why I'm here. Grumbler picks up a baby magazine—the only kind on offer—and starts flicking through that. He's not self-absorbed, instead he includes me.

"Will you look at that?" He points out a crib. "Electric. It's even got a built in MP3 player and rocks the baby to fuckin' sleep."

I get the feeling that raising a baby seventeen years after my last would be a somewhat different experience.

"Of course," he continues in a serious tone, "it would have to be a Harley Davidson one."

"Do they make them?"

"Fuck knows," he chuckles. "But nothing would surprise me now."

"Mrs Styles?"

Hearing my name, I stand, suddenly feeling shaky. I still have no idea what I want the doctor to say.

Well, the long and short of it is that I am pregnant, but only four weeks—too soon for a sonogram to pick up a heartbeat.

Whether I should continue with the pregnancy, well that's quite a different thing. Miscarriage is highly likely. Weirdly, if I was forty-five, the problems would be less, but those two years apparently make a heck of a difference, or so the doctor said.

Grumbler, hands clasped between his knees, is listening to everything, and now adds a question of his own.

"I'm fifty-seven, Doc. I smoke occasionally, much less so than in the past. I've ridden a motorbike for damn near forty years. Even thought my swimmers might be fried, I'm not an angel, I drink. Not enough to be an alcoholic, but enough. What's the chances of my sperm causing a defective baby?"

Doctor Woodward smiles, and starts drily, "Seems like your sperm are working perfectly, Grumbler. Though, it's a valid point. There is some research that shows there is a higher risk of babies being born with genetic abnormalities once a man is over forty. That goes for the woman as well. So, in your case, your chances are increased of having a baby with birth defects or health problems. These could show up before birth, or once the baby is born."

"Is there a chance the baby will be healthy? Or is everything stacked against it?" he asks.

"Of course there is." The doctor smiles at us. "You might notice I'm no spring chicken myself. I've seen many births in my time, and babies often surprise me."

"But it's a risk?"

She nods. "One you should take into consideration." Her features rearrange into a frown. "You asked me to paint a picture of what you're in for should you go ahead with this pregnancy, so I'm trying to do that. First, Mary, it will have great demands on your body. You've been pregnant before. Well, this time, fatigue is likely to hit you badly. You may have to give up work, and that's if you get very far along in your pregnancy. Mother Nature often steps in. If a foetus isn't viable, you may lose it, however careful you are." She pauses, then resumes, "There is a high chance that the baby won't form properly, and we may need to step in, and perform an abortion."

I shake my head. "If I continue with this baby and don't lose it naturally, I wouldn't want to abort it. I'd want it to be born."

She nods, not upset by my outburst. "Quite right. And we'd do everything we can to facilitate that. But, worst-case scenario? I've seen a case, not age-related, just sheer bad luck, where a baby's organs formed outside its skeleton. There was no chance the baby would survive. We can work miracles with surgery, but to correct that when the brain, liver, kidneys and lungs are all outside the skull and rib cage? Impossible. If the baby is born, it will live minutes, maybe hours, and in excruciating agony."

"What about in the womb?" Grumbler asks. "Would it be in pain there?"

"There is evidence they can feel pain at twenty weeks."

I want to understand everything. "Say my baby was badly deformed as you say. If I carried it to term, would that mean it might be in agony for another twenty weeks?" If so, I'd be sentencing it to a living hell even before it's born.

"To what extent, I can't say. But on the other hand, you may go on to deliver a baby that's perfectly healthy. We'd help you all the way. You may need to be induced early to give him or her the best chance to survive and may need a C-section in any event as your uterine muscles may be too weak to push the baby out. But Mrs Styles, we have a lot of experience with pregnancies. If you want to continue, we'll do all we can to achieve a healthy result."

"But you can't guarantee it?"

"I can never guarantee how any pregnancy will proceed," she responds honestly. "Taking into account your age and its toll on you, as well as the possible genetic problems with a baby, if you don't want to continue, it won't be a problem. This will have a major effect on both your lives."

She's not kidding. Of course I had worries when I was carrying Alicia, what mother doesn't? But it had been a smooth pregnancy, and an uncomfortable but not difficult birth. What I hadn't done was stress out for nine months about whether I'd made the right choice and expected nothing other than a healthy baby at the end of it.

"My job," the doctor leans forward, "is to give you all the facts. You've both got a lot to think about. You could look at this as an unexpected blessing, or the outcome of a mistake you didn't expect to make with ramifications you can't live with."

Grumbler raises his fingers. "Is there a risk to Mary? Could it affect her health? Could she…"

As his voice trails off, the doctor looks sympathetic. "Carrying a baby isn't easy, even for a woman much younger. Yes, there will be a strain on your heart, Mary, as well as on your back. You will need more monitoring than you did with your daughter."

"You've given us a lot to think about," Grumbler states, reaching over and squeezing my hand. "In the meantime, while we're thinking it through, are there any dos and don'ts? Can Mary ride on my bike?"

Dr Woodward laughs. "Yes. Just avoid anything too strenuous, have a good diet and take the vitamins I'll prescribe. Listen to your body. If you get tired, rest, if you're fine, get on and enjoy life. Stressing out and worrying won't be good for any of you."

I think I'm in a daze as I exit the hospital carrying my bag of vitamins. Both of us remain silent until we're in the car.

"We need to talk."

"Too fuckin' right," Grumbler grumbles. As I start to bristle, thinking he's going to tell me the pregnancy can't proceed, he surprises me. "Look, Mary. I know you loved Dave and that I can't replace him. Don't want to. I want my own space in your heart which is big enough for us both. But I don't want to hear one more person call you Mrs with a name that's not mine. Next time we fuckin' come here, I want you to be Mrs Winslow."

I gasp in air, then splutter out, "Did you just ask me to marry you?"

"That's what I said, isn't it?" He shakes his head, then, cautiously looks at me, his eyebrow raised in challenge. "So, what do you say?"

We've got a heap of issues to work through. We could decide to go ahead with the pregnancy and lose the baby and have to deal with the grief. We could decide there's too much risk involved and end any possibility now and always live with the regret. But as I look at the handsome man sitting next to me, I know I can get through anything with him beside me.

So what answer can I give, but throw myself into his arms, and sob out a *yes?*

When Dave died, I never thought I'd find happiness again. Loneliness had driven me to go looking, but in the wrong direction as it turned out. I'd never have given a biker a second look, or not one that wasn't to ensure he wasn't heading in the same direction as I.

He might not be the smoothest talker in the world, his manners might be gruff, but he's the man I want in my life.

When he finishes ravishing my mouth, I pull back, holding him at arm's length. "I love you."

"Kinda guessed that," he smirks, "with you having my kid and agreeing to wear my ring on your finger. But, if we're into big declarations, I love you, too."

I can give as good as I get. I roll my eyes. "Kinda guessed that," I reply.

CHAPTER FORTY

Grumbler

Jeez, where does the time go? It's been four weeks since we handed over Devon, and the days have flown by. On the personal front, things couldn't be better. Mary and Alicia have moved into my house, with the result that it's become a home. It feels warm and welcoming every night when I return. Almost daily, I notice little changes, a vase of flowers here, a throw cushion there, each addition being an enhancement.

I'd bought the place so long ago with dreams I've long since forgotten. I might have had to wait almost a quarter of a century, but it's all come together now. I love having my two ladies there, and they in turn have settled in well. Which, on Alicia's part might have a lot to do with the small car I'd bought for her. Oh, and the thousand dollars I'd passed on to her—her share of the money I'd got out of Devon.

I'm slowly coming to terms with the idea I might become a dad, and I'll be fucked if I don't like it. The only cloud being, neither Mary nor I can get our hopes up. Nature might put an end to our dreams any day now. It's going to be a long seven months. It's a tough situation to deal with, but I'm determined to be her rock, to be there for her whatever the outcome.

The hardest part is not hovering over her, trying to ensure she doesn't do too much. A smile curves my lips. Last night, she chased me out of the house with the fucking hoover when I tried to take over. I hadn't gone far, just to the barn I'm fixing up so I can work on bikes at home. I have a need to be close to her, even though I might drive her crazy at times.

How did I, a wizened biker who thought the best of his life was over, end up with so much to look forward to? Mary's stolen my heart, and I, lucky bastard, appear to own hers.

I still work, splitting my time between home and the club so neither suffers. My brothers mean no less to me now, it's as though my heart's been augmented. There's space for both.

Currently it's club business which absorbs me. I'm seated in church listening avidly to the update Prez is giving. Today we're finding out if handing Devon over alive was worth it.

"Utah wants to remain under the radar, so they're working with Devil's team—Sean and Nessa Cooper in particular—and passing the info to the feds that way. The feds have launched an intensive national operation to raid the homes of the users who downloaded the content, and having passed the information on to Interpol, similar operations are continuing in other countries.

"Christ, that must be a shit ton of work. How many fucking feds are involved in this?" Bones asks, after sniffing and rubbing his nose.

"Enough to take the heat away from RICO investigations against MCs I would hope," Pennywise states.

"From your mouth to God's ears." Salem grins broadly.

I agree with the sentiment but sincerely doubt any great man upstairs would be listening in. If he is, he may want to cover his ears.

"What about the people who maintain the site?" Token leans forward, clasping his hands on the table.

Prez nods at Blaze. "They were the first people arrested. Feds stepped in and continued maintaining the site until such time as they rounded up what they could of the subscribers."

"And Devon?" I ask.

"Sung like a fuckin' bird according to all accounts. He's in protective custody now."

But he won't be forever, and I think Swift will make good on her word. I remember how coldly she'd told me, *child abusers don't last long inside.*

"So, to my mind, all's good," Prez sums up. He raises his eyes and looks around the table. "I think us working with Utah has borne results. It's shown what can be achieved when we all pull together and work to each other's strengths."

He won't get any objection from me. It was down to Utah that Alicia's future is now secured, with no porn video waiting in the wings to come back and bite her.

"They're certainly less secretive now," the VP observes. "And, what's more, Snatcher passed on his thanks for our involvement. Seems we've cultivated some mutual respect."

"Drummer's well pleased," Prez agrees. "And there are doubts that Utah is shielding Stormy now. Maybe he really is dead or out of the country."

I tend to agree. If Swift knew where the man was, she'd make sure he took his punishment. That man's a darn coward for running, and she'll have no time for such men.

"They still looking for him?" I ask.

"According to Snatcher, yes. But as he said, they can't focus on finding a man who doesn't want to be found, not when there's other important business to conduct. I tend to agree with him, and so does Drummer."

"But we'll all be keeping our eyes out?"

Prez raises his chin. "Of fuckin' course." He rubs at his

forehead. "It might be out of our hands now. Drummer's going to be speaking to the Wretched Soulz as soon as Snatcher declares him out bad."

If he crosses the dominant's path, they're not going to buy him a beer. But the man brought it on himself by disappearing. Briefly the table goes quiet.

"Prez?" Salem waggles his hand and breaks the silence. "I'd like to propose something." He pauses, then shakes his head. "Hate to admit it but Swift's one in a million. I reckon there's a lot I could learn from her. I was wondering if she could run a course on interrogation techniques. It's possible other enforcers will be interested."

The table erupts in laughter.

"Run a fuckin' course? You'll be wanting to take health and safety next, Brother," Snips chuckles.

"Sounds like the Satan's Devils are trying to join a corporate world. Perhaps we should think about what fuckin' courses we could run?"

"Bondage, courtesy of Kink." Scribe answers Brakes with a smirk.

"Pole dancing from the VP's woman." This is from Token.

Dart sits forward and growls, "I'll bleach your fuckin' eyes if you've been ogling my ol' lady, asshole."

While Bones shakes his head, he says "Swift doesn't need any lessons from her. Did you catch sight of her on that fuckin' pole?"

"Sure did," Deuce confirms, grinning widely. "It was then I stopped wondering what Road saw in her." He gives a soft whistle and makes an immature pumping gesture with his hand.

"She'd break off your fuckin' dick." Reboot rolls his eyes.

"Getting back to Salem's suggestion…" Niran's voice is serious. "I think it's a great idea, and I'm sure there are other suggestions she can pass on to the enforcers. Hell, that woman hasn't just read about them, she's fuckin' lived them."

"I agree," Lost says. "I'll speak to Drummer about it."

"Like anyone would want to learn from a woman." Snips eyes have opened wide.

"Were you not fuckin' there?" His eyes might be wide, but mine are rolling. "I admit I was one to reserve judgement until I met her, but from what I could see, I have no problem riding with her as I would any brother."

"Me neither." Salem backs me up. "And if anyone else wants to call me a pussy for wanting to learn from her, I'll see them in the ring after this meeting. Starting with you, Snips."

Snips raises his hands, palms forward. "Hey, I was just making an observation. Didn't mean anything by it. I can't afford to lose more teeth." He smiles a goofy smile, showing he's making a good point and also demonstrating that two weeks back, we knocked him out and dragged him to the dentist. The offending tooth couldn't be saved and had to be removed. Strangely, he's not thanked us for it, though his pain level has decreased.

Salem snorts. "I'll leave your teeth alone, but that doesn't mean I don't have other targets."

"That's no fun, Brother. We already know the outcome. Snips will be screaming and crying, not even worth betting on."

"Give him a one-time pass, Salem," Dart suggests. "Maybe when you learn those torture techniques, you can use him to demonstrate on. It might make him reconsider whether Swift knows what she's talking out."

"I like that," the enforcer replies, and gives a grin better seen on a Halloween skeleton.

Snips has gone white. We all give him a moment, then the table, once again, erupts in laughter.

"Your fuckin' face!" Keeper calls down the table.

Prez's head moves side to side, and for a moment his eyes go to the ceiling, then he bangs the gavel. "Okay, is there any other business, or can we wrap this up?"

Brothers shrug, Token closes his laptop. I'm the only one to raise my hand.

"Sergeant-at-arms?"

"Yeah. Well." I gather my thoughts. I'm normally a private person, but the coming months might mean I need my brothers around me, and I want them to be prepared.

"Mary and I have spent the past few weeks coming to some decisions, and she's given me permission to share them with you." We'd gone back and forth about whether to keep things to ourselves, but in the end, we decided we needed support. "Some of you have been badgering me to share shit with you, but until now, I've stayed quiet. The long and short of it is, while it was highly unlikely, Mary's pregnant."

"She is?" Dart's eyes widen. "Didn't think it was possible, Brother."

"Old man's still got it. I'll be damned." Bones is smiling.

I don't take offence at either comment, it had surprised me too. "It was confirmed two weeks ago. There are risks to her and the baby. For a while, we didn't know which way to go."

"She's keeping it?" Niran asks, quietly.

"May not be the most sensible thing, but yes. *We* are." I change the pronoun to show I'm invested in this as well.

"Is that dangerous?"

I grimace. "It could be. Pregnancy at her age will be harder on her. She might miscarry any day, in fact, that's highly likely. Or, we could find out the baby's so poorly, the pregnancy has to be terminated."

"Or, you could end up with a precious bundle of joy?" Bones queries.

"And I fuckin' hope we do." I don't want them to doubt it.

"You need time off to be with your ol' lady?" Lost asks.

"Maybe. I want to be there for all her check-ups. They'll be monitoring her carefully. It will hit us hard if anything goes south, however much we think we're prepared for it."

Salem leans back, clasping his hands behind his head. "Christ, Brother. You're wanting us to be there for you. You don't need to ask us, that you already know."

I nod. I do know, but if they understand our worry, then that's a weight off my mind. I don't like hiding that I have shit going on in my private life. Now I know, if the worse comes to worse, they'll understand.

Prez drums the table with his fingers. "Take what time you need, Brother. If it comes at a bad time, Niran can step in and deputise for you."

"You want me to step down?" I've no doubt Niran would be able to take on my role.

"No, I fuckin' don't," Lost replies firmly. "But if you're called away when shit hits the fan, it's good to have a backup plan."

"What can we do to help?" Dusty asks.

This I've been thinking about. "We've kept ourselves to ourselves while wondering what's best to do. I know you think we're probably crazy, but now we've both come to the decision to let Mother Nature play her hand, it's meant us doing some hard thinking. Now we've got our path planned, I want us to come out of hiding. I'd like Mary to become comfortable around the MC."

"You've not brought her here," Scribe points out.

I shrug. "As I said, we had to get our heads on straight. This kind of blindsided both of us."

"And she knows we know?" the VP asks.

"Yes. She knows I'm telling you now." And hell, I've got it easy. Mary wanted to talk to Alicia by herself and should be doing that now.

"Well the answer's simple, isn't it? She's got to get her

patch, and what better time than at a party to welcome you both?"

"Might be more than that." I grin. "I've asked her to marry me. We're going to the courthouse next weekend."

Lost's eyes narrow. "Is this our official invite, Brother?"

I nod. "I suppose so, if any of you want to go."

"You fuckin' what?" Brakes eyes widen comically. "Of course we fuckin' want to go. And afterward, a double party. Your wedding and you officially putting your patch on her."

Now I've got them just where I want them—a party, a celebration—exactly the right way to welcome my old lady.

"Sounds fuckin' ace, Brother." I glance at Prez, making sure he's happy about this.

Reading my unspoken question, Lost snorts. "It's been a while since we had something to celebrate. You really think I'd say no, Brother? Let me be the first to say how fuckin' happy I am for you." A cloud passes over his eyes. "The next few months are going to be fuckin' hard for you both. Goes without saying we'll be here for whatever you need. I'm glad you didn't try to keep that to yourself."

"Hear! Hear!" Salem bangs the table loudly.

"One more thing." I eye my brothers one by one. "You can say what you want to me in private but leave the 'old' jokes aside when you're in front of Mary. She doesn't need to be reminded of that every day."

"Compared to you, Brother, she's a fuckin' baby."

I roll my eyes. I don't need to be reminded I've cradle snatched—not when Mary's worked so hard to convince me it's how I feel in my mind and not in my body. I'm not considering hanging my motorcycle boots up, can't ever see that time coming if I'm honest. I'm determined the kid will give me a new lease on life and will do everything I can to keep up with him or her.

"So, this party. Alicia coming along?"

"Can't leave her out," I reply to the VP. As far as I'm concerned, Mary and Alicia are a package deal.

"Okay. So we keep it PG. Old ladies and kids, hell, I'll bring along Tyler. He'll be well up for that." Dart pauses and looks at Kink, raising an eyebrow.

Kink raises his hands. "I hear you, VP. Any pets will be fully clothed while the old ladies are present." He grins quickly. "After that, all bets are off."

How does he get all these females to get naked for him? I know brothers don't object, hell, even I've been entertained before, but what's in it for them? That's always been a mystery.

"One last thing, Prez?" I pause, knowing my two worlds are going to collide, but it's a promise I made to Mary. Mary makes few demands on me, so when she requests something, I'm more than happy to do it. Not that I'm sure of the wisdom in this. "I've got some friends, civilians. They've got a band. Any objections to having them play at the party?"

"Friends?" Bones leans forward and looks down the table. "Since when have you had friends outside the club?"

"You been holding out on us, Brother?" Brakes shakes his head. "Going to gigs without taking us?"

I bow my head and rub my temples. "These friends and I go way, way back, but I only connected with them recently. Three years back if I'm going to be honest."

It obviously doesn't need a genius to work out what I'm talking about.

"You ran to your friends because of the betrayal in the club? We weren't enough for you, Brother?" Snips shakes his head, looking disgusted.

Lost raps his knuckles on the table. "I think we can all accept what happened with Snake affected all of us, and we dealt with it in our own ways. I'd have handled it better had I had Patsy beside me."

"I had Alex, she helped me," Dart butts in. "Can anyone truly say there was a right or wrong way to deal with it? I think we all needed to examine our loyalty to this chapter and whether it was worth fighting for. If Grumbler needed to leave club matters behind him for a spell, I can't see there's anything to criticise."

"I'm still in contact with my old Army buddies," Niran offers. "You going to have a go at me for that?"

"We're already going to be on our best behaviour with the kids and old ladies," Bones points out. "I, for one, don't object to a decent live band. As long as they're not rubbish. If Grumbler assures us they're worth listening to, it might be a fun night."

It seems that's a point well made as no one raises any more objections. As to the talent, I can make no assurances about that.

Lost ends the discussion with one last request. "Let us know the time of the fuckin' wedding. We'll all be there, Brother."

If they're all coming, then there's something else. I raise my chin at Salem. "I'd be fuckin' honoured if you'd stand up with me, Brother."

"Fuck, man, you don't need to fuckin' ask. It's me who's honoured." Salem beams.

I realise Lost hasn't quite finished. "Grumbler's getting his happy ending, so I think it's time, while he's in a good mood," he smirks at me, "that we discuss something else. It's long past time we brought Wrangler to the table. His time has come, he's either in or out."

All eyes come to me. I shrug. "Christ, Prez." I rub my hand over my face. Truth is, I am happy. Happier than I've been for many years. I can't continue to hold on to a grudge. I hope that the prospect learned his lesson and won't again be turning away a young girl in need. "Patch him in, he gets my vote."

It seems like he also gets everyone else's.

"Road name?" the VP asks.

"Asshole," I mumble.

"Seconded," Keeper shouts.

But it seems we're to be voted down. Shame.

Various suggestions are put forward, but none of them stick.

In the end, it's Niran who raises his hand. "I'm in the company of one, here, without a road name. Why not keep it as Wrangler? Sounds like a good handle to me, and there's nothing more suitable."

"Except Asshole," I put in again.

Prez ignores me, raising his chin at Niran. "Road names can be earned anytime. I agree with Niran. Wrangler stays Wrangler. Now, who wants to bring him in?"

It's a great end to the meeting. I doubt there's any of us who don't like fucking with a man's head. When Keeper goes out and returns with a worried looking prospect trailing behind him, all expressions are stern.

Prez does a great job, staring, unsmiling, toward the end of the table. "Prospect. We've been discussing how you fucked up. And, what we're going to do about it."

He doesn't have to explain. Wrangler's eyes meet mine, but he pulls his shoulders back and keeps his back straight.

"You going to fuck up again?" Prez asks.

"No," the prospect mumbles. "No," he says a little firmer. "Love this fuckin' club. Respect all the members. I know I fucked up, but I won't make that mistake again." He knows because I don't let him forget about it.

Lost stares at him, as do all of us, stretching out the moment until Brakes cracks up.

"Oh to hell with it." Prez glares at Brakes. "Pass him his colours."

CHAPTER FORTY-ONE

Mary

The decision we were going to let nature take its course wasn't a conscious one, more a creeping realisation that neither of us wanted to take any pre-emptive action. I saw the way Grumbler's eyes lit up when he imagined himself with a child of his blood, and I knew, if it was possible, I wanted that for him. On my part, I could picture myself with his baby.

Grumbler's house was the perfect place to raise a child—plenty of outdoor space for him or her to enjoy. We'd made plans that were dual purpose. Grumbler would rebuild the barn giving him somewhere to fix up bikes so he could work at home more if necessary, or if he just wanted to be close to me and Alicia. A room was identified as a nursery, though it wouldn't be painted or furnished until the last moment, both of us all too aware that any day could see the end to this pregnancy.

I was on board with Grumbler's suggestion not to keep this quiet. I'd also given in to his demands for a wedding—not that that was going to be anything like my first. When I'd married Dave, I'd had a dream ceremony—a white dress, a big cake and a reception full of friends and family. The only guests I was inviting this time were Kristen and Terra. Just a quiet exchange of vows, that would be enough for him, and sufficient to give Grumbler what he wanted, me taking his name officially.

That he'd managed to grab a cancelled slot had brought forward the agenda, another couple backing away before tying the knot had granted us the opportunity.

Today, Grumbler's telling his brothers everything, and wants me to become more of a part of the club. Strangely enough, the men no longer scare me, not when I'm going to be officially part of his life.

These past few weeks, Grumbler and I have kept to ourselves, needing no one else's input while we make our life-changing decisions.

Now, I've one more hurdle to jump. My hands are sweaty, and my heart's beating fast. "Alicia?" I call up the stairs in the house which has so quickly become home. We'd gone back and forth about telling her, but with me starting to be sick in the mornings, and tiredness already taking its toll, soon she'd be aware things weren't normal.

"Coming."

I don't know what it is. The change of scenery? The fact Grumbler pays her so much attention may well help, providing a buffer between mother and daughter who go head-to-head so often. Or it may be that he's bought her a car. Whatever it is, Alicia's been a pleasure to live with since we moved to this spot. It does help that Marisa likes to stay here a lot, being envious of the huge room and private bathroom my daughter now has.

"Whatcha want, Mother?" *Some things never change*, I muse, watching her make a beeline for the cupboard and pulling out a bag of chips. Her eyebrow cocks when she sees the smirk on my face.

"Sit down, I've some things to discuss with you."

"Uh oh. Sounds serious." Suddenly her hand stills even though it's in the bag. "You and Grumbler aren't splitting up, are you?"

My eyes roll. "You think?"

She shrugs. "You can't keep your hands off each other, so I'd like to say no, but adults are so damn confusing at times."

I swallow hard. "You like him, don't you?"

She nods, unable to speak as she's resumed eating the chips.

"Would you mind if we got married?"

"Well, duh. Of course not." Her brow furrows. "Though shouldn't he ask me for your hand or something?"

I'm sure that can be arranged. "Actually, he's managed to get a date at the courthouse… next weekend." My voice rises, making it almost a question.

Her eyes snap to mine. "That fast?" She digests that for a moment, then, says with a laugh. "Is there anything I should know, *Mother?*"

I didn't raise a stupid daughter, she'll know, especially when a blush appears on my face.

"Oh my God, Mom. There is. Don't tell me you're pregnant?" Her eyes study me, waiting for a denial I can't give.

"Mom!" Her voice is so shrill it's like fingernails on a blackboard.

Damn my expressive face and my reddened cheeks. "Alicia, you know those talks we had about sex. How I always told you to be careful."

She shakes her head. "Time and time again. Are you going to tell me you didn't take your own advice?"

I bite my lip. "Grumbler and I have been careful, but not careful enough." I glance up at her through my eyelashes.

"You're really pregnant?"

For a response, I nod, then hold my breath as I wait.

"Is that why you're getting married? Is that what you want, or because you were careless, and he knocked you up?"

"We weren't careless." Well, maybe Grumbler was by not checking the expiration date on the condoms. "We were unlucky. But no, Grumbler and I would get married, whether I was pregnant or not."

"Christ, Mom. I don't know what to say or think."

It's hard to tell whether she's disgusted, or pleased, or something in between.

"So, I may have a baby brother or sister?" Her brow furrows as she ponders on that, and I watch while she comes to a decision. "Cool."

"But, I'm not young, Alicia. I could lose the baby. The doctor doesn't give very good odds."

"Mom." Alicia puts down the chips and moves closer to me. "Is it dangerous for you, at your age? Would it be safer to terminate? I don't mind what you do, Mom. I'm just worried for you." She's the adult now, taking my hand and squeezing it, then she looks into my eyes, examining what she reads there. "You really want this, don't you?"

"It's crazy, sweetie, and sometimes I think I shouldn't. But I do. Grumbler does too." I still can't work out whether she's happy or not, or worried for me.

"Just promise me something?"

"Anything."

"If the doctor advises it, you won't carry on. I," her voice breaks, "I've lost my dad, I can't lose you."

That's an easy assurance to make. "I'll do everything the doctor says, Alicia."

Her head bows, and again I can't read her. But when she looks up, a grin lights up her face. "I want a sister. Not sure about a brother, but I suppose I'll put up with him. I hope it works out, Mom."

Relief floods through me as the sound of a motorcycle reaches my ears. *Grumbler's home.*

Alicia jumps up, ready to greet him at the door. As soon as he walks through, she pokes her finger in his chest. "Hey, big man. You've got something to ask me."

Grumbler's eyes come to me, his brow raised in question. Then he looks back down to my daughter. "What?"

She punctuates her words with more pokes to his chest. "Permission to marry my mom."

He grins. "Okay, so I'm asking. Can I take your mom's hand in marriage?"

Her head tilts to one side. "You going to look out for her? Care for her? Love her?"

His smile widens. "What do you think? I love your mom, kid." Then he puts his hand on her shoulder. "Love you as well. Don't know how you both fuckin' did it, but you've made this old man the happiest alive."

Alicia humphs and takes a deep breath. Her eyes rise to his. "I know you've knocked her up."

"Alicia!"

Grumbler winks at me over her head. "That I have," he agrees.

Her finger is back to poking his chest again. "Next time," she says, warningly, "wrap it up."

I snort. Grumbler chortles, and Alicia looks triumphant.

"Oh, and one last thing. I'm giving her away at the wedding."

And here I was thinking she'd insist on being a bridesmaid, but I don't have a problem with that.

"Too right you fuckin' are," Grumbler agrees, beaming widely.

The next few days fly fast. Another doctor's appointment, this time a sonogram works, and while invasive, we both hear what people mistake for a heartbeat, but is an undeniable indication that there's a baby growing inside of me. It affected both me and Grumbler, his whispered words as we left the hospital *we're really doing this* bringing home that bizarrely, in a few months, we could be parents.

Then Alicia was dragging me out to get dresses for us both, and wanting her hair done, so I had mine done as well. I didn't even mind Grumbler disappearing in the evenings, knowing he was only doing what I'd asked.

Before I knew it, the day had arrived.

Grumbler drove me and Alicia to the courthouse where a surprise was waiting for me. Not only were my own guests, Kristen and Terra waiting there, but the whole of his MC, and the three friends of Grumbler's he invited who stayed in the background.

I'm wearing a nice new dress, not flamboyant, but something I was comfortable in. Grumbler is wearing clean jeans, a button-up white shirt, and, when he got out of the *cage*, he slid into his cut. I took a moment to lick my lips. I hadn't wanted him to dress in a suit, although he had offered, as I hadn't wanted to marry a stranger. I wanted to marry the man with whom I'd fallen in love.

"Mary, this is Salem," Grumbler informs me as a man steps to the front. "I've asked him to be my best man."

"Mary." Salem raises his chin toward me, then leans forward, asking conspiratorially, "You sure about this? There's still time to run."

I snort in an unladylike fashion, but his words break the ice. I don't reply but running is the last thing on my mind.

Then I stare, open-mouthed as his leather-clad brothers form an escort. Grumbler, I, Alicia and Salem walk past them, Grumbler pausing to shake a few hands and receive back slaps.

We head to the front, while everyone else crowds into the room behind us. Turning, I see Kristen and Terra in the first row, Kristen's tongue all but hanging out. Jeez, I hope she behaves herself back at the clubhouse.

Then the brief ceremony begins. It's over fast, and in no time at all, I have his ring on my finger and a new name, Mary Winslow, as we walk out into the sunlight.

"I took some shots." A biker called Blaze waves his phone at me. "But we'll take more at the clubhouse." He winks. "I've got it all set up."

Unsure what that wink means, I just thank him.

"Shouldn't you have your bike?" I ask Grumbler, spying all his brothers getting on their rides.

"With you in that dress?" He grins broadly. "Not having you flash my brothers. What you've got under there is all mine. And what about Alicia? Nah, I'm good Mary. I can suffer a cage with you and her with me."

We do, however, lead the convoy of bikes, Grumbler holding tight onto my hand as he drives as if he never wants to let me go. I feel the same way about him. I don't think I've ever been happier, or not in recent years.

I smile broadly when it becomes clear what Blaze had been talking about. We reach the clubhouse to see Grumbler's bike in pride of place. As Grumbler parks my car out of the way, his brothers circle around it, lining up their bikes behind his.

It's there the main photographs are taken. It's fitting that his ride is part of this, it was her who brought us together after all. *It's strange how things work out,* I muse, as photo after photo is taken.

If Grumbler hadn't been getting a tattoo that day, his bike would never have been spotted by Devon. If I hadn't allowed Alicia to model, then some other girl would have been there. I'd have never met the biker who'd seemed so scary at first.

Would I change it? To save Alicia from being used, I might. But then, I wouldn't have met Grumbler, and wouldn't be where I am today.

"One more," someone calls out. "Mary, get on the bike with Grumbler."

"I'm wearing a dress," I yell back.

"We're gentlemen, we won't look," an anonymous voice assures me.

"Speak for your-fuckin'-self," someone else says, followed by an oomph.

I laugh, realising this will be my adopted family. In the end, Alicia saves the day, coming forward and shielding me so I can get on behind Grumbler without showing too much flesh. Nevertheless, my dress is hoisted up around my thighs and I am showing a lot of leg. Alicia hands me back my small bouquet.

Then, before she steps back, she quietly asks, "You doing okay?"

I make a circle with my finger and thumb. "More than okay."

Grumbler turns and winks at me. "This is the wedding photo we're going to have framed."

"Sergeant-at-arms!" His prez's voice booms out. "Your woman's fuckin' naked."

I'm not showing that much, am I? Glancing down I check my boobs are constrained as Grumbler tenses. Then, I feel him relax.

He dismounts and takes something Lost is holding out. Alicia laughs loudly, as he helps me into the leather cut he'd obviously had prepared for me. On the back it says *Property of Grumbler.*

He walks around me as I'm still sat on the bike. "Fuckin' beautiful," he whispers to me. "Never thought I wanted a woman of my own, but I was just waiting for you, Mary." His forehead touches mine. "I was going to give you my rag later, but this works." He swings his leg back over the bike. "Take more pictures, Blaze."

Blaze does. More than one click show others are doing likewise. Laughing, I glance around and see Kristen giving me a thumbs up.

"Throw your bouquet!" It's Patsy's voice.

With a laugh, I do, blindly throwing it over my shoulder and hearing a scuffle behind me.

"What the fuck? Asshole. One of the girls was supposed to catch that."

"That was mine!" I hear Kristen complaining. "Mary, throw it again."

Twisting my head, I see Dusty gripping my wedding bouquet tightly, holding it triumphantly high, up and out of Kristen's reach. She places her hands on her hips and glares at him.

"She can't throw them again. It would be bad luck," Grumbler says, holding his stomach as he's laughing so hard. "Seems you're jinxed now, Dusty."

"What?" Dusty, who'd probably leapt for the flowers as a prank, seems flummoxed. "That's just superstition, isn't it?"

"No," I call out. "You caught the flowers, you're next."

Then I'm clutching my man's back, laughing just as hard as he is, while the handsome long-haired biker stands, looking bemused.

CHAPTER FORTY-TWO

Grumbler

I told Mary she'd made me the happiest man alive, and that was only the truth. I'd laughed at Dusty's confusion and knew we were all going to get mileage yanking his chain about him catching that bunch of flowers. Yeah, fun times to come.

But my amusement pales into insignificance as I lead my wife, my old lady, into the clubhouse, suddenly choked up.

No more will my big two-wheeler be the only female in my life, though she'll still have a place in my life. I've two flesh and blood ones to care for now, and who knows, in the future, maybe one more.

The club girls, who today are fully clothed in quite passable dresses, together with Patsy and Alex have spent time getting the clubhouse ready. There are banners and balloons, as well as a large table overflowing with food. And fuck me, I didn't expect that, a cake decorated with a bride and groom on a Harley.

As everyone comes up to us in turn, my attention is on making sure my old lady is greeted respectfully, which she is.

I take a moment to nod at Fagan, Jon Boy and Kurt, who

start carrying in equipment, then busy themselves setting it up, for once obscuring Alex's pole which she uses for dancing. I have to jump back as Tyler comes running past.

"Hey, Tyke," His dad stops him with a hand to his shoulder. "Take it slow, okay?"

Mary's eyes follow him, and then her hand goes to her face. "Oh my, he's so damn cute. He's got his own cut."

I eye the kid knowing well his leather bears *Junior Prospect* on the back. I think he's up to the fifth or sixth version now. "Long story," I speak into her ear. "But a good one. I'll share it one day."

When we've greeted all the brothers, I lose sight of my woman, seeing her after a moment with her friends, Kristen and Terra. I grin again. I may not be close enough to hear the conversation, but Kristen is glaring, and miming trying to catch the bouquet. Switching my gaze to the other side of the room, I see Dusty, who's still carrying said flowers as though he doesn't know what to do with them.

Then I'm caught up, accepting more congratulations.

"Nervous?" Mary asks when she returns to my side and we get a moment to fill our plates with some of the amazing spread.

"Fuckin' terrified," I admit.

"You used to be used to this," she says, with a smile.

I did. But that was many years back. "Never faced an audience like this, babe." Not one I know could make my life a living hell if I make a fool of myself. A club full of strangers is different. If you fuck up, you can forget it once you walk out.

Jon Boy waves his hand, indicating the guitars on their stands. I raise my chin back and watch as he carefully tunes them.

The jukebox is playing. After looking around, making sure most people have had their fill at the tables. I know it's time.

The drum kit is set up ready to go, I note, checking with

expert eyes. Kurt's picking up his bass, and Jon Boy has the strap of his own guitar already slung around his neck.

I kiss Mary, hard, as though taking strength from her.

"Good luck," she tells me, holding onto me for a moment.

"The things I fuckin' do for you, woman." But in truth, I'd probably do anything if it puts a smile on her face.

Moving closer to the stage, I give my old friends the prearranged signal. Jon Boy steps to the front of the stage.

He taps the mic. "Good evening. First, congrats to the lovely couple and thanks for letting us join in the celebrations today." He raises a beer bottle in a toast, then places it on one of the speakers. "I'm pleased to introduce for your entertainment tonight, Spitting Gravel."

I snort. They've used our old band name. The name that came from my gravelly voice and our even then love of motorcycles.

Then, as Fagan hits the drums commencing with a drum roll then setting up a basic rhythm, and Kurt joins in on the bass while Jon Boy starts strumming chords, I, unnoticed make my way to the stage and take the two steps in one with my good leg leading.

Then, before anyone can exclaim, I select one of the guitars and place the strap over my shoulder. Fagan pauses his drumming, silencing the hi-hat with his hand, then clicks his sticks together above his head in a four-beat countdown. While my brothers are staring up at me mouthing *what the fuck?* we launch into our own blasting version of *Born to be Wild*, me belting out the vocals.

Ignoring everyone else, I focus on my old lady, *my wife,* seeing the love beam from her eyes. Alicia pulls her mom closer to the stage, gives me two thumbs up and starts moving energetically to the beat.

When I look away, I notice Salem and Pennywise standing with their arms folded, and I know they're thinking I've been holding out on them. Right now, I don't give a damn. All I'm focused on is doing the favour I promised to do for my wife.

We give *Highway to Hell* a good shot, then I slow it down, swapping out my Strat for my Les Paul and making that guitar sing as I launch into the haunting *MainStreet* which I know Mary loves.

The club girls are standing together with linked arms, swaying to the beat. Lost and Patsy are slow dancing in each other's arms, and, following their lead, Dart and Alex do likewise. Then Dart steps away to allow Tyler to dance with his mom. Alex is short, and while the kid's only nine, the height difference isn't very remarked. I don't miss Dart taking Isla from Eva, and is now dancing with her. From the way her head's thrown back, the toddler thinks it's great fun.

I glance behind me, catching Fagan's eyes—they're alight and gleaming. He's enjoying this as much as I am. Kurt plays that bass like a master, and Jon Boy makes the rhythm guitar come alive. Suddenly I realise how much I've missed playing to an audience.

Not that I'd parade myself on stage in front of strangers, but this? Well, if the brothers want us back, then I'd be happy to oblige.

It's only then I wonder whether I'm making a fool of myself, and any seeming enjoyment is pretend. *Let the old man have his moment.*

Suddenly something lands at my feet. Half expecting a rotten egg, I glance down to see it's a pair of panties. Looking up, I catch Mary's mischievous eyes. *One's she's been wearing?*

Not to be outdone, suddenly the sweet butts are reaching under their dresses and skirts and several more pairs fall at my feet.

I grin wide. *Guess the old man's still got it.*

Doubling down, I give everything I've got, feeling my

voice strain, belting out the songs as we go down our playlist. When I'm almost at the end, I step up to the microphone.

"Folks, only a few more songs to go." I pause to allow the welcoming groans and protests sound. "As today is my wedding day, I'm going to play a song for my wife."

Another guitar exchange, this one for my acoustic. Somehow someone dims the stage lights so I'm in the spotlight, my band members in shadow. Then I launch into *If I Were a Carpenter*. When I sing the line, *Would you marry me anyway, would you have my baby?* my eyes fall on my beautiful wife, and my voice cracks a little as I think for not the first time, *how the fuck did I get so lucky at this stage in my life?*

Alicia puts her arms around her mom whose eyes are glistening.

Then I signal to Connor who seems to have taken over the lighting tonight. He illuminates the whole stage as we launch into *Born to Run*, my voice augmented by everyone in the clubhouse. When the final chord rings out, I start to take off my guitar.

"More! More! More!"

Voices are chanting, boots are stomping, and Fagan starts to play a beat I recognise instantly. Again, we get the whole club, members, prospects, sweet butts, old ladies and visiting guests singing along to *Born in the USA*.

When it ends, they continue clamouring, so I move toward Fagan. Jon Boy and Kurt draw close. I whisper to them. They grin widely and nod. It seems a fitting end to play *This Life*, the theme song from the popular MC series.

"Amen, Brother!"

"Right fuckin' on!"

As cries of approval ring out, whistles come from mouths and fists are raised in the air, I call out loudly in response, "Ride Satan's Devils. Satan's Devils Ride together!"

They pick up the call I've started as fists now slam against hearts. The chorus echoes around the walls of the clubhouse, and I feel a wave of emotion. That's my wife right there, and these are my brothers.

I'm living the life, and will until I die.

I wait for a moment, then replace my guitar on its stand. The bass and rhythm guitars are likewise put away safely, and Fagan puts down his sticks.

A slow hand clap starts, and feet stomp again.

I step back to the microphone. "That's all for tonight, ladies, Brothers." I pause for a beat letting the cries for more wash over me. "I need a fuckin' drink, and then I'm gonna fuck my wife."

Mary's hand covers her face, Alicia's mouth falls open, but then she's doubled up laughing.

As I descend from the stage, I'm subjected to back slaps which almost have me stumbling. Glancing behind, I'm pleased to see my bandmates are being subjected to similar treatment, though perhaps more lightly.

There's only one place I'm heading for, my old lady, needing her more than that drink, more than air probably. As soon as I get close enough, I pull her to me.

"You were amazing." Her shining eyes, her whole expression shows that she's being truthful.

"Not bad for an old man, huh?" I ask, winking. Then voice the question that's been burning inside me. "Were they a spare pair," I jerk my head toward the stage still littered with panties, "or the ones you were wearing?"

She bats my arm. "That's for you to find out."

Smirking, I put my arm around her, moving my hand down to fondle her ass.

"Not cool!" Alicia objects loudly, rolling her eyes. "Kids present." She points at herself.

Her fake objection makes me chuckle, but I move my hand

up again, unfortunately before having obtained my answer. Never mind, I'll soon find out.

"Grumbler."

I turn around, only to receive Salem's fist in my stomach. I'm lucky, he pulled it.

Even so, slightly breathless, I ask, "What the fuck?"

"That's for you holding out on us," Salem explains. "Why the fuck did we not know about this? Is this what you do when you disappear 'for a ride?'"

He's got me there. But hey, that excuse had worked.

"Yeah, Grumbler. Your fuckin' voice, man. Never knew you had it in you." Pennywise is shaking his head. "And how you make that guitar sing? Fuckin' ace."

I do owe them an explanation. "I thought it was time I let my past and future come together. I didn't set out to keep it a secret. Thanks, babe." The last is to Mary who's miming drinking and pointing to the bar. "Bird knew, but it's tied up with some shit from before I joined the Army. Just never wanted to make it a part of who I am in the club."

"Looked fuckin' good up there, Brother. We going to see more of that? You going to be gigging here regularly?"

"Prez." I raise my chin. "Maybe. But nowhere else. Jon Boy, Fagan and Kurt, well, we're quite happy jamming alone." I turn back to Salem, speaking to the three of them. "Lost touch with the band for decades. Bumped into Fagan when I had gone for a ride. He invited me back to his place. It was just after Snake betrayed the club. I needed an outlet, I suppose. Music calms me."

"Fuckin' Snake." Pennywise spits on the ground.

Salem nudges him. "But it seems we've one thing to thank him for. If it hadn't been for him, Grumbler would never have shown that talent he has."

I've played on stage, had panties thrown at me before. Had even thought I was going places before all that was taken from me. But no crowd's adulation has ever pleased me more than the enforcer's endorsement of my skills.

"Anything else you're hiding?" The VP had been standing behind me.

Turning I wink at him. "Only those talents I share with my ol' lady."

"Eww."

I chuckle, having forgotten Alicia is still standing next to me.

As I put my arm around my stepdaughter and pull her to me, she states drily, "And we all know where those talents have gotten you."

Salem snorts, and Pennywise cracks up. Dart's grinning widely, while I just shake my head at her audacity. Fuckin' kids. Got to love 'em.

When Mary returns with my much-needed beer, one by one, brothers come up to me, the main theme being they hope this isn't the last fucking time the Spitting Gravels will be playing here. I keep an eye on my bandmates, but they seem to be getting along fine, having equally impressed my brothers. Catching Fagan's eye, I raise my beer bottle in his direction. Grinning broadly, he lifts his back at me.

It's not long before Alicia starts yawning.

"Right kid," a female voice sounds. "You're coming home with me."

"Do you mind?" Mary asks Terra.

"Of course not." She leans in and says in a stage whisper, "Your old man is fuckin' hot."

Mary giggles. "Saw you getting up close with the drummer."

Terra smirks. "I've got his number."

It takes a few minutes for the hugging and goodbyes between Mary and her friends and Alicia. When they leave the clubhouse, it seems to be a signal. The jukebox is turned up, and the sweet butts look like they're about to go hunting. I notice Dart, Alex, Tyler and Isla have disappeared.

"Come on," I say to my old lady. "Need you upstairs now."

"Yeah?"

I only hesitate for a moment, assessing her weight and whether my leg can take it, then I put a shoulder in her stomach and hoist her over my shoulder in a fireman's lift, slapping her ass for good measure. I carry her across the room to hoots and catcalls, but knowing the stairs will be too much for me, put her down on the first step.

Raunchy suggestions which are both practical and impractical follow us as we walk side by side up the staircase.

Once in my room, I close the door, then just hold her at arm's length. "What the fuck do you see in me? Whatever it is, Mary, I fuckin' love you. You make me so damn happy."

"I could ask you the same. As for me, I've got my very own Rockstar biker. You looked amazing up there tonight."

"Yeah?"

"Very sexy," she purrs.

"Still want to know, babe." As I speak, I bend slightly, taking hold of the hem of her dress and pulling it up. I chuckle softly. "Knew it. You were a coward." I can see she's still wearing panties.

"The sweet butts weren't so shy." She rolls her eyes, but there's laughter in them. "And I can rectify that now."

She helps me take her dress off her, and then, she rolls her panties down her legs, kicking them off along with her shoes. Next goes her bra, and she's standing naked in front of me. I love that I've reassured her she has no need to be shy.

"Your tits are bigger," I observe.

Glancing down, she shrugs. "Sensitive," she warns me.

"Yeah?" I bow my head, gently sucking a nipple into my mouth.

"Grumbler," she exclaims.

My hands start wandering. "You're fuckin' wet for me."

"Of course I am, you should have seen yourself on that stage."

When I was a teenager, I'd been only too well aware of how to make the best use of what had been given me—the ability to play guitar and a gravelly voice which would make hearts throb. I'd taken advantage, of course, I had. But now there's only one woman I want to have that effect on, and fuck me, if it works, I'll play every weekend if necessary, and serenade her in private every day of our lives.

I'm overdressed. I rectify that immediately, not immune to the way she devours my newly revealed body with her eyes. Naked, I lead her to the bed, pushing her down gently.

There, in my room, in the clubhouse, while the music's thumping beat shows downstairs the party is continuing, I ease into her gently and make love to her, my wife.

We come together, it's perfect, just the way I knew it would be. She's been made for me.

Smoker would have cheered for me, I think, as I'm on the edge of sleep. *He wouldn't have wanted me to be lonely.*

I never looked for a woman of my own, never thought I needed one to be happy, but I'm glad I took my time waiting. Mary is exactly what I needed.

While the path ahead looks rocky, nothing for certain, nothing guaranteed, we'll handle whatever life throws at us.

Together. The perfect team.

STORMY'S THUNDER

#2

How can one body take so much punishment and not die? If I hurt, does that mean I'm still alive? If I'm already in Hell, it's worse than I expected.

I've been an asshole all of my life. I came out of the womb that way, or so I've been told. I'd rather believe it was down to nurture, surely men aren't born bad? Perhaps it's too late for redemption, but I'd hoped for absolution before I died.

I need to come back to life, but the struggle is hard.

I need to fight, if only for her and not myself. Death can't take me. I need just one more chance, else she won't survive. Just a few words uttered out of my mouth will assure she's safe. Then I can die peacefully.

But it might already be too late, for me and for her.

OTHER WORKS BY MANDA MELLETT

<u>Blood Brothers – A series about sexy dominant sheikhs and their bodyguards</u>

Stolen Lives (#1) Nijad and Cara

Close Protection (#2) Jon and Mia

Second Chances (#3) Kadar and Zoe

Identity Crisis (#4) Sean and Vanessa

Dark Horses (#5) Jasim and Janna

Hard Choices (#6) Aiza

Satan's Devils MC - Arizona Chapter

Turning Wheels (Blood Brothers #3.5, Satan's Devils #1) Wraith and Sophie

Drummer's Beat (#2) Drummer and Sam

Slick Running (#3) Slick and Ella

Targeting Dart (#4) Dart and Alex

Heart Broken (#5) Heart and Marc

Peg's Stand (#6) Peg and Darcy

Rock Bottom (#7) Rock and Becca

Joker's Fool (#8) Joker and Lady

Mouse Trapped (#9) Mouse and Mariana

Blade's Edge (#10) Blade and Tash

Heart Mended: A Satan's Devils MC Novella

Truck Stopped (#11) Truck & Allie

Satan's Devils MC Boxset 1 Books 1-5

Satan's Devils MC Boxset 2 Books 6-8

Satan's Devils MC Boxset 3 Books 9-11

Satan's Devils MC - Colorado Chapter

Paladin's Hell (#1) Paladin and Jayden

Demon's Angel (#2) Demon and Violet

Devil's Due (#3) Beef and Steph

Devil's Dilemma (#4) Pyro and Mel

Ink's Devil (#5) Ink and Beth

Devil's Spawn (#6)

Satan's Devils MC - Next Generation

Amy's Santa (#1) Wizard and Amy

Hawk's Cry (#2) Hawk and Olivia

Satan's Devils MC - San Diego Chapter

Being Lost (#1)

Satan's Devils MC - Utah Chapter

Road Tripped (#1)

ACKNOWLEDGMENTS & AUTHOR'S NOTE

I should start this note with a disclaimer. Devon Starr is not based on any of the amazing photographers who I've had the pleasure to work with. He's completely a figment of my imagination.

The darker parts of this book are fiction, but are unfortunately grounded in reality. Kids do disappear crossing the border and are prime for being targeted and abused.

In real life, people you'd never suspect in a million years are suddenly arrested for having child porn on their PCs – I sadly know, it happened with someone I thought was a good friend. That happened a few years back, but it plays on your mind. *Why didn't I know? What had I missed?* Unfortunately, there were no clues. It shows there are monsters everywhere.

I apologise if these scenes upset you, but you know me by now, I don't shy away from difficult topics.

As well as shocking you, I hope the lighter parts of this book made you smile.

I loved writing about Grumbler. So many people facing a milestone in their life measure where they should be in life by the number of years that they've lived. But why should the best of life be behind them? I wanted to give Grumbler a new lease on life, and Mary as well. I do love writing older characters as I've lived through what they're experiencing.

Don't worry, you've not seen the last of Grumbler and Mary, we'll be checking in with their story in future San Diego books.

I'm currently writing the second Utah book, *Stormy's Thunder*. Yes, we're catching up with Stormy and finding out why he left the club, and what he's been up to. He's an interesting character with one hell of a story to tell – I hope I'll be able to do him justice.

On to the thank yous.

All my beta readers are amazing, but Sheri and Danena deserve special mention. Without their talents at spotting where I've gone wrong, this book wouldn't have come together. You both help keep me on the straight and narrow, so thank you both for helping me sort all the details out. Thanks also go to Tami, Alex, Nicole, Terra, and Zoe. Your reactions showed me I'd got a storyline which works.

Maggie Kern, thank you once again for being such a pro-active editor. You really helped me shape the book. I can't recommend you enough as an editor and am proud to call you a friend. You go out of your way to help me.

I've reconnected with Melanie Darrow for the proofreading of Grumbler's Ride. Thank you so much for your timely responses and suggestions. I've enjoyed working with you again.

The cover image was provided by Golden Czermak of Furious Fotog. As before, he had the perfect model, Fred Dibella. I'm sure you agree, he makes a perfect Grumbler. The cover was brought to life by Dar Dixon of Wicked Smart Designs. Thank you all.

Finally, last as always, but definitely not least, thanks to all of you, my wonderful readers who've taken a chance on this book. If it wasn't for your encouragement, I wouldn't keep writing. I have recently received messages and emails telling me how much you like my books, and I love reading every one. A positive message inspires me to write more.

This book, like all of my works, has been to beta readers, through editing twice, to a proofreader and then to ARC readers, but there could still be the odd typo that's crept through. Please message me if you've found anything so I have a chance to correct the book. I love to hear from readers, even if you're pointing out something I've got wrong.

If you've enjoyed this book, please consider writing a review. Reviews are essential to us authors, and I appreciate and read them all.

This book may be done, but don't worry. There'll be another Satan's Devil coming along very soon.

STAY IN TOUCH

Email: manda@mandamellett.com

Website: www.mandamellett.com

Sign up for my newsletter to hear about new releases in the Satan's Devils and Blood Brothers series.

Facebook reader group: https://www.facebook.com/groups/mandasbadboys/

facebook.com/mandamellett

twitter.com/manda_mellett

Photo by Carmel Jane Photography

9 781912 288830